# Jump at the Sun

# KIM McLARIN

# Jump at the Sun

WILLIAM MORROW

*An Imprint of* HarperCollins*Publishers*

This book is a work of fiction. The characters, incidents, and dialogue are drawn from the author's imagination and are not to be construed as real. Any resemblance to actual events or persons, living or dead, is entirely coincidental.

HarperCollins books may be purchased for educational, business, or sales promotional use. For information please write: Special Markets Department, HarperCollins Publishers, 10 East 53rd Street, New York, NY 10022.

FIRST EDITION

Printed on acid-free paper

Library of Congress Cataloging-in-Publication Data

McLarin, Kim.
    Jump at the sun/Kim McLarin.—1st ed.
    p. cm.
    ISBN-13: 978-0-06-052849-2 (acid-free paper)
    ISBN-10: 0-06-052849-4 (acid-free paper)
    1. African American women—Fiction. 2. Mothers and daughters—Fiction. 3. Race relations—Fiction. 4. Identity (Psychology)—Fiction. I. Title.

PS3563.C38357J86 2006
813'.54—dc22

2005056256

06 07 08 09 10 JTC/RRD 10 9 8 7 6 5 4 3 2 1

*For S and I,*

*I sure do love you*

Mama exhorted her children at every opportunity to "jump at de sun." We might not land on the sun but at least we would get off the ground.

—ZORA NEALE HURSTON, *Dust Tracks on a Road*

Even/after all this time
The Sun never says/to the Earth
You owe Me
Look what happens/with a love like that
It lights the Whole Sky.

—HAFIZ, *The Gift*

# Prologue

MISSISSIPPI, 1941

He was not the first man to slither up behind in her in a field of whispered white and throw her down upon a cotton sack. But he was the teacher's son.

That meant he was educated; at least he was more educated than most of them sharecropping the plantation. More educated than Rae, who at fifteen had long since given up on what good could be located on the inside of schooling books.

Rumor had it, too, the teacher's son was leaving soon, taking off when picking season ended. Headed beyond the railroad tracks. Rae had a notion she might go along.

She was eating when he came, finishing the wedge of corn bread she had cut that morning and wrapped in a bit of clean cloth and tucked into a pail for noontime food. The bread itself was hours old and hard as tack—Eba's bread. Folks joked Eba's bread was good for taking to the field; what didn't get eaten could always be used to kill a snake. But Rae had soaked her slice in molasses, had tipped up the small, tin bucket, and let the blackstrap flow until the golden bread was black and glistening. Eba would have a conniption fit when she saw how much was gone, but that was later. Rae sat in the hot dirt between two rows of cotton and ate her bread as sweet and moist as cake and licked her fingers one by one and listened for the teacher's son.

"Baby Rae," he whispered, reaching her with soft words and hard arms. He threw her down upon the empty cotton sack; she let herself be thrown. Had she filled her lungs and screamed, someone would have heard her. It was early September in Holly Ridge, Mississippi, with the bolls all swollen and just beginning to crack; still a week or two before all other life halted and King Cotton summoned all around. But her uncle and a cousin or two were close at hand, just up a ways eating their lunch beneath a stand of sweet-gum trees. If she screamed they would come. If she yelled she could stop him, or if she raised her hoe and laid it upside his head. She was a little piece of leather but well put together and she could do damage. If she wanted to.

But she did not scream or hit or push him away, but only looked up at the great and hazy Delta sky. Up there in the endless expanse, clouds scudded past, cotton plucked and floating free. Traveling north. Rae watched them racing, watched them making their way, then looked down and watched her fingers rake the rich, black Delta dirt. The teacher's son fumbled with her skirt, threw it up to her waist, wrenched down her underthings. His hands were rough and callused from too many cotton thorns, but then again so were her own.

"This . . . what . . . you . . . want . . . Rae?" he grunted, slamming himself into her, thumping her into the land. Sweat dripped from him and fell onto her neck and rolled with her own into the dirt. His breath smelled greasily of fatback and black-eyed peas; the teachers's son, he'd been home for noontime meal.

"This what you been asking for? You want it. I know you do. I know you do."

Picking season would begin soon. Days and days of working from can to can't, from when a body could see at sunup to when a body couldn't see at sundown. On her best days Rae could pick three hundred pounds or more of cotton, as much as many a man, though she stood barely more than five feet. The soft, white puffs reminded her of the dumplings her long-dead mother used to make; when things got tiring, when her back began to moan from too much stooping, she just got down on her knees to reach the waist-high bolls, narrowed her eyes, and pretended her fingers were snatching dumplings from the pot. She had a grasp, Rae did. Everyone said so. Her grasp was something to see.

The teacher's son thumped and thumped upon her. Then he stopped, moaned high, trembled. With a whimper he fell atop her, crushing her with his weight. She pushed him off, pulled down her skirt. In a field to the right a mockingbird jawed away.

"I heard you leaving," Rae said. The teacher's son lay catching his breath.

"Yeah," he said finally. "Going north. There's gonna be a war. Them Japs and Germans getting bad."

She had no idea what a Jap or a German was and didn't much care; it affected her life not one whit. One thing Rae knew was how to stay focused, like when she was picking cotton all she saw was cotton, not the stalk, not the leaves, not the dirt, not the other people around. Just the puff.

"You gone fight?" she asked.

The teacher's son laughed. "Hell, no!" he said. "I'm gonna get me a job making guns! Guns and boats and planes. Somebody got to build them."

Now it was her turn to laugh. Even educated Negroes could be fools apparently. "What makes you think the white man gonna let colored folks get any of that?" she asked.

The teacher's son sat up abruptly, began shoving his shirttails back into his pants. "Ignorant gal!" he sputtered. "See how much you know. The president done made an order they have to let colored folks work in them places building stuff for the war. Heard Mr. Burch cussing and fussing about it weeks ago!"

"For true?" she asked.

"You'll see how true when all I am is dust."

She considered this for a moment. The teacher's son was hardly good-looking; his ears stuck out from his head like tobacco leaves and his legs were as skinny as a crow's. But he was nineteen or thereabouts and he seemed to know where he was going. He seemed to know what he wanted, and that was something. Rae didn't know what she wanted—she didn't even know what there was to want—but she knew she wanted more than this.

She scooted across the Mississippi dirt to get next to him, took his hand, placed it on her leg. Let it slide again beneath her skirt. King Cotton danced and whispered in the wind. "How about I come along?"

# Book
## One

# Chapter One

My mother says: Be careful what you do on New Year's Day. Be careful because you'll find yourself repeating those actions for the rest of the year. New Year's Day is a template, a groove worn in twenty-four short hours, and thereafter impossible to escape. If you wake to find yourself licking the bathroom tiles, look forward to a year of drunkenness. If you're in the kitchen until dinnertime, whipping up a feast for the gathering hordes, prepare for twelve months of domestic servitude. If you are praying, that's good, and if you are in the hospital, that's unfortunate, and if you're traveling, you might as well go on and keep those bags packed. Or so my mother says.

My mother, Mattie Jefferson, is sixtyish, Southern and black, a child of old Jim Crow, and this was only one of a vat full of superstitions in which she was steeped as a girl. I, on the other hand, am a modern woman, a rational, highly educated *Brown* Baby, the fulfillment of so many, many dreams. I have tossed off the weight of superstition, I chose logic and rationality. I do not believe. I do not believe eating collards on New Year's Day will fatten my wallet or that consuming black-eyed peas ensures good luck. I do not believe if the first person through my doorway that primary morning is a woman, misfortune will surely follow yapping on her heels. (Let's pause a moment to acknowledge the misogynist riptide swirling under *that* particular belief. My mother used to keep us locked down on New Year's morning until our neighbor Mr. Bones—red-eyed and stinking from the night's festivities—could stagger down the street to our house and free us with the gift of his testosterone.)

I believe none of it, and still I soak the peas and wash the greens and even let my husband step out to the front walk for the newspaper if he is up and about. I tell Eddie the reason is not superstition but tradition: a harmless bit of Southern black cultural heritage to pass on to the kids, one of the few gifts my grandmother gave to me. I tell him we are a disconnected people, severed from our rich African legacy, reaping still the whirlwind of all that fracturing and rootlessness. I tell him human beings need ritual to frame and navigate the chaos of life, and that our children especially and Our Children particularly must be given these touchstones in order to survive. I remind him I am a sociologist and thus trained to see these things. But Eddie is not stupid; he knows there is more to it than that. And so do I, though what the more is I could not precisely say.

All of which is to say when I found myself trapped in the basement on New Year's Day, I might have known trouble was coming. I might have known chaos would rule the year.

Also because I feared I might be pregnant again. And while this should have been good news—*was* the best of all possible good news to my husband—and while I wanted it to be good news to my own scarred heart, it wasn't.

Also because I woke that morning thinking, *I could leave them. Grandmother did.*

Which scared the piss out of me.

And so, the basement. It began when Eddie and the children went off to brunch at his mother's house, leaving me alone.

"Sure you don't want to come?" he asked as he bundled Paula into her coat. He was asking not because he desperately desired my company but because he disliked taking the children out into the world unassisted. And also because he knew his mother would be disappointed and Eddie hated to disappoint his mother. She would take my absence as a slight; I'd have to grovel for days or weeks to regain a place on her slightly more pleasant side. Still, I begged off. "Tell your mother I'm sick," I said. "Tell her I'm not feeling well."

"She won't believe it," said Eddie.

"Then tell her I'm prostrate with menstrual cramps."

He made a face. "I don't think I can say that to her."

Eddie's mother was what my mother would call—had called, at our wedding in fact—high siddity—a Vineyard-summering, hyperarticulating, card-carrying member of the Boston black bourgeois. Her maiden name was Harrison and she liked to affect that her family had come down directly from the president, though how, precisely, such a thing might have happened she did not like to say. Her husband's name was Monroe and she had aspirations about that, too, but none that she could prove. The first time we met she asked who my people were and where we hailed from, and when I told her she gave her son a look of such raw, withering disappointment I wanted to drag myself out behind the barn and put me down. When we told her I was keeping my own last name of Jefferson, she smiled and said, "That's probably just as well, dear."

I knew Eddie would rather burn his lips with a hot poker than say the word *menstrual* to this woman. And she would rather that he did.

But that was their problem. I had my own, potentially, and I wanted everyone out of the house so I could sit in peace with it and figure out what to do. "Then just tell her I'm having a nervous breakdown," I said. "That'll make her day."

Eddie was struggling to stuff Paula's hand into her mitten, but he paused long enough to search my face. "Is this about last night? You're not still worried, are you?"

"I'm fine," I lied. "You guys go and have a good time." Because even in marriage, there comes a time when it is every person for herself.

*I went down into the basement in search of a box. I went down* swinging the door closed behind me to keep our cat, Prince, from following me down and casing the place. I went down and pulled the door shut because in our old house the basement door did not lock from the kitchen side, or even lock at all.

I had this crazy idea of contacting a former colleague of mine, this white guy, an English professor and acquaintance back at UNC who had moved to Boston five or six years before we did. His wife, whom I'd met several times at faculty cocktail gatherings, was a gynecologist. If I could find his information, which he'd sent in an if-you're-ever-in-Boston card shortly after he left and which I stuck into my address book and never looked at again—I could look them up. Give them a call. Make my way through pleasantries and chitchat. Ask for her help.

What I wanted—what I needed—was a prescription for the morning-after pill. Under normal circumstances I would just telephone my own gyn or even my primary care doc and ask for help, but the days and months postmove are never normal; we'd been in our cozy little Boston suburb only a few months and I'd had no time to focus on my own health needs. The children, as always, came first: a preschool for Harriet, a play group for Paula, a dentist, and, most important of all, a pediatrician. It had taken weeks of investigation and asking around, not to mention double-checking with the

HMO, to get the kids into a small, parent-friendly, highly regarded practice in Hyde Park whose doctors all had props at Children's Hospital and which had twice been voted Best of Boston in a local magazine. All of which did me no good unless the pediatrician on call that weekend was willing to write me a script for emergency contraception. Which I doubted. Although she should.

So I went down into the basement in search of a box stuffed with items from my previous life: books and papers and computer disks and scholarly journals and my old address book containing the contact information for the gynecologist wife of a man with whom I'd been only marginally friendly and to whom I had not spoken in several years. That's how desperate I was.

I might have even telephoned her. I might have choked down my pride and gulped my humiliation and called, but I could not find the card. After digging for a while, I found my address book, stuffed with a dozen business cards and several scraps of paper with names and addresses scribbled on them but none from the gynecologist and her man. The idea of calling directory assistance passed through my mind, but I did not know if they had settled in Boston proper or one of its many suburbs. I didn't know if they were listed or unlisted, I didn't know if they were still in the area or had sickened of New England winters and moved to Mexico. I didn't know if they were both still young and vibrant or if one or both of them had hit black ice coming home one winter night or had mutated cancer cells or flown the wrong plane from the wrong airport on the wrong day or gone vacationing in the Amazonian rain forest and snuck away from the tour leader seeking snapshots and been snapped by a poisonous snake.

So that wasn't going to work. I would have to find some other means to save myself.

I sat on the steps, thinking and looking around. The basement, like everything else in the house, had been renovated by the previous owners, renovated to within an inch of its life. The floors had been excavated a foot to ensure plenty of headroom, then tiled an elegant blue gray, the walls paneled in honey-warm oak, the furnace and hot-water heater removed to the far north section and artfully tucked away in their own, custom-built armories. There was a bathroom complete with shower and a kitchenette with Italian marble on the breakfast bar and windows on three walls. The windows were new and high and vinyl and shiny white, and cranked open just enough for ventilation but not enough for handy-dandy burglar access, as the Realtor had pointed out. "Not that we have any problems of that kind in this town," she hastened to add. "My goodness, I think the worst thing on the police blotter page in the paper last month was an unlicensed dog."

Eddie planned to outfit the place with a billiards table, black leather couch, wide-screen television, and, in the south corner where the laundry room had been (shifted to the second floor to ease the load on the previous owner's wife, or, more likely, their maid) a small putting green. But at the time of my imprisonment the only furnishings were two old window air conditioners we no longer needed and a dozen empty boxes from the move. Eddie and I were still debating what to do with them. He wanted to cut them up and put out for the recycling truck; I wanted to save them. At two bucks a box, which was what the movers had charged, we were talking a nice little bit of pocket change.

"But we can afford it now, Weezie," Eddie had bragged two days after our move as we stood among the empty boxes, debating their fate. He stuck out his chest and cocked his elbows behind him and did a little lap of his George Jefferson strut. Ever since we'd closed on this four-bedroom, two-bath dream home of his, he'd been calling me Weezie and yelling for Florence and breaking into off-key renditions of the old Jefferson's theme song. He did it with hip-rolling, eyebrow-wiggling exaggeration and I was supposed to think he was being tongue-in-cheek, but we both knew he was serious.

"You need to calm down, George," I told him. "That paycheck only feels heavy because the ones before it were so light."

"Ouch," he said. "Would you like to kick me in the other one, now?"

I smiled, to show I meant no harm, and reached over to rub Eddie's back. Part of a wife's job, wasn't it—protecting a man's ego? I remembered an African woman at a feminist conference I'd attended once long before saying as much and how I'd scoffed at the idea. Wasn't a man's ego his own responsibility? But no; no, it wasn't, not in a marriage, apparently. "I'm just saying we need to be careful. The fact that you are pulling in more than we were making together in North Carolina just means we weren't making that much. Plus, this area is a much more expensive place to live. We need to be careful, especially until I find something."

Eddie put his hands around my waist and pulled me toward him for a kiss. "We've already found it," he said with a smile. And, I could see that he had. After many years of sojourning down in the Southern wilderness, Eddie had returned triumphant to the city of his birth—or, better yet, to a suburb of that city. He had a job he loved at a money-churning pharmaceutical company, an impressive house he adored, and, except for the missing son, an enviable family. His mother was pleased, his sister disdainful, his childhood friends close and envious. Eddie had achieved the dream and saw no reason to wake from it. He had, if not precisely transcended race, at least muted it. He was good to go. And thought I was, too.

Remembering that conversation on New Year's Day, I got up to go upstairs, planning to have a cup of coffee and figure out plan B. But when I put my hand on the doorknob it would not turn.

I twisted, I shoved, I banged, I cursed. But there I was, trapped in the basement on New Year's Day. A clearer message could not be sent.

Walking back down the stairs, I realized Eddie and the kids could be gone for hours, could end up staying at his mother's until it was time for bed. I had no telephone, no computer, no morning-after pills, nothing even to read or study or write, nothing but a toolbox and the future to occupy my mind. I was as mentally horse-healthy as the next black woman, I had never suffered claustrophobia or any related fears, but all of a sudden it got close there beneath the surface of the earth, the room grew stale, the air tasted gritty and metallic, like dirt. I tried climbing on a box to crank open the windows, but the box collapsed beneath my weight and I banged my knee against the lovely Italian tile.

Through the window I saw the snow had begun, the weatherman predicting six to eight. To keep myself busy I sat again on the steps and began mentally arranging furniture throughout the house. I put Eddie and some friends right there in the basement on the black leather couch watching football and drinking beer. I put the children upstairs in the carpeted family room, bickering about who would get the red construction paper and who would get the green. I put myself in the eat-in kitchen, hands in soapy water at the double, stainless-steel sink, staring out at a half-acre lawn blanketed in snow, thinking about my childhood plans for myself, my great expectations, the life I would carve from the world. I put Eddie in the box in which he planned to leave the house and myself in there beside him and the lid slammed down and I couldn't breathe. I wanted to scream but I could not even breathe.

I stumbled up from the steps, began pacing the basement. A plan, a plan, I needed a plan. And then one came.

All I had to do was locate the closest Planned Parenthood. The sooner the better; I wasn't sure of my window of opportunity but I knew it wasn't long. I'd get the pills, I'd take them. Eddie would never know.

Later on, after he released me, Eddie joked that my imprisonment was divine punishment. It was well past nine in the evening, more than twenty-four hours since our rendezvous, and all I could think of was tracking down the closest clinic. So when

Eddie spoke of punishing I thought he meant for what I planned to do.

"See," Eddie teased. "That's for forcing me to lie to my mother. God don't like ugly."

"God forgives," I told my husband. "After all, it was New Year's Day." Maybe God would set a template for the year.

# Chapter Two

What happened was this: Friday, New Year's Eve. The children were finally in bed. I was exhausted after a week of no school and family festivities and feeling like a slug. An antisocial slug. Then Eddie, swinging home from the office holiday party with flowers and tiramisu and two bottles of champagne. All so cliché and predictable as to be embarrassing.

But when Eddie first came through the front door, whistling and wriggling his eyebrows, it was all I could do not to laugh. "You're joking, right?" I asked him. "I'm so tired I can barely stand."

"Then sit," he said, taking my hand and leading me upstairs. He ran me a hot bath and put me in to soak. He lit some candles, he refilled my glass. Clearly he'd been reading magazines. "I'm going out for kindling for a fire," he said, kissing me.

By the time Eddie came back in, the cold clinging to his shirt, his face smelling sharp and fresh as the midwinter night, I'd put away half the bottle. "Slow down," he said, filling my glass to the brim. I sipped some more, feeling comfortably loose. Loose enough to let him scoop suds onto a washcloth and rub me. Loose enough to let him rinse my glistening skin. Loose enough to recognize how hard my husband was trying, and how much I needed to go along.

And by the time I let Eddie wrap me in my terrycloth bathrobe and lead me back downstairs to the fireplace, the champagne bottle was empty and I felt as pliable as well-chewed gum. I let him kiss me, let him open my robe. "I miss you," Eddie murmured. "So much."

But I was not loose enough to have unprotected sex. I kissed my husband, then tried to stand, feeling so light-headed I thought I could simply float back upstairs to the master bathroom for my diaphragm. "Be right back," I murmured.

But Eddie pulled me back onto the blanket. "Don't worry, I've got it under control." He pulled the packet from his back pocket and dangled it between his fingertip, looking both sheepish and weirdly proud. I knew this, too, was a gift to me. Like every other male on the planet, Eddie claimed to hate condoms. This had never been a problem for me, since Eddie and I had connected before AIDS reared its terrible head and since from the age of seventeen until Harriet's conception I had been on the pill. I considered going back on after Paula was weaned, but concerns about the health risks of longtime pill use—and the infrequency of sex with my husband—made me decide otherwise. I figured careful and consistent use of the diaphragm would do the trick.

Looking at the condom in Eddie's hand, I laughed. "How long has that thing been in your wallet, mister?"

"Since nine A.M. this morning," he said. "It's fresh off the farm."

I leaned back and closed my eyes. Letting go for once. Giving in. "Okay."

And of course the damn thing broke. Apparently, that was what you got for ceding control.

I knew it right away. Moaning ceased, panting ebbed, mind

and body reconnected, and mind pointed out that things were far more sticky than they should have been.

"No," I whispered. "Please no."

Eddie opened his eyes and pulled back to look into my face. "What's wrong? Did I hurt you?"

Body said: *Don't move and nothing bad will happen.* Mind said: *Get up and get to the bathroom, quick.* I pushed my husband off.

"What's wrong?" he asked again, sounding frightened, but I had no time to waste calming his fears. There is a moment when disaster happens, a moment before knowledge or logic or training kicks in and tells us what to do when pure animal panic is running the show. This was the moment I was in. All I could think was that I had to get to the bathroom and get some spermicide into my body before the hole from which I was climbing caved right back in upon my head. But by the time I got the bathroom door closed and the cabinet door open and the spermicide in hand, reason had returned, smirking. You can't outrun sperm; the brainless little monsters swim astonishingly fast. They can gallop up those long, long tubes and breach the fort in thirty minutes, they can hide for days in secret corners, lying in wait. Pumping spermicide after intercourse was closing the barn door while the horse galloped on down the lane. I did it anyway, then sat on the closed toilet and held my head in my hands.

Eddie knocked on the bathroom door. "Baby? Can I come in?"

I said nothing, and when the door opened and closed I did not look up. "I'm sorry," Eddie said to the back of my head. "I really am." He paused. Then, as if he could not help himself, he added, "Guess we got a little too enthusiastic, huh? That's your fault, for being so beautiful."

I looked up, found him trying to suppress a grin.

"You think this is funny?"

The grin vanished. "Of course not. I'm just saying it's no reason for panic. There's only an eight percent chance of pregnancy from a single act of unprotected intercourse."

I did not have to ask how in the world he might know such a thing because I knew. He would have remembered from something he read when we were first trying to get pregnant with Harriet. My scientist husband, my research scientist, my brilliant mathematician, who loved knowledge for knowledge's sake, who never forgot a number, who put such faith in quantification and his own ability to calculate life. But numbers were relative; even I knew that much was true. An eight percent chance of rain was insignificant. An eight percent chance of winning the lottery was not enough to stay up and watch the power ball drawing. An eight percent chance of being pregnant when you did not want to be—that was huge.

Eddie bent down to take my hand. "Besides," he said, looking into my eyes, "would it really be so terrible?"

A traitorous thought slunk into my head. Had this been truly an accident? Or was it a devious plan on my husband's part?

"We've been so blessed, Grace," he said. "Shouldn't we share those blessings?"

Dear, sweet Eddie, wanting a son and fearing my hardening heart, deciding to take matters into his own masculine hands. It was possible. I imagined him in his ergonomic chair at his sleek black desk in his Swedish-furniture office, plotting the attack. Food and drink and the melancholy madness of New Year's Eve; the old pin-in-the-condom trick, which, if it worked, would work. Because being educated, progressive black folks, my husband and I danced on the pinhead of the abortion issue: supported abortion rights on the one hand; deeply opposed the idea for ourselves. I made a mental note to add this to the book of advice I was writing for my daughters: always buy the condom yourself. Useful advice was one thing I knew I could give my daughters. My own mother used to say things like "Whatever doesn't kill you makes you stronger" and "Get up! Plenty of time to sleep when you're dead," but such admonitions did not, strictly speaking, qualify as advice. More like warnings. Predictions of doom.

"Look at all we have been given, Grace," Eddie said, sweeping the air with his hands. I knew he meant the house and not the bathroom; still I followed the arc of his sweep with my eyes. The bathroom was big enough for six to stand comfortably and had been done over in French Country, with marble floors and tumbled marble walls and a sink that sat on the counter like a big, glass bowl. And stenciled chickens running all over the place. Not my taste at all. "That's okay," Eddie had said when we first looked at the house. "We can remodel. You'll have fun." My heart had sunk a little at that, because the old Eddie, the Eddie of our first connect, would have been sickened by the idea of spending money on something so bourgeois and self-indulgent and ridiculous. Something his mother would so love. Ten thousand dollars to make it look like Provence and another ten thousand to make it look some other way and, in the end, still just a place to shit.

"Grace," Eddie said, calling me back to the present. "We have the resources for another child."

On the night of Paula's birth, Eddie had labored mightily to hide his disappointment at the fact that our second child had come to us without a penis. With Harriet we'd learned the sex beforehand; with Paula we decided to put it off. Or Eddie decided; I went groggily along, acceding to his unspoken hope that delay might somehow transform even the stubbornest X chromosome into a Y. When our beautiful Haitian doctor announced "It's a girl!" I saw the pain in my husband's eyes, though he quickly roped it and stuffed it away. He kissed our new bundle with a grin. "She's healthy and she's beautiful," he said, then said it again. "She's healthy. She's beautiful. Thank you, God."

Had it been a boy, we'd planned to name him Paul Laurence, after the great Paul Laurence Dunbar. We had not gotten around to settling on a girl's name. When I suggested Paula Laurence, Eddie had looked stricken. And betrayed. Just as he looked betrayed now at the idea of me not wanting another child.

"We could raise a strong black man who would go out and help his people," he said.

"Don't."

"Don't what?" he asked.

"Don't use race," I said, suddenly angry. "Also, in case you've forgotten, we already have two daughters. Can't they help their people? Or will they be too busy mopping the floors?"

Eddie jerked to his feet. "Don't try to turn this around," he said. "Wanting a son doesn't make me love our daughters any less."

That was true; I knew it. Still, I kept a tactical silence, waiting to see what might be revealed. Eddie said, "Maybe God wants us to have another child."

Though he was a scientist, Eddie saw no disconnect between his vocation and his faith. In Eddie's world there was room enough for all. It was one of the things I admired about him. But I lacked the focus to try to read God's mind.

I went to the bathroom door. Eddie came to stand beside me. "I guess I just don't understand why this scares you," he said. "I don't see why you resist it."

"I know."

"What's wrong?" He stood there beside me, bewildered and hurt, waiting for me to speak. My husband the scientist, who'd run the numbers on having a third child and found they all added up for him. I should have said "I don't know" because that was the truth. But that would have only frightened him more. I kept my peace.

"I know they're hard right now," he said. "They're so young, they need so much."

"Probably that's it."

"All parents struggle at first."

"I know."

"It doesn't mean anything at all."

"I know."

"And you love them," he said. It was a statement he was fighting to keep from being a question and it sliced me—his asking, his thinking, the possibility. Sliced straight across my heart. I pressed my hands to my face.

"Oh God," I said. "Of course, of course."

Eddie pulled my hands away and kissed them. He was smiling now, smiling through tears of relief. "Of course you do," he said. "You love them and you would not be able to imagine your life without them. I know that."

I nodded and let my husband hold me, but I knew what he said was not completely the truth. Yes, I loved my children. God, I loved my children. I would have flayed my own loins for them, hurled my body between theirs and danger, tossed myself into the river Charles to save their lives. Every day hummed along on a buzz of constant low-level anxiety for their safety; some days it rose to fear. And every night I got down on my knees and prayed for their whole delivery into adulthood and beyond.

But those were prayers offered up for what existed, for what breathed and laughed and lived. In truth, I could imagine a parallel life for myself, a life in which the two bits of unrealized humanity that were egg Harriet and egg Paula went down that river of blood like so many before. In this life, I never met Eddie, or maybe I met him and we dated but in the end went our separate, amicable ways. I joined the faculty at some esteemed university, received tenure in record-breaking time. I wrote a book that not only revolutionized racial dynamics in the country and transformed the urban educational system but inspired a generation of African-American youth to redirect their lives in a positive way. I lectured and traveled, testified and taught. In the winters I took off a month to fly to Brazil and lie upon the hot white sand. In my spare time I read and visited museums and hiked the winter slopes. I learned to meditate. I treasured silence. I baked bread for myself and ate it standing over the stove. I saw my mother four or five times a year, had love affairs but did not take them seriously though sometimes I wanted to. Sometimes I was lonely and even sad. Sometimes on rainy Sunday afternoons I put on Billie Holiday music and poured myself some wine and sat down before the fireplace and imagined myself a parallel life. A life with a husband and a home. A life with kids.

Eddie went out and I climbed into the shower, turning the water all the way to hot to scald myself. Really, what was my problem anyway? House too big? Bills too paid? Kids too healthy and well fed? I was a sociologist, a kind of societal shrink, and as capable as anyone of casting a skeptical eye over the specter of middle-class American malaise. My life was good, objectively speaking. Enviable even, exceedingly blessed, and I damn well should have been able to appreciate it. Outside my door more than three million black American children were living in poverty, and that was poverty as defined by the government, which wouldn't even get a person past those grip-and-grin greeters at Wal-Mart. In some cities more than fifty percent of black men were unemployed. Fewer than fifty percent of black Americans owned their own homes, compared to three-quarters of our white friends and neighbors. I, on the other hand, had a chemist husband with a new job in corporate America, a new house, and two healthy, beautiful children who had never missed a meal. Boo hoo hoo.

Even the fact of my unceremonious dumping by the Duke department of sociology and our subsequent retreat to Boston fell about a million leagues short of tragedy. When one was first scaling the walls of academia one assumed copious amounts of scholarship, rigorous teaching, and persistent if unspectacular publishing would see one safely to the top. That, of course, was naive. Hard work was not necessarily rewarded; the cream did not always rise, or if it did, it could be easily shoved right back down again. Folks got denied tenure all the time, as it turned out, even ambitious, accomplished folks. Their lives continued. They moved along and tried again at some other, lesser university or became permanent adjuncts or hired themselves out to corporate America or agreed, in a moment of emotional weakness and desperation, to stay temporarily at home with the kids. It was hardly the end of the world.

It wasn't like it was 7 P.M. in South-Central and I had to hide the children in the bathtub because the gang wars were raging again.

It wasn't like I was a Tutsi and the president had just been killed and the streets were boiling and the Hutu radio was broadcasting vitriol. It wasn't like I was in tower number one and the stairwells were filled with smoke.

It wasn't like I was in the field picking cotton with my children and the slave auctioneer just rode past on his horse, headed up to the big house door. It wasn't like I was uneducated or living on a pitiful government handout or struggling to raise a gaggle of children all by myself.

It wasn't like I was my mother. It wasn't like I was living my grandmother's life.

# Chapter Three

Here's what I know about my grandmother: she was born Royal Rose Polk in 1925 in a Mississippi Delta sharecropper's shack with dirt floors and cypress walls and a roof of corrugated tin. The walls had gaps so wide you could look out and see who was coming up the road, the floor spaces so big you could look down and see the chickens roost. The nearest town was a one-road backwater called Freedom, and the nearest town of decent size was Holly Springs. The nearest city was across the state line in Tennessee: Memphis, rich and beckoning, sixty miles away.

Her parents named her Royal to lessen the sting of having white folks address you by your first name no matter how old you were. (Among her brothers were Judge, Doctor, and King.) She was the youngest of nine, all but three of them boys, two of them dead before the age of sixteen. She never grew taller than a minute but she filled out a dress by the time she was ten and plumped sassier by the year. She was an ordinary, kinky-haired, brown-skinned girl at a time when such were crushed underfoot by the hour. They called her Royal or Roy or even sometimes Queenie. But mostly they called her Baby Rae.

I know that at fifteen she ran away to Memphis with the teacher's son. Fifteen then was not what fifteen is now, here in the dawning years of the twenty-first century, here at the end of the world. Back then fifteen was both a far more tender and a far less innocent age, and I imagine that at fifteen my grandmother knew some things about life I have yet to learn.

The year must have been 1941. The country geared for war. President Roosevelt, desperate to avert a threatened Negro march on Washington ("Ten thousand black Americans!" cried the great A. Philip Randolph), signed an executive order banning employment discrimination in the defense industry. Maybe the teacher's son heard about it. Maybe he dreamed of running north and finding a job in a defense plant. Maybe my grandmother went along for the ride.

## MISSISSIPPI, 1941

She woke up alone in the room with gunnysack curtains, woke up tender and swollen and sore in a Memphis boardinghouse, and looked across to where the teacher's son's black woolen coat had hung on a hook. It was gone, just like she suspected it would be. It was gone but at least she'd had the foresight to steal the bastard's stash.

Not that it was much money; eight dollars and some change. She had slipped it from its hidden place deep inside his tobacco pouch when he went down the hall to do his business. She had taken it because he'd slapped her, hard and twice across the face, for laughing at something stupid he said. But then he'd kissed her and stroked her and pushed her down on the bed and afterward she felt a little bad about the stealing. She told herself she'd put it back in the morning. But in the morning he was gone.

*Let that be a lesson,* Rae told herself as she pushed back the gunnysack curtains and slipped out the window. From the hallway came the footsteps of the landlady, clumping up the stairs. Let that be a lesson right there: God helped those who helped themselves.

She stayed in Memphis until the money ran out, which was a day after she spent $4.50 on a pretty little navy-blue gingham suit from Sears. She put it on and walked out of the store with her head held high. She had been gone thirty-eight days from home.

It took her two days to get back home, catching a ride where she could and walking where she could not. More than one white man stopped to pat the seat next to him, his face all loose and shining, his hat tipped back. These she declined, politely if she could or by veering into the fields. In her sack she carried her shoes, her second dress, a few underthings, a comb for her hair, and a bright blue scrap of satin given her by the teacher's son. She had asked for a dress; he'd laughed and said he had no money for such foolishness. But then he'd taken her into a dry-goods shop and told her to pick out a scrap of fabric to make herself a scarf to cover her head.

On the second day she swayed a little as she walked, dizzy. *I'm hungry,* she told herself; *hungry, that's all.* But she already knew what it really was.

A gray-haired man who reminded her of her grandfather took her as far as Freedom in his wagon. She thanked him and walked the rest of the way. It was twilight and the sun fell down in the sky as she walked up the road toward her Eba's house. She knew the world would be outside on their porches, sitting, smoking, talking, easing up from a hard day. Everybody would see her come.

It was November and the air was dry and cooling. As she walked dust flew up into her face and mouth as if mocking her, calling *you back you back.* No dust in Memphis, paved streets she had walked and walked with the teacher's son, marveling at stores. *Welcome home, welcome home.* She threw her head high. When she got to the fork in the road she saw a figure coming toward her in the gathering darkness. It seemed to have two heads, one normal and one on its right shoulder, and it limped, dragging its right foot heavily through the dirt. An evil spirit, she thought. Why not?

But when she got closer she saw it was only Hootie Taylor, coming out from the woods. He had a rifle slung over one shoulder, a sack hung heavily beneath it, a pail swinging in his hand. He'd been hunting and the sack was full.

"Hey," he said, stopping before her.

Rae wasn't scared. She had known Hootie all her life. He was two years older than she was, or maybe three—nobody knew for sure, not even him. He was the last of twelve children, and by the time he was born his mother was so worn out she stopped marking things like names and birth dates. She died three months after he was born. His father died six months later, out hunting for his hungry children when he tripped and fell on his rifle. The older boys took over the cropping and the older girls took over the house and nobody paid much attention to Hootie except to feed and diaper him and finally name him Hootie when he was two and hooting around the house like an owl.

"Hey," she said, and moved to go around him, expecting Hootie to continue on his way. But to her surprise he fell in line with her, walking.

"You back?" Hootie asked.

"Looks like."

She waited for him to ask what happened to the teacher's son, why she had come back alone. But Hootie, he was silent, the only sound his steady breathing as he walked. And she remembered men were not like women in that way. They wouldn't be the ones whispering behind her back, calling her fast, smiling to her face; they would take out her humiliation in a different way, or try to. She didn't have to worry about that mess from the men. She had only to wait until they came around.

"Evening, Hootie!" It was Miss Grant, calling from her porch. "What that with you? That Rae?"

"Yes, ma'am!" Rae called before Hootie could answer. She would speak for herself. "It's me."

"You back, gal?" Miss Grant called. It was not so much a question as a triumphant statement of fact. No doubt Miss Grant had predicted just this thing. Rae raised her head high and called, "Yes, ma'am, I'm back!" and did not slow her pace. Miss Grant cackled her glee.

They passed on from sight of Miss Grant's house and kept on walking. After a moment Hootie said, "Carry your bag?"

She tried to look at him through the twilight, but darkness was falling now and it would be a moonless night. She could not see his face. The sack wasn't heavy, she barely felt its weight against the strength of her back. And anyway nobody had ever asked to carry something for her before. That was the way men were when they wanted something. From any other man Rae would have guessed what he wanted, but Hootie was—or at least folks *said* Hootie was—slow.

"You want to carry my sack, Hootie Taylor?"

"Want to marry you, too," he said plainly.

She couldn't help herself; she laughed. Stopped right there on the road and busted out laughing. It was so far from what she had expected. Hootie stood next to her, staring off a little into the darkening field as if watching a picture show.

"Marry me? Boy, you crazy!"

But Hootie did not laugh. He put down his head, spoke to the dirt. "Got me a mule while you was gone."

Darkness had fallen completely now, folks were going inside. From their path on the road Rae could barely see the houses as they retreated into the gloom. All that was visible was the glow from kerosene lamps inside. Hootie started walking again and she fell in step beside him.

"Gonna get me a plot," he said. "Already talked to Mr. Burch about the one down near the creek. Gonna start cropping for my ownself."

A late last mosquito, putting off his winter death just one more night, flew down from the darkness and bit Rae on the neck. She slapped it hard, then picked it off, feeling the calluses on her fingers against the soft skin of her neck. She thought of a black woman she'd seen in Memphis rubbing some kind of cream into her hands. When Rae had asked her what it was for the woman said, "Mens like their women soft, sugar. Even their hands."

"You'd be a big help to me, Rae," he said. "And I'll take care of you."

They rounded a bend in the road. She knew that up ahead and just off to the right stood Eba's house, though she could not quite make it out in the gloom. Not that she needed to see it to know it was there; it stood stark and clear in her mind's eye, even clearer now, it seemed, than before her thirty-eight days of escape. The split-rail fence weathered to grayness, the beaten dirt path to the porch. She saw the sagging steps, the tar-paper roof, the loose weatherboarding on the sides. She saw the four pine poles propping up the roof over the porch, poles against which she had leaned a thousand times staring down the road

She saw the two clustering rooms inside, always close and dark, the potbelly stove Eba used to cook and heat. She saw the iron bed in the back room, the pallets on the floor, the barley sacks they used for pillows. She saw the walls covered from ceiling to floor with yellowing newspaper, newspaper Eba carried home from the white families whose bathrooms she scrubbed, and wet with cornstarch paste and slapped up against the wall against the winter wind.

She saw, out back and up the path, the outhouse with its stench of piss and shit and lime, its hoe propped up just inside the door for killing snakes.

She saw, too, the cotton fields on every side; they pressed right up against the house like weeds against a tomato plant, trying to suffocate it, trying to steal its air and light. The fields were red brown now and barren, stripped and fallow, miles of ugly endless dirt. In the spring they'd be planted and all through the summer they'd be chopped and in the fall they'd be picked over and over again. She'd always thought cotton fields in winter an ugly sight.

"You got a house?" she asked.

"Gonna build one. Right off."

She was quiet a moment, listening to the wind.

"I want four rooms," she said. "And a brick fireplace and a decent cookstove. And a big front porch, big as the house for sitting on."

He handed her the bag. "All right, then," he said.

With no other word Rae turned and went up the beaten-dirt path to Eba's house. As she walked she thought it funny that folks said Hootie was none too smart, for he seemed plenty smart enough for what he needed. She saw quite clearly, for instance, how he had gotten himself two mules for the price of one.

# Chapter Four

On my first day of graduate school a professor opened class by saying "Nobody ever grows up wanting to be a sociologist." The class erupted in laughter, as if this was the funniest thing any of us had ever heard. Later on I realized this was more than just grad-student sucking up to the faculty; it was the sound of the greatly relieved. Misanthropic psychologists, disenchanted philosophers, panicky historians staring unemployment in its hissing, yellow eye—these were the lost souls who, wandering the bright hallways of academia, found their way gratefully to the dim sociology floor. Put a hundred sociologists into a room and fifty of them will sip a scotch and tell the lighthearted tale of how they Became A Sociologist By Accident. Try that with doctors. Or firemen. Few other fields can boast such a high stumble quotient.

Perhaps it is because, in part, no one really knows what sociology is. Sociologists themselves have trouble agreeing on a definition. Is it the study of human society? Of the interaction that occurs within and between human social groups, which is slightly different? And if that is so, what differentiates it from social psychology? From political science? Is sociology more precisely the study of social order, seeking to understand how the components of society, the social relationships and institutions, support or undermine "society"? Is it all of the above? Does anybody care?

"The softest of the soft," Eddie liked to tease, displaying his natural scientist's disdain for the human sciences. Even applying the word *science* to sociology or psychology or poli sci made him laugh, and no rigorous study, no theory, no carefully crafted method of research could shut him up. "Where's the empirical evidence?" he asked. "Where's the predictive measure? Where are the experiments?"

Back in the early days of our relationship, back when we still had the energy to explore each other's inner life, Eddie and I sometimes wondered aloud about the inappropriateness of our respective career choices. Eddie the extrovert, the people person, believing in human goodness in spite of it all, spending his days alone with his computer and his numerical modeling and his algorithm analyses. And me, the strong, silent type, the cautious introvert, the most-people-are-more-trouble-than-they're-worth cynic, spending her days up to her armpits in the magical mush of human connectedness.

But for me sociology was a way to connect the dots of a badly fractured world. A biologist looks at human behavior in terms of physiological process, the churnings of our physical selves. To a biologist we are depressed or hyperactive or alcoholic because of the chemicals zapping through our brains. A psychologist delves into the muck of human behavior and comes up grasping the individual psyche, the single ego as it has developed from birth to adulthood. To a psychologist, it's not so much about biology as biography.

But sociologists believe no social group—not black people or white people, not baseball players or academics or nuns—can be understood simply by examining the characteristics of the individuals within.

Émile Durkheim, a pioneering sociologist of the nineteenth century, compared the nature of a social group to bronze. Bronze is formed from melted copper, tin, and lead. But a metalsmith cannot understand bronze simply by understanding any one of its component parts: bronze is harder than copper or tin or lead and reacts in different ways from each of them.

Furthermore, even individuals themselves can't be understood out of the context of their social groups. You can't understand Bill Clinton without understanding white America and Southern America and rural America and poverty. You can't understand George W. Bush without understanding white America and New England prep schools and privileged Eastern wealth. Try and you will only be led astray.

*As it turned out, Planned Parenthood was closed on New Year's* Day. This fact struck me as plain bad management, not to mention wholly irresponsible. It was like a doctor closing his office during an epidemic or a church closing its doors on the day of a national tragedy. If there was any day such an organization ought to be present and accounted for, if there was any hour of great need, it was that ugly, blinkered morning after, January 1, the day of national regret. Released from the basement but not from anxiety, I went to bed early that evening, trying to rush forward the coming day.

But the next day was Sunday and—astonishingly enough—the local office remained closed. I could not believe it. I stood in my kitchen that morning and listened to the recorded message over and over and over until the words were like beetles crawling up my spine.

"You okay?" Eddie asked, coming into the kitchen.

I started, slamming down the telephone. "What?"

"I dropped my spoon and you nearly jumped through the roof," he said.

I tried to smile. "Sorry. Just daydreaming I guess."

He nodded and poured himself another cup of coffee. We had decided to skip church, spend the day relaxing together as a family. At least that's what I'd said.

He poured the coffee, added some cream. The kids were in the dining room, finishing off the waffles I'd prepared. Unable to eat more than a bite, I'd already scraped mine into the trash.

"So what's the plan for the day?" Eddie asked. "Sledding?"

"Maybe."

"A movie?"

"We'll figure something out," I said.

Eddie looked at me. "The kids want us to do something together," he said. "All of us."

"Did they say that?"

"Yes."

Part of me didn't believe him. The fear of being pregnant was somehow making it hard for me to sit with the girls and maybe they sensed that. What did the parenting magazines say—children were sensitive? They picked up on things? Maybe my beautiful, sensitive daughters could tell I was feeling the weight of this potential baby like a stone around my neck. At breakfast I'd sat in a kind of zone watching Harriet saw at her waffles and Paula drip syrup all over her shirt as she fed herself until Paula snapped me out of it by pointing at my untouched plate. "What's the matter, Mommy?" she asked. "Don't your waffles taste as good as mine?"

I touched Eddie on the arm. "We'll do something fun," I told him. "Why don't you finish the paper first. I need to take a shower."

Eventually Eddie and I planned to carve twin offices for ourselves out of the house's vast, unfinished, walk-up attic. But in the meantime we had set up the computer and our bookshelves and our overflowing filing cabinets in the spare bedroom at the top of the stairs. It was a small room, scarcely big enough to hold a twin bed and dresser but with triple windows along one wall overlooking the backyard. The walls were still papered with huge pink peonies from the previous owner, two-dimensional flowers as big as my head. Ripping down the paper and repainting the room were on my list of things to do, my happy homemaker list. I was forcing myself through the list one by one by one.

The Planned Parenthood Web site listed a call-in phone line for emergency contraception but it operated only between nine and eleven weekdays and Saturdays; requests on Sunday would not be processed until the workweek resumed. I would either have to wait, or try my luck with a list of local physicians who would call in a prescription for an emergency contraceptive. I got up to ease shut the door to the room, then sat and double-clicked the list.

The answering services at the first three numbers said the doctors were no longer offering the service or had left the practice. The fourth number was for the student health center at Boston University; they still offered the prescription but only to students. By the fifth number my stomach hurt. I could hear Eddie and the children below me, wrestling on the living room rug, giggling. I dialed the number and explained the situation to the woman from the answering service. To my surprise she put me on hold. A few minutes later, a man's voice came on the line—abrupt, older, accented in some unidentifiable way. I imagined him snatching the phone as he hurried down a hospital corridor.

"This is Dr. Aranki."

"Oh. Hello, Doctor," I said, immediately cowed. I had my PhD, was, of course, also technically a doctor, but everybody knew it wasn't the same, and in speaking to physicians, I usually caught myself slipping into the role of supplicant just like everybody else. "My name is Grace Jefferson. I need a prescription for the morning-after pill."

"The what?" he demanded. Behind him was a noise that sounded like pots and pans being slammed together. I couldn't tell if he could not hear me or was simply furious.

"The morning-after pill?" I said. "Emergency contraception?"

"What do you need that for?" he snapped.

"Because I had unprotected sex?" I was so taken aback by his tone it came out as a question instead of a statement, and I heard myself rushing to add, "With my husband."

Another loud clanging and then, sweetly, the shattering and tinkling of glass. The doctor snorted in disgust; whether at the person who had dropped the items or me I could not tell. I was torn between the desire to curse him out for his rudeness and to burst into helpless, feminine tears.

"Did I call the wrong—" I began, but he cut me off.

"What is your name?" he demanded.

"Grace Jefferson. Like the president."

"Give me the phone number of your pharmacy."

The relief was like a breeze then. I gave him the number, pausing between each numeral to make sure he got it right. When I was finished I held my breath and prepared for a lecture or a curse or something from this lunatic physician. Whatever it was I would take it, because he was saving my life.

But all he said, after repeating the number back to me, was, "My mother hoped I'd write poetry." Then he hung up.

We all went sledding at the park, and when we returned, I told Eddie I suddenly remembered I had promised to make up a batch of play dough for Harriet's preschool and needed cream of tarter. It was the absurd specificity of the lie that made it work; Eddie nodded and waved me out the door.

At the drugstore I sat in the parking lot holding the first two pills, so pale and weightless in my palm. The informational pamphlet said the pills were most effective when taken within twenty-four hours after unprotected intercourse, but could be taken up to seventy-two hours afterward. I was thirty-eight hours and counting and I didn't even go back into the store for the water I'd forgotten to buy but gathered my saliva and forced the pills down. According to the directions, I would need to take the second dose twelve hours later. And to prepare for the possibility of nausea and vomiting. And because of who I was and where I lived and when, it was really that simple. As simple as one, two, three.

Sitting in the parking lot with my coat pulled tight around me, I wondered what my mother would have done with such a modern miracle, with such a painless little escape hatch wrapped in shrunken foil. My smart-but-hemmed-in mother, whose own body remained a dark and dangerous mystery to her. How about my grandmother—what would she have done? Or my ancestors, those nameless slave women huddled in their slave shacks, praying the master did not come tipping down the lane. Pregnancy was such calamity for them so much of the time. Fulfillment, too, of course; joy and determination and love and stupid, stubborn hope but also calamity. Disaster. Every birth a knife aimed at the heart because the master could always sell that child away. Every birth a chain around the ankle, because with children to love and worry you couldn't risk the run to freedom, or just walk into the river and die. You had to stay and suffer. Would those women still have chosen to be pregnant if they'd had an easy choice? Would they have kept on making those generations, or swallowed the pills and called the whole damn thing to a halt?

*I spent the rest of the day waiting to be nauseous. Not that I wanted* to be sick, but it would have made me feel the pills were working. Also, a little nausea seemed the least I should expect to pay. By that evening I was exhausted from the waiting and the willing and the anxiety.

Even in the best of times it was the longest day, Sunday. The most intimate, the most claustrophobic: the day of no escape. Saturdays could be difficult, too, but at least Saturday—regular, nonholiday Saturday—came after Friday and Friday contained a few hours of solitude if Harriet made it to preschool and Paula consented to a nap and so I felt buffered for Saturday. And also Saturday—regular, nonholiday Saturday—skimmed along on a river of activity: dance class for Harriet, swimming lessons for both girls, birthday parties and grass mowing and park visiting and housecleaning and escapist trips to the grocery and hardware stores.

But Sunday stagnated. Sunday was one big, gunky, swamp of family life. The day began with children crawling into our bed and went on and on from there. Even when I rejoined the church, in part—tell God the truth now—to have someplace to take the kids, the day still lingered. By Sunday evening I had sunk so far down into the morass of family, had spent so many hours no more than a foot away from the three of them, that I felt like a claustrophobic in a mining shaft. By Sunday night it was all I could do to stay civil. By Sunday night I was done. And still nausea-free.

Sunday evening I went for a run, then drank two mugs of steaming water—old wives' tale—and curled up on the couch to watch television in an attempt to distract myself. Eddie was down in the basement, setting up his toys. The children were in bed. Two flips of the channel and Sidney Poitier's beautiful, royal face flashed onto the screen. *Guess Who's Coming to Dinner.*

The movie was more than half over, things were rising to a climax. Sidney and his father went into a room in the lovely and sprawling home of Spencer and Kate to have a father-son heart-to-heart about this crazy idea of Sidney marrying a white chick. The father, a retired mailman, took the moment to lay out for his wayward son all the years of hard work and sacrifice he had undergone to give him the very advantages in life that had caught the white girl's eye, how he lugged that damn mailbag around for forty years, not to mention shoveled coal on the weekends, so Sidney could go to college and medical school.

"You owe me," the father says.

And, of course, Sidney explodes, but elegantly. "I owe you nothing! If you carried that bag a million miles, you did what you're supposed to do! Because you brought me into this world. And from that day you owed me everything you could ever do for me like I will owe my son if I ever have another. But you don't own me!"

Sidney Poitier was one of my mother's favorite actors, but she had always hated this particular movie; and for the first time I could see why. It had nothing to do with the fact that the movie never questioned what a man like Sidney's character—a wildly sophisticated, intelligent, and successful international physician—saw in the flippy little white-girl idiot he so adored. Or maybe it had something to do with that, but now I saw that maybe it was also how Sidney treated his father that got my mother's goat. In the confrontation scene between the two, Sidney stands lithe and elegant and as cool as Italian ice while he demolishes his stubby father, with his slumping shoulders and his fake, powdered-gray hair. The movie takes Sidney's side. This is America, where no one owes anyone anything. Least of all family.

For the first time, I could see the father's point. Yes, he'd brought his son into the world and in doing so had incurred certain obligations. But to his way of thinking, he'd signed a contract on the day of his son's birth, a contract that said: I will sacrifice everything for you, I will lay down my own impossible hopes and dreams for your achievable ones. And in return, you owe me a slice of yourself. You will always consider, you will never abandon, you will try not to disappoint. You will not pack up my sacrifice when its time has passed and toss it away. And if his son had no say in the terms, well, what was that but the unfairness of life? Talk to a black man born in 1910 about life being unfair.

What the father was asking of Sidney might have been unfair, but was it really unreasonable? If I'd given up my whole life, I'd sure as hell want a return on my sacrifice. Which was a scary thing to realize. I turned off the movie before the final, gushy makeup moment and crawled upstairs to bed.

Hours later I woke with a dull pain at the bottom of my gut. Yes, I thought, excited even in REM stage. But when I opened my eyes I saw the pain had an external cause: Harriet's foot. She and Paula had crawled into bed and were snoozing contentedly between Eddie and me.

I looked at the clock: 3:20 A.M.

The day I told my old former department chair back in North Carolina I was pregnant with Harriet he smiled and said, "Kiss your last decent night's sleep good-bye." I thought he was exaggerating, trying to crank me up; he was an idiot who disliked me intensely and the feeling was mutual. But the man was the father of four children, something I failed to consider at the time. Even a stopped clock is right twice a day. Just as we finally got both children sleeping through the night, Harriet suddenly developed nightmares: bogeymen and robbers slinking through her window and carrying her away. We got that settled down—kind of—and then Paula graduated from her crib to a twin bed. It was like moving John Dillinger from Alcatraz to Barney Fife's house for safekeeping. Now Paula came wandering every midnight hour, bright-eyed and chatty, astonished at the wonders of the night. All of which meant that more nights than not we ended up three or four to our queen-size bed.

None of this bothered Eddie, who could sleep through a tornado. But the family bed was not my idea of a good situation. When I made the mistake of letting this heresy slip in front of my sister-in-law Hollis, she graciously lent me her dog-eared copy of *The Family Bed.* Being well raised, I received it with thanks and a smile and later tossed it into the recycling bin.

"The last thing I need is a book about family beds!" I ranted to Eddie. "I know everything I need to know about family beds. I grew up in one, only we didn't call it that. We called it poverty!"

Eddie just smiled and went to sleep.

For the bulk of my childhood I shared a single bed with at least one and often both of my sisters and I disliked it. I disliked it because it was a struggle. I disliked it because Lena hogged the blankets and Dot whimpered and shuddered in the night, jiggling the bed. Most of all I disliked it because, as television clearly showed me, every other child in America got to sleep in his or her own neatly tucked single bed and the fact that we had to share was just more embarrassing proof of our weirdness and our poverty, which seemed the same thing. I wanted to be Cindy Brady, to come home from school one day to a house transformed into an expansive California ranch with open stairs and a maid's quarters and a slant-ceilinged room for my sisters and myself. The room would have pink curtains and a matching vanity and a rose-printed bedspread draped regally across my bunk. The top one, my own. My sacred, untouchable space.

But in reality I slept with Dot or Lena in one bed, Sidney, because he was a boy, slept in regal splendor in the other and our mother spent most of her nights curled on the living-room couch. Why she did not claim one of the two beds for herself is something I never wondered about. Not as a child.

My mother always held out college as our salvation, the thing that would lift us from the muck and misery of our lives. I didn't take much convincing, but it would have been even easier had she thought to mention the dorm-room bed. That first night freshman year, while my roommate prowled the hallways, breasts bouncing, beer mug in hand, I lay between my brand-new sheets, still creased and starchy-smelling (I didn't know you were supposed to wash them first); I felt such joy I thought my heart would crack. That was the night I realized something about myself: I slept much better alone in bed. I slept better untouched.

But try saying that to a five-year-old.

Harriet stirred a little, whimpering in her sleep. Nightmares are common in preschool children, the books all say. All that furious learning going on during the day, all that acquisition of language and understanding and identity has to work itself out somewhere, has to find release. Dreams are our way of making sense of a nonsensical world. Harriet whimpered again and reached out for me.

I took her hand, held it, smoothed her forehead with a kiss. But the clock read 3:35 and the day was coming. I couldn't sleep in that bed, hemmed in on both sides. I would have to leave.

My plan was to slide down, swing one leg up and over Harriet to the floor, and then push my body clear. If I could do it without touching her or shifting the bed too much, maybe she would not wake up and my escape would be clean. I might have made it, too, had Eddie not chosen that moment to snort in his sleep. It was like a tractor trailer shifting into gear beside your ear. Harriet opened her eyes.

"Mommy?" she murmured.

"Shush."

"Mommy, where you going?"

I put Pooh in her arms, pulled the blanket up, and tucked it around. "It's okay," I whispered. "Go back to sleep."

"Don't leave," my daughter demanded, so sleepy she slurred the words like a drunk. "Mommy stay."

I knelt beside the bed and put my hand on her back. "Shush."

"Stay," she said again.

If there was a Ten Commandments of modern American parenting, a set of rules for soccer moms and softball dads, then commandment number one was surely this: Don't lie to your children, especially not about leaving. I had read as much in more parenting magazines than I cared to remember and been lectured on the point on the first day of Harriet's's preschool. "Never sneak out," the teacher warned as we all stood there, dazed and bewildered among the ankle-high chairs, our children clinging to our legs. "It may seem easier, but when your child realizes you are gone he will feel deeply, deeply betrayed. And he will never ever trust you again. Or anyone else, for that matter. For the rest of his natural life."

"Mommy, stay," Harriet mumbled. She was five years old now, pointed like an arrow toward kindergarten in the fall and then to the world beyond. Old enough to lay down memories that would stand the rest of her life: the smell of paste on construction paper and the taste of licorice, the feel of a best friend's hand in her own, the sound of a mother sighing in frustration and pain. Everything counted from here on out.

"Shush, go to sleep," I whispered. "Just going to the bathroom."

When her breathing steadied I grabbed a blanket from the chest and fled downstairs. The living room was pitch-black but I didn't need the light. I felt my way toward the couch, lumpy in the middle and sagging at the ends and just big enough for one.

*Three hours later I woke again, this time to the sound of the pipes* creaking as water rushed from the basement to the shower upstairs. With the blinds drawn in the living room I could not tell if the gray light seeping in around the corners was just the gray of an early-winter morning or the warning gray of rain.

I pulled the blanket over my head, wondering what would happen if I just lay there all day or all week, if I simply refused to face the world for a while. I imagined poor Eddie in a panic, not knowing who to call or what to do. He could handle the basics of dressing and feeding the children, but pretty soon things would start tumbling: doctor's appointments and oil changes, school meetings and laundry and having the chimney cleaned. All officially my responsibility now that I wasn't working but even back in North Carolina, even when I was carrying eight courses a year, I'd done the same things. This was a common complaint, of course; the bane of modern womanhood, how we carried so much more than our husbands, how we shouldered a disproportionate share of the weight. All my friends back in North Carolina and the few acquaintances I'd made so far in Boston said the same thing. But it was easy to tell which women secretly thrived on being indispensable, which ones deep in their hearts loved being the Big Boss, ultimately responsible. They were the ones who chuckled when describing how their husbands walked past the dog vomit on the stairs, twice. Me, I gritted my teeth.

Curling deeper beneath the blankets, I thought how wonderful it would be to just give in to depression, to just sink into its warm and watery depths. But of course I couldn't. "Don't ever have that first breakdown," my mother had joked when we were teenagers. "They'll never let you forget it." I had no idea what she was talking about then but now I did. *Be strong,* she was saying. *Cry if you have to but keep on keeping on.*

Black women and their damned, exhausting strength.

I threw off the covers, forced my feet onto the freezing floorboards. I would get Harriet off to preschool, run Paula around at the park for an hour, then feed her and get her down for a nap in time to have an hour to myself that morning. I would work on my CV. I would think about starting my book, an as-yet-undefined examination of the black middle class. I would get a grip.

Propelling my body across the living room, I checked the thermostat, then reached the stairs and began to climb. At the second floor, I turned onto the landing and glanced out the window to check the sky, but I couldn't see it. All I saw was snow. The world was white with it. Which meant no school.

"Crap."

When I reached our bedroom, it was empty. A minute later Eddie came bounding in, a towel draped around his waist. Eddie took the fastest, most efficient showers of any human being I had ever known. Navy showers he called them, though the closest he had ever been to a submarine was when, as a child, he visited his seaman father at port.

"Where are the kids?" I asked

"Hmm? Oh, I carried them back to their beds last night," he said. "Didn't you see them when you passed their room?"

I shook my head. I'd walked right past their room without even checking. Very nonmaternal.

Eddie strolled to the window and pulled up the shade with a resounding thud. "Coming down like a mother out there! They're predicting eight to ten by afternoon." He unwrapped his towel and tossed it onto the foot of our cherry sleigh bed. "Schools are closed."

I had the urge to pick up the towel and thwack him, but I fought it away. "If we're going to live in a place that shuts down every time it snows, we might as well go back to Durham."

Eddie smiled but I could see what he was thinking behind it: he was wondering if this was going to become a theme with me, this might-as-well-go-back-to-North-Carolina tune.

"There's the little matter of school buses," Eddie said. He was pulling on his snow-day business attire: black dress slacks, crisp white oxford shirt, black boots. Eddie always dressed two notches better than the other people at his level, the other math geeks and chemistry geniuses at the chemical-industry research firm. Like Eddie, they were all holding their first big jobs, their first jobs worth holding, pulling in money that made their sweat-labor wages back in prestigious academia look anemic, but they were, all of them, white and they slouched in wearing Irish knit sweaters and khakis or even jeans. But it was a point of pride for Eddie to do better, to dress like a professional. Not that it was demanded of him or expected, or anything like that. No, in science Eddie thought he'd found a sphere in which race would sift away.

Such dreams men had.

I went to my dresser for a pair of woolen socks. When I turned back into the room, Eddie was studying me. "You look tired," he said. "Sleep okay?"

I knew what he was getting at, what he was hoping for. "Fine," I said. "Just need some sunlight to perk me up."

He smiled, came over to sit beside me on the bed. "So what else is new with you?" he asked.

"Not much," I said.

Some women I knew complained that their husbands never talked to them. That wasn't a problem with Eddie; he talked all the time, and listened as well. He wanted to communicate.

When I was five months pregnant with Harriet he would wake up some Sunday mornings, kiss me on the forehead, wrap his arms around me, and ask how I was feeling, what I was feeling, what I was thinking about, what was going on. I would wake up and think, *Why is this person talking to me?* Part of that was just a personality clash: Eddie was the chirpy morning bird while I was the nightest of owls. But some days the feeling would stretch past my shower and past my coffee and straight on into noon. I'd be reading on the living room couch or at the computer doing work or at the kitchen table contemplating space and Eddie would say something and the irritation would just crawl up my back. I would think: *Can't you just leave me alone? Why are you talking to me, anyway?* And then I'd think, *Oh. Because that's what couples do, you lunatic. Get hold of yourself.*

Not only did couples *talk*, but women *loved* it when they did. Wasn't that what the seventies were about—women finding their strength and men finding their emotions? Becoming more *available*? I would read a novel or watch a movie and some woman would be clawing at her strong, silent type, trying to pry him open, trying to make him spill all over the floor and my stomach would clench. *Leave him alone!* But this was wrong: unwomanly, unnatural. I told myself it was the hormones. Every one of my emotions was zooey; they'd settle down after the baby was born. Only they didn't; some nights at dinner I'd look around the table at the children, chattering gaily and competing for my attention, and at Eddie, beaming at me across the salad bowl and I would think, *Why do these people keep insisting I interact?* And then I'd tell myself, *Because that's what families do, you lunatic. Get hold of yourself.*

"Got any projects in the works?" Eddie asked. "How about finding someone to work on the attic?"

I stood up, pretending to stretch. "Actually, if I get a minute today I'm going to work on my CV," I told him. "Update it, put it in the mail to a few places. If I get a whole ten or twelve minutes to myself I might even try to piece together some thoughts for a book."

Eddie stood, too, moved to his closet for a tie. "No hurry on sending out the CVs, though."

"Fall semester's not that far away," I said.

"But if you—" he stopped, started again. "I mean, you'd hate to start working then have to take maternity leave a few months later."

I began yanking the covers up on the bed. It would be easier to tell him if I was not facing him, and I needed to tell him. This needed to stop. "Eddie. You're getting way ahead of yourself. I—"

But he came up behind me and put his arms around my waist, cutting me off. "I know, I know!" he said, lifting me a few inches in the air then putting me down again. "The chances are minute. But I can't help it—it feels like something's happening. It feels like the boy is on the way."

He turned me around to face him and I saw the happy tears standing in his eyes. Had it been anyone else, the cynic in me might have thought such an overt display manipulative. But Eddie's emotions were always right there on the surface, and they were always genuine. It was one thing that always caught me by surprise about him.

In my social construct, crafted during childhood and resistant to alteration ever after, the male of the species rejected feelings. Men were immune to love. Loving and committed husbands, beaming, cheering fathers—these were legion on television when I was a girl but I never made the mistake of believing in them any more than I went whistling for Scooby-Doo down at the park. Boys wanted beneath your skirts and they might even be tricked into a relationship for a while, but they never came willingly and they could walk away at a moment's notice, even from their children, without a hiccup of regret. Women were the lovers, men the beloved, and the beloved had no good reason to cry.

"Of course, I have no scientific basis for that assumption," Eddie said, grinning. "But science isn't everything. Is it?"

But over the course of our marriage I had come to see that men were, in fact, the more vulnerable of the sexes. All the bluster and strutting was really just to cover their great and yawning need for us; not just for our love but also our belief in them, our adoration and delight. At a conference on multicultural feminism once, at the start of my career, a woman from Ghana had defended both the practice of polygamy and the traditional role of the African wife before a politely hostile audience. "It is a wife's job to protect her husband's dignity," the woman insisted, her chin raised and her own voice dripping with dignity. The woman sitting next to me, an older colleague battling through an unpleasant divorce, leaned over and whispered, "In other words, it's the wife's job to keep her husband from the sure and certain knowledge of his own idiocy." I laughed but my colleague was serious. "Really, Grace," she said. "If a woman can just do that, without resentment and maybe even love, they'll both have a happy life."

Turning to Eddie, I said, "No. Science isn't even half of it."

The problem was, I didn't seem to have the muscle for such behavior. Maybe the ability to adore men was best developed early in childhood, like learning a second language or taking on the piano. Maybe it required a father or other doting male figure, someone to cart you on his back and tickle your toes and buy you ice-cream cones. My muscle had never been properly flexed, and so it had atrophied. And no amount of exercise now could get it back.

But Harriet and Paula would have that muscle; I saw it developing every evening when Eddie came through the door. Maybe that meant they'd have an easier time with this thing called marriage. If I could only stick it out.

I forced my arms up around my husband's neck and kissed him. Then I had to step away, because a strange little fillip of anger was threatening me. It was all his fault, anyway, Eddie's. For choosing me in the first place. Why would he pick someone incapable of love, at least love the way he needed it: open, embracing, without reserve or silent place. Why hadn't he chosen better? Why hadn't he picked someone else?

Eddie must have felt it. He walked to his dresser and lifted his wallet into his hands. "I wish I could make you happy," he said.

"It's not your job."

"But I want to."

"I know," I said.

"I love you."

I knew my line; there was only one possible response if the union was to stand. "Me, too," I said. Then: "I better go check on the children."

Eddie looked at his watch. It was brand-new and elegantly expensive, his gift to himself. "I better hit the road. The streets will be bad."

"You driving?" I asked. Eddie normally took the train into the city, though we owned a second car, an ancient hatchback.

"Gotta work late," he said. "Plus the T will be crazy. Actually, mind if I take the van?"

Some men would rather chew bricks than be caught driving a minivan, but Eddie loved our spanking-new family mobile. It was heavier and far more stable than his car, and sported all the bells and whistles our demographic was supposed to demand: antilock breaks, all-wheel drive, a CD player, and heated seats.

"With the snow and everything, you guys are probably staying in today?" Eddie asked.

I had discussed the possibility of actual coffee at an actual coffee shop with my friend Valerie the day before. But she disliked driving in the snow. So that was probably out and he might as well be safe.

"I mean," said Eddie, "you don't have any place to go. Right?"

Our bedroom faced south and from the window I could usually see all the way to the stop sign and even beyond that a little. But today the snow blocked from sight everything beyond the stop sign.

"Right," I told him. "No place at all."


*"Hey, Mommy," Harriet said when she woke up. "What are we going to do today?"*

This was often the first question my children asked me in the morning, followed later by What are we going to do next? and I'm bored; can we do something now? Some days I felt less like a mother and more like a cruise ship director, tossed before a crowd of bickering old farts. *Entertain us now!*

"Is it a school day?" Harriet asked, as she did each morning.

"Normally yes. But it's ..." I paused, braced myself. "It's snowing outside."

Harriet leaped to her feet with a scream. "Snowing! Yeah!"

"Your school is closed."

"Yeah!" she screamed, bouncing up and down on her bed. "Can we go sledding?"

I stood up to keep my teeth from being knocked through my gums. "We'll see."

"Can we play Candy Land?"

Oh, how I hated Candy Land. The most mind-numbing of all mind-numbing children's games. "Let me get some coffee and we'll see," I said.

"Can we do arts and craps?"

I smiled. "Arts and craps it is. But coffee first."

We headed downstairs, me to the kitchen, Harriet to join her sister on the living-room couch, where I heard her explaining the day's itinerary. "Mommy's making us breakfast and then I get to stay home from school because of the snow and we get to play all day. We're gonna play Candy Land. Tell Mommy you want to play Candy Land."

In the kitchen a greasy pan sat on the stove; Eddie had fried himself eggs for breakfast again, despite warnings from his doctor about his climbing cholesterol. I moved the pan to the sink.

"Breakfast!" I called, pulling down a box of Cheerios from the cabinet. I looked out the window at the sky, leaden, at the back-yard, already blanketed. The snow blew sideways now, coating the bare, brown bones of the trees. Not for the first time I wondered how something so pretty could also be so encasing, so treacherous. I had already learned to hate the way the world narrowed in a New England winter, the way it contracted in upon itself. In summer I might be able to choose one of the two paved paths and countless grassy ones between my front porch and the escape of my drive-wayed car, but in a New England winter there was only one path between point A and point B, one path, shoveled by Eddie, who thrived on doing such manly, manly things.

The morning crawled by in a haze of childish bickering. I set up the easel for painting; Paula tipped over the yellow, slapped a brush full of red onto her paper, spattered some blue, and announced she was done. Harriet spent two minutes painting a garden scene, then dissolved into tears when blue sky dripped into her sun and turned it green. I sent them into the living room and cleaned up the mess.

We made oatmeal cookies and I cleaned up the mess. We made paper snowflakes and I cleaned up the mess. We read a book then had a snack of wheat crackers and orange slices and juice. Harriet spilled her juice on the floor. Paula, only recently trained, got so involved in the book she forgot she had to pee and urinated in her chair. I cleaned up the mess.

At ten, having exhausted both ideas and patience, I dumped a box of LEGOs on the living-room floor and fled to the kitchen for a cup of tea. When the telephone rang I debated not answering it, just allowing the answering machine to pick it up. Screening calls was a habit into which I had fallen recently, after it dawned on me that probably seventy percent of the time I answered the phone I

My mother drew in her breath. "The baby okay?"

"She fine," I said. "I think Harriet took a toy from her."

"Oh."

More silence. In the kitchen the clock ticked away.

"Mom?"

"You should not say things like that," my mother said. "When you say things like that, you sound just like your grandmother."

I winced. When we were young and did something selfish or hurtful, when we called one another vicious names or pinched or hit one another, my mother could chastise us with a torrent of words ending in the phrase *just like your father! You get that mess right from him.* Since our contact with our father was spotty at best, we had to take our mother's word that such behavior was indeed like him and was also something dark, something to be struggled against. "You are just like your father" was enough to shame us back into line until the day Lena yelled back, "Good! Better him than you!"

But being like my grandmother was infinitely worse.

"Some folks only care about themselves," my mother continued. "The world is full of people like that."

Opposite me fine rivulets of something brown and grainy, chocolate perhaps, ran down the wall. Who knew how long I had let it sit there? Who knew what legion of disgusting roaches and ants I had failed to notice it drawing to my house.

"I hope I didn't raise you to be one of them, Grace," my mother said.

I reached over and scratched at the brown stuff, driving it beneath my nails. "I love my children," I said.

My mother gave a dismissive laugh. "The last thing my mother would say before she ran off down the road was always 'Mama love you.'"

I imagined her, my grandmother. Sashaying down some red-dust Mississippi roadway on her way to adventure while behind her a child sat on a porch and cried.

"Love means next to nothing," my mother said. "Duty is what counts."

*After hanging up with my mother, I sat in the hallway a few minutes,* wondering for the first time in a long time about my grandmother. My mother, and as far as I knew the rest of my mother's family, had been out of touch with her for years. Nobody wondered, nobody mentioned, nobody talked about her and neither had I; for a long time, neither had I. But that didn't mean I couldn't start.

# Chapter Five

Here's something else I know about my grandmother: she gave birth to the first of her seven children in 1942 in a Mississippi Delta sharecropper's shack and named her Mattie Mae. The man who gave that child her last name was not the baby's father but he was the first and last man to treat her well—or so the child believed. And of course, believing makes its own kind of truth. I wonder what my grandmother thought about the men in her life, about their purpose and duty toward her. I wonder if she thought partnership was possible. Or had too much damage been done to ever recoup the loss?

### MISSISSIPPI, 1947

*Folks said Rae didn't cry when Hootie died but that was just idle* minds and vicious mouths. In the dark of her bedroom, in the comfort of her bed, she cried a river. Losing Hootie was far from the first hard thing to happen to her, but it was always one of the worst.

Hootie had treated her well—no beatings, no slipping out, no throwing her down anyway when she said no, and he never asked her to rise earlier or work harder or sweat longer than he did himself. He said he would build her a house and he did and it was a good sight better than Eba's shack. It had four nice rooms instead of two: one big room with a fireplace for heating *and* a woodstove for cooking, and three skinner rooms, sitting side by side off the back wall. One of the rooms was their bedroom and one of the rooms was for washing up and one of the rooms Hootie said could be her own for sewing and mending and storing food and more children if they came along, which they didn't, and for woman times, which made her laugh. The baby Mattie slept on a pallet near the woodstove in the big room and in the wintertime they slept there, too, and dragged the washtub there to bathe. He put in two windows in the front and two windows on the side and glass where he could instead of tar paper or boards. He built a fireplace from bricks he carried home from here and there, and built the walls tight to keep out the wind. He built her a table from scrub pine and a bed from oak.

He wanted another mule and he wanted to own his own land and he wanted her to get what she wanted, too. He promised to take her to Chicago someday, to buy an automobile and ride up there in style, and he would have, too, except he got sick. One day he was fine and the next he was sluggish and the next his whole body swole up and he could barely move. She made him stay in bed, told him to eat and drink water, but it did no good. Two months later he was dead.

She found him in the morning after she came back from pumping water from the well. She pulled the curtain to the bedroom door, went outside to the yard where Mattie sat on the stool making pies of mud, took the child by the hand, and set off toward Eba's house.

"Where's Mr. Hootie this morning?" Mattie asked as they walked.

It was her favorite question: *Where's Mr. Hootie? When's he coming home?* From day one the child had been crazy about the man, so crazy Rae swore the first word out of the girl's mouth wasn't mama or dada but Hootie. *Where's Mr. Hootie?* Hootie never pretended he was her father, never told her to call him anything but his name, but he treated her like his own. Fed and sheltered the child, gave her piggyback rides, and carved her whistles from pecan sticks and brought her home sugar cubes smuggled in the pockets of his overalls. He built her a little three-legged stool to sit on by the fire, told her it was hers and hers alone. The girl carried that stool everywhere she went, all around the house and out to the field and back, until the wood was rubbed smooth and shiny from her little hands.

"He'll change when his own come along," Eba had warned. "He'll make a difference between her and his own blood."

Maybe Hootie would have changed when his own was born, but that never happened. When a year had come and gone and no babies, folks started whispering. Hootie hung his head but she pushed it up again. "Don't make you no less of a man," she told him in their bed at night. "You plenty man enough for me." What she didn't tell him was how glad she was for what he lacked.

"Where's Mr. Hootie this morning?" Mattie asked again. The girl had let go of Rae's hand and was skipping along the road the way she often did. "Mr. Hootie," she sang. "Mr. Hootie is his name."

Rae let the child keep on. It would probably be the last skipping she'd do for a while. Maybe ever; a heart had to be weightless to drift above the world and no woman Rae knew had a heart any lighter than a Mississippi barge. It was a shame the girl had to start becoming a woman at only five years old, but there it was. Life. Womanhood. Becoming a woman was like breaking a mule; you had to start early, before the mule got too strong. Because a too-strong mule wouldn't break and an unbroken mule was useless, an unbroken mule could not exist in the world. It would not be allowed.

"Come here," Rae said after they had gone another few feet. "Stop that jumping around and come over here. Got something to tell you."

Mattie ran to her mother's side. Forever and always the obedient child. Rae bent toward the child but she did not touch her. "Something's happened. Something bad. I'm going to tell you and it's going to hurt and you're just going to have to bear it. Mr. Hootie is dead."

Mattie said nothing, just stood looking into her mother's face.

"He died this morning," Rae went on. "I just saw him, back there, in the house. You know how he's been sick? Well, whatever sickness it was has carried him off and he's dead."

"He's dead?"

"Yes," Rae said.

For a long moment neither one of them spoke. Then Mattie asked, "Mama? Will you be mad if I cry?"

Rae stood up straight, took Mattie's hand, and started walking again. "If you want to cry, go ahead and cry," she said, looking now out over the fields. "Crying ain't good or bad. But nothing is going to change what is, Mattie. Hootie is dead and nothing will bring him back."

They buried him the next morning. Eba, who had stayed the night, helped Rae dress. "I'll watch the baby," she said, taking the heavy, black woolen shawl she'd been holding in her hands and draping it over Rae's head.

Rae, who had already been perspiring, began sweating even more beneath the shawl's heavy weight. Not even eight o'clock in the morning and already the heat was like something alive and hungry. They had to get Hootie into the ground.

"You go stand by your husband one last time," Eba said.

From the front room came the sound of women murmuring,

neighbors dropping by with pots of collard greens and buckets of freshly fried chicken and towering white cakes. They were preparing for the feast. After a funeral there was always a feast.

Rae gathered the ends of the shawl in her hands. "Then what?" she asked her sister. "After I stand by him one last time, then what do I do?"

"Then you go on," Eba said.

She went to say good-bye to Mattie and found the girl curled up like a newborn calf in a corner of the bedroom Rae had shared with Hootie, hiding beneath a pile of his clean work clothes, crying silently. Rae thought about what Hootie would have done had he been there instead of dead. He'd have scrunched up his eyes and puffed out his cheeks and raised his voice like a screech owl and cried, "Mattie! Did you know there was water leaking from your eyes!" Then he would have scooped up the child and tossed her high in the air until she laughed. Rae just sighed and turned to leave. But Mattie's voice stopped her.

"I want Mr. Hootie!" Mattie cried. "Make him come back."

"Can't make him come back," Rae said. "He gone for good. Gone up to the sky to be with God."

"Then I want to go, too! I want to go with him!"

Rae looked at Mattie or what she could see of the child: her legs, thin and ashy and long for her age. Her arms, clutching the cotton sacks. The top of her head with its pale, white cross of scalp dividing her reddish hair into four equal parts. Sometime between yesterday and now Eba had found time to plait the child's hair.

"Soon enough for that, Mattie," Rae said. "In the meantime, you still here. You still here and you better keep on going long as you are. Don't crawl in the grave with nobody."

During the funeral Hootie's five sisters, who had teased him mercilessly as a child and ridiculed him relentlessly for marrying Rae, wailed and screamed and cried and fell out so bad their husbands almost broke their backs trying to hold them up, and the preacher had to shout just to be heard. Rae watched it all from the suffocating shelter of Eba's hood and thought about Hootie. About how he kept promising to take her to Chicago, at least to visit. After the war.

When it was her turn to walk past the grave she carried a branch of honeysuckle she'd snapped from the bush behind their house and dropped it onto the plank-wood coffin. Hootie always said honeysuckle reminded him of her: sweet and abundant and smelling so good.

"Bye, Hootie," she whispered, dropping the branch. "Bye."

They sang "Swing Low, Sweet Chariot" and "Precious Lord" and a few other songs and then the preacher closed his Bible and breathed, "Amen." For a moment no one moved; in the woods behind the graveyard a flock of birds set up a terrible racket, as though to get all their singing out and done with so they could sleep the long, hot afternoon away. Then, as if in agreement, everyone rose and began shuffling back toward the gate. They would be going to Rae's house for food and drink.

"Can I walk with you?"

It was Clarence, the oldest of Hootie's three brothers. He stood beside her, dressed in a clean pair of overalls and a faded black jacket whose sleeves climbed nearly to his elbow, but, unlike most of the other mourners, he was also wearing shoes. Rae noticed them right away. Shoes meant that at some point he'd been able to scrap together enough money to buy a pair. This put him one up on most of the other folks around the plantation. As they liked to say, "Ain't nobody on the place got shoes but the hoss and the boss."

"Come on," he said, stretching a hand toward her arm. "Let me take you home."

Rae looked up at him. Of all the boys Clarence looked the most like Hootie, which was strange given the space between their births. Clarence was the oldest of the family, Hootie the baby; between them there lay a dozen years and a sack of expectations. Where Hootie had grown up as the slow, dull one, everybody had always thought of Clarence as sharp: sharp-looking, sharp-talking, extra sharp with the girls. He'd started cropping his own forty acres at sixteen and swore up and down he wasn't going to be like everybody else, end up three steps behind instead of ahead every year at settling time. He was going to work hard and outsmart the boss man; he was going to clear enough to buy his own land. Except that it never worked out that way. He was down to twenty acres now and at settling time every Christmas he slumped out of the plantation office like everybody else.

But he was still sharp with the girls. When Rae hesitated he put his hand on her elbow and smiled. "You need somebody," he said.

She looked at him. "What make you think that?"

"To walk you home, I mean."

Well, why not. It was what everyone expected her to do; to wait a few months for decency then find another man and move him into Hootie's bed. How else could she keep cropping that big old plot of land? How else was she to live?

"No, thank you," she said, stepping back from the brother's grip. She felt every eye in the graveyard upon her. "I want to walk a ways on my own."

She went straight out through the gate and down the road as fast as she could, not waiting for anyone. When she reached the turnoff for her house she passed it by without even slowing down. The heat and the hurry made her feel heavy in her chest, but she treasured it. She opened her mouth and drank down the sticky air like it was honey. She was aboveground not below. She was alive and she was glad.

She took off the shawl, tossed it onto the branch of a nearby tree. Her dress, made from cheap, brown muslin but cut by her own hands to fit her figure, lay plastered against her chest and belly. She broke a branch of magnolia to fan herself and headed into town.

They would wonder where she went to but not right away and not for long. They would bustle into the house and all around it, talking about Hootie and what a good man he was. They would fill their plates with chicken and potatoes and sliced tomatoes and sit out on the porch eating and laughing, happy for the day off. A little later they would bring out the whiskey and sip it. Somebody would get a harmonica and start to hum. They would sing and maybe dance. The sisters would fan themselves furiously and remember to cry.

Eba would push them all out when it got too late and she was tired, and she would take care of Mattie, too. She'd feed the child and wash her up and put her to bed on a pallet in the back corner where it was cool.

It was the dead of the afternoon and blistering hot when she got to town. Two dogs collapsed in the shade of an old oak tree barely raised their heads as she passed. Where was she going? She still didn't know, having walked the long, dusty road with her mind replaying only over and over again the feel of Hootie's brother gripping her arm.

"Thought you was burying your husband today, Rae?"

She looked up. Standing in the doorway of the hardware store was Mr. Burch, the boss man. Owner of the land on which she'd lived her entire life. "What you doing in town?"

"Hootie's buried," she said. She had learned a long time ago that when white folks began to question you about something, it was best not to say too much to them, to answer one question at a time, keeping the sentences short. It made them think you were ignorant and they left you alone.

"Ain't there a wake going on at your house? Saw all the food going in when I drove past this morning."

Rae found a spot in the hardware-store window just behind and off to the right of Burch's wheezy, red face and stared at it. She gave the smallest of shrugs. She moved her feet and let her mind roam on ahead to the rest of the day, the rest of her life, how she had to figure it out. She didn't think another second about Burch. This would be over soon.

But it wasn't. Instead of shaking his head at what an ignorant nigger she was and going on back into the store the way she expected, Burch just lingered there in the doorway, saying nothing. Not turning away. After a few minutes she realized he wasn't going to leave. Then she heard his breathing; it was deep and ragged, as though he had just run someplace. She felt his gaze upon her body as surely as if they were his hands.

When he spoke his voice was different. "So. You figure out what you plan to do?"

All at once she sensed the danger, like a snake she had stupidly stepped over in the tall grass. She dropped her eyes to the road, tried to round her shoulders so her breasts wouldn't shout so much. She wished for the shawl. "Not yet," she said.

Burch stepped closer. "Maybe I'll come on out to your house tonight and we can talk about it."

She faked a cough into her hand and used the movement to inch away, but Burch followed. Down the street a white man she did not know ambled out of the barbershop, paused to wipe his face, then climbed into his car and drove away. "Got folks there tonight," Rae said, remembering the funeral guests.

"Tomorrow night, then," Burch said. "You know, Hootie was giving me eight or ten bales off that plot. You can't do that on your own." He quickly glanced up and down the street and then, before she could move, reached out his hand and brushed it across her breast. "We might have to work something out."

Not thinking, just reacting, she stepped away. He stepped after, not touching her again but standing close.

"Where you going?" he said. His voice was low and a little breathless, as though he had run up and down the street in the hot summer sun. She sneaked a look into his face, trying to see if he was crazy, if he really planned to try something right then and there in the middle of the street. What would she do if he did?

No one would help her, that's for sure. No white man would lift a hand or black man either, for different reasons. Her only hope was if a white woman came along and shamed him into backing down, shamed him for daring to do in daylight what was usually left to the dark.

"I always did say that Hootie was a lucky man." He was so close she could smell the onions from his lunch on his breath. The stink of them and him made her stomach turn, her palms itch. She had the sudden, terrifying urge to slap his face, but that, of course, was death. Instead she turned her face away.

"What you say, Rae?" he breathed.

She would run. She would just start running and not stop. She started to turn, but before she could take a step she heard a different voice.

"There you are!"

She turned around. Clarence came sauntering down the street with his jacket slung over one shoulder and his sleeves rolled up and his left hand plunged deep into the pocket of his overalls. And he was smiling. Smiling like a man who'd just been out behind the juke joint and heard a dirty joke. It was the smile that lashed at Rae, the smile that made the dogs raise their heads and the day hold its breath. Colored people never smiled at white folks, never. Grinned, yes; they grinned if they could stomach it. A grin was always sure to please. But if they could not grin they allowed themselves no sign at all of knowing merriment or discontent. They kept their eyes and the corners of their mouths pointed down into the dirt.

Clarence kept walking until he was standing by her side. Then he reached out and put his hand—the same hand she had just rejected—on the crook of her arm. "Where you been, Rae?" he asked. He was talking to her but the frightening thing was, he was looking at Burch. He was looking at the man, looking soft and smiling and dead into Burch's washy gray eyes.

"We all waiting for you back at the house," Clarence said.

She tried to open her mouth to answer but it would not open;

it was as if it had been soldered closed. Maybe something had happened to her. Maybe she'd had a stroke like Miss Hyacinth from down the road. Or maybe she couldn't speak because it was impossible to talk to a dead man, and that man holding her arm was dead. She didn't want to be dead, too.

"You ready?" Clarence asked.

She nodded, used every ounce of strength in her body to make her legs move. As she turned she sneaked a look at Burch; he looked as though someone had splashed a drink into his face and forgotten to take out the ice cubes first. He stood before them with his pale lips parted, his face an angry, blotchy white. Shock, Rae knew. He was in shock and that was the only thing saving them. That and the fact that no one else, no witnesses to his humiliation, stood in the street.

Forcing herself to move, Rae grabbed the brother's arm and pulled. "Let's go. Folks are waiting." As she turned she mumbled, "Thank you, Mr. Burch," in the tiniest, most wheedling voice she could manage. Maybe it would do some good.

"Mr. Burch," Clarence said, finally dropping his eyes.

Burch, still staring, pushed back his hat. "Clarence," he said slowly. Then, when they had taken a few steps, he seemed to snap back into himself.

"I'll see you later," he called down the street after them. Rae knew he was talking to them both. When they had gone a half mile out of town and she had cleared the fear from her throat enough to speak, Rae said, "That's trouble."

Clarence did not answer, so she went on. "White folks already crazy about all the soldiers soon to come home. Afraid they going to be uppity. They all been looking for something to set them off."

Clarence turned to her and smiled but she could see that he was frightened. His hands trembled a little until he shoved them into the pockets of his pants. "Well, guess I got to run," he said. "Never in my life been further than the next plantation over, but I guess now is the time to go."

Rae looked at him. He wasn't Hootie, she could see that much. He would not be nearly as good to her. But he was right, he had to run if he had any hope of seeing the sun rise another day. Even now Burch was probably sitting in the town bar and stewing on what happened, working himself into a white moonshine rage. Sooner or later he would come looking for Clarence. And sooner or later he'd coming looking for her, too.

"Where you think you might be heading?" she asked Hootie's brother.

He shrugged as he walked along beside her. "I don't know. Got some kinfolks who moved off a few years back. Heard they went about sixty miles south of here."

For a long time they walked along in silence, past the dogs and out of town and down the cotton-lined road. When they reached the tree where Rae had thrown the shawl, she stopped to retrieve it. Turning to Hootie's brother, she laid a hand upon his arm. "You ever been to Chicago?"


*She stayed at Eba's house that night, told Clarence to come for her* there when the moon was up. She was ready to go. She didn't want to spend one more night hearing the kudzu slither up the walnut trees or smelling the hogs from down the road. She convinced Hootie's brother that Burch might be drinking right then and there, might be working himself into a white, moonshine rage against the nigger who dared step between him and his prize. "We need to go," she said to him. "We need to go."

To Eba she told some version of the truth: that Hootie's brother had stood up to Burch and had to run; since he had stood for her, she would go reluctantly along. Eba stared down her long nose. "That's why you going? 'Cause he stood for you?" She sniffed as if she smelled something bad. "Your man barely cold in the ground and you running off with his brother. It's a sin sure as I'm standing here."

Rae said, "Whether it is or not I'm going anyway."

He came about an hour after dark. She had already packed, had thrown into a croaker sack her two dresses and underthings and sewing needles and a pail for dipping water and a tin plate for eating on. On top she'd placed, neatly folded and wrapped in clean muslin, the three yards of pale, blue silk Hootie had given her on their wedding night. "You make you a pretty dress," he'd said. But she never had because she'd wanted it to be the dress she wore when she and Hootie were finally leaving the plantation, when they rode out of town for good.

Mattie lay asleep on a pallet beneath the room's only window, a window open hopelessly against the heat. The room smelled sharply of the lemongrass Eba rubbed on them all to fight off mosquitoes. She was in the back room, pretending to be asleep.

"We're ready," Rae whispered. "I was just gonna wake the child."

Rae had started toward Mattie but stopped when he said, "Don't."

"You plan to carry her asleep?" she asked. "Because let me tell you, the child might look like a stick but she gets heavy after a few miles."

"We can't take her," he said, his voice low and urgent.

Rae stepped back to stand beside Hootie's brother, tried to search his face in the lamp's flickering light. She wanted to be sure she was hearing him straight.

"What?"

"We don't know where we're going, don't know how we're going to live when we get there," he said. Already his voice sounded less sure than it had this afternoon, less brave. "I don't have God's faintest idea what I'm walking into."

"We're going to Chicago," she said. "They got children in Chicago, I'm sure."

"I don't even know if I can take care of you and me," Clarence said. In the shadowy light of the room he sounded nothing like the man who had stood to Burch that afternoon. He sounded like somebody older, somebody weaker. He sounded afraid.

"We can send for her later," he said. "Right now we have to leave her here."

Rae looked from his shadowed face to Mattie's little legs. Nobody in the family could figure out where the child got such skinny, bowlegged legs; certainly not from Rae, who even as a child had been soft and rounded and dimpled from her knees to her chin. The little sticks Mattie ran around on were tougher than they looked, but they were still the legs of a child, a baby. A baby could only go so far. Some days, when Eba was off washing clothes in some white woman's house, Rae would take Mattie into the field with her to chop cotton. Rae worked fast; she was strong and she hated the job and her feeling was to get it over and done with, but with Mattie along she always had to slow down. It was hard for the child to keep up with her. She had the desire, no doubt about that. But desire only got a person so far in a world of ability and might.

"All right," Rae said. Eba would take care of the child. Eba was better suited to it anyhow. Eba was built for giving herself away.

Rae turned to pick up her sack but stopped when she heard a sound, a cry like the wind in a storm. It was Mattie. Before Rae knew what was happening, the girl was up from her pallet and across the floor. "Mama!" she screamed, clutching at Rae's dress. "Don't leave me! Don't!"

"Shut her up!" Clarence hissed. He cracked the door and peered into the night one long moment before closing it again. "Come on, Rae, we got to move. Forget the girl and let's go!"

Rae looked down at her daughter. The girl was sobbing so hard she could barely stand up; only her death grip around Rae's knees kept her from falling down. "Ma . . . ma," she blubbered.

"Hush!" Rae ordered. "Hush up, now! Stop all this foolishness."

"Don't leave me!"

Rae pried the child's fingers from around her knees, led the girl back to her bed. "Who told you to be awake, anyway? Listening to grown folks talk. Stop that crying and come on and lay down."

She pushed the girl down onto the blankets, trying to stroke her into calm.

"Hush up, now," she said.

"But, Mama—"

"I said hush." Rae reached into her bag and pulled out the yards of silk. She folded it neatly into a pillow and slipped it into Mattie's arms.

"Here," she said. "Hold on to that for Mama tonight. Now hush up and stop this nonsense. You go right on back to sleep."

She stroked the child's back over and over and over until her sobbing eased. "Hush up now."

"Mommy . . ."

"Shush," Rae whispered. "Close your eyes. Your mama ain't going to leave."

When the child was sleeping she picked up her bag and left.

# Chapter Six

On the night of Paula's birth I sat propped in bed, flipping rest-lessly through the channels on the hospital's cable TV. My vernal daughter lay nearby, dozing in her lucite bassinet, exhausted from her trip down the birth canal. Eddie and Harriet were gone home, Eddie disappointed but still grateful, Harriet cuddling her new giant teddy bear, blissfully unaware of the seismic shaking of her world.

The night nurse had already made her rounds and would not be seen again that evening; with your first baby they're buzzing in and out every hour to check on things, but with your second kid, apparently, it's either sink or swim. I was tired but couldn't sleep, I had a journal and a pen but couldn't write and a stack of *New Yorkers* but couldn't read. I was aching and sore and harmoniously daffy and I needed something to divert my mind from the reality of now being responsible for not just one small life but two. I skipped past sitcoms and nature shows and some kind of extreme sporting event and there it was: *Imitation of Life*.

It was a movie I had not seen since childhood and scarcely remembered: all I knew was it had something to do with a black girl passing for white. But that turned out to be just the secondary plot.

The main story revolved around Lana Turner, an ambitious blond bitch who paused just long enough in her relentless climb to the top to dump her child into her black maid's lap. That we were supposed to hate Lana was obvious. Who in the hell did she think she was, anyway, turning her back on hunky whatever-his-name and tossing aside little Sandra Dee for the sake of her stinky old career? Our sympathy was saved for—was shoved toward—Annie, the ever-humble black maid, the avatar of loving female self-sacrifice. See Annie holed up in Lana's natty little apartment caring for Sandra Dee and her own fair daughter while Lana claws her way to the top. See Annie wash and clean and smile beatifically. See her fall all over herself trying to please her daughter, Sarah Jane, who wants nothing to do with darkie Mom. See her offer a lifetime of servitude to Lana and Sarah and Sandra Dee then die with angelic grace, having thoughtfully arranged her own funeral and left Sarah Jane all her worldly goods. "I want the rest to go to Sarah Jane," she says, groveling to the end. "Tell her I know I was selfish, and if I loved her too much, I was sorry."

It was a good thing none of the maternity nurses came in while I was watching; they might have mistaken the stricken look on my face for postnatal complications and called a code blue or whatever it is they call. Because I was horrified, so horrifically mesmerized I watched without moving the first two-thirds or so and only tore my eyes away from the spectacle at that point because Paula began to wail her tiny, tinny newborn cry. I got up then, picked her up, climbed back into bed, and latched her to my breasts. She was what the lactation consultant called a seal gasket; her little rosebud mouth latched on to my nipple perfectly. My eyes dragged themselves back to the television screen. Looking back now, I see I was in the grip of plunging hormones, my estrogen spurting, my blood volume plunging, all the fluids and swellings of pregnancy falling away. I was so whacked-out those first weeks after my kids were born that baby-shampoo commercials made me weep, and the sight, one day, of a dog wandering alone down the sidewalk made me wail. Looking back now, I see the movie was just a movie, some man's florid vision of 1950s womanhood, but on the night of my daughter's birth I saw it as an enchiridion on motherhood, a primer on my life to come, a manual from which no deviation was allowed. I saw it carving back the hokum and laying bare the simple choice at the heart of motherhood, which was that, in the short term at least, somebody had to be sacrificed.

My mother sure loved that movie, though.


*Paula wandered into the hallway and wrapped her arms around my* neck. "Let's play in the snow!" she said.

I just barely managed to squelch my groan. "Maybe later."

"No. Now!" She lowered her head so she could look up at me through her lashes; barely out of diapers and already a coquette. "Please? I'll let you come to my party." Ever since Harriet had celebrated her fifth birthday, Paula had been planning her own shindig—never mind that her birthday was still six months away—and using the guest list as a means of manipulation.

"Later," I said, trying for loving firmness. But Paula scrunched up her eyes, opened her mouth, and began to wail. "You hurt my feelings!" she cried.

I took her into my lap and sighed. Any minute Harriet would come racing into the hallway, not because her sister was crying—she could care less about that—but because she was being comforted. She and Paula both had an astonishing radar for maternal affection; they could smell its dispensing three rooms away.

Sure enough, ten seconds later, Harriet hurtled through the doorway. "I want to sit in your lap! I want to sit in your lap!"

They jostled for position, then settled down, one to each thigh. They wrapped their arms around my neck and burrowed into my body, eyelids fluttering in ecstasy. "We love Mommy," they cooed in syncopation. Two junkies firing up the mommy pipe.

Some women, when they are rubbing their motherhood into the faces of their childless friends, like to gush about finally knowing what it means to love and be loved unconditionally. Before my own children came along, I would hear these comments daily from the secretaries in the sociology department at UNC: middle-aged white women who needed something, some weapon honed and keened, with which to cut my educated black ass back down to size. *You can't know until you've felt it,* they said to me. *You simply cannot know.*

When I eventually became pregnant these same women loved nothing more than to get me into a corner somewhere and pour out their horror tales. How their feet spread and their nerves pinched and the skin on their hips and stomachs stretched silvery white. They told me about their deliveries, how they screamed for ten hours and split themselves so badly it took twenty stitches to close them up and still they feel as roomy as a bucket down there. They told me every ugly, messy detail they could remember about the physical effects of childbearing, but when it came to feelings there was still only one word. *Love. You will love your children like you've never loved anyone before in your lifetime,* they said. *The very depth of it will take your breath away. Unconditional love.*

But even then I remembered how many children I'd seen stumble through the door of that mental health clinic when I was in college. Children who'd been coked up in utero, then beaten, berated, burned, or simply left alone in some rat-infested boarding-house with a soda and a pack of chewing gum once they emerged to face the world. And I remembered how all these children, all these damaged babies, all these splintered young souls, loved their mothers. Loved them like you would not believe, loved them so fiercely they fought and cried and screamed to be back in those skinny, indifferent, crack-addicted arms. I remembered that, and when my own children came along and loved me, I loved them back. But I couldn't really take it personally.

I kissed Paula and Harriet, then pried their hands from my neck. "Maybe some fresh air would do us good. But we're not staying out long."

It took us twenty minutes to track down and pull on the vestments of winter: long underwear, snow pants, boots, jackets, hats, mittens, and scarves. I managed to convince Paula to leave behind the tattered pink security blanket she carted everywhere, telling her I didn't want it getting lost in the snow. We'd barely stepped off the porch when Paula began to dance the pee-pee dance. I looked at her and sighed. My fault for forgetting rule number 56 of motherhood: Always make the kids piss first.

Ten minutes later we were back outside. The snow fell in fat, boggy flakes, joining the four inches or so already whitening the ground. While the children chased each other and made snow angels I grabbed the shovel and tried to clear the walk. Then I got the Flexible Flyer from the garage and pulled the children around the yard. The runners needed waxing; something else to put on the list.

The third time around my back began to ache. Dropping the rope, I said, "Time to go in."

"No!" the children howled together. Their first act of sibling cooperation for the day.

"I said we were only staying out for a minute."

"We don't want to go in!"

The parent magazines suggested taking a deep breath to steady oneself when dealing with recalcitrant kids. But when I tried it, the icy air made my forehead throb.

"Here's what we're going to do," I said. "I have to mail some letters I've been holding in my pocket for a week. We're going to walk to the mailbox, and when we come back we'll go inside and have hot cocoa. Okay?"

"Yeah!"

It was bribery but I didn't care. It worked. At the mailbox I pulled the stack of letters from my pocket and handed some to each child. Pulling open the mailbox door, I said, "Okay guys, put them in and let's get home to that cocoa!"

Paula crossed her arms. "I wanna open it!"

With a sigh I bent to lift her. "Go ahead. Hurry up."

Paula opened the slot and peered inside. "Where does it go, Mommy?" she asked.

"It's just a box," I said, shifting her in my arms. My feet were turning to ice and now I had to pee. "Mail the letters and let's go."

"Okay," she said. But instead of stuffing the whole group through the slot, she peeled off a single envelope, examined the stamp, flipped it over to examine the back side and then flipped it back again, then slid it slowly into the mailbox slot inch by incremental inch until she was grasping the last corner snippet by her pudgy little fingertips. "Good-bye, letter!" she called. "Good-bye, good-bye, good-bye!"

Breathe, I told myself. Take joy in this childlike exploration of the world. Still, by the time she sang farewell to her fourth envelope I thought I was going to scream. "Okay, Harriet," I said, setting Paula down in the snow. "Your turn. Hey! Bet you can't mail them all at the same time!"

But Harriet threw back her head and stared up at me with the outrage of a soap-opera queen. "Paula got more!" she said.

"What?"

"More letters," she cried. "She got four and I got three!"

It was to moments such as these my mind flew whenever I heard some woman gush about how she had never had a job more rewarding than motherhood.

"Please," I cried, doing the pee-pee dance now. "Just mail the stupid letters and let's go home."

But the injustice of the situation was too much for Harriet. She wasn't giving up without a fight. "It's . . . not . . . fair!" she wailed, crossing her arms.

Paula, delighted to have the upper hand for once, decided to pounce. "Nah nah ne nah nah!" she taunted, sticking out her tongue. "I got more letters!"

"I hate you!" Harriet screamed. "I hate my sister!"

"Stop it, you two," I said.

"Paula is dumb!"

"Harriet, mail the letters."

Paula burst into tears. "Mommy, she called me dumb!"

"You got more letters than me!" Harriet countered.

"Stop it, I said!"

"She's a big baby! Look at the baby cry!"

I slammed the mailbox door so hard it hurt my wrist, then slipped on a patch of ice and had to flail to keep from falling on my ass. All of this ridiculous movement probably took less than fifteen seconds, but in those fifteen seconds I managed to control myself enough not to slap my children, but not enough to keep from yelling at them. Nor enough to keep my pelvic muscles, weakened from childbirth, from giving way against the tide.

Wet, tired and pissed, I turned on the kids. "Oh, stop bickering! You make me sick with all that noise!" Even as the words left my mouth I regretted them, but I was cold and tired and pissing myself like a two-year-old, and no matter how you sliced it, it was a ridiculous argument. Just because they were children didn't make their childish behavior any less irritating. "Just mail the letters!" I snarled at Harriet.

She did.

We headed back to the house, the children silent, the streets silent, me waddling like a duck trying to keep my clammy pants from chaffing my thighs. Where was everybody? I wondered. Where were the other mothers of the young children in the neighborhood? But of course I knew the answer—they were locked away inside their homes with their own set of bickering kids. How unnatural to lock a woman and her children in a house with only one another for company. How against the whole long course of human history, this idealization of the nuclear family. The word *family* itself originally referred to a band of slaves; so much for Ozzie and Harriet. On the front porch we paused to stomp snow from our boots and Harriet took the opportunity to hiss into her sister's cold-reddened ear: "Next time I get more letters, dummy!"

"Not fair!" Paula bawled. Harriet stood catching snowflakes on her tongue in perfect innocence. "She called me dummy!"

"She got more letters than me!" Harriet cried.

"Mommy!"

"Mom!"

As calmly as I could, I said, "You know what? I really don't give a damn."

Paula burst into tears. "Mommy doesn't give a damn!" she wailed. "Mommy doesn't give a damn!"

Monster.

I bent to pat Paula's back, but Harriet was already on the case. She wrapped her arm around her sister and squeezed a little. "Don't cry, Paula," she said with great authority. "She's the mommy. She has to give a damn."

I glanced at my watch: 1:30. Five more hours until Eddie returned home, excited about some new research project or frustrated at office politics. When he asked about my day I would tell him I'd conducted a series of mailbox negotiations but that they had not gone well. Perhaps some person somewhere—perhaps the sociologist, James Q. Wilson, who argued it is the mother's task to establish the bonding process that makes human society possible—could argue seriously that time spent deciding who mailed three bills and who mailed four was time valuably spent. But I didn't buy it. The truth was, even Harriet and Paula would have forgotten by dinnertime.

We were at the front door by then. I opened it and the children rushed into the hallway, kicking off their boots. I let them go first, let them in out of the cold into the security of the house, while I remained on the porch for a moment. Ignorning my clammy pants. Letting the snow kiss my face. Holding the door. Then, just to see how it felt, closing it.

The air, which before had merely been cold, was suddenly bracing, the tang of it in my nose and my lungs tasted sharp. The snow-covered ground dazzled, the low sky brightened, the birds sang, or so it seemed, so good, so thrilling the moment felt. Still holding the screen door open, I inched a bit away from the door and closed my eyes and lifted my face to the falling snow. I had a vision of myself as Tim Robbins in that movie *Shawshank Redemption,* crawling through the sewer line to escape prison, finally reaching freedom and raising my arms to the cleansing, falling rain.

It took the children four or five minutes to notice I was gone. Through the mail slot in the door I could hear them giggling and squealing as they unbuckled and unzipped, the mailbox debacle already forgotten, plans for the afternoon already under way. Finally, though, Harriet must have glanced behind her at the empty hall.

"Mommy?" she called casually.

I said nothing. I kept my mouth closed. Testing.

"Mommy?" called Paula.

"Mommy," called Harriet again, and this time worry shaded her little voice. "Mommy, where are you?"

Paula's voice came closer to the door and I could tell it was hovering on the verge of tears. "Mommy! I want Mommy!"

And still I didn't move. I stood there on the porch with hand on the doorknob, not thinking, not moving, neither coming or going nor intending to. I don't know how long I might have stood there, how much I might have been willing to hear my frightened children scream before I moved. But Paula—my star-bright child—pushed open the mail slot and saw me.

"Mommy's outside!" she called to her sister, giggling. "She's playing hide-and-seek! Found you!"

I went inside and called my sister Lena. She wasn't in her office, so I left a message saying I was just checking in and would call back later. The next time I spoke to my mother I could at least tell her I'd tried. Duty counts.

# Chapter Seven

About my grandfather I know little—next to nothing, in fact. Only that he was a teacher's son, that he and my grandmother were not married, that after sowing his seed, he disappeared from view. If my mother knows more than that herself, she has never shared it with us. She has never even mentioned his name.

The one she talked about was Hootie. And, to a lesser extent, Hootie's brother Clarence, the man who brought her temporarily back into her mother's life. "He just showed up one day at Aunt Eba's," she told me once, in a rare talking mood. "Just came walking up the path with that beaten, old hat pulled down across his face. Aunt Eba said the minute she saw him she knew Rae had run off and left him crying in some hole someplace. But he came up to me and hugged me, then handed me a wad of money wrapped up in a handkerchief and told me where my mother was living. He told me if I wanted him to, he would put me on the bus. And of course I said yes."

Of course, I thought at the time, sitting between my mother's knees while she braided my hair. Of course. Of course.

## Memphis, 1949

*His name was Clarence but she always thought of him as Hootie's* Brother, even years and years after they'd fled Burch and Mississippi and cotton fields. They'd been headed to Chicago but only got as far as Memphis before he began trembling and dragging his feet. To keep him from bucking altogether and running back to Mississippi, she told him they'd settle in Memphis awhile. Find someplace to live. Get jobs. See the town. She thought at first he would be like her—thrilled to have escaped the hard, dirty work of picking cotton, hungry for new sights and new ways—but she saw quickly that he was not. He was, in fact, afraid. What he needed was a job, someplace to be and something to do and somebody standing over him to make sure he did it right.

"HB is like a mule," she told her friend. "He don't know nothing but dumb, hard work."

That's what she called him in her mind—HB. Once, in bed and not thinking as he nuzzled against her breasts, she cried out, "Oh, baby, oh, HB!" He thought she was calling another man and slapped her so hard he split her lip. Blood, red and bright, misted the sheets.

"I guess now I know what you be doing all those nights running the streets!" he raged. "I guess now I see!"

He was wrong. There was no other man while they were married, not in the way he thought. Yes she loved to put on a pretty dress and shine up her shoes and straighten her hair with the hot comb and curl it around her face and go out, but she wasn't looking for some man. Sure, the men came around, and sure she danced with them. The whole point was to dance. The point was to be out in the world in those early days with the boys rolling tall and handsome home from the war, their uniforms starched, their eyes unshuttered, their heads up. Their heads dangerously, thrillingly up. How could a body stay home in some room when the whole world was kicking up its heels? How could a person stick his butt on a chair in a room and stubbornly refuse to dance? No, it wasn't the men but the party she lusted for, the wholehearted gobbling up of life. She had a chance to live and she was taking it. One chance was more than anybody she ever knew ever got.

But HB would not come along. "Why I need to go to some club and spend my money on watered-down liquor?" he asked. "Watch some damn Negroes strutting around like peacocks just 'cause they been in the war? I'd been in the war, too, not for this foot. I'd have killed more Japs than all them!"

She supposed that's what she got for trying to drag a country Negro to the city. No sooner had they got themselves married by a colored preacher and found a room in a respectable boarding-house and Hootie's Brother got a job washing dishes in a fancy restaurant down on Front Street—no sooner than all those good things happened than he was moaning about going home. Home! Rae could not believe it.

"What's back there?" she asked. "Tar-paper shacks? Snakes everywhere you turn? Doing your business in a hole in the ground? Look what we got here!"

To make her point she opened the door of their room and pointed at the toilet room just down the hall.

"Indoor plumbing!" she cried. "Indoor plumbing!"

It was, for her, the best thing of all good things about city life. Every morning Rae opened her eyes in joy, knowing she did not have to go out into the yard and fight off snakes to do what needed to be done. But HB just shrugged.

"I could get you that back home," he said. "I could figure it out."

He was a fool. She closed the door. "What's back there, Clarence? A lynch mob?"

HB crossed his arms and stuck out his lip. "Least a man can

walk down the road without bumping into fifty people," he said. "Least a man can breathe sweet air."

"Breathing from the end of a rope," she said. "Don't forget about Burch."

She knew he remembered Burch. Still, he was so miserable in the city he might have gone off that first year and she might have let him—might have gone off herself with one of the boys who sniffed around her on Saturday nights—if she had not found herself carrying Hootie's Brother's child. When she first noticed the slow leak of energy, the softened belly, the tender breasts that meant she was carrying, Rae was so angry she could spit. It had been her understanding that Hootie's Brother, being Hootie's brother and being, it seemed to her, old as the hills, would be like Hootie in that way, unable to make babies. It was one of the things she had liked most about him: that she could really let herself go free in bed and have a good time without worry. She had bargained for a neutered bull, but what she got was a snorting stud.

The child, a girl, was born on a blistering day in July in the maternity ward of the colored hospital because their landlady didn't want any birthing screams in her house. They named the baby Josephine.

"Guess you'll be settling down now, huh?" Hootie's Brother asked, tickled pink. He held the baby in his enormous arms and blinked his big goat eyes at her and shook his head and waggled his flabby tongue. Rae wanted to smack his face.

"I done let you roam and carry on this little while, but a woman with children don't need to be running the streets," he said. "She needs to be at home with her children."

"Children?" Rae echoed. "This just one child," she said, though she did of course occasionally think of Mattie, back home with Aunt Eba. She thought of Mattie and the baby just born and then she thought about how she could avoid having any more.

Their landlady told them they would have to leave. She could not have babies crying and carrying on, could not have children running through the living room. She had respectable clients, teachers and nurses, folks who needed their rest. They would have to go. It nearly broke Rae's heart because the rooming house was so nice and well kept and relatively cheap—the landlady only took in select people and charged them reasonably.

"Maybe we ought to go on home," Hootie's Brother said. "Maybe God is telling us . . ." But by the time he finished his musing, Rae was already out the door searching for a new place. What she found was a first-floor flat in a two-story brick tenement. It was a little dingy and run-down and had only a kitchen and a bedroom as living space, but there was indoor plumbing and flower boxes hanging out front and it was less than half a mile from Beale Street. Still, when Hootie's Brother saw it he sat down in the middle of the empty floor and put his head into his hands. "Don't make no sense to live like this," he said.

"Wait till I fix it up," said Rae, looking around the room. She'd scrub the walls and floors, find some furniture, make new curtains of silky blue. Just the other day she had spent an hour wandering the aisles of a fabric store, a store filled with bolts of material finer and brighter than back home had ever seen. "I'll make it nice."

"At least at home a man can smell the earth," said Hootie's Brother. "At least at home a man can raise his own food."

Rae took a breath and let it out slowly, fighting to keep from rolling her eyes in disgust. It was all she could do not to scream at him to take his sorry, gloomy butt on back to the cotton fields he loved so much. But no other man would want her now, not to marry. She had to hang on a little while.

"Clarence," she said, going to him and placing her hand upon his head. "The Bible says man don't live by bread alone."

"But by the word of God," he said. "I don't see God in this place."

She tried another tack. "There's a whole wide world out there. Don't you want to see none of it?"

Hootie's Brother looked up at her and she saw, as she always did, how yellow his eyes were, how veined with red. "You think that world was made for the likes of us, Rae?" he asked.

She shrugged. "This dress weren't made for me either. But I'm wearing it."

"So you think *you* going out there and those white folks going to hand *you* the key?"

"I know damn well they ain't coming down to Mississippi to put it in my hand."

Hootie's Brother shook his head. "Who you think you are, gal?" he asked, but he was grinning now, clearly tickled despite himself. She knew she had won.

"All right," he said. "I'll live like this for now. I've lived in worse. But you have to do right, Rae. If we stay here as a family, we have to be a family. You have to be like a woman should be."

She smiled down at him, took his arms, and wrapped them around her hips. As far as she was concerned, a woman should keep her man fed and clean and satisfied. She did all that and she'd keep on doing it. But that didn't mean she was going to be his slave.


*Douche, her girlfriends told her. Every other day and always, always,* always right after doing it, immediately, and she'd have nothing to worry about. Sure enough, it seemed to work, at least for a while, for eight whole months, and then it stopped. She was pregnant again. A boy this time; they named him Clarence Jr. Rae got up twenty-four hours after his birth and went back to work at Steinman's department store, leaving the children with Stella upstairs, who had four of her own and, for a few dollars, did not mind another two.

"Quit," said Hootie's Brother. He didn't like her working at Steinman's, though she made more money there than cooking in some white woman's kitchen. He didn't like her to dress so nicely or to make new, unmarried friends. He didn't like her sitting at the kitchen table smoothing cold cream from the makeup girl, cold cream that smelled of cherry almonds, onto her hands. He muttered about how she had not needed soft hands back home, how soft hands would bleed digging cotton from the bolls.

"Quit that job and stay home with your children," he demanded. "I can keep this family. You quit that job."

But the money Hootie's Brother made kept the family only in housing and food and shoes, not in wool dresses or hats for church or curtains of silk.

"I will," she promised him—and got up and went to work.

*The night before HB finally left her for good she went out to dance.* She went out as usual with some of the other girls from Steinman's department store and danced as usual with men who'd seen death piled up like cotton bales in the fields of Normandy, so much death and so much frightening freedom that even seven years later they were still busy lapping up life. And as usual, HB stayed home and sulked.

She went straight on from work, stopping by a friend's apartment to wash her face and do her makeup and to slip off the ugly, gray smock she was required to wear as a Steinman's seamstress. The salesgirls got to wear soft, pretty dresses of royal blue that showed off their shapes and matching pumps, but of course the salesgirls were all white. The seamstresses were colored. Apparently the lovely ladies of Memphis did not mind colored fingers upon their bodies, only upon their cash.

She went to her friend's place to change not because it was closer but because she knew if she went home to her own little hole in the wall, Hootie's Brother would be on her the second she set foot inside the door. He would demand she stay in for the evening; he would cry and beg and plead, shaming himself and irritating her. If he was really worked up he might even strike her, hoping to blacken an eye or mark a cheek and thus have embarrassment pin her at home. One time he had tried such a thing, and she had yelled she was going out anyway and he had grabbed her forearms in desperation and wrestled her right on down to the kitchen floor. She wrestled back, snapped and thrashed and dug her fingernails into whatever soft flesh she could find, but he won easily, being more than twice as big as Rae. She, on the other hand, was more than twice as smart; she simply stopped coming home on Saturday evenings. That took care of that.

"Ain't you afraid he going to walk out on you, Rae?" her friend, whose name was Arlene, had asked her once. "I don't mean no offense and I ain't wishing it on you. But most mens won't be taking this kind of thing for long."

Arlene was a sweet girl, older than Rae and never married, with big front teeth and a jutting, blocky chin. Rae looked at her and saw what it was to be without a man—struggling by day, alone by evening, afraid by night. Vulnerable and aching in that place down deep only a man could touch. Not that Arlene never got loving; she did most Saturday nights, always with somebody new. But Rae went out dancing and still had somebody at home paying the rent.

"And he ain't going nowhere. Once he gets planted someplace, he's planted. It would take a hurricane to blow him off his root."

The juke joint was packed so full there was barely room to dance. Anybody who worked in a store or a restaurant or a barbershop had the next day off and was determined to spend it recovering in bed. Anybody who cooked or cleaned didn't have to show her face until noon at the earliest; still plenty of time for recovering.

At two in the morning Arlene disappeared with the trumpet player and Rae walked herself home. She found HB sitting fully dressed at the kitchen table, his arms crossed before him and his head laid down, a low rumbling snore coming from his mouth. This was the way he often waited for her to come home, fully dressed and snoring, waiting to either slap and curse or weep and moan.

She would not have thought two seconds about it other than to wonder which fate awaited her that night—even if it was slapping, it would be quick and quickly followed hard by weeping, manless guilt—except for the sack. Beside HB's foot, braced against a table leg, slumped the same burlap sack he had carried up from Mississippi years before. She had tried time and again to throw the thing out—it was ratty and country and ignorant, it embarrassed her just to look at it—but he had clung to it like a baby kitten clinging to its mother's back. Had hung it right out in the open on a nail hammered into the wall. Now it sat stuffed full with all that he possessed in this life: an extra pair of pants, a couple of shirts, some socks, his whittling knife, a can of snuff.

For days and weeks and months and years he had talked of leaving her, of escaping this city he loathed and going home. Twice before he had gone so far as to take down the sack and hold it in his hands. He'd put it back, of course, though both times he had slapped her before doing so to save the shame.

Rae looked at the bulging sack and then walked on past and into the bedroom. She needed to change her party dress in case of blood.

Because there was only one bedroom, they all had to share it. HB had scrounged from somewhere two twin beds, which they shoved against opposite walls of the room, trying to create the illusion of distance. The children slept in the bed on the right, the baby at the top and blocked in by walls and blankets, Josephine at the foot. Rae glanced at them as she stepped from her dress. Josephine slept the way she always did, butt raised high in the air and face mushed into the pillow. It was the most uncomfortable-looking way to sleep. Hootie's Brother couldn't stand it; he was forever trying to ease the child down, getting frustrated when she popped back to her knees. Rae, on the other hand, left the child alone, figuring she knew how she wanted to sleep.

Rae left the room, buttoning her house dress. Hootie's Brother was awake. He reached down and grabbed the sack but made no move to stand up. He seemed very calm.

"Got me a letter from Billy today," he said. "Burch is dead."

In the quiet of the kitchen she heard her stomach gurgling. She hadn't eaten supper, only a piece of buttered bread at Arlene's house and that had been hours ago. Most nights she went out dancing she made somebody buy her dinner: a plate of ribs and greens and corn bread from Shorty's, some fried catfish and black-eyed peas from Mama's Place. They couldn't go into any of the major restaurants downtown, of course, but they could sure enough dress up and slip on over to Bim's Eatery for some sweet-potato pie. She usually made somebody at least run out and get her a plate, but when a man fed you as well as danced with you all night, his expectations got as big as his head and it took a lot of slipping and sliding to deal with that. Tonight she hadn't had the energy, so she hadn't eaten. Now she was hungry and she was tired; she wanted to go to the icebox and drink a glass of milk and then she wanted to go to bed.

"Never meant to stay up here, in this place," Clarence said. "Now Burch is dead and buried we can go home."

She laughed. "And do what? Start cropping again?"

"Better than this." He stood, swept his hand over the room with a look of disgust. "Better than living where you can't breathe sweet air. Where you can't walk down the street for folks cussing at you. Where you always got to have fancy clothes and fancy shoes and fancy things I don't even know what the use of them is."

Rae shook her head. "Go on, fool. Go on back to living in the dirt if you want," she said. "I'm staying here."

"I'm a simple man, Rae. I want a simple life."

"You simple, all right," she said.

He moved away from the table. In the center of the room Rae braced herself for the slap. A slap and some tears and it would all be over, she could go to bed. But to her surprise Hootie's Brother stopped well away from her.

"You ain't coming?"

"No."

"That's what I knew you'd say," he said.

The musky sweet scent of whiskey floated across the air and she realized with a start that he had been drinking, something he rarely did. Because they kept no whiskey in the house, he would have had to go out and get it, or bring it home with him from work that afternoon. She looked around for a bottle, saw only a kitchen swept clean.

"That's what you always say," he declared. "But this time I'm really going. I'm going on back home and I'm leaving you here alone, with two children to raise in this terrible place. Two children and nobody to sit here with them while you out running the streets. And we'll just see how long you last."

"Get out," she ordered.

"We'll just see how long you last. You come back home before when a man left you. That's how Hootie got you—bided his time."

She looked at him. "You figured that out, huh?" It was, for HB, a pretty good guess. But he had waited too long to get smart. She said, "Get on out."

One after another pictures of Hootie rose in her mind: Hootie on the road coming toward her, Hootie swinging a hammer to build her house, Hootie grinning at her in the moonlight sweetness of their bed. But as quick as the pictures came Rae shook them away. No sense crying over spilled milk. She thought instead of the young girl she had been the first time she left Memphis. Pregnant and no man in sight, shoeless and ignorant, a country girl who knew nothing but plucking cotton and living in the dirt. That girl was as dead and buried as Burch, as Hootie. Rae meant to keep her in the ground.

"Rae?"

But what about that baby? Mattie who would now be almost ten years old. Ten years old was plenty enough to be a help around the place. She could look after the little ones, do the shopping, maybe even earn a little money doing piecework if Aunt Eba had trained her right. And Aunt Eba would have. It was Aunt Eba who had forced Rae to learn to sew.

"Rae, you gone let me go?" All of a sudden he was just inches from her face. "You really going to let me go?"

"Leave me alone, Clarence!" she cried, jumping back. If he was leaving she would not be slapped. "Don't you touch me!"

He looked at her and she could see he had wilted, had collapsed in upon himself. He was like a plant ripped from the dirt and left to lie in the garden path. All the sun and rain and blue sky in the world would not do it any good because its roots weren't where they needed to be.

"Go on now, Clarence," she said. "Go on home."

"You really ain't coming with me? You really truly ain't coming home?"

Rae shook her head. "Only way I'm going back there is in a pine box. Maybe not even then."

He stood before her mute and wounded, the sack hanging limply from his hand. After a minute he pushed a foot toward the door and then another one.

"You can do something for me, Clarence," she said. "When you get home. If you would." She knew it was a lot to ask, that most men would spit in her face, tell her to go to hell.

He stopped with his hand on the doorknob but did not turn. "What's that?"

"Tell Aunt Eba to send Mattie on up here to me," she said. "Buy that girl a ticket and put her on the train."

He laughed bitterly. "Oh, you want her now. So she can sit here with these others while you run the streets."

"It was you made me leave her," Rae said. "I wanted to bring her along."

He turned now. His face was hard and his whole body strained toward her, as though he wanted to strike her with his words. "Like hell you did!" he hissed. "A regular woman, decent one, woulda made me take her child."

Rae rocked back on her heels, absorbing his anger. Then she folded her arms. "Put the girl on the train, Clarence. Do that for me."

He stared hard at her for a minute, then shook his head. "Yeah, I'll send her. I'll put her on the train. But I'll make sure to tell her to keep her bags packed. 'Cause soon as the next man roll around you'll likely be sending her back."

# Chapter Eight

By Tuesday I had given up on the nausea; nausea at that point would have been a bad sign, the opposite of what I hoped for. Nausea was a variable, as Eddie might say.

On the upside, the streets were clear, the snow plowed up against the sidewalks like white elephants. For some crazed, don't-tread-on-me, New England reason, it was not against town law to leave your sidewalks covered with snow, so half the folks in town declined to shovel, which made walking tricky, unless you didn't mind battling SUVs for gutter space. Still, the buses could roll and the schools were ringing their bells. I planned to drop Harriet off at the preschool and grab a cup of coffee with Valerie, then scoot home and, while Paula napped, telephone my aunt Josephine at the small bridal store she owned and ran in downtown Memphis. She was nine years younger than my mother and a hundred years less intense. If anyone knew where my grandmother was, it would be her.

But the best-laid plans began to falter the moment I went in to wake Harriet. She opened her eyes and said, "Mommy, I feel funny."

"Funny how?" I asked. "Does your head hurt?"

"No," Harriet said, sitting up. "I just feel funny."

"Does your tummy hurt?"

She considered a moment, then said, "No."

I kissed my daughter's face. Her forehead radiated either the slightly elevated warmth of a child just waking from sleep, or a fever that would spike twenty-six minutes after she got to school. I sighed.

The winter before, at Harriet's old preschool back in North Carolina, a mother had been caught spiking her son's thermos with Tylenol. I didn't know the woman but I knew that like myself and unlike most of the other mothers—snooty, university wives—she worked, except I was a professor and this woman seemed to be, from the incandescent green of her polyester blouse, a rental-car clerk. She never lingered in the mornings, never plopped down on the bright red "sharing" rug and read aloud to her son as though auditioning for a Broadway play. She dropped and ran, no doubt to a job she needed desperately. She must have figured a dose of Tylenol in the kid's thermos would get them both through the day.

But a teacher must have figured it out somehow; maybe they routinely taste-tested the children's juice boxes, on the lookout for refined sugar and artificial flavoring. At any rate, outrage rippled through the school. You would have thought the woman had laced vodka into zippy cups. One sharp-faced, Botoxed woman cornered me one morning—as the only black mother in the school, I was constantly and adamantly included in all kinds of things I didn't want to be—and hissed, "Isn't it awful?"

I had finally managed to pry Harriet from my leg by wiggling a chunk of pink Play-Do before her eyes. She sat at one of the little round worktables that dotted the school, blue plastic knife in the air and a wistful, bemused look upon her little face. She seemed to be trying to remember what activity was currently called for—having fun or pitching a fit. I wanted to make my escape, but the woman kept hissing in my ear.

"Isn't it terrible?" she insisted. "What kind of mother would do a thing like that?"

"A desperate one," I said. "Cut her some slack."

That backed Pinch Face up off me, which at the moment was my prime concern. I slipped out the door and gave the matter little more thought. But now, sitting on Harriet's bed, my morning of solitude crashing around me, I saw the working mother's true failure, her biggest misstep: she should have given the kid ibuprofen instead of acetaminophen. Ibuprofen lasted all day.

"Let's go downstairs and get you some breakfast," I told Harriet. "Then we'll see how you feel."

She perked up considerably at the breakfast table, downing a full glass of orange juice and half a waffle, less than her usual amount, it was true, but kids waxed and waned that way. I dropped her off at preschool with a guilty kiss and a cheerful good-bye for the teachers. No words of warning. If they needed to know, they would know.

By the time I dropped off Eddie's dry cleaning and made it to the coffee shop, Paula was dozing in her car seat. I still had fifteen minutes before Valerie showed up, so, with the car running wastefully for the heat, I picked up my cell phone and dialed the number to my aunt Josephine's shop.

"Proms and Promises," said the voice that answered the phone. I was confused. I thought I recognized the voice, though my aunt and I usually communicated through my mother. But my aunt's shop had been named Classy Lady Bridal for the past five years or so.

"I may have the wrong number," I said. "I'm trying to reach Josephine Grant."

"You got the right number and the right chick," she said, and I laughed. That was my aunt Josephine all right. "Is this Grace?"

"Hi, Aunt Josephine," I said. "You confused me with that Proms and Promises stuff. What's that?"

"Running a business is like being a shark," she said. "You got to keep moving or die. How's life up there with all that snow?"

I gave her an abbreviated version of life since our move from North Carolina then asked about her own family. Aunt Josephine had divorced two husbands before calling it quits. She had only one child, a son. The little prince, my sisters and I used to call him when we were kids. He was ten years younger than us, and good-looking, and had all the latest toys and even his father around; whenever we went to their house we'd return home sick with jealousy. He stumbled in high school, though; tripped and fell against the wall that stopped so many black boys, the wall erected by race and class and low expectations and reinforced by his own self-annihilating friends. Aunt Josephine and his father managed to pull the little prince through an early and frightening brush with the law, and to shove him through to graduation, but after that everybody was exhausted. They took a break, which was where they were when I called Aunt Josephine. The little prince spent his days hanging out with his friends, halfheartedly taking community college classes and helping Aunt Josephine in her bridal store.

When Aunt Josephine finished with her update, I took a breath. "This might seem kind of out of the blue, Aunt Josephine. But I was wondering if you had a telephone number for Grandmother. Or an address. I'd like to get in touch with her."

There was a silence, during which I could hear, in the background, Al Green singing, part of the sweet, rhythm-and-blues music Aunt Josephine kept playing on low in her shop to get her customers in the spending mood. After a moment my aunt asked, quite casually, "Why?"

I'd guessed this question might be coming, but now that it was here I found myself getting on the defensive. "She's my grandmother and I haven't talked to her in probably fifteen years. Isn't that reason enough?"

"I don't know—is it?" Aunt Josephine asked. Then: "Your mother know about this plan?"

"It's not a plan," I said. "Just something I thought about today. No big deal."

"Uh-huh. Hold on a sec." I heard her put her hand over the receiver and speak to someone in a sharp tone of voice. "I'm back," she said a few seconds later. "Folks think they can come into a store looking skunky and try on a three-thousand-dollar dress with no bra and no slip? I don't think so."

Behind me Paula stirred in her car seat. It was occurring to me that anything I said to Aunt Josephine would go directly to my mother. And my mother would be upset. I should have found another path to tracking my grandmother down. "Listen, Aunt Josephine, on second thought, never mind. If you don't want to give—"

"Honey, I'd give you her address if I had one. What do I care? But the truth is I haven't heard from my mother in about a year, and the last time I tried to call her at the last phone number I had for her, it'd been cut off."

"Oh," I said, surprised. "Should we be worried?"

Aunt Josephine laughed. "Maybe. But it wouldn't do no good. She's done this before, you know. She'll show up sometime. I'll get a phone call or a letter or a telegram talking about some new husband or asking for money."

"And will you send it to her?"

"She's my mother," said Aunt Josephine.

I waited for her to say something else, but she seemed to think the answer sufficient unto itself. So, after a moment I said, "How is it, Aunt Josephine, that my mother is so . . . angry at Grandmother and you aren't? She left you, too, didn't she?"

Aunt Josephine expelled a short burst of air. "Honey, who knows?" she said. "Maybe because I was older when Mama left me than Mattie was. Maybe because I knew who my father was; he claimed me. Maybe because I had Mattie around when Mama left, and I knew Mattie, for one, would never leave. Who the hell knows?"

There was a small commotion behind her on the line, a gaggle of voices raised in squealing delight. "Gotta go, baby," Aunt Josephine said. "Got a fool customer dragging a five-hundred-dollar train across the floor."


*I'd known Valerie Jackson since my third week as a new New Englander.* We'd met at the park down the road from our house, a place to which I had begun taking the children every afternoon. They needed the fresh fall air and exercise; I needed to wear them out. We hoped eventually to install a small swing set in our small backyard, but that was a few house improvements down the road; in the meantime, the park it was.

As parks went, it was shabbily functional, the way public services often are in towns full of wealthy folks. It was a simple patch of dirt, carved out of a small set of woods and outfitted with two sets of swings, a modest wooden play structure with a swinging bridge, and two weathered rocking horses on rusty steel coils. Decaying wood chips covered the ground beneath the swings, and in the middle of the area a sandbox was filled with discarded pails and shovels. Off to the side were two peeling benches on which the nannies but not the mothers perched. I could tell they were the nannies because they were (a) black, (b) Carribean, and (c) weary, while the children in their care were not, not, and not. I could also tell they were nannies because they watched over the children without making frantic googly eyes with every push of the swing or flinging their padded bodies down the slide with forced whoops of glee. I had a great conversation with one of these women, Gloria, but two days after we met she got fired for raising her voice to the little brat in her care and disappeared. (I overheard the details from two white mothers at the park.) After that, the nannies seemed to stop coming and mine was the only black face among the maple trees until the day Valerie rolled up in her sparkling white minivan. Three boys came roaring out once the doors were open, startling two white mothers pushing their toddlers on the baby swings. Valerie pointed her boys toward the play structure then came and sat on the bench next to me.

"Thank goodness this park is not being renovated, too," she said. "The one down the street from us is closed this week. I was pretty certain if I didn't get my boys out of the house they'd rip it apart."

It turned out she lived on the opposite side of town, a distance of maybe five miles, but really several worlds apart. When Eddie and I were house hunting, the word we'd gotten from colleagues wishing us well was that while our side of town, the side closest to Boston, was livable, the other side was the place the whites who stoned buses in South Boston in the 1970s had finally gone to escape. But here was Valerie and she said, when later I asked her, she never had a moment's unease. "Oh, you know, you get looks sometimes. But most people mean well," she said. "They're just afraid. Fear and ignorance are terrible burdens. You have to help people get them off their backs."

"Valerie," I told her, "you are a far better woman than I."

A better mother, too; that much was clear from that first day at the park. Her boys—Travis, Jason, and Michael, ages nine, five, and three—were sweet and loving and lively without being wild. They came when she called and left when she told them they were leaving and stopped hurling fists full of sand at one another the second she raised her fingers and snapped. She never yelled to get their attention. When Harriet whined that she was hungry, Valerie pulled out a Baggie full of apple slices and a juice box, plus a package of baby wipes. When Paula tried to climb up the slide and skinned her knee, Valerie handed me a pack of tissues for her runny nose, a tube of antibacterial gel, and a Band-Aid shaped like Mickey Mouse.

"You're making me look bad," I told her, wiping Paula's face.

She laughed. "With three boys it's self-preservation," she said. "Trust me, it's not innate."

But I wondered about that. Valerie seemed quietly happy shuttling her boys from place to place. No matter how closely I scanned her for signs of resentment or boredom or desperate bewilderment—and I did—they never appeared. She had a master's degree in education from Boston University and had taught in the Boston schools for nearly a decade before Travis was born, but once he arrived she quit her job and never looked back. "Better to spend the days taking care of my monsters than taking care of society's," she joked. And maybe that was it.

Or maybe it was not so much that she had been born to motherhood as that she had been born with the capacity for a certain kind of love. Because Valerie not only delighted in her children, she delighted in her husband. Which was, sadly, equally astonishing to me.

They had been married nearly fifteen years. But unlike most of the married women I knew, she never complained about him, never bitched, never rolled her eyes or sighed or snarfed when the subject of men arose. She occasionally mentioned his domestic ineptitude or his weight gain or his ability to watch twelve straight hours of televised golf, but did so with such loving gentleness she seemed not so much blind to her husband's faults as enamored of them. Once, as we sat talking at the park, her cell phone rang and she glanced at the screen and her eyes lit up. "It's Howard!" she said, and answered with a coo. Watching her, overhearing the conversation (about dinner and basketball practice), was for me like stumbling across a leprechaun: if I had not seen it for myself I never would have believed it. But there it was, it existed: a marriage in which love—and not duty or obligation or inertia or convenience or lack of knowing what else to do—still reigned at the core.

If such a thing really did exist, and if one's own marriage was not like this, then logic would suggest one had, perhaps, married the wrong person. But what if it wasn't the person but the marriage, the connection, that was the problem. What if some people were simply constitutionally incapable of long-term love? I thought of my mother. I thought of Grandmother Rae. I hardly dared to think of myself.

I intended to talk to Valerie about these thoughts. But the minute she walked into the coffee shop—Michael on her hip and Jason at her side—I knew something was wrong. She was as nicely dressed as always: black boots, black tapered corduroys, pale green cashmere sweater beneath a long, black woolen coat. But her face was drawn and her eyes seemed slightly puffy and her hair, which usually swung around her face in an impeccably relaxed bob, was pulled back into a tight ponytail. Still, she smiled and kissed my cheek and clucked Paula beneath her chin. We got the two boys and Paula settled over warm cocoa and cinnamon rolls, then pulled our chairs close together on the opposite side of the table.

"Valerie." I leaned in. "What happened? What's wrong?"

I had yet to meet her husband. Men were still largely invisible during the day in the suburbs, and it was easy to know a woman for months without meeting the man attached. But I had seen him once, driving past our house with Valerie smiling beside him in the car.

"Did someone hurt you?" I whispered, not wanting the children to hear.

Valerie took a sip of her coffee. "Not as much as I might have to hurt him," she said in a low voice. Then, trying to smile: "Are they are doing arts and crafts here today?"

"I'll check," I said, and went up to the counter. It was a small, old-fashioned coffee shop, comfortably seedy. To fend off competition from the new Starbucks two blocks away, the owner had hired a local college cutie to bounce around in a tight T-shirt (for the men) and to lead the children in an hour-long art project every Tuesday while the mothers drank their coffee in peace. Once Valerie and I heard about it, we never missed a week.

The girl behind the counter said she could be out in a few minutes with her box of rounded scissors and yellow construction paper and glue sticks. When I got back to the table Valerie was wiping Paula's sticky hands with a baby wipe.

"She'll be right out," I said.

Five minutes later the girl bounced out, art supplies in hand. "Art time!" she cried. "Who here wants to make some kitty cats?"

The children squealed in delight. "We'll be right over here," I told the girl, steering Valerie toward a lumpy brown couch near the front window. When we'd settled in I asked, "What's going on?"

She took a breath and let it out. "It involves my husband," she said, carefully. "Who is, after all, a man."

"Oh, Valerie."

"Right," she said, then glanced out the window. I could tell she was fighting back tears, so I let her sit for a minute or two. After a while she turned toward me, skirmish won, though perhaps not the war. "Not an affair, he says. Just a onetime slip. A year or so ago." She chuckled, as if remembering a joke. "Just when Michael was learning to walk."

I watched her carefully, trying to figure out how she was going to take this thing. It felt as if I had known Valerie forever, but in reality it had been only a few short months, and in that time, the worst crisis I'd watched her weather was Travis's case of chicken pox. She'd seemed rock solid to me, but people could fool you. We all worked so hard and consistently at putting on a show.

"I was organizing our files last night," Valerie said. "Howard pays the bills, but every now and then I have to go in there and straighten the place up. He's so disorganized at home."

It was the first even remotely critical thing I had ever heard her say about her husband, and I found it hard to reconcile with the image she had painted before. Howard was a corporate attorney, high-powered and apparently meticulous about his looks, his clothes, his clientele.

"I found a stack of old credit-card bills, and on one of them was a charge for a hotel room." Valerie paused and looked at me. "Am I boring you? Is this so pathetically movie-of-the-week?"

"Valerie," I said. "That's the last thing you need to worry about now."

She tried to smile but failed. "To be honest I didn't think much about it. I mean, if you were going to screw around wouldn't you have sense enough to pay cash for the room? Or at least tear up the bill? I thought maybe it was for his sister. She'd come to visit us around that time, but she always says she can't stay in the house because of the dogs. I thought maybe he'd paid for her room and didn't want to tell me because he knows I think she's a hypochondriac flake. I just left the bill on the desk next to the computer, thinking I'd ask him about it later and then I forgot about it. But he must have gone in there and seen it and gotten worried, because after I got the kids in bed I was down in the basement doing laundry and he came down and confessed. Just spilled it all right out on the floor while I stood there holding the bleach. He's lucky I didn't toss it in his face."

"Indeed," I said. I knew I was supposed to be outraged on her behalf, but what I mostly felt was a kind of weary sadness, not only for Valerie but also for Howard and for anyone who had ever been married. It was not for the faint of heart.

I glanced at the children, who were happily cutting out pictures of kittens and gluing cotton balls around their heads as fur. Gingerly I asked, "Do you believe him? About it being a onetime thing?"

Valerie shrugged. "Does it matter?"

Now it was my turn to shrug, because I could tell from the way she tensed her shoulders that it wouldn't matter, not to her. Back in North Carolina I'd known a white woman in my department, a close colleague if not precisely a friend. One day over lunch in the faculty dining hall she confessed her husband had had an affair. It had been devastating, she said, but they'd gone to counseling and worked things through and in the end it had served to make their relationship stronger, to keep both of them from taking for granted what they had built. Listening to her, I tried to think of any black woman I knew taking a view like that. My friends and family seemed to stand at one extreme or other on the issue of infidelity. I had a good friend from college whose mother had pulled me aside at my wedding and told me to expect that Eddie would eventually stray: men were men, it meant nothing, as long as he kept it out of my face and respected our home. On the other hand, I had girlfriends who declared World War III if their men so much as glanced at another woman. It could never be a mistake; it was a betrayal. It was proof black men were unsalvageable dogs. You couldn't be expected to live without them, but you'd better remember at all times, even with the good ones, that it was you against them.

Valerie was bending and unbending the plastic top of her coffee cup. "Right before I kicked his ass out of the house he said something about feeling neglected, about me being so wrapped up in the kids all the time and forgetting about him."

"Oh, please," I said.

"Yeah, I know," Valerie said. "Spoiled babies, all of them."

For a moment we were both quiet. Then I asked, "What are you going to do?"

The plastic top Valerie was worrying broke in two. "I always said if a man cheated on me I'd kick him to the curb so fast his head would spin. Second chances are for suckers, I always said." She dropped the top on the table before us, closed her eyes. "But that was before the children came."

I nodded. "Amazing how they complicate things."

Valerie opened her eyes. "Was your father around?"

"No," I said.

"Mine either. It's like an epidemic among us."

"Yes," I said.

She looked at me closely. "It's not very fashionable these days, is it? Staying together for the kids. I suppose you'd think I was a fool."

I couldn't help myself, I laughed. It was the idea of Valerie worrying about what I might think of her that seemed so ludicrous. "Lord knows I have neither the position nor the energy to judge you, girl. Most days I don't know if I'm coming or going! You do what you need to do."

Valerie smiled. "Well, you might not think I'm a fool, but my sisters surely will. One of them just got divorced. Our mother tried to talk her into staying married for her daughter's sake—my niece is six—but my sister said she would not be doing her daughter any favors as unhappy as she was. She says children never benefit when their parents are unhappy." She paused. "Do you think that's true?"

I looked over at Paula. She had a glue stick in one hand and a cotton ball in the other, and she was giggling. Was it true that children were sensitive little seedlings, alert to the slightest change of wind in a household? Or was that just what we told ourselves to help ease our way out of marriages that no longer fit? In the absence of physical or emotional violence, of one parent hurling insults or a man slugging his wife across the living room floor, did children really care? Did they even notice? Maybe adolescents could piece together the separate bedrooms, the mumbled greetings, the deadened kisses on the forehead for appearance's sake, but by then they were on to their own emotional issues: friends and classes, the turmoil of puberty. Young children, though, were oblivious. Young children didn't really care if their parents were happy or not. What they wanted was Mommy and Daddy at home.

After all, I'd been struggling for months by then, and Paula and Harriet were still bubbling along.

"Take some time," I told Valerie.

She nodded, but it was clear her thoughts were far away. "All the time he was standing there telling me, I was getting more and more furious," she said. "I've never felt that way, so angry I could barely control myself. My thoughts were flying all over the place. I was going to blind him with that bleach. I was going to get into the car and go find that woman, whoever she was, and blind her with the bleach. I was going to march upstairs and break every single one of his precious jazz albums into bits."

"That's normal, Valerie. That's normal to feel that way."

"I even—" Valerie broke off her own sentence with a barking laugh. "I even—just for a second—I even thought about leaving, just packing my bags and hopping a plane someplace and leaving him with the children. I was thinking that would show his ass! Like to see him trying to get some action with three children hanging off his neck! That's how crazed I was, Grace. I mean, I would never, ever do something like that!"

I looked across the room at the children, who were finishing their project. The clerk was giving me and Valerie the eye, trying to signal that she'd had enough of our children for now. "Of course you wouldn't."

Valerie followed my gaze and smiled tiredly at her boys. "Children need their mothers more than anything," she said. "They wouldn't survive without me."

I nodded, and looked across the room at my daughter. Paula stood up and ran toward me just as my cell phone rang. It was one of the teachers at Harriet's preschool. My daughter had a temperature of 100.5.

*When I got to the school all of the children except Harriet were in* the large room the school used for free play and exercise on rainy days. They were, apparently, imitating dinosaurs; growls and roars reverberated off the bright yellow walls. Harriet lay in the reading area on a mat, one of the teachers by her side. "Mommy, I feel funny," she said, raising her arms.

The teacher aimed an eyebrow at me. "Her temperature's up to a hundred," she said.

Paula clung to my leg. She had decidedly mixed emotions about the school, always fearing she would be left to fend for herself among the raucous boys and prancing, princess-outfit-flashing girls we encountered when dropping Harriet off. I had to pry her away so I could bend down to lift Harriet into my arms. "Poor baby," I said.

"Strange how it just came on suddenly like that," the teacher said. "No sign or warning or anything."

"Kids." I staggered toward the door, one child in arms, the other grafted onto my leg. "Thanks for calling me."

"If she still has a fever tonight I wouldn't bring her in tomorrow!" the teacher called after us, but we were outside by then, the wind humming, the cars squishing past on slushy asphalt. I pretended not to hear.

At home I put Harriet on the couch with a blanket and a juice box and got Paula some lunch: yogurt, pretzels, the last of the applesauce. I tried telephoning Valerie, but her answering machine picked up. I left as casual a message as I could and hung up the phone. Thinking of Valerie and whatever was going on with her made me think of my sister. I telephoned Lena and got her answering machine as well; it was as though every woman I knew had gone into hiding, had decided to withdraw from the world. "This is Lena Washington of Record Real Estate," my sister said in her bright, hypercultured Realtor's voice. "Leave me a message and I'll get back to you as soon as possible."

At the beep I said, "Hey, girl, give me a call. Just checking up on you."

In the living room I bent over the couch to check on Harriet and my heart skidded. Heat was rising from her little body in waves. "Mommy," she moaned, sounding wilted. "Mommy, I'm hot."

It took me ten seconds to reach the bathroom, grab the thermometer, and get back to my daughter's side. The thermometer was a digital creation, sleek and white and serious. The numbers leaped, from 95.3 to 99.5 to 101. At 102 I became concerned. At 103 concern climbed to worry. At 104 worry flamed into fear. At 105 I dropped the thermometer and lifted my daughter into my arms, terrified. "Honey, guess what you get to do?" I said, taking the stairs like Rocky. "You get to take a little bath."

"Don't wanna take a bath," Harriet mumbled.

"I know, but the water will help you feel cooler." I struggled to keep my voice light. Harriet was the kind of child who picked up on the slightest hint of worry and magnified it. I thought of a story my mother had once told me, about going in tears to her doctor when Dot was three months old and colicky and crying all the time. The doctor, an old white man, took one look and said, "Now one of you is going to have stop crying. One of you is going to have to stay calm."

I tried to stay calm. On the way to the bathroom I grabbed the cordless phone.

"Don't wanna bath."

"Just let me pull off your shirt. Here you go, sit down. That's a good girl. Doesn't that feel nice? Just relax."

Dialing the pediatrician's office, I wondered if this was God punishing me for having doubts about being a mother. Would God do such a thing? The sins of the mother, slammed upon the child?

By the time the nurse came on the line, I was close to hysteria. The nurse, by contrast, might have been inquiring about the weather, or the phases of the moon. "What's her temperature now?" she asked. "Did the bath bring it down?"

"Yes, it's about a hundred and one now. But it was a hundred and five!" I was perched on the side of the tub, swishing water over a droopy Harriet, and I could not believe the nurse's nonchalance. What was her problem? Why didn't she have the paramedics on their way?

"Did you give her Tylenol yet?"

"A few minutes ago. Her temp was a hundred and five!"

"That should bring it down more."

"From a hundred and five!"

The nurse made a shushing sound. "Don't worry," she said. "Dry her off, keep pushing fluids, and bring her in."

I got Harriet out of the tub, dried and dressed and on the couch, then got Paula up and downstairs. It had begun to snow again and I had to race outside to brush the snow from the car and start the engine, panicking all the while about leaving the kids alone inside the house, but the only alternative was to put them in the car while I brushed off the snow—and that was no good. Earlier in the winter a child had died from carbon-monoxide poisoning inside his mother's SUV. She had placed him there and left the car to idle while she cleared the driveway, not noticing that the car's tailpipe was blocked by snow. The newspapers were full of it; the television reporters swarmed the woman's house, banging on her windows, rapping on her door. Nobody blamed the mother straight out, but in the fake sorrowful tilt of the TV reporters' heads, the implication was clear.

In decent weather, which Boston enjoyed maybe three weeks a year, the pediatrician's office was eight minutes away. It took us twenty-three, sluicing and sliding along the slushy streets, pumping the brakes, pumping my prayers up to God. At one intersection the light cut maliciously from green to yellow and then straight to red as I approached. I knew the car would fishtail if I jammed the brakes, so I kept moving and nearly plowed into a man on cross country skis who was fording the street. I swerved at the last minute. The man gave a mighty push and sailed onto the sidewalk and in an astonishing feat of skill and speed had his right glove off and his middle finger in the air in no time flat.

By the time I reached the doctor's office I was as flushed and sweaty as my child. More so, in fact; Harriet, when I reached into the backseat for her, was no longer as toasty as she had been. Holding her on one hip and Paula, who never walked when somebody else was getting a ride, on the other, I staggered through the parking lot.

The lobby smelled of wet carpet and doggy pee, presumably from the veterinarian's on the first floor. It took five minutes for the elevator to come. While we were waiting Harriet raised her head and asked, "Mommy, if everybody we knew, everybody in our family, all got together and blew on the fire in our fireplace, would it go out?"

I looked at Harriet. Was she delirious? "What made you think of that, baby?" I asked, but Harriet just shrugged.

The L-shaped waiting room held two separate clusters of chairs, one designated for sick children, the other not, but I could never remember which area was which. Probably no one else could either, since most people seemed to cluster on the side closest to the doorway leading to the exam rooms. On this day the far side of the room was occupied by a young, anxious-looking couple who sat rocking a baby in a car seat, while the near side held a nursing mother and another woman, a curly-haired blonde in winter-white wool pants and a cashmere sweater the color of cream, who sat nuzzling noses with a miniature version of herself. I checked in with the receptionist and lurched toward the near side of the room.

"How you feeling, honey?" I laid my palm to Harriet's forehead. She felt ten degrees cooler and her face was no longer flushed. Tylenol the wonder drug. By the time we got in to see the doctor my child would be a Sno-Kone and the nurse would look at me as if I were some neurotic hysterical nut.

Paula said, "Mommy, I'm hungry."

"We'll get something as soon as we're done here," I said.

"But I'm hungry now," she whined. "I want a snack."

With a sinking feeling I opened my purse and began rifling through it, praying for something, anything: a peanut, a fuzzy Tic Tac, a dried-up stick of gum. Here I was with one sick child and another hungry one and nothing to feed her. I had broken the first rule of motherhood: Never leave home without Goldfish. The tyranny of the snack.

Paula was sniffing my bag like a dog, diligently working herself into a state. She balled her fists and tensed her arms straight down at her side, the way kids did. You could pick her up by those arms when she did that. "I'm hungry! I'm hungry!"

"Paula—"

"I want crackers!"

Hopelessly, I looked again but came up empty. Even the bag of pulverized oyster crackers I'd been hauling around for six months was gone, tossed in a fit of cleaning three days before.

"We'll get something to eat after this," I said, trying to give her a hug. "It won't be long."

Paula burst into tears. "But I'm hungry now!" Then she went down on the floor for maximum tantrum effect and I remembered that in the car, in the glove compartment, was a granola bar, the kind Eddie liked and kept stashed all around the house. I'd seen it while rifling around in search of the ice scraper to clear the windshield. Had I been more focused, I would have put it in my purse. To get it now, I'd have to bundle up the kids, drag them back down the elevator and out into the snow, then hope to get back inside before Harriet's name was called.

In another time or another place I might have been able to go by myself. To zip right out and zip back in with no problems, but in America in its declining years of the twenty-first century, a mother did not dare leave her children unattended. Not for a second. Not anywhere. Between the pedophiles and the police you were surely doomed. I knew a woman at Harriet's day care who left her sleeping twins in their car seats while she ducked into a storefront Starbucks for a cup of coffee and returned to find a police cruiser flashing nearby and a grim-looking officer jimmying her lock. He radioed child welfare, then stood there lecturing her and scanning the traffic for the social worker while the mother sobbed and begged. After fifteen minutes or so he called the social worker and canceled, letting the mother off with a warning. By the time she made it to the preschool to pick up her son, she was a molten mess. I told her the cop probably hadn't really called child welfare; once they're notified they have to show up. He was just trying to scare her and she was plenty scared. A few other mothers gathered round, cooing their sympathy, but I could sense, and so could she, the disapproval behind their smiles. *Get over it,* they were thinking. *Make coffee at home or go without or drive the eight miles out of your way to a drive-thru Dunkin' Donuts like the rest of us.*

  But this was different. This was not a car exposed and vulnerable on the street; this was a pediatrician's office, the welcoming workspace of people sworn and dedicated to the idea of child betterment. Was there a safer place in the world to leave one's kids? Just for a minute, just for two? I could ask the receptionist if she would mind. Tell her I just had to grab something, my car was just outside, it would take far less than a minute, I'd be back before the kids realized I was gone. I could leave my purse as insurance, grab just my coat and my keys. Not even wait for the elevator, take the stairs two at a time and push through the glass door out into the bracing air of a snowy world. Get in the car and close the door. Start the engine. Look straight ahead.


*After a few minutes of Paula's screaming a nurse came and led us* into an exam room. "Poor baby," she said on the way. "She's probably hungry, Mom."

  I looked at that nurse with more animal hatred than I had ever felt for anyone in my entire life. "You think?" I asked. The nurse nodded sincerely, then went off to scrounge up a candy bar. I had to break it in half to split it with Harriet so she would not, in turn, pitch a fit. It took another fifteen minutes for the pediatrician to finally show. He cruised in reading a chart, mumbled hello, plunged his otoscope into Harriet's ears, and diagnosed a virulent double infection. Paula whined and stomped and rolled around on the floor demanding Oreos until the doctor—not our usual young, honey-voiced, ample-breasted, earth-mother pediatrician but her fish-breathed, tufted-eared semiretired partner—turned around, fixed my child in his watery gaze, and said, "See this?" holding up his stethoscope. "This is my magic wand. It turns whiny little girls into toads." Wildly unprofessional, probably even a little cruel. But it worked. Paula climbed into my lap and sat wide-eyed and silent for the rest of the exam. I should have been outraged but what I wanted was to kiss the doctor's warty old hand.

I paid for it, though. It was twilight by the time we got outside, the sky murky and low, the air bitter, the snowfall eased up to near nothingness, and the minute Paula reached the car she began to howl. The streets were slushy but tractionable, the salt trucks had been past though the plows had yet to catch up and most folks had already hit the supermarkets and gone home, so traffic was light. I drove to the pharmacy closest to our house, dragged the children inside, dropped off the script, grabbed a box of Nutri-Grain bars—glorified cookies but I pretended to believe otherwise—opened them right in the grocery aisle. Paula and Harriet shoved them into their mouths and for one, glorious moment there was peace. I stood there in the aisle, watching my giddy daughters as they wandered a little away from me in their sugar buzz. They seemed so small and vulnerable, out there alone in the dark woods of the world—but then, of course, they were not alone. I was with them, they were with me. I watched as they walked hand in hand up to the checkout aisle, leaving behind a trail of crumbs.

# Chapter Nine

I became a sociologist by accident, having entered college with a half-formed intent to pursue psychology. Much of what I knew about the field I'd gotten from watching the old *Bob Newhart Show;* still, it seemed a good way to become a doctor—thus pleasing, or at least, relieving my mother—without undergoing the scientific rigors of medical school.

My older sister Dot had been the first in our family to go to college, and my mother had spent those four years not so much proud as terrified, holding her breath. *Be careful be careful be careful,* she would caution my sister during their weekly telephone calls. *Keep your head down. Don't mess up!* Then she'd hang up the phone, sighing heavily. *She's not going to make it,* she would tell us, bracing herself. *Probably none of y'all are.* I was fourteen by then and beginning to realize that for all of us, especially the girls, my mother held high hopes but low expectations. This hurt, until I figured out, much later in life, that this view had less to do with us and more to do with her pain-filtered view of the world.

Dot responded to this maternal view by pursuing the most practical four-year degree she could think of: a bachelor of science to become a registered nurse. My sister Lena responded by climbing into a stolen car with her renegade boyfriend after high-school graduation and driving off into the sunset. My mother, already depressed—though we did not identify it as such at the time—responded in turn by becoming even more so. Dot transferred to a college in Memphis and moved back home. Sidney, twelve years old and the only boy, disappeared into his comic books. I watched *Bob Newhart* and decided everyone I knew could use some mental-health help. Including me.

But during a summer spent interning at a mental-health clinic between freshman and sophomore years, I realized psychology was not the path for me. For one thing, saving one person at a time seemed too glacially slow for the state of crisis in which black people in general seemed to live. The clinic was located in a rough-and-tumble section of Memphis, and almost every person staggering through the door was black. That summer the entire race seemed to be coming apart at the seams, ripped asunder by booze and heroin, by knife fights and petty jealousies, by molestation and oppression and simmering anger and its desperate acts.

Then, too, the people we saw were a mess: hostile, demanding, self-pitying. Taken one-on-one they were hard even to tolerate, let alone feel compassion for. One of the cases that put me over the edge was a guy of about thirty-five or forty who came every week for an anger-management group I helped the staff psychologist organize. One day as he waited in the waiting room he encountered his daughter. She was eleven or twelve; she didn't live with him, but when she saw him she ran over, excited and grinning, and tried to hug him and then asked for fifty cents so she could get a Coke. And he just stared at her for a minute, just stared with such naked hatred and disgust I nearly came out from behind my desk, and then he reached into his back pocket and pulled out a wad of papers, all folded and stained and creased. "You see this?" he asked, unfolding the papers. "This here the paper the judge give me when I left your mama. It say I'm supposed to give her fifty dollars a month to take care of you. And if I don't, I'm going to jail. They going to put me in jail just like if I don't do this thing now and sit and listen they going to put me in jail. So I give it to her, your mama, that bitch. So if you want a Coke, you go find your mama and tell her to break off a little chunk of that wad I give her because you ain't getting one more dime out of me!"

I watched all this through a doorway as I was setting up for the anger-management group. *Have compassion,* the psychologist was always advising me. *These human beings are damaged and need our help.* But I could find no compassion in my heart for that man. He reminded me of my father. I left the clinic and went searching for another field.

I considered law, political science, the complicated dross of public policy. Then, junior year, I stumbled into a class on African-American history.

The professor, Dr. Eric Madison, took a liking to me, and urged me to study history. He was an elegant older black man with slender hands and precise diction and the kindest voice I had ever heard, and I so wanted to please him I ended up majoring in history as an undergrad. But two years of studying two hundred years of America left me alternately angry and depressed. *The past is prologue. Those who do not remember the past are condemned to repeat it.* I knew these mantras as well as anyone, believed them as much as any twenty-two-year-old ever could, but still, I thought, once you had the general gist of genocide and forced removals, of slavery and oppression and naked greed, what else was there to learn? What was *to be* learned from those abominations? What possible use was to be made of them?

So the study of history led me to the incomparable W.E.B. DuBois, and the study of DuBois led me to the field of sociology, a field he helped to pioneer. I read his great work, *The Philadelphia Negro,* in which he rejected the racist theorizing that dominated social research at the turn of the century and advocated statistical methods in social research. I learned how he combined social observation, statistics, and a desire to advance the status of African-Americans into work that could be ignored but not denied.

When I told Dr. Madison I was giving up history to pursue a PhD in sociology he said, "Don't forget DuBois was first and foremost a historian. The past has meaning in the present, whether the present acknowledges it or not. Especially for the done-tos."

He had a whole theory about history being divided between the doers and the done-tos. It was a great theory, very encompassing and meticulous, and it was one of the things that depressed me most.

"Without history we are simply lost," Dr. Madison said. "Don't forget."

"I won't," I swore, with great solemnity. But secretly I had already left history behind.

*Wednesday and Thursday were sunny and cold, but on Friday it* snowed again: six inches this time, frosted by two inches of hail. Eddie was up and out before I finished showering, calling through the wall of water that he was taking the good car. *A winter for the ages!* chirped the guy on the radio. *The kids'll be in school till the Fourth of July!*

I got us out and down to the park for sledding, but Harriet hit an icy patch on the second run and scraped her face. On the walk home Paula wet her snow pants, then sat down on the sidewalk and refused to move. I ended up having to carry her. By the time we made it home it was hard to tell whose mood was more miserable, theirs or mine.

When I asked Harriet to help me carry the load of snow pants, jackets, mittens, hats, and wet socks down to the basement to put in the dryer, she balked. "I don't want to," she whined. "I don't like going into the basement."

A wise and decent mother would have gotten down to her daughter's eye line and explained in kind and loving words why we all had to work together as a family to make the household run. I said, "What the hell has that got to do with anything?" It was my mother speaking, except that my mother would have gone on for five minutes, running down for me a heated list of all the things she didn't like to do in a given day but did anyway, including cooking or cleaning or otherwise caring for my ungrateful self. That I managed to stop myself short of that kind of tirade was progress. I supposed.

I bent over to try to gather the bulky coats into my arms without tripping over the boots the girls had left sprawled just inside the front door. Harriet stuck out her lips. "Why doesn't Paula have to help, too?"

My mother had never justified to us any action, or word or thought or least of all command. "Pick up your pants and Paula's and let's go," I ordered.

Harriet crossed her arms over her little plane of a chest. "It's not fair!"

"Just do it," I said.

"I always have to do stuff and she never does!"

I stepped closer to her and hit a puddle of melting snow with my foot. "This is my last warning."

"But why do I have to? Why? Why?"

"Dammit! Because I told you to!" Not the first time I'd heard those words coming from my mouth, words I'd hated in childhood. But I got it now, got why mothers the world over resorted to the phrase. Because you wiped their butts and scrubbed their grime from the bathtub and sponged up their vomit when they were sick and you did it because you were supposed to and maybe you even did it with love, but the least they could do in return was pick up a pair of stupid snow pants off the floor when you asked them to.

With a sigh Harriet bent over and dragged her hand across the leg of her snow pants. *"Because I told you to,"* she mimicked. Not quite under her breath.

I covered the three or four feet between us before the last syllable fell from her lips. "What did you say?"

My hand gripped her upper arm, my fingers clenched oh so easily around the tender flesh. I squeezed. And then I shook her: once, twice, three times. Her feet danced back and forth across the floor. I had some dim awareness of restraining myself, of holding back from using all of my strength. But not as much as I might.

"Were you mimicking me?"

She shook her head, too terrified to speak.

"If I ever hear you talk to me that way again I will spank your little behind!"

She tried to shrink away but I held firm, unmoved by the fear in her eyes. "You little brat! When I tell you to do something, you do it. Understand?"

She nodded once.

"Understand?"

She was crying now, and the tears seemed to release her voice. "Yes, Mommy," she whimpered. "I'm sorry, Mommy."

I let her go, then gathered the great pile of winter clothes. My hands were trembling. I threw the clothes down the basement stairs and considered, for a moment, hurling myself down after them in full self-disgust. Instead, I made myself turn around and touch my daughter's hair. "Go on in the living room," I said to Harriet. It was the best I could do. She looked up at me, her tears easing up.

"Go on, honey," I said. "Go play with your sister."

If you are a decent person, the kind who stands for old folks on the bus and brakes for squirrels and gives quarters to homeless people knowing nine times out of ten they'll spend it on booze but giving for that tenth burger time anyway, you will think, before you have children of your own, that anyone who could be cruel to a child is the worst possible kind of human being. You will listen to that Suzanne Vega song and that Natalie Merchant song and that Tracy Chapman song and you will hum along with all those sanctimonious lyrics and you will believe it is beyond your capability to ever harm a little person in word or deed. You will stare at the newspaper mug shot of a child-abusing mother and mutter, "Monster!" and shake your head.

But to have children is to understand the impulse toward child abuse. As a parent, you will say and do things to your children you would never say and do to anyone else—because society would not allow it; because no one can rattle you the way your children can; because from adults you can always walk away. But you cannot walk away from children; children reveal you to yourself. So if you are a decent person, the kind who walks instead of drives to save the environment and who gives to the United Way, you will be surprised at the visceralness of your reactions sometimes. You will be horrified at the way you behave.

*By dinnertime all I could think about was getting the children into* bed. It struck me, as I filled a pot with water and opened the fridge, how much of my day centered on looking forward to the end of it.

I fed them spaghetti and carrot sticks. I bathed them, zipped them into their footed jammies, herded them downstairs for graham crackers and milk and right back up again. I read *Three Little Pigs* and *Madeline* and *Goodnight Moon* for the three-hundredth time, pausing on each page to let Paula find the mouse. The children snuggled against me as I read, smelling of peachy soap and watermelon shampoo and outrageous possibility. I brushed their teeth, I tucked them in, I stood in the doorway while they sing-songed their prayers. *Now I lay me down to sleep.* Harriet hugged me furiously before I left the room. Paula laid a trail of cottony kisses across my cheek.

"I love you, Mommy," Harriet whispered.

"I love you, too, peanut," was my response, and it was not a lie. Loving my children was easy at bedtime. Loving my children was not the point.

Downstairs in the kitchen I headed straight for the bottle of wine chilling in the refrigerator door and poured myself a glass, not using a wineglass—they were in the dining room and too far and too delicate and too nice—but at least using a glass tumbler instead of one of the red plastic ones from Burger King.

Glass in hand, I sat down at the computer to check my e-mail for the tenth time that day. The longer I stayed at home the more compulsive about checking I became, though I rarely heard from anyone other than Dot or sometimes Sidney or some Nigerian banker needing a secure and trustful place to stash his cash. Lena did not believe in e-mail, and my mother had no interest in anything electronic at all. This night I had two new messages: one a vacation offer from AAA, the other a jumble of symbols and text having to do with Viagra and something hot. I deleted them both, went to a nationwide white-pages Web site and typed in my grandmother's name.

Or at least typed it in as best as I could remember. Royal Rose Polk Van Buren, unless she had married again. Would she use all those names? Surely not. Did she, after leaving the last husband, go back to her maiden name? I doubted it; that was not her generation. I typed in every name I could think of and came up with more than three hundred names across the country. Scanning the list, I felt like a fool. It was ridiculous trying to track my grandmother down that way, cold, like a detective with only the sketchiest of clues. It was ridiculous that I didn't even know what she called herself.

I was about to log off when I noticed, at the bottom of the last page on the screen, a listing. For one Royal R. Taylor in Providence, Rhode Island. I took a drink. Providence, Rhode Island, was forty-minutes from our front door, at the most. Though of course the chances that this Royal R. Taylor was my grandmother were infinitesimal. Probably a lot of black families had named their children Royal once upon a time, and anyway, why would my grandmother be in Rhode Island, of all places? Why, at all? Still. Providence. I wrote down the name and address and clicked the computer off.

In the living room I collapsed on the couch with my glass between my thighs. Eddie would be home within the next half hour, was probably already on his way. The stove was off and the iron unplugged and the children asleep—all was well in the little house, all settled for the evening, another day passed and done. If I rose from my couch and walked out the door, just took my purse and coat and nothing else and walked down the street, chances were good nothing bad would happen between the time I left and the time Eddie arrived. The children would sleep on, the furnace would pump, the gas would stay inside its pipe. I could even hide across the street and watch, just to make sure. I was their mother, after all. I could do that much.

People grew from love. Love was supposed to fill you up; that's what I'd learned from the only places I ever learned anything tangible about that bewildering, four-letter mystery: television and the movies and books. My mother never mentioned the word. My teachers did not discuss the topic. The church of my youth had nothing whatsoever to say about the matter, though plenty to advise about the wages of sin and the unforgiving horror of death. But if love filled you up, why did I feel so damn drained all the time?

I got up and put on my jacket and my hat, took my wallet and keys from inside my purse. I opened the door; I stepped outside. The night crackled with cold, the stars snapped and popped with iciness. Down the steps I walked, past my withered azalea, brown and skeletal. Too many grubs in the soil below, eating up the nutrients. It wouldn't come back in the spring.

Maybe, I thought, it was simple after all, as simple as this: those who fainted at the sight of blood should not try medical school and those who hated arguments should stay away from the law. Panicky people made bad air-traffic controllers. The blind made dangerous crossing guards. The lame found the army hard. Not every person was cut out for every job. Not everyone was suited; we had to accept that. That was life. Not everyone should try.

As I stood there, not moving, glancing down the street, a car appeared. It was Eddie's; he pulled into the driveway and opened the door. "Hey!" he called. "What are you doing out here in the freezing cold?"

I looked at my husband. He took a step toward the spot where I stood.

"Grace?"

I raised my hand. "Just getting something from the car!" I cried, waving my wallet wildly. As if that was some kind of proof.

# Chapter Ten

On Saturday morning I awoke to a brilliant sun shining through the curtains and to the feel of hands roaming across my hips. "Morning," Eddie murmured, kissing me. It was toasty beneath the double comforters and even toasty without; the furnace hummed in the basement, heating up the house.

"Mmm. Your body feels so nice and soft." Eddie burrowed his head against me. "Especially your breasts. I think they're getting fuller."

I opened my eyes. "Eddie, they're not. They are not getting fuller." I tried to speak meaningfully. I pushed against his chest, tried to look him in the eye, but he was goofy with sleep and lust. He nuzzled me through my nightshirt.

"I think they are," he said. "I think they're ripening like peaches."

I laughed. "Peaches?"

"Mmm," he murmured. "A man can dream." He started yanking at my gown, trying to pull it above my head, but I resisted.

"If you're going to be like this I'll have to go back on the pill," I said, sitting up. "Be back in a second."

I tried to stand up from the bed, but Eddie grabbed my hand. "You don't have to go. I mean, maybe it's not an issue anymore."

I waited for the little zap of guilt to reach my heart. When it did, I raised my husband's hand to my lips and kissed it before dropping it back onto the bed. "It's always an issue," I said. "Be right back."

Afterward we lay together for a minute, listening to the muted cries of the television one floor below. Then Eddie kissed me and heaved himself from bed. "Sleep awhile. I'll get breakfast for the kids. Oh, and don't forget my mother is expecting us for dinner tonight."

"She is?"

"Didn't I tell you?" He stood in the sunshine, looking so innocent. "Well, just a quick, family meal. It'll be painless."

"That would be a first," I said.

But the good news was that in exchange for agreeing to attend the family suffering, I received from Eddie a free afternoon. He took the girls for a hike in the snowy Blue Hills to work off some of their energy, then out to lunch. "You've got three hours," he said before leaving. "Make the best of it."

Two minutes after they left I got in my car. Just the action itself, just opening the door and climbing in without children to herd or car seats to wrestle, was exhilarating. I felt as if I was seventeen and driving my mother's car for the first time alone, my license still crackling new inside my purse. Reaching the highway, I turned the radio up high and cracked the window so I could feel the air on my face, though it was barely forty degrees. I didn't let myself think about what I was doing, or what I would say if I actually found my grandmother, or why I did not simply pick up the telephone instead.

Traffic was light and my foot heavy. I made the outskirts of Providence in thirty-six minutes flat. It took another fifteen or so to locate the address using directions from an Internet Web site, which, amazingly enough, proved accurate. A left and a right, three miles, six stoplights, another turn and first the street and then the block. I found a parking space across the street from number 19, but did not turn the engine off.

It was the projects. Not the worst I had seen, not the horrific high-rise barracks of Chicago or Philadelphia or New York, but the projects nonetheless. These were two-story row houses made of brick, with cracked concrete steps and barred windows and front doors that had once been painted green. They ran along both sides of the block and also the next one and the one after that, an entire neighborhood of public housing, probably built in the 1940s or 1950s for all those soldiers coming home. The city fathers who oversaw construction would have meant them to be temporary, a leg up and into real home ownership. They also would have meant them for white people, not black. Though we inherited them.

A group of boys sauntered past, startling me from my zone. They all had sweatshirt hoods gathered around their faces against the cold and they were laughing about something, laughing and shouting loud. Nigger this and nigger that, they called. One of them, the smallest, led a pit bull by a chain. I watched them strut on down the block, claiming it for all it was worth, which wasn't much, and then I looked back at number 19. It occurred to me that I had not bothered to think about what I might say to my grandmother because I had not really expected to find her there. But what if she was? What was I there for—to reconnect? Was this some *Roots*-like exploration, or was I kidding myself? What did I really want from this woman I scarcely knew—an explanation? Some understanding? Forgiveness for what I myself was fighting not to do?

A man in a leather jacket and red running shoes came out of the door next to my grandmother's. He turned up his collar against the wind and stood on the stoop for a moment, lighting a cigarette and looking at me. His face was blank—not angry or hostile or even curious—but he was looking straight at me, directly into my face. I realized I'd been sitting there, a stranger in a strange car, the engine running, for ten or even fifteen minutes by then. Back in my little burg the police would have already been called. I shut down the engine and got out, waving my color before me like a flag. The man blew out a puff of smoke and moved off down the block.

I stopped just short of the stoop. For some reason it had never occurred to me that my grandmother might end up in such a place. Though, of course, it should have. A crafty woman, from what I knew, but craft against race, age, minimal education, was a sucker fight.

Back in Memphis there was a public housing project of so-called garden apartments a half mile from our house: the E. H. Crump Homes. Some kids at my school called them the dump homes and laughed at the boys and girls who came from there. We never laughed, not because we were sensitive or noble but because the homes frightened us. They frightened us because every time we drove past, our mother got quiet and nervous and something dark and twitchy came over her face. Sometimes she even went out of her way to avoid the neighborhood, as if some band of monsters lurked within. We never asked her about it as children, of course. But when I was older I asked why the homes had seemed to bother her so. "Because we were always about two steps away from ending up there," she said. "Some months it was only one step, and I knew I couldn't save y'all if we did. I knew if we went into a place like that, not all of us would make it out again."

I made myself move forward, across the tiny yard and onto the stoop. There was a lot less snow on the ground than in Boston; I could see the bare, packed dirt in the front scrap of yard before my grandmother's house. The doorbell was broken; the little button looked as though someone had gouged it out with a knife. I opened the screen door, which was missing its top section of screen, and knocked. Plastered to the door beneath the small window was a bumper sticker, a yellow circle on a white background with the letters *WTF* and a question mark: WTF? It took me a minute to figure out what it meant or might have meant, and when I did I had to think it didn't sound like my grandmother. But then again, what did my grandmother sound like? I knocked again and then, after a few minutes, a third time. Finally I heard sounds within, feet moving closer. My heart skidded across my chest.

There was the clanging of chains and the turning of locks. My stomach flipped. The door opened. A hand, a chest, a neck, a face, a woman of about forty, standing across from me, rubbing her eyes against the daylight.

"Yeah?" she said. She wore gray sweatpants and a baseball jersey and her hair stood on end in broken, overrelaxed little spikes. She was easily six feet tall. She was not my grandmother.

"Oh," I said.

The woman dropped her hands, awake now. She reached out for the screen door and pulled it closed, forcing me to step backward and away from her. "Can I help you?"

"I'm ... I'm sorry to disturb you," I finally managed to say. "I'm looking for Royal Taylor."

"Why?"

"It's personal," I said. "Is she here?"

The woman pulled herself up straight and squinted behind me into the street. She was thinner than I had first thought; she had no bust to speak of, no waist or hips. It was as if someone had squeegeed every spare ounce of fat from neck to foot. She looked back at me, her face hardened now. She crossed thin, ropy arms across her chest and raised her lip. "You from DHS?"

"What?" I was taken aback. "No."

"Don't try to pull no stuff," she said. "If you from DHS you got to prove it. You got to let me see your card."

A cold gust of wind rose up, slapping us both. The woman shuddered and closed the door a fraction. I could tell she wanted to close it all the way, was itching to do so but she was afraid. As big as she was, she was afraid. And not of me. "You wasting my heat," she said.

"I'm not from DHS." I raised my hands, palms out, as if this would convince her. "I'm just looking for Royal Taylor for personal reasons. For my family."

The woman eyed me carefully. "I don't know you," she said.

"You're Royal?" I asked, though of course I'd known the moment she opened the door. "Royal Taylor?"

"I'm gonna ask one more time what you want, then I'm shutting this door." She glared at me again, but I was already moving, already backpedaling across the stoop.

"Nothing," I said. Suddenly I couldn't wait to get back into my car and out of that place. "Wrong address, I guess. Sorry I bothered you."

At the edge of the stoop I turned and leaped to the sidewalk, skipping a step. I might have kept on leaping right across the street but a car was passing, forcing me to stop, and before it could pass I heard the screen door creak. The woman's voice called behind me. "Ain't too many people named Royal."

When I turned around she was on her porch, shoulders hunched and arms crossed against the cold. Out from behind the cage of the screen door she looked far less menacing and younger than I'd thought. Maybe right around my age; maybe even a few years less.

"I never met anyone else in my life with my name," Royal Taylor said. Now that I was going, now that the threat had been turned aside, she wanted to talk. But I did not. My car called to me from across the street, clean, contained, secure. I wanted to get in and drive away from that place as quickly as possible. For the first time since leaving home I was really afraid. Not for my safety, but for where my thoughts might lead.

"You looking for your mother?" she asked.

I looked at her. Sociologically speaking, we were very much the same: both black, both women, both mothers, both Brown Babies, born at the dawn of our legally ensured civil rights. We stood there looking the same and breathing the same and yet, of course, not: not the same at all. I had left history behind but she had not. Like my great-great-grandmother, like both our ancestors, this woman was raising her children in a society in which her rights to her children were in constant jeopardy, but I wasn't. Not really. My rights had been reasonably secured; nearly as secured as any white woman's. Her fight was to keep her children. Mine was not to flee them, not to run away and leave them both behind, and I had to wonder: if I stood where Royal Taylor stood, would I still feel the same? Weren't all these free-floating problems—alienation, dissatisfaction, a fear of being slowly, slowly suffocated, of being squeezed beneath the weight of motherhood—were these luxuries of the middle class? Weren't these feelings the direct, if unintended, result of being able, for the first time in history, to lift my head and feel?

Then again, the other Royal had stood where this one stood. And then she'd gone.

"My grandmother," I said. "I'm looking for my grandmother."

Royal Taylor frowned at me. "Your grandmother?" she repeated, and then she laughed. "Hell. Those usually easy to find."

It took more than an hour to get myself home.


*Eddie's mother lived even farther out in the burbs than we did, in* one of the tony and deadly dull "W" towns surrounding Boston I could never keep straight. Three towns and twenty miles to the south. It wasn't the house or even the town Eddie had grown up in; it was his mother's dream home, the one for which she and Eddie's father had worked all their lives, the one they had been saving for since that first day Eddie boarded a school bus and rode out to kindergarten in that same, tony, magnanimous "W" town, part of a plan to save a handful of inner-city children by giving them a taste of the educational good, good life. While leaving the Boston public schools to ruin the rest, of course, but never mind. At any rate, Eddie graduated from the "W" high school and went off to college in Washington, D.C., and his parents escaped to the burbs. At least, Louise escaped there. Eddie's father, Mason, spent most of his time commuting the forty minutes to his job as a supervisor for the Boston transit system, and drinking or sleeping it off with one of his buddies in the old neighborhood. Louise continued pretending, and continued to pick up substitute teaching slots in the Boston public schools whenever she could stand it. Otherwise she spent her time decorating the house with a fearsome, triumphant pride. This went on six or eight years, until Mason got sick.

We pulled into the circular driveway behind the sleek gray Accord Eddie had talked his mother into buying—she had wanted a BMW or Mercedes, but this was more sensible given her fixed income—and another car: a black SUV the size of a small battleship. Eddie got very busy unbuckling the children's seat belts.

I said, "You didn't tell me your sister would be here."

"Didn't I?" Eddie gave himself a comical smack to the forehead. The children giggled. "Goofy Daddy goofed again."

Eddie's sister, Hollis, and her husband, Michael, lived somewhere in the hinterlands of western Massachusetts, an hour or so away. Pleading winter weather and the long process of settling in, Eddie and I had so far managed to avoid a visit, but I knew that would not last. Not that it would be so bad. Hollis alone was fine—a little ditzy, a tad self-righteous, but easily contained. It was the combination of Hollis and her mother that made me want to go lie down somewhere. Together they were bleach and ammonia: the fumes could put you out.

"I don't know if I have the energy for this."

"We won't stay long," he promised. "Just dinner and we're out."

Hollis was seven years older than Eddie, seven years in which she had reigned as the indulged and pressured only child. My guess was that when Eddie came surprisingly along, she was not so much jealous as relieved. She thought it would take the pressure off, and it did, but only for a moment. Then Louise got some sleep and it was right back to nightly math drills and piano lessons, to Saturday tutoring in history and logic by the retired lawyer up the block (for whom her mother provided baked goods in return), and French tapes from the library. Hollis went along without complaining, until one morning when she was fifteen years old, she woke up and decided to hurl everything at hand straight into her mother's face. Her mother hoped for her to attend some elite, cultured, cloistered (in her mind) women's college like Smith or Wellesley; Hollis hightailed it five miles over to Northeastern University and worked her way through school. Her mother hoped for her to marry well, meaning a manicured, three-named, Oak Bluffs type on his way to Harvard Law; she grabbed the biggest, blackest, roughest (in her mind) Negro she could find, a man who grew up in the projects of Providence and made his escape to Boston, a man who wore his hair in dreadlocks that hung down past his shoulders and whose flawless, blue-black skin seemed to positively absorb all light. (That Michael had once planned to be an actor was even better as far as driving her mother crazy was concerned; a starving artist. The fact that he now made a respectable living as a voice-over artist, flying to New York once or twice a week to use his melodious baritone to entice America into buying disposable toilet wipes, was just an unfortunate bit of luck.)

Most of all, I thought, Louise hoped Hollis would grow to despise her father once she learned the truth about his drunkenness, the truth Louise had worked so hard for so many years to conceal. But even when the man lay dying of cirrhosis of the liver, his children still adored him. Far more than they ever would Louise.

"Two hours," I told Eddie as we stomped around the house and up the steps to the side porch. "Two hours and I am gone."

Louise opened the door in a knit dress of forest green and matching sweater and a look of astonishment. "You made it! I wasn't sure you'd come; the weatherman is predicting more snow later tonight. The streets will be terrible."

Eddie ushered the children into the mudroom and kissed his mother on the cheek. "The sky is perfectly clear," he said.

"But Storm Reynolds is never wrong," his mother said. She was referring to the local dean of weathermen.

"He's been wrong three times in the last month," Eddie told her. "Anyway, we're not staying long. We're both a little beat."

His mother gave a delicate shrug, then turned to me. "Hello, Grace."

"Hello, Louise." Deciding on my tack for the evening, I smiled. I smiled again when she asked if we'd brought salad like she asked—we hadn't; Eddie had forgotten to tell me—then worried aloud that the few, meager vegetables in her refrigerator would not be enough for all of us. I smiled again when she kissed Harriet and said she looked too thin. I smiled again when she took Paula by the hand and declared her fingers frostbitten. "They are not frostbitten, Mother," Eddie said. "They're just cold because she made a snowball on the way from the car."

"The child needs a better pair of mittens," she said.

"She has excellent mittens," Eddie said. "She took them off."

Switching gears, she eyed Paula's security blanket. "She's still carrying that thing around? Do you think that's wise?"

Standing between us, Paula clutched the blanket tighter. I reached down to smooth her hair. "It's fine, Louise," I said.

"You don't want her to become dependent."

"It's fine."

"Also, you have to be careful about germs."

I smiled. "Why don't I set the table? Which dishes should I use?"

We got through the predinner talk okay, though there were a few tense moments when the subject wandered from Harriet's ear infection to childhood infections in general. Eddie's sister, Hollis, had found, out in their Berkshire wilderness, a homeopathic pediatrician who recommended against the usual childhood marathon of measles-mumps-rubella-polio vaccinations, and therefore none of Hollis's children, with the exception of Devin, the oldest, had been vaccinated at all. As far as I was concerned, this was their business, as was the fact that the youngest three kids always seemed to be as sickly and pale as ghosts. Eddie, with his scientific brain, had taken a week when Harriet was three months old and researched everything he could find about the risks of vaccines, including the alleged links to autism and other childhood disorders. To that we added our deep belief in the overweening greed of the pharmaceutical industry and the tendency of Western medicine to think all could be resolved by a pill or a shot. On the other side we placed the elimination of polio, the astonishing health of the average American child, and the very real ravages of measles and pox I'd witnessed on a trip to India my senior year in college. We decided to get our children vaccinated. Hollis reacted as if we'd tossed a coin and signed the kids up for a stint at the local crack house. That had been four years ago and she was still trying to convince us, as if our decision somehow challenged her own. This was one of the great problems with twenty-first-century American parenthood: the inability to row your own damn boat.

"But I read just the other day about a woman in New York whose son was perfectly normal until his third birthday. He went to the doctor and got his shots and the next thing they knew he was rocking back and forth and staring at the wall all day."

We were sitting in Louise's immaculate French Country living room. The kids had been shunted downstairs into the basement rec room Louise had outfitted and reserved for entertaining her grandchildren. There was a television with a Game Boy, a kiddie ice-hockey table, and two bookcases stacked with toys, all sitting atop a cheap, wash-and-wear carpet from Home Depot. Louise had also craftily installed a table and chairs, making the eating of dinner down there "an adventure" that just happened to protect her cherrywood dining room.

Eddie sighed. Illogical thinking made his hackles rise. "You're assuming a causal relationship where one does not necessarily exist," he said.

Hollis made a face and pushed her glasses back up her nose.

Though it was to risk your life to say so, she was the spitting image of Louise: long-faced and square-jawed, with a broad nose, a high, high forehead, and round, wide, luminous eyes, the only thing saving them both from total mannishness. Hollis's skin was half a shade fairer than her mother's and freckled with tiny brown dots, and she wore her curly hair in a no-nonsense little 'fro instead of a relaxed bob—much to her mother's dismay and probably at least partially for that reason—but otherwise they could very nearly be twins.

"All I know is that my doctor did not vaccinate her children and they grew up just fine," Hollis said.

"Because everybody else in town did, thus keeping disease under control and giving infection no base upon which to build," Eddie explained. He was using the slow, science-for-idiots voice he slipped into sometimes. "It's called herd immunity. If everyone stopped vaccinating, disease would proliferate. By assuming the risks of vaccination, my children are, in effect, protecting yours."

Michael stepped into the room and took a seat next to his wife. He'd been downstairs with the children, but since he rarely said much of anything even when present, no one had noticed him gone. Now, however, he decided to speak. "Never considered it that way, brother," he intoned, nodding his head solemnly. "Never at all."

"I remember when Hollis got measles," said Louise. "She was eight years old and Eddie was one and I was terrified he would get it, too, and it would be much worse for him. I kept you on the second floor, Hollis, and Eddie on the first and I spent three days running up and down between the two of you, washing my hands with bleach in between. I didn't sleep for seventy-two hours straight."

"The sacrifice of motherhood," said Michael, nodding sagely, his locks dancing along the shoulders of his shirt.

"Impossible," dismissed Hollis. "No one can stay awake for seventy-two hours."

"Well, I did."

"It's physically impossible," Hollis insisted. "A person would go insane. Isn't that right, Eddie?"

"Actually," Eddie began, but his mother gave him a look and he shut up. I wished for a glass of wine, red and mouthy and lush, but Louise allowed no alcohol in her house. Not a drop.

Louise pulled her sweater tighter against her chest. "I'll just say I was grown and you were a child and delirious at that, so I think I know what was what. At any rate, my point is that in my day, our children got mumps and measles and got over it. We didn't need shots for everything; we didn't try to shelter them from every little bump in life."

"We're not sheltering our children," Hollis protested, as if she had suddenly switched sides. "We're being responsible."

But Louise just shook her head. "My goodness, next thing you know they'll have a vaccination for teething pains! For when you fall down learning to ride a bicycle. For your first crush!"

Louise tittered, amused at her own wittiness, and we all smiled along, all except Hollis, who rolled her eyes to the ceiling as though she were fourteen instead of forty years old. "Well, there's no need to exaggerate, Mother," she said. "Please. It's not that bad."

Louise's smile tightened. Then, after a moment, she clapped her hands together and stood. "Let's eat," she said.

Dinner was rosemary roast chicken with mashed potatoes and gravy, butter beans, homemade biscuits, and a lettuce-and-tomato salad Louise had whipped together after our failure to produce one ourselves. While Hollis and Louise served, I ferried hamburgers and oven-baked french fries down to the kids. Hollis's oldest two, boys, barely looked up from their video games, but the rest of the children crowded eagerly around the plastic tabletop. Harriet, beaming, sat next to Hollis's daughter, Atalia. Atalia was eight years old, the spitting image of her father and snotty as a used handkerchief. Of course my daughter idolized her.

At the table Eddie carried the conversational ball with talk about his job for a while. Louise said, "My friend Harris's son just got tenure at Yale. Now that's job security." Then Hollis made some crazy talk about homeschooling her oldest. Louise said, making a face: "Homeschooling is wonderful until the children have to go out in the real world. And Teavon is already so sensitive." Then Michael came down from his cloud long enough to mention a new series he'd auditioned for, something about an animated, hip-hop bar of soap.

"Not exactly Ibsen." He smiled. "But it pays the rent."

Hollis said, "You can say that again." Nobody wanted to ask which part of the sentence she felt needed reiterating.

Louise, taking a sip of her ginger ale, said, "My friend Helen and I saw a play last week at the Majestic. There was a very handsome black man in it. His name was Wilson Freeman and he was . . . magnetic." Louise had put down her drink but kept her hand on her glass, and as she talked she stroked it absentmindedly. "So tall and handsome and clean-cut, just beautiful really. All through the play I couldn't take my eyes off him. I kept thinking he reminded me of someone I used to know . . ."

She let the sentence drift away and for a split second I thought I saw something girlish in her, a softness I had never seen or perhaps never noticed. Then she gathered herself with a shake. "Finally I realized it was Colin Powell he looked like. So upright and clean-cut. The audience loved him. I'm sure he'll go far on the serious stage."

I glanced over at Michael, to see how this little dart had struck, but he just smiled and speared another piece of chicken with his fork. He was, without doubt, the most insouciant human being I had ever met, so consistently glazed and unflappable that for years I'd assumed he went through his days on a marijuana high. But since our move to Boston, I'd revised my opinion of my brother-in-law. I'd come to see him not as a pothead but as simply wise, a deeply advanced human being who knew what it took to survive the life he was in. His wife he handled, at least in public, with detached interest, as if she were some kind of astronomical phenomenon to be observed and possibly enjoyed, but certainly not worried about. Louise he just let roll right off his back. I admired that. I wanted to emulate him.

But Hollis didn't. "Well, that's about the most self-loathing thing I've heard this week," she said.

Louise looked startled. "What?"

"Admiring this man because he's light-skinned and has wavy hair." Hollis gave a light, contemptuous laugh. "How sad we as a people are."

"I said no such thing," Louise protested. "He was a fine actor, that's all. A serious one."

"As opposed to?"

"As opposed to nothing," Louise said. "Can't I make an observation in my own house? Am I supposed to just sit at my table and keep my mouth shut?"

"What you can do—" Hollis began, but her husband cut her off.

"Baby, could you pass the butter beans?" he asked, using his soothing milk-of-magnesia voice. "Or perhaps Grace. Grace, you're down that way, too. Did you try the butter beans, Grace? Eddie? They're delicious, the best I've ever tasted." He went on like that, even after I'd handed him the bowl, pouring his voice all over all of us. "Louise, you've outdone yourself tonight. Everybody should have some of these beans. Everybody should just put a few on their plate and savor them. Everybody should just focus on the beans for a minute and be glad."

*Outside it was a crystalline night, cold and clear, the sky a glittering* black. The children stomped their feet and pouted at having to leave, but by the time we eased our way through the still-slushy streets of Louise's neighborhood onto the main roads, the girls were both asleep in their car seats. We drove in silence for a while, the only sounds the white roar of the heater and the swishing sound of the tires. As we reached the highway, Eddie reached across the seat to squeeze my hand.

"They just get worse and worse, don't they?" he asked. "My mother and my sister. Going at each other like cats and dogs."

Not exactly cats and dogs, I thought. The tension between Hollis and Louise was marked and sometimes awkward, but I'd seen worse. Of course, Eddie had not. Eddie could not imagine.

"Hollis blames it all on my mother, of course," he continued. "She says she's incapable of ceding control and resentful of having to hold it."

I shrugged. "Might be some truth to that, I guess."

"Hollis says if it weren't for the Game Boy she wouldn't even be able to get Teavon and Devin to come visit their grandmother anymore."

"That's too bad."

"If she's not careful she'll drive everyone away," Eddie said.

I let the wipers swish a minute. "I feel sorry for her."

"For Hollis?"

It was starting to snow again. Flakes came at the windshield and swirled around beneath the highway lights, but the streets and the sidewalks were clear; it seemed to have gotten too cold to stick.

"For your mother."

"Really?" Eddie's voice was surprised. "Somebody must have spiked the ginger ale."

It *was* surprising, my sympathy for Louise; it surprised even me. Lord knew she could be hurtful, my mother-in-law, could be casually destructive even when she meant to be nice, throwing her spiked arms around you and leaving little wounds all over the place. She was, as Eddie said, a critical, negative, sometimes bitter old woman. But maybe she hadn't always been that way. As revelations went, this one was paltry. That Louise had once been a sweet, optimistic young girl, that she'd had a life before the one we knew, should not have hit me with the rattling force of a two-ton meteorite. I was long past adolescence; I was old enough to know how dreams got crushed and goals shoved aside and all the best-laid plans crumbled into dust.

But listening to Louise speak dreamily about the actor onstage who reminded her of someone—I didn't for a minute believe it was Colin Powell—brought the understanding right on home. What part of life had caused that sweet young girl to sour? I wondered. The big struggles or the little ones? The burden of living with and hiding an alcoholic husband, or the constant everyday naggings of motherhood? The hovering specter of poverty, or the ordinary female sublimation of her own hopes and dreams? Louise had guided two children through a decaying neighborhood and an indifferent school system, and also been the one to notice the dog vomit on the stairs.

So, yes, Louise was a negative, critical old woman whose children barely tolerated her and whose grandchildren snickered and sneered behind her back. But what if it was motherhood that had made her that way? Wouldn't that be ironic? Wouldn't that be hilarious? Wouldn't that be a big, fat, heartbreaking kick in the ass?

Eddie asked, "You okay? You didn't eat much dinner."

He tried to keep his voice neutral, but I could hear the hope, heard it warming and expanding him; every day that passed without a tampon wrapper in the bathroom wastebasket, he puffed up a little more. A good wife would ease the pressure, would tell the truth and forestall a painful pop. But I could not tell him about the morning-after pill. And if Eddie really had sabotaged the condom, he deserved to suffer a little. Plus I didn't know I was not pregnant, not for certain. Really I was hoping, too.

"I'm fine. Just a little tired," I said. Let him take that as he would.

At home we carried our sleeping children inside. Paula nuzzled against me as I climbed the stairway to her bedroom, reminding me of the baby who had so recently nursed there at my breast. They grew so quickly, so everybody said. Don't blink, they warned. Don't blink, don't blink, and if it was only the span of a blink, why couldn't I enjoy it? Why couldn't I endure it? What the hell was wrong with me?

I tried to ease Paula into her bed as gently as possible, but when her face touched the cool pillow she opened her eyes.

"Shhh. Go back to sleep, sweetheart."

"I want my blanky."

Eddie, who was pulling the covers up over Harriet, looked across the room and I knew he and I were thinking the same thing: *Please, don't let us have left that thing at Louise's house.* He whispered, "I'll go look in the car."

When he was gone I sat rubbing Paula's back, humming, trying to ease her back into sleep. If we had left the blanket and if she came fully awake and realized that absence, there would be no sleeping for anyone that night.

"Blanky," she murmured.

"Daddy's getting it." I kept rubbing and humming. "Shhhh.

By the time I heard Eddie's footsteps on the front porch, the child had drifted off. I got up and tiptoed from the room, leaving the door open behind me. Downstairs I found Eddie on the couch, the blanket beside him.

"Oh, good, you found it."

"Yeah," he said. "And something else."

He held out a piece of paper, a little booklet really, folded accordion style and printed with some words I couldn't make out. I had no idea what it was, not at first, but I could tell from Eddie's face that it was nothing good.

"What is this, Grace?"

I narrowed my eyes, looked again. "What?"

"This!" he yelled, waving the booklet in the air. And then I knew. It was the informational packet from the morning-after pill. In my greed and relief I must have dropped it in the car, kicked it beneath the seat and forgotten it there.

My heart thumped hard and my vision seemed suddenly to blur. When it cleared, I thought, *I'm tired.*

"You lied to me," Eddie said.

*So tired. Of all of this.*

"Eddie . . ."

"All this time."

"I told you I didn't want another child. I told you I didn't think I could handle it."

"So you killed it?"

It was a slap and I took it as such. I turned my head and began walking around the living room turning off lights. Whenever Eddie came into a room he always turned on every lamp and every switch in the place, as though the world could not be bright enough for him. "You know better than that," I said. "It was forty-eight hours after intercourse. The egg didn't even implant."

Eddie crumpled the paper and hurled it across the room. He hurled it away from me. He was not a violent man, but still I flinched. "I see," he said, "that you have the science of reproduction down pat. Good for you."

"Eddie—"

"The fact remains you lied to me." He was sitting now on the edge of the couch, both hands pressed into his knees. I could tell he wanted to stand up but was keeping himself from doing so. "You went out and unilaterally decided not to be pregnant and then you let me go on thinking you were."

"I tried to tell you not to get your hopes up."

He threw up his hands, barking out a laugh. "Oh! Right! Thanks for that!"

From upstairs came the sound of one of the girls shifting in her bed. I imagined Harriet sneaking to the top of the stairway and listening in as her mother and father fought. "Maybe we should calm down," I said. "Maybe we should talk about this tomorrow."

He sprang up, finally, but kept his arms stiff at his side. "We don't have to talk about it at all. We don't do that, apparently."

"I'm sorry," I said, but he raised his hands as if to brush my apology from the air.

"I'm going to bed," he said, pushing past me in the doorway.

The air between us seemed to vibrate with his anger. He smelled like the snow. I stepped aside.

At the bottom of the stairs he stopped and turned around. "If you're so miserable," he said, holding my gaze with his eyes. I could tell he was fighting, fighting to hold on to his anger so he would not cry. "If you hate this life so fucking much, why don't you just leave?"

I opened my mouth but nothing came out. What was there to say?

"If you don't love us," Eddie said, "what in the world is keeping you here?"

He went up the stairs, not stomping but softly, thinking probably of the kids. I sat on the couch and held Paula's blanket in my lap. I did not think.

After a few minutes the phone rang. It should have made me jump, coming in the silence of the late evening, but it didn't. It seemed the most natural thing in the world and I got up to answer it as if I'd been expecting it all along.

Later, though, in the irrationality of grief, part of me would blame my husband. I would think if he had answered as he usually did, if he had rushed to stop the ringing with his hands, things would not have been as they were. He was a man who still believed the telephone brought mostly good things and so it did, to him. But I did not believe.

"Hello?"

"Is this Grace Jefferson?" It was man's voice, one I did not recognize. Had it been family I would have been frightened, but it was a stranger and so I was reassured. Just a telemarketer, calling late. I put on my getting-ready-to-be-pissed voice and answered, "It is."

"This is Howard Jackson," the voice said. "Valerie's husband. I'm sorry to call you so late but . . . there's been an emergency."

His voice was very formal and contained. All I could think of was how strange that Valerie, who for all her good grooming and matching shoes, was anything but formal. "An emergency?"

"Valerie . . ." he began, but his voice broke. A sinkhole opened in my heart and for a second I couldn't breathe. I looked toward the stair, looked for Eddie, but I could hear him in the bathroom brushing his teeth.

"Valerie has suffered some kind of . . . incident," her husband said after a moment. His voice had regained itself, though it still shook. "She's on her way to Beth Israel. I need someone to come to my house and watch the children, so I can go be with her."

# Book
# Two

# Chapter Eleven

I t took more than a year of being married before I could say the words *my husband* without wanting to laugh. *My husband, my husband.* I might as well have been saying my wings, my third arm, my peaches-and-cream complexion, my Republican membership— it was just that strange and nearly that unthinkable. Much easier to avoid the declamation altogether, to go around it. "The guy I married," I said sometimes. My other half. The guy at home. Or, most simply, Eddie. Allowing the ring on my finger and known history to speak the rest.

The ring itself was another issue. I never liked wearing rings, had never been able to get used to the heavy, constricting feel of them around my fingers, and so was forever taking them off and leaving them behind on desktops and tabletops and bathrooms and in other people's living rooms. I lost my high-school class ring that way, plus more cheap craft-fair rings than I can count. I worried about losing my wedding and engagement rings. Especially the engagement ring; it belonged to Eddie's grandmother on his father's side, a beautiful, unpretentious, old-fashioned ring, white gold with a modest center diamond and two smaller ones clustering on either side. The twin wedding rings Eddie and I picked out were even simpler: silver bands engraved with a wriggly black line that jolted up and down again like the line on a heart monitor. "Will that mean our marriage is always on life support?" Eddie asked me, grinning, when I pointed to the ring in the jeweler's case.

"It means marriage is a series of ups and downs, peaks and valleys," I said. Just as if I knew what I was talking about. "But see how the line never breaks."

At first I tried to keep the rings on all the time, the way you were supposed to. But that didn't work; I couldn't wash dishes with them on or make meat loaf or lift weights at the gym. So then I tried wearing the rings the way I did earrings and my watch: putting them on in the mornings as I dressed for work, taking them off when I came home. But even at the office I had trouble. Teaching a class or advising at student in my office, I would twist and tug and pull at the rings absentmindedly until I ended up taking them off. More than once I accidentally left the rings on my desk overnight, not noticing until I went to wash dishes or brush my teeth for bed. The next day I'd find the rings placed deep inside my top desk drawer along with a note from Jesse, the cleaning woman. *Girl, you lucky it was me cleaning this office but I might not be here every night. Keep these rings on!*

By the second year of marriage I had pretty much stopped wearing the rings altogether, save for special occasions: family events, department parties, a night on the town. Sometimes I wore them to work and sometimes I didn't, depending on what the day might bring. A meeting with the dean, yes. A conference or paper presentation or faculty meeting, probably. Strong women frightened some people; unfettered ones really gave them the creeps. But if the day foresaw only the usual four hours of trying to shove a pellet or two of education down the throats of my sullen undergraduates, I might not bother at all.

"Do you mind?" I asked Eddie once. It was maybe a little over two years into our marriage. I was twenty-nine. "Do you mind me not wearing the rings?"

"Nope," Eddie said, pulling me into his lap. His own ring never left his finger, though I suspected that was as much from inattention as anything else: he simply forgot the thing was there. That was the way he was: a brilliant man who routinely left car doors open, towels on the floor, the refrigerator ajar. "I know I gotcha. I don't need a piece of jewelry to tell me that."

"How romantic."

"Of course you might want to wear it when the children start coming along," he said. "I don't want anybody thinking my kids are fatherless bastards. You know how these Southern crackers are."

"Not only Southern ones," I said.

Eddie had been in North Carolina for years by then and liked it well enough, but like most Yankees he persisted in his belief that race relations in the South were inferior to those up north. An interesting perception from a Boston native, but there you were.

Eddie shook his head with a smile. "I think you're wrong," he said. "But I won't argue the point."

"Why not?" This was one of Eddie's little emotional habits that made me furious. It wasn't so much that I liked arguing as that I could not understand how a person could believe he was right about something and still refuse to stand up for it. "Argue away."

But Eddie just shook his head, smiling still. "The racial predilections of my hometown are beside the point," he said. "The point is I want everybody everywhere to know my children have a proud, black father standing behind them. I don't want anybody thinking my brood comes from a broken home."

"Brood?" I tried to say it lightly, smiling, to show my heart had not hardened on the topic, although of course I feared it had. "Did we discuss a brood?"

"Now, Grace."

"Funny, I don't even remember discussing a single chick."

In those days I often felt besieged by baby fever. Everyone I knew seemed to either have a baby, be having a baby, or be talking endlessly about the day she would finally reproduce. A friend of mine attended two churches, left her own washing machine idle and trucked her clothes to various Laundromats, joined three dating services, and even took a class in auto repair—this from a woman who never pumped her own gas—in her relentless quest to find a husband and thereby leap the biggest hurdle along the path to her true goal: motherhood. She harangued me for being married and not knocked up. She herself wanted babies the way a dog wants bacon on Saturday mornings: bad. The smell of infants made her twitchy and wiggly and wet-eyed with lust. The same smell just filled me with dread.

The women in my department who had children—mostly adjuncts, I noted, or women who had put off baby making until after tenure showed its pretty little head—held their baby pictures to my face as if warding off a vampire with a crucifix. Ha! *Take that,* their eyes cried while their mouths bleated platitudes about maternal tenderness and knowing, for the first time in their lives, what it meant to give and receive unconditional love. That was the favorite, the biggie everyone seemed to repeat. "If I had never had kids I would never have known what it means to love and be loved unconditionally," one woman gushed at me. As if either one of those things was actually true.

Eddie pushed, too; gently at first, hardly seeming to, then more and more and more. One night on our way to a restaurant, we passed a movie house; some kiddie matinee was just letting out and the sidewalk overflowed with fathers lifting their children to their shoulders, balancing them high above the crowd. At dinner Eddie started in about how, unlike his father, he intended to spend quality time with his son. Or daughter; it didn't matter to him. Then he turned those doe-brown eyes on me, all moist and shining, and my blood ran cold.

"I don't think I want children," I told him.

He fought to keep his face from crumpling. I looked away, pretended to examine the massive aquarium across the room. It was the least I could do, fiend that I was.

Finally, voice wobbly, he said, "I love you, Grace."

I held my breath and waited. I knew there was more to come.

"Please," Eddie said. He had gotten control and his voice was steady. "Please. Don't make me choose."

I kept silent but what I thought was: *Someone has to.*

Even my mother got in on the act, telephoning me weekly with suggestions for jump-starting what she assumed must be my stagnant fertility. Eat yogurt. Bathe in baking soda. Drink eight glasses of water a day.

"To keep your system flushed out," she said.

"My system is fine," I told her, but she didn't hear me.

"So you can get pregnant," she said. "Trust me, it will help."

"It might," I said. "If pregnant was what I was trying to get." Pouring gallons down my throat might help if I didn't, every night before bed, brush my teeth and wash my makeup away and open that sweet little white compact and punch out one of those dream-colored little pills and swallow it like a devout Catholic swallowing the Host. Ninety-nine percent effective if taken properly and I took it properly. Faithfully. Religiously. "Zealously," joked Eddie. "One might even say obsessively." When we still joked about the subject.

"That is, if you're not already pregnant," my mother said. "Are you?"

"No, but if it happens, you'll be the third to know," I told her. "The first to know will be Eddie. The second will be the guy who manufactures the pill."

"If you don't have children, you'll regret it."

"Or vice versa."

"The Bible says be fruitful and multiply."

"Maybe King James's translators got it wrong," I said. "Maybe the original text said multiply and be fruity. Have kids, go nuts."

"Now, Grace," my mother said.

"Now, nothing," I responded. "Don't you of all people start with me."

At the time of that conversation I was twenty-nine years old and had, to my pride and great relief, sixteen years of flawless contraception upon which to count. The pill, the diaphragm, the sponge: these were my friends, and we were very close. I knew how they worked and why they worked and what would make them cease to work and thus what to avoid. I knew my cycle as well as my name. I owned a dog-eared copy of *Our Bodies, Ourselves*. I'd held a hand mirror to myself and looked. The female body stood a mystery to my mother and grandmother, but I came of age in the long, roiling, wake of Betty Friedan, and I had broken my body's code.

Only the heart remained unfathomable. And one day, out of the blue, the heart said, *Sure. Why not?*

Astonishing really. The ticking clock, I suppose. The will of life to reproduce itself. The exhaustion of tenure seeking and the creeping fear it might not be on the way. Whatever it was, even Eddie was surprised at the swiftness of my turning, though he soon leaped upon the boat and paddled hard. *Yes,* I decided. *Yes, I would have children.* And I would do better than was done before. Not perfect—I never deluded myself into believing a perfect motherhood was possible—just better. I would not be dragged down. I would not be consumed. I would redeem my mother's life by not repeating it. And so pregnancy became a goal, a project to tackle and then complete. Just like my senior thesis, my BA, my dissertation, my PhD. Just like tenure, toward which I thought I was still striding. I went off the pill, began charting my cycles, choked down folic acid by the ton. I read and exercised; I learned what a teratogen was—substances or chemicals capable of causing birth defects—and avoided them like the poisons they suddenly were. Raw fish, tuna, bleach, gasoline, the pesticides sprayed carelessly upon my neighbor's lawn—all suddenly anathema to me. I became so attuned to the complex workings of my womanly flesh that I could actually feel the delicate twinge behind my kidneys at the exact moment one of my ovaries released its tiny egg. Mittelschmerz, my dear husband. Come to bed.

Not like my mother at all.

Here's what I know about my mother: when she was twenty-two she married and when she was thirty she divorced and by the time she was thirty-five she had sacrificed all the bits of life that gave her joy: a job she liked, a man who loved her, a sense of herself as whole in the world. What she had left was us.

Here's what else I know about my mother: it was abandonment that shaped her life. Her stepfather died, her mother, my grandmother, left twice that I knew of when once was more than enough. When we were little, when I pouted or Sidney grumbled or Lena muttered beneath her breath, when one or the other of us tossed a hissy fit about not receiving some new fabulous toy, or complained about our Goodwill clothes or Goodwill shoes or Goodwill life, sometimes when these things happened my mother would cross her arms and fix us with a look that, at the time, would scare and bewilder me but that later, when my own children came along, I grew to recognize. "At least," she would say, "at least I'm here."


## KNOXVILLE, TENNESSEE, 1960

*She was in chapel when it happened. It was well past noon but the* Sunday service, mandatorily dull for all students at the Mary Todd Lincoln College for Negro Girls, was still going strong. In the first pew the college president sat nodding in his seal-gray morning suit, his otterish wife slick beside him in a blue feathered hat and white opera gloves. In the second row perched the dean and vice dean and their unfeathered wives; in the third, fourth, and fifth rows hovered the faculty. In the sixth row, just behind the biology professor and his fiancée, sat Mattie, fighting to keep bile from rising in her throat.

In the pulpit Reverend Jamison preached from Matthew, the story of Peter climbing from the boat at Jesus' command to walk upon the troubled waves. Those first few steps were no problem; those first, sweet steps upon the parlous sea were just fine. Peter was doing it. But then he looked around at the fearsome waves cresting above his head and he got worried. He took his eyes off Jesus and put them on the world and that was the moment, the single moment, when he began to sink. He was going down, the preacher said, going down because he lost faith.

Mattie tried hard to take the lesson of the sermon to her heart, but it was hard to concentrate on anything but the mounting crisis in her body. Her throat was closing, her stomach twisting in upon itself like a snake. Her mouth felt like the inside of a field hand's pocket, though she had brushed twice that morning, brushed and gargled and flossed. Her eyelids seemed suddenly to weigh ten pounds each. All she wanted in the world at that moment was to lay her head upon the pew and sleep a thousand years.

A great, gasping yawn rose up in her throat and roared toward her mouth and Mattie raised her hand to smother it, forgetting her purse and the gold-tipped Bible in her lap. Both tumbled to the floor. The Bible landed flat-backed with a thud just as the minister was pausing, uncharacteristically, for breath. The purse spilled its lipstick and pencils and handkerchief and a single dime that rolled straight back through the chapel and seemingly out the door. Heads swiveled, beheld Mattie straight-backed and lockjawed and barely breathing, swiveled back. All except that of her dorm mother, Mrs. Strand, whose glance lingered just long enough. Mattie dropped her eyes. There would be words that afternoon. She would be called alone into the parlor and reminded about proper behavior, about the need for absolute ladylikeness, about representing Lincoln Dorm and the Todd College and the Negro race, and at the end of the talking Mattie would be sent from the parlor and the girls who had achieved gracefulness that week would be invited in for tea. And Mattie would go to her room and lie on her bed and cry, not because she had let down the dorm or the college ' or the race but because she had let down Mrs. Strand.

The Bible had fallen open to Psalms. *The thing I feared most has come upon me.* Too fast Mattie bent to retrieve her belongings, and dizziness reared up like a dog and grabbed her by the neck and in that instant she knew the problem, in that one, swift moment she knew precisely what was wrong and she bit the inside of her cheek to keep from crying out. It was the autumn of 1960 and she was twenty years old and a junior in college and that close—that close.

Up in the pulpit Pastor Jamison's mopped his face with a handkerchief, caught the president's warning glare, worked to squelch the joy in his feet. None of that hysterical, screeching emotional nonsense during worship at the Todd College for Negro Girls.

*My father's name was Cush Breedlove.* He and my mother stumbled across each other in the great navy town of Virginia Beach one summer when she was twenty-two. He was there with his ship. She was there cleaning house and watching kids for a wealthy family, great white benefactors of her small, black school.

That my mother even made it to college was a miracle, one transmitted, primarily and improbably, through the auspices of a Burch. Melanie Anne, maiden daughter of the old man himself, dedicated the bulk of her childbearing years to improving the conditions of the colored folks upon whose backs her father had built the family wealth. In Mattie, who returned to the plantation after four years in Memphis with Rae, she saw an opportunity for redemption, a chance to alleviate guilt and establish herself as a woman of independent thought. Melanie Anne decided Mattie would not only attend and complete the local colored high school, but would go on from there. And when, the summer of her sophomore year, Mattie needed a job, it was Melanie Burch who made the call to her close friends the Ravenels of Virginia Beach.

Such great friends of the colored people were the Ravenels that they not only hired Mattie for the summer, they actually let her have Saturday nights off. She usually spent the time in her room above the kitchen, reading or sewing or writing secret poetry. But one Saturday night two of her friends, also college girls, also working for friendly white families in town, came to her room, removed her curlers, dragged her out for a drink and a dance. In telling this story to us, my mother always added, "I haven't spoken to those people since."

She saw him the minute she stepped through the door and so did her girlfriends; he was hard to miss. Tall as an oak tree, broad in the shoulders, dressed in navy blues so crisp they crackled, and the gold piping around the collar was like a mantle some great king had placed upon his back. He stood at the bar with two friends, also sailors, also dressed in blue. Somehow they faded into the club's smoky darkness while he stood out.

"Look at that," said one of her friends, a slouch-shouldered, flat-nosed girl named Mabel. "My, my, my."

Her other friend glanced over, glanced away. Her name was Ruby and they all agreed she was the prettiest of them, though once Mabel said to Mattie, "You know, you're actually prettier than her when you smile. You just don't smile and she does."

"Too dark," Ruby said now, shaking her head. "Black men are trouble. Make ugly babies, too. And look at that head!"

"That's the navy, girl. You know they don't let them conk their heads in the service."

"Yeah, they want us to look like we just crawled out of the jungle somewhere. Easier to shoot that way."

"You are crazy!" Mabel laughed. "Anyway, looks like he has eyes only for Miss Mattie here."

Mattie looked up. He was sipping his drink, watching her over the rim of his glass with a blind man's gaze, both penetrating and blank. Her knees felt oddly loose, her palms strangely numb. She had the urge to retreat.

"I think we should—" she began, but her friend had grabbed her hand and was pulling her deeper into the club.

"A table right up front!" her friend squealed. "This night is meant to be!"

The band was blistering. The crowd danced and clapped and sang along, but Mattie turned down every offer until he came over and held out his hand.

"I'm Cush," he said. "Want to dance?"

He said his name came from the Bible, the Book of Genesis; Cush was a son of Ham. She was impressed that he knew the Bible and that he didn't make up some stupid, sleazy explanation for his name, like "It means cushion, baby, because my love is so soft." She took it as a sign of integrity. After they were married, she realized it wasn't integrity but a lack of imagination on his part.

As they danced he told her his story: youngest of eight, four boys and four girls. Though it was impossible to believe looking at him then, he swore he'd been small for his age through most of his childhood. This smallness of stature led his sisters to treat him like a Betsy Wetsy doll and his brothers to regard him as the family punching bag. In this they took after their father, who seemed to hate the way his wife doted on her youngest son, and went out of his way to balance the scale.

"Last time he hit me was the night I left home," Cush told her. "I was sixteen. He came behind me in the garage, yelling some mess about gas in the car and disrespect. I told him not to put his hands on me. I told him I'd make him swallow his own blood, and I did."

That night he lied about his age and joined the navy to see the world; he'd hardly been home since. "But I intend to go back," he said. "And I'll have something to show for it when I do."

He drove a white Ford, old but pristine inside and out. He picked her up that Wednesday evening and that Saturday afternoon and every Wednesday and Saturday for a month afterward, and they went driving—into town for a movie or out to the beach for a picnic or along the highway to catch the air. Once they drove all the way down to New York to ride the elevator up to the top of the Empire State Building and eat lunch in a Times Square diner and then leave because they were so identically uncomfortable in the city, so hectored and squeezed and unable to breathe. Another time they double-dated with Ruby and her latest beau, and on the way out to dinner stopped at Cush's apartment so he could switch out of his uniform and into a cheap and shiny suit. It turned out Cush disliked wearing his uniform off base; he did so only when changing at home was too much trouble. Mattie tried to tell him how good he looked in it, how distinguished, but she could tell he didn't hear what she said.

Cush had just been promoted to corporal and had moved off base in search of privacy. The apartment was small—one main room, Pullman kitchen, bathroom the size of an envelope—and sparsely furnished, with a bed, a small table just outside the kitchen door, and a blue armchair stationed in the corner beneath a lamp. But there was a dish towel neatly folded in the kitchen, and curtains, plain white muslin curtains, hung from the window near the bed. And Mattie noticed that what the place lacked in decoration, it made up for in cleanliness. It was, in fact, scrub-brush spotless, the bed so tightly made Ruby's beau tried to bounce a quarter off it and succeeded, the kitchen so organized the three cups in the cupboard all faced handle out, the bare wooden floor so clean it squeaked when Mattie scuffed it with her shoe. It was probably cleaner than Mattie's own room and that was saying something big. She was a person who believed in cleanliness and order, in the calming, steadying effect of having a place for everything and everything in its place. She believed in beating back chaos with a broom and a mop.

"Man, you got a maid?" cracked Ruby's beau. "Or does your mama come up here to clean for you?"

"Neither one," answered Cush, taking the crack seriously. "I do it myself."

Ruby's beau grinned. "And you'll make someone a fine wife someday, too!"

Ruby let out a bark of laughter and squealed, "Hush up!" Mattie giggled, too, but stopped when Cush looked at her.

"What's so funny?" he asked.

"Nothing." She laid her hand on his arm. "Nothing. I'm sorry. Let's go."

On the way out Mattie noticed, by the side of the blue armchair, a small three-legged stool. It was crooked and roughly hewn but with a seat made from a slice of oak so golden warm it nearly glowed. Even from across the room she saw its beauty. She wanted to touch it, to lift it up and feel its heft. But Ruby and her beau were still giggling to themselves and Cush was shoving them all out the door. He was still angry, she could tell. She had hurt him and made him angry, and she would have to make it up.

Which she did two nights later by letting him take her to his room. They'd had dinner, danced awhile at the club. Cush had ordered champagne and Mattie, who never drank, had let two whole glasses of the liquid magic slip past her lips. She asked about the stool, and he said he would show it to her.

In his room she avoided the bed, which seemed to loom twice as large as it had before, and aimed her body straight toward the blue armchair. Cush pulled out the stool, sat on it, took her hand in his. The stool, he said, was the first thing he'd made in shop class in seventh grade. He'd made it for his father, back when he still hoped they could get along. He'd made it for his father to have something to rest his feet on while he watched television, but his father had taken the stool down into the basement and never brought it up again. Cush didn't see it again until the night he left home. He went into the basement in search of a suitcase and found the stool, shoved behind the hot water heater. It was covered with grime and dust. He took it with him when he left.

"Never seen nobody so interested in a stool," Cush said.

She tried to smile a sophisticated, movie-star smile, but ended up giggling instead for some reason. "I used to have a stool like that. When I was little. Somebody made it for me."

"Oh yeah?" Cush inched the stool forward. She could smell his cologne, something spicy and like cinnamon.

"He made it just for me. Just for me and nobody else!" Her hand flew away from Cush's and landed on her hip and she was four years old again, standing on the porch yelling at Annie Lou from down the road to put down her stool, stop touching it, it was special, her daddy made it for her, and Annie Lou was yelling back that it was just a stinky old stool, who cared, and anyway Hootie wasn't even her daddy at all.

"What's wrong?" Cush asked. She felt his hand, enormous and warm, brush across her face. "Why you crying?"

She tried to smile again, hoping for giggles, but none would come. "Being silly, that's all," she said, brushing away the tears with the back of her hand. "Over a stool."

"Did you lose that one?"

"I guess," she said. "I don't remember."

"You can have this one." He stood up then. "You can have this one and I'll make you a dozen more if you want. Just for you."

He'd come late from work and was still reluctantly wearing his uniform, his dress blues, and he looked so incredibly handsome, so mountainous and solid and fully grown. He pulled her into his arms and drew her into him.

"Let that be a lesson to you," she would later warn her daughters. "Never marry a man in uniform until you first see him out of it. A lot."

But it wasn't really the uniform that made her marry him; it was my sister. Seven months later in a hospital in Virginia she gave birth to a baby girl; Cush waited outside. "A girl?" he said when Mattie showed him the baby.

"A girl," she said. "What should we name her?"

"I don't know," he said, befuddled. "A girl."

Mattie named the child Dorothy, after Dorothy Dandridge, who was gorgeous and talented and seemed to be making it in the white man's world.

She didn't know much about the body, or how it worked; she knew very little about operations "down there." So she did the things women said would stop the babies from coming. She ate no meat. She got up after lying down with Cush and washed herself; she went to the kitchen and squeezed a lemon and sucked the juice. She knew there were things a man could wear, but Cush refused to wear them and she didn't know anything else, so when Cush missed the point of a joke or used *lay* for *lie* or stumbled over a word in a sentence he was reading aloud, she laughed at him, hoping he would strike her, knowing she would fall, praying something inside would break. Oh, but the will of life. Next came Lena, named after Lena Horne, and then came me. Named Grace, after no one in particular. Just because there seemed so little of it in the world.

*He was a sailor who hated traveling. Join the navy and see the world,* except the more he saw, the more he only wanted to come home. Whenever he returned from a tour, exhausted and sour and rubber-legged, he would fall into bed and sleep for twelve hours straight. She would gather up his clothes, hold them to her face. It wasn't him she wanted to inhale, but the places he had visited. For a while after they were first married she would pepper him with questions whenever he returned from tour. What did they wear in China, what kind of clothes? Did they really eat dogs? Did they have trees in Morocco or was the whole nation engulfed by sand? What did it smell like in the streets of Turkey? What color was the sky in Greece?

"The sky?" he'd answer, irritated. "The sky is blue, just like here. Don't be dumb."

Or: "How would I know? I volunteered for watch duty. I stayed on the ship where it was clean. Unlike around here."

Or, if some eager friend did manage to drag him from his bunk into the world: "Crowded and dirty." Crowded and dirty he said of Shanghai, of Cairo, of Freetown, of Paris, France. "And foul. I don't know how people live like that." Saying this, he would glance around the living room, at the crust of bread deposited by Dot upon the couch, at the bits of shredded newspaper in the corner on the carpet where Lena sat playing Snow Day. Mattie had cleaned up the room not thirty minutes before, but short of locking the children in their rooms, it was impossible to keep them from messing up as they went along.

"You'd probably like it, though," Cush said. "You'd fit right in."

Sometimes, when he was feeling generous, he brought home souvenirs, trinkets mostly, things he picked up last minute from barefoot children and old women in black shawls hanging around the docks: a rubber doll in a red paper kimono, salt-and-pepper pyramids, a pair of plastic maracas, cracked and spilling their dark red beans when he pulled them from his bag. Once he brought home a conch shell small enough to fit into the palm of her hand. On its back of speckled caramel some lonesome sailor long ago had scratched out the Lord's Prayer in impossibly fine and flowing script. The best thing he ever gave her, brought home his first tour after they were married, was a cuckoo clock from the Black Forest of Germany. She loved the beautiful wooden house with its delicately carved leaves and dangling pinecones and red-beaked cuckoo darting out to sing the hours racing past. She hung it high upon the kitchen wall, away from the children, away from the heat and grease of the stove, visible through the short, bright hallway as soon as one stepped inside their door. The rest of these objects she set carefully upon the top shelf of the china cabinet, the only safe place in the house.

*He walked around the house silent and brooding, never meeting* her eyes except to point out something she had done wrong. His shirts weren't starched enough. There were applesauce handprints on the bottom of the door. One day he yelled for fifteen minutes because dinner wasn't ready, stormed out of the house, stormed back in and yelled again because the gas tank in the car had fallen below half-full. "How many times do I have to tell you to keep it full?" he cried. The children were outside, making mud pies in the backyard. Something else he would yell at her about and maybe strike her for. He had struck her once or twice.

"Cush, I'm sorry." She used his name deliberately, to calm him.

"Yeah, you sorry all right," he said. He never used hers anymore. She could go for weeks in her house hearing only "Mommy, Mommy," never hearing her own true name.

"Dot has an ear infection," she said. "She was screaming and crying all the way home from the clinic. I couldn't think."

It was a partial truth: Dot did have an ear infection and she had screamed all the way home from the clinic. But the child's screams had scarcely penetrated Mattie's brain on the drive home. *Congratulations, Mrs. Breedlove,* the clinic doctor had said. *Maybe this time you'll get your boy.*

"Couldn't think? What's wrong with you?" Cush looked her up and down. "When I met you, you seemed so smart," he said disgustedly. "I thought you were smart."

So had she.

*For their anniversary he took her out, a surprise. She didn't want* to go; she was exhausted and worn and sick from being pregnant, but she had yet to share the news and so had no excuse. They went to dinner and then on to a club. She wanted to sit and listen to the music, but he wanted to dance and pulled her into his arms. He smelled of cinnamon and musk, the aftershave she'd given him for Christmas. She leaned into his arms. He put his lips to her ear.

"You smell nice," he whispered.

She felt herself blushing and buried her face into his shoulder to hide it. An outsize reaction, she knew, for such a little compliment, but then he rarely found anything about her worth complimenting. Even something so basic as her smell.

The compliment gave her courage to talk to him, to try to connect. "This is nice," she said. "Being like this."

"The way we used to be." He pulled her closer. "Just me and you. Nobody pulling on us, tugging on us all the time. It was sweet, wasn't it, baby?"

She closed her eyes, nodded her head against his shoulder. It *had* been sweet, hadn't it? She could barely remember through all the pain and acrimony of the past few years, but yes, there had been a time when she thrilled to see him and, she still believed, he had felt the same way about her. Why had they lost that? Whose fault was it?

"Sometimes I wish it could be that way again," he said to her.

"Me, too."

The band, a quartet, segued from an instrumental into a Sam Cooke song. A skinny, tired-looking woman in a sequined dress took the microphone and started on the lyrics from "Somebody Have Mercy." Cush stroked Mattie's back and nuzzled her neck. "We could be that way again," he said. "If you want."

She thought he meant they could be nice to each other again. Maybe they could never get back to those early days of infatuation, but they could put down the daggers, they could stop trying to break each other's heart. Did she want that? Did she want to get through the days without crying? Did she want to wake up in the morning without a rock on her chest? "I do, Cush," she said. "More than anything."

He let out a little laugh and spun her around on the dance floor, nearly bumping her into another couple, who were so engrossed in pressing their bodies together they barely noticed. "I'm so glad you feel that way," Cush said. "I didn't think you would, but I'm glad."

She laughed, too, suddenly delighted. Maybe now she could even tell him about the baby and it wouldn't be terrible. Maybe now he might actually be glad.

"Will your mama take them?" Cush asked.

But the spinning and the wine and being pregnant had made her a little light-headed. She closed her eyes, then opened them again. The air was blue with smoke, and it took her a second to get her focus. "Take who?"

"The children," he said. "Luke and Nellie sent their boy down to Luke's mother in Georgia. Nellie says it's just for the summer, but Luke says if he got anything to say about it, the boy's staying right where he is."

The singer ended her song with a flourish. Everybody around them stopped dancing to clap. The noise made Mattie dizzy. Why was Cush talking about some friend of his and his whorish drunk of a girlfriend?

"Don't you think your mama would take them for a little while?" Cush was saying. "Seems to me she owe you at least that much."

The band got up to take a break. Somebody opened a door somewhere, and she felt a rush of air, not cool but cooler than the sweaty, breathed-up air all around them. She looked up at her husband, saw his wide, dark, handsome face. "My mother? You want to send the children away to her?"

"So we can be alone," he said. "You can go back to school instead of sitting around the house all day."

She stumbled a few steps back, away from him. Without thinking, she said, "I'm not sending my babies away."

Something swept over his face then; the lover of the early evening was gone; back was the man who came through the door every afternoon full of rage and disgust. The change pierced her so much she tried to beat it back. "I mean, my mother isn't . . . she isn't like Luke's mother. She wouldn't take them anyway."

Cush curled his lip as he stared at her. "That's right," he said. "I forgot. Your mama tossed you out and you're her daughter. She didn't love you, so why should she love your nappy-headed kids?"

He turned and walked away, leaving her alone on the dance floor. When she got back to the table he had ordered another beer and had already gulped down half of it. They stayed until the band returned, Cush silent and drinking, Mattie cradling her unconsumed glass of wine in her trembling hand.

Later that night he came to her, tripping his way up the basement stairs. Light from the streetlamp seeped around the edges of the window blind. Mattie closed her eyes against it, turned her head into her pillow, shut her eyes tight. He had been drinking steadily since they came home, down in the basement. If he was drunk enough he would fall into bed already asleep, and then she could rise and go sleep on the carpet between the children's beds.

The bedsprings creaked. "Mattie Mae," he whispered.

She kept her eyes closed, tried not to breathe.

"Baby," he said. "Mattie Mae."

She braced herself for what she knew would come. He would grab her by the hips, pull her out of her fetal curl. Push her back into the sheets. She would not resist but she would keep her eyes shut tight.

But his touch, when it came, was gentle. He laid his hand upon the swell of her hip, curled his body against hers, laid his cheek against her own. He smelled sourly of beer and mustily of the basement and he was crying. Hot tears fell on her neck. "How come? How come? How come?"

She had never known him to cry, not from joy when the babies were born, not from grief when his father died. In shock she turned to face him. "Cush?"

He took her face into her hands and held it. "You and me," he whispered. "We'll show them all."

He placed his mouth on hers and kissed her, and it was all she could do not to gasp. When was the last time he had kissed her? Before Grace was born? Before Dot? She could not remember. They still had sex two or three times a month when he was home, but even then Cush rarely met his face to her own. In bed he was all hands, tugging her this way and that, positioning her body for maximum efficiency. It was, she supposed, the way men were, the way things were supposed to be. She would close her eyes and concentrate on infertility.

But now as he kissed her she found herself kissing him in return, gently at first, then harder. She felt his surprise, felt his quickening response. Cush nibbled her bottom lip, moaned her name. His breath, so hot and yeasty from the beer, made her dizzy. To stop the world from spinning she raised her arms and circled Cush's back just as, from down the hall, came a noise: the sharp, anguished sound of a child crying out in her sleep.

Mattie froze; Cush kept kissing. She couldn't tell whether he had not heard the cry or was ignoring it.

"Aaahhh!"

Mattie knew right away the cry came from Grace. Lately the child had begun waking in the middle of the night and refusing to go back to sleep until Mattie lay down beside her in her twin bed. The first few times it happened Mattie drifted off to sleep herself and stayed in the girl's bed until morning. But after a while Cush complained. He said Grace, at three, was big enough to sleep by herself, and that all Mattie was doing was spoiling the child. He said if she needed a body in the bed she could sleep with one of her sisters. But the child was a wild sleeper; she kicked the covers off and thrashed around, so neither Lena nor Dot would share a bed with her. Mattie defused the issue by going to the girl in the night but lying down atop the covers, so that if she fell asleep, the cold night air would wake her and she could slip back into her bed.

"Mommy?" Mattie could tell the child was awake now and getting scared. She was used to her mother appearing more quickly than this. "Mommy!"

"I have to go," Mattie said. She waited for Cush to move away.

"Mommy!" The child had ascended to wailing and was already passing that landmark, climbing on toward hysteria. Any minute the other children would wake, too. "Mommy!" she screamed. "Mommy!"

Cush's eyes were open now, his hands fumbling with the zipper of his pants. He found the release, pulled the pants down to his ankles. He climbed on top of her. "Stay here with me," he pleaded, pushing up her gown.

Mattie kept herself still. She didn't fight, she didn't help. "She's calling," she said.

"She's fine."

"She's not fine!"

"She'll go back to sleep."

"No," Mattie said. "She needs me."

Cush let out a groan. "Can't you forget her?" he cried. "Can't you, for one damn minute, just forget about those kids?"

All at once she remembered a room, a darkness, the warmth of the night and the cool of the floor. She remembered the smell of honeysuckle, the scratchiness of a croaker sack against her cheek. She remembered velvet stars against her eyelids as she squeezed them tight and a voice she did not know making her mother choose.

*Forget the girl and let's go!*

"I'm your husband," Cush was saying. "I'm a man!" His hands were on her breasts; the rough, scaly touch of them against her skin enraged her and she struck at them wildly, fought them down.

"Let me up!" She hurled her body at him, her hands and her elbows, her fists and her knees and her teeth. "Get off!"

His body went rigid with shock. She tried to use the moment to get at his face. She wanted his face; every cell in her body yearned to reach up and rake it with nails. But Cush grabbed her flailing wrists before she could do damage. "Stop it!" he yelled.

Down the hall rolled a silence, a great, breathless pause before the storm. Then Grace gathered herself and let out a yell so piercing it could set dogs to howl. Immediately Dot and Lena were awake and screaming, too.

"Get off!"

"Mattie! Calm down!"

"Mommy! Mommy!"

My mother put her hands against my father's chest and pushed.

# Chapter Twelve

Valerie's church was vast and bright, a modern warehouse of worship with stadium seating and video screens hanging from the rafters and room on the dais for a choir of one hundred and a twenty-piece band. Funerals were normally held in the smaller chapel, but a sound system was being installed, so we clustered together at the front of the main sanctuary and the vastness made us seem fewer than we were, scattered lifeboats full of shocked survivors, adrift in an endless sea.

The family—Howard, his three heartbreaking boys, his mother and father and sisters and brothers and Valerie's mother and sisters and a niece or two—all huddled forlornly in the first pew, dark and miserable against its gleaming blond-wood seat. On the row behind sat more family, cousins and uncles and aunts. On the row behind that sat Valerie's father and his third wife, a shiny, brittle thing in a wide-brimmed hat and cheap, overpriced suit dabbing her face with a black lace handkerchief. I recognized the father from a photograph Valerie kept on her piano, stuffed in among the babies and the children and the nieces and nephews and aunts as though they were all one big happy family. I had been surprised to learn from Valerie that she and her father were estranged. Surprised not just because of the photograph, which she said she kept around for her children, but because of what I'd thought was her boundless capacity for love. People were complex.

I sat alone a few rows back, behind a group of mothers I recognized from the park. Eddie had coolly and dutifully offered to accompany me to the funeral, but had refused to let our girls attend. "They're too young to be confronted with death unnecessarily," he said, a little angrily. "How could you even ask?" We had not had the time or the opportunity or the courage to discuss the true source of his anger, so we both decided to pretend this was it. "You're right," I told my husband. "Why don't you stay with them today? I can go alone." Which, of course, was a relief in a way, going alone. How much easier it was not to have to think about the children at such a time. How much easier to focus on myself, to cry and shudder and curse in luxuriant selfishness. How much easier to pick up my grief like a porcelain cup and carry it solo into that church.

Scattered elsewhere around the church were maybe fifty or sixty people. Was that a lot of people or a little for a lifetime? It seemed pathetically few for the great heart Valerie had been, but a lot compared with the number of folks I was sure would show up for me.

The minister was a tall, angular man with a mustache and flowing black robes. I'd seen him before, once when I came to church with Valerie. He was one of those preachers who ran back and forth across the pulpit while he preached, who screamed into the mike and jumped up and down and waved his arms and whipped up the crowd. The first time I saw him I caught myself wondering if all the drama was for real—and even if it was, whether it was necessary. Not that I hadn't seen such zeal before; it was what

I'd grown up with, but light years away from the restrained, staid, quiet Methodism I'd chosen for myself as an adult. But I tried to keep my mind neutral, not being stupid enough to sit in church and criticize a man of God, and I thought I'd done well. But Valerie must have noticed my skepticism, because after service was over, as we were leaving, she'd smiled at me and said, "Don't get too siddity for God."

During the funeral, though, the preacher held himself still behind a lectern draped in mournful purple cloth. When he announced he would begin his homily by reading from Proverbs, I knew immediately what the passage would be. It made me angry, a little. I wondered if Howard had requested the verse, or if the pastor himself had decided it would be appropriate.

"Who can find a virtuous woman?" the preacher began, and the words rose up to greet me from a hundred Sundays of my childhood. I always listened intently when the virtuous woman came up, because she and Mary, the mother of Jesus, were the only two women in the Bible for whom the pastor of my childhood church had any respect.

"Who can find a virtuous woman?" read Valerie's preacher. "For her price is far above rubies. The heart of her husband does safely trust in her, so that he shall have no need of spoil. She will do him good and not evil all the days of her life." The preacher read all twenty-one verses, slowly, reverently, pausing between each one to scan the congregation as if sizing us all up.

As the preacher read, my eyes kept wandering to Howard, who sat with his arms crossed and his hands tucked tightly beneath his armpits, as if he could barely stand even to breathe. I remembered how he had met me at the front door of his house that terrible night, eyes wild with fear. I was trembling myself, trembling and praying, and I tried to offer him a face devoid of judgment, a face full of nothing but concern. But he looked at me and knew that I knew, and it seemed to infuriate him. "I love her!" he shouted, as if I had insisted otherwise. "I love her! I always have!"

Without thinking, I said, "She knows." I meant it as comfort; later I realized he might have taken my words a different way.

"God, help me," he cried. "I never—"

I pushed him out the door before he could say anything else. "Go," I ordered. And he did, sprinting down the driveway to his car and roaring off toward the hospital. When he was gone I checked on the children, who were sleeping, then headed down to the living room to wait. As I sat there staring out the window at the streetlamp and the telephone wires stretching down the block, I had all kinds of wild, waking nightmares about what had happened to Valerie. I imagined a fight with Howard, a brutal slap or a storming off into the dangerous night. I envisioned some drug-crazed carjacker slipping up through the shadows as she sat idling in traffic or some self-destructive little Negro punk trying to prove his manhood by spraying bullets as he drove through the neighborhood. Even in my confusion I recognized that all the images were bizarrely violent and horrible, as if that made it easier. As if my mind could more easily accept a friend betrayed from without than from within.

But in the end it was Valerie's body that had turned on her, a body only three years older than my own. She had suffered a massive ischemic stroke; a brain attack, what happens when an artery carrying life-sustaining blood to the brain is suddenly blocked. She fell into an instant coma, and was gone by the time the ambulance reached the emergency-room door. The doctors themselves were surprised, not at the stroke but at her dying. Most people, they said helpfully, just end up severely impaired. The whole thing seemed outrageous to me; the idea that a woman could stroke out and die without warning at the age of thirty-nine seemed impossible. But no, no, apparently not. Not if you were a black woman with high cholesterol you'd told no one about and were halfheartedly monitoring. Not if your blood pressure had always been borderline. Not if somebody, without intending to, had just stacked a pile of bricks upon your heart.

Watching Howard's back at the funeral, I wondered if he would ever recover from the guilt, or if it would haunt him the rest of his life. I wondered which Valerie would have wanted. She was one of the kindest and most loving women I had ever known, but that meant nothing. Love sometimes made monsters of us all.

The preacher finished the passage and closed his Bible with a dramatic thump. "Valerie Jackson was a virtuous woman," he said. "She dedicated her life to her husband and her children. They knew it. We knew it. God knew it, and God does not forget. In His own time and His own season He has called her home, and although we are sad, although our hearts are heavy and our spirits low, we must rejoice for her. For ourselves we are in grief, but for Sister Valerie we celebrate. The virtuous woman has gone home to be with her Master and Lord."

The preacher made a small bow downward, toward the bier. It stood just below the altar, draped in gold, and as I looked at it I thought, angrily, *Why not white? Why not go all the way? Why not the angel in the house?* But what good was that, anger? It was really just the first stage, wasn't it? I wiped my eyes and looked again at the coffin, a polished, gleaming, gilded-handled thing, massive and closed. I'd been surprised, upon first entering the sanctuary, to see a closed coffin. Surprised and relieved and ashamed at my relief. Death was easier to deal with when you did not have to look it in the face.

When Eddie's father had reached the end stage of his liver disease and all the doctors shook their heads, Louise moved him, not home, as her daughter wanted, but to a hospice three miles away. Hollis's wrath was withering, but Louise withstood it; she would visit her dying husband thrice a day, she said, but she would not oversee a death brought on by the bottle she had spent twenty-five years trying to pry from his grasp. "We reap what we sow," said Louise.

Eddie had visited his father every evening after work, but I was not allowed to come along. Mason was too proud, and too humiliated, to let anyone outside the immediate family witness his fearsome decline. It was not until he lapsed into a coma that I got a chance to say good-bye. As I sat at his bedside, holding Eddie's hand, I thought how amazing it was that we—Eddie and I—had reached our midthirties before confronting death. How old had my mother been? How old my grandmother? How old most contemporary children of Africa? And even though we were there, Eddie and I, for the grit of the dying, it was the nursing-home staff who managed the muck of it, who wiped the blood and cleaned the shit and emptied the piss bag. We stepped outside while these things happened, grateful to be spared. A former colleague who taught the sociology of dying told me once that nearly eighty percent of Americans died in institutional settings. "Then the body gets whisked away to the funeral home, where they clean it up nice and pretty and make the corpse look as if he were sleeping," he told me. "Nobody denies death like America does."

The preacher finished and bowed his head, lifting his hands as if to collect the sighs and murmurs and mournful *amens* rolling his way. Suddenly Valerie's mother burst into a sob, and it was as if a latch had been unhooked, a signal given. All around me people who had been dabbing their eyes and sniffling burst into raw and open tears. Howard pitched forward, slamming his head into his hands. He seemed about to cry out, to sink into his grief, and I steeled myself for it. I stiffened my back and bit my lip and clenched the handkerchief in my palm. But it did not come. Howard kept silent; he sat like that the rest of the funeral, collapsed inward upon himself. I wanted to look away, to raise my eyes to the cross behind the pulpit, but for some reason that felt like a betrayal of Valerie, a glancing away from what she had been. So I made myself keep watching Howard. I made myself keep my eyes locked on him as he withered. I made myself watch my friend's husband because the only other place to bear witness was there in that pew right next to Howard, Valerie's children, and I couldn't look there. I could not, in that moment, bear to see what children looked like when they had been left alone.

*It was a nice day for January in Massachusetts, insultingly nice:* low forties, sapphire sky, a tender wind. We stood at the graveside without shivering, those of us who had caravanned out and hiked the snowplowed paths to the site. It had occurred to me in the car to wonder if they would be able to actually bury Valerie, this being winter in New England. But at the cemetery I saw a hole had already been clawed from the frozen earth by some kind of machine, mercifully hidden from view. One last benefit afforded by life in the twenty-first century.

The brief ceremony passed in a blur. The minister, so thundering and certain in his pulpit, stood muted in the great vault of nature, cradling the Book of Common Prayer in his black-gloved hands. Without pausing for breath, he read, "I am the resurrection and the life, said the Lord. He that believeth in me, though he were dead, yet shall live, and whosoever lives and believes in me shall never die. We brought nothing into this world, and it is certain we can carry nothing out. The Lord gave and the Lord hath taken away. Blessed be the name of the Lord."

When it was over we all trudged back to our cars and drove slowly to Valerie and Howard's house. By the time I arrived, the driveway and the street in front of the house were stuffed with cars; I had to park two blocks away. It was a relief to turn off the engine, to close my eyes and rest my forehead on the steering wheel. It was only midafternoon by then, the sun just beginning its retreat, but I wanted to crawl into bed and sleep until dawn. I couldn't, though; the sisters and the sisters-in-law, not knowing what else to do, had been cooking and baking for days. I had at least to make an appearance. Plus, I did not really want to go home and face Eddie. My husband, so cold and disappointed and unreachable.

One of Howard's sisters greeted me at the door with a handshake. She looked just like him, right down to her short, neatly trimmed Afro. "I'm so sorry for your loss," I mumbled.

"Thank you for coming," she said. "Please have some refreshments."

"Thank you," I said. "Is Howard around?"

"Howard has gone upstairs to rest," the sister answered, eyeing
me carefully. "The refreshments are in the dining room."

Dismissed, I moved toward the dining room to get something
to drink. I had wanted Howard to know I was there in case he
needed someone nonfamily to talk to, but the sisters had clearly
closed ranks and that was fine. They'd outdone themselves with the
cooking also; every horizontal surface in the dining room groaned
beneath the weight of food. Ham and turkey, baked macaroni and
cheese, sweet-potato casseroles and lasagne and greens and biscuits and coconut cakes and apple pies. People milled around the
table with their plates piled high, murmuring.

I poured myself a glass of seltzer and wandered toward the
family room, normally cluttered with toy trucks and random rocks
and little plastic game pieces that would never be restored to their
rightful place. Today the room was pristine in appearance, not a
toy or a crayon or a sock in sight. The sisters had done their job
well. At the far end of the room a pair of patio doors looked out
onto the enormous backyard play structure. The first time I'd seen
it I asked Valerie why she even bothered taking the kids to the
park. She'd laughed. "It's called socialization, Grace," she said.
"They can't spend their lives playing by themselves." Now, looking out at the slide and swing and tarp-covered fort, I noticed that
Valerie's boys were playing there, released from the suits they'd
worn to the funeral and back in jeans and pullover fleece. Michael,
the five-year-old, was on one of the swings, pumping furiously with
his head thrown back, as if he were trying to gobble up the sky,
while Travis was helping his baby brother race up and down the
slide. All three were laughing; the door was cracked open and I
could hear their laughter. I stopped where I was and just listened,
tried to block out all the other sounds of the house—the shuffling
feet, the whispered conversations, the jazz playing softly on the

stereo. It seemed critical that I really hear it, that I soak the sound of those boys playing into my skin; and I concentrated so hard I didn't even realize I was crying until another one of Howard's sisters, not the door one, came into the room and handed me a clean handkerchief. She looked much younger than Howard, twenty or twenty-five at most, and she stood next to me, fighting back her tears. "That's the worst part of it, isn't it?" she asked me, looking out at the boys. "I mean, I don't have children but I imagine how terrible it is for them. Being left alone like this."

I wiped my face. "They have Howard."

The sister made a little noise of exasperation. "Oh, of course they do," she said. "And all of us. But it's not the same as having your mother. Is it?"

"No," I said, because that much was truth. It was not the same.

The sister crossed her arms in triumph. "No, it's not," she repeated, shaking her head. "They'll never get over it."

The youngest one must have heard her voice because he suddenly stopped climbing and looked toward the house. I smiled and waved and then closed the door to show him we weren't calling him in. I thought how many times Valerie must have stood in that doorway, watching her boys, adoring them.

"Never," the sister repeated. There was a kind of grim insistence in her voice, the lost, unshakable clarity of the young and child-free. It left no room for argument, so I didn't argue. I just stood there watching as the oldest boy ran up and grabbed his brother's hand and together they went laughing up the slide.

*Eddie and the children were out when I got home, a little gift I* hardly seemed to deserve. I stumbled up the stairs and fell onto my bed, dragging the comforter around me. But just as I was drifting off the telephone rang. Dragging myself back to consciousness, I strained to hear the answering machine downstairs. There was no one I wanted to talk to at the moment, but when you are a parent and your children are out of the house, the telephone is a potentially dangerous weapon that must not be ignored.

"Hi, Grace," I heard. "It's your mom. Just checking in to see if you've had a chance to call Lena. Dot still hasn't heard from her and neither have I."

I had closed my eyes but opened them now. Some quality in my mother's voice, some underpinning of weariness and concern, forced me off the bed and to the telephone. "Hey, Mom."

"You are home!"

"I was just resting," I said. "Closing my eyes."

"In the middle of the day?" my mother asked, sounding genuinely surprised. I wondered if this was because I rarely napped or because she never did. "Everything okay?"

Everything was not okay, of course. But I did not want to tell her about Eddie; she would either tell me it was over, that I needed to pack my bags and clean out the bank account, or she would tell me I was crazy for messing things up with such a good man, a man so unlike my father, or maybe she would tell me both. But I didn't want to hear it. Nor did I want to mention Valerie. My mother would be sympathetic there, would listen to the horrible details and maybe even shed a tear at the forced abandonment of those three beautiful children, but I was barely standing up, barely holding it together. Her sympathy would put me on the floor. So instead of answering my mother truthfully, I lied. I cleared my throat and lied.

"I'm fine," I said. "Just tired; Harriet had a toothache last night and didn't sleep well. What's up with Lena?"

"That's what I want you to find out," my mother said. "She's never in her office and never at home when I call."

"So you haven't heard from her? At all?" This *was* unusual for Lena. We were neither the closest nor the most estranged of families, but one thing we always did was check in with one another. We, none of us, went too long or too far without letting somebody know, without leaving at least a message and a telephone number on an answering machine. This was something our mother had drilled into us as children, that the world was a vast and dangerous place and that you'd better stay at least tangentially in touch.

And sure enough my mother clarified. "I haven't talked to her," she said. "She did call yesterday morning, right when I was driving Tamieka to school. Left a message saying everything was fine but she was just really, really busy, so if I couldn't catch up to her for a while I shouldn't worry. And not to bother calling her office because she was out a lot."

I relaxed a little. "So she's fine. She's just busy."

"Maybe," my mother said. "Funny, though, that she called then. I'd left her a message on her machine the day before saying I'd be home all day except from seven to eight because I had to drive Tamieka to school."

But my worry about my sister had abated with news of the message on my mother's answering machine. Lena was fine, probably just busy with the muck and mire of everyday life. Not wanting to get into it with my mother, not wanting to lay out whatever struggles she was facing, didn't mean anything serious was wrong. It just meant she was hiding a little. I could understand that.

"I'll call her this afternoon," I promised. "And why are you driving Tamieka to school, by the way? What happened to her bus?"

"They kicked her off for fighting," my mother said matter-of-factly. "Jumped on a couple of other girls, though Tamieka claims they started it. She says she was defending herself."

I gritted my teeth. My mother's foster children were a source of constant stress. "That doesn't sound good, Mom."

"Not good at all," my mother said. "They found a box cutter on the floor of the bus and other girls claimed it belonged to Tamieka. They almost kicked her out of school. I had to fight to make them just suspend her a week instead."

Now, instead of irritation, I felt only alarm. "A box cutter?"

"She says it wasn't hers."

"And you believe her?"

My mother chuckled. "Daughter, you know me better than that."

I looked at my bed, tired, so tired and so suddenly furious; weariness and fury broke over me in subsequent waves. It occurred to me that the children assigned to my mother had grown not only steadily older but steadily more troubled—resistant, withdrawn, angry, damaged kids. For the first few years the children she took in were babies—four, five, six, small and bewildered, dropped off with their black garbage bags full of cheap clothes and cheap shoes and cheap toys, because even the urban poor in America came overburdened with consumer goods. If these children acted out their pain it was by scrawling on the walls with crayon, or flinging their broken trucks against the window or jumping too hard on the bed. Now, though, they carried box cutters and sneaked out at night and got banned by frightened bus drivers. And now my mother was nearing sixty, with stiffness in her joints and heaven knew how much pressure in her blood.

"Did you know she was violent when you took her?" I demanded. "Did they warn you? Because if they didn't, if they tried to sneak—"

My mother, rising to my tone, cut me off. "I saw her file, Grace. I knew what was what."

"And you took her anyway."

She said flatly, "They're paying me an extra five hundred a month."

My voice went up. "Oh, for heaven's sake! Stop always talking about the money, as if that was the only thing that mattered!"

Utterly cool, she said, "Your father used to say the only people running around saying money doesn't matter got plenty in the bank."

I was so incredulous, I laughed. "Since when do you quote him?"

The silence was her rebuke. "Okay," I said, trying to calm myself down. "Mom, I can send you some money. Eddie and I can send you . . . two hundred a month. No, three hundred. And I'll call Dot and Lena and Sidney, they can send some, too. We can cover that five hundred easily, Mom. You don't need to keep doing this."

But of course we'd all made this offer before; a few years earlier Dot and I had gone so far as to begin sending money in an attempt to get our mother at least to cut down the number of children in her care. It took us only weeks to realize she had no plans to get rid of anybody, and months to learn she was simply tearing up the checks without depositing them.

"We can help you, Mom," I said. "If you let us."

My mother sighed. "I know you want to, Grace. I know you do."

It was the sigh that killed me, the sigh that made me want to crawl under my bed and howl. "But you don't trust us," I said, my voice rising again. "You think we'll start off sending the money fine, but then as time goes on we'll forget or get too busy or want to buy a Mercedes instead. Is that it? Is that what you think?"

"I think on this earth the only person you can depend on one hundred percent is the one standing in your shoes," my mother said. "I hope I taught you that much."

And of course she had. Only too well. I thought, too, about how Dot and I, after realizing our mother would never take our money, had opened a retirement account in her name, promising to deposit two hundred dollars a month each. I couldn't even remember the last time I had written a check. Four months before? Five? It was down there somewhere among the cracks of my life.

I felt like crying. Instead I tried to make a joke. "But what's the point in having children if they don't care for you in your golden years?" I asked. "When are you going to start collecting on what we owe?"

"Honey," my mother said, "don't worry about it. I'm not going to collect because you could never repay me. Never. Not in a million years."

She spoke lightly, as if she were playing along, but we both knew she meant every word. And because she meant it, it was true. We could never repay her; maybe we shouldn't even try. She had sacrificed everything for us, not least her life; the least we could do in return was to owe her eternally. *Never,* she said; in that word I heard an echo from earlier in the day. Nobody ever got over being unmothered, Howard's sister had said. But maybe nobody ever got over *being* mothered, either. Maybe either way it went, you were screwed.

# Chapter Thirteen

There is, in sociology, a concept we like to call the Sociological Imagination—a fancy phrase for some fancy common sense. The man who coined the phrase—C. Wright Mills—described it as a quality of mind enabling its possessor to see the bigger picture, to grasp how intimately connected is one's personal biography to the larger, historical scene.

Most people live their lives in a series of close-ups, wrote Mills. Job and family, church and school, city and neighborhood: these are the private orbits in which we rotate, going round and round and round each day without ever raising our heads to examine the universe beyond. And yet there are huge, seemingly impersonal changes in that universe, in society itself, which exert tremendous influence upon our lives. "When a society is industrialized, a peasant becomes a worker; a feudal lord is liquidated or becomes a businessman," wrote Mills. "When wars happen, an insurance salesman becomes a rocket launcher; a store clerk, a radar man;

a wife lives alone; a child grows up without a father. Neither the life of an individual nor the history of a society can be understood without understanding both."

Yet, most people persist in thinking that their lives are strictly their own. They think their troubles are personal, their failures exclusive to themselves. What they fail to see is how often those troubles are intricately connected to the social issues of the day. One man's joblessness is his own problem—unless that man is black and fifty percent of black men in New York City are also unemployed. One woman's homelessness is her own sad concern—unless the supply of affordable housing in a city has dwindled to near nothingness. One child flunking a standardized test is the headache of that child's parent exclusively—unless sixty to seventy percent of the children in the Boston public schools also cannot pass the test. People mess up their lives, that's true. But clearly, in the latter cases, something bigger is going on, some larger social issue is at play.

Of course, nobody really wants the done-tos of society to realize that their troubles and their failures are not simply their just deserts. If that ever happened, if the sociological imagination ever gained mass currency, there'd be hell to pay.

When I first encountered Mills, he failed to make much of an impression. It was during an Origins of Sociological Theory course and I was swimming in Marx, Durkheim, Weber, Simmel, Herbert Mead, and Adam Smith, being tossed about by class and its vicissitudes, by division of labor and social control; I could scarcely keep my neck above the waves. The first year of graduate school is a miserable time, full of fear and hunger, of teaching sniveling undergrads and encountering bafflingly hostile professors and of the creeping realization that the experience will not be what you imagined. It will not be a life of the mind; the mind is secondary in graduate school. Indoctrination, figuring out how the game is played and entering the fray—these are the primary purposes.

It wasn't until I staggered out of the cave six years later that I was able to give Mills a fighting chance. Against all odds, I had managed to secure a position in my field, an assistant professorship at UNC. Eddie had landed a two-year postdoc at a university only twenty miles away. Giddy with relief, we settled down in a two-story Victorian between the towns to play academics in love. I knew the tenure battle still loomed, but I thought I could take a few months off to enjoy my accomplishments, teach the hell out of a few undergraduate courses, and breathe. That summer, in preparation for my fall classes, I dug out some of my old undergraduate textbooks and reread them. *The Sociological Imagination* was top of the list.

It was the summer of the O. J. Simpson trial, the summer America sat before the television, slack-jawed and mesmerized, surreptitiously fondling itself at the sight. Half the sociologists I knew were trying desperately to make hay while the O.J. shined. The Sociology of the News Media. The Sociology of Race in Criminal Trials. The Sociology of Sports Stars Gone Bad. For my part, I wanted none of it, not just because it was sordid and pathetic and far, far beneath the life of the mind I thought I'd fashioned for myself, but because it was also, of course, personal. O.J. was black and I was black and so it was personal. If I didn't know that, my mother reminded me each time I telephoned. My mother was fasting for O.J., she told me; fasting and praying that the Lord would bring him through. When she told me, a little bomb went off at the top of my skull, poof. *Fasting for that murderous thug? Suffering and praying for that brownnosing ass-kisser, that Uncle Tom, that nose-thumbing traitor to his race?*

"Are you serious?" I asked. "Why in heaven's name?"

"Because they're after him and he needs some help."

It took me a few hours after that conversation, but eventually I managed to talk myself down from my pique. Consternation at such a thing was small and meaningless, I told myself. My mother was my mother, and I myself nearing thirty, a married woman with a Ph.D. in understanding. I told myself to let it go.

Instead I focused on the upcoming semester, went about creating lesson plans. In doing research, I came across an exercise by sociologist David S. Adams that involved having students construct a time line of the past five decades in America. On one side they were to indicate significant events—the end of World War II, the civil-rights movement, the dawn of Reagan's America—in the United States over the past fifty years. On the other side they were to write down significant events in their family's lives: marriages undertaken, homes bought or abandoned, careers launched or collapsed. Finally they were to write an essay, using the time line and the research required for it as material. This essay would be one in which the student would connect family events and changes in fortune, for good or ill, to the world in which those family members lived and worked. And they were to use their sociological imaginations in making sense of it all.

The exercise intrigued me; I wondered how my students would react to it. In America we embrace our constitutional right to ignorance, and none do this more fiercely than the young. How many times in my class had a student, after spouting some gooey, half-formed social theory and being questioned firmly but kindly on the point, responded by crossing his or her arms and jutting his or her chin and saying "Well, that's just what I think!" They were especially resistant to the idea of structural inequalities in the world they now called their own (as opposed to the old world of their parents), believing, for example, that racism and sexism and classism could be (had been) best solved by individual rejection of prejudice against blacks and Hispanics, against women, against people from the wrong side of the tracks. The cultural anthropologist Judith Shapiro calls this sociological illiteracy. We are a nation of sociological ignoramuses, and proudly so.

Still, I determined to use the exercise. And like any ethical scientist, I believed I should not subject my students to an experi-
ment I was not first willing to undergo myself. So on the day
O.J. stood before a jury of his peers in Los Angeles and tried to
force his bloody hand into a glove, I sat down at my sun-splashed
kitchen table in North Carolina and forced myself to connect the
events of the past fifty years to my family's life. I forced myself to
see my mother in a way I had not before, in a way wholly different from the image formed when I was young. When I was child
I spake as a child, I understood as a child, I thought as a child,
the Bible says.

My mother was seventeen when *Brown v. Board of Education*
came down; too late to challenge the separate education she'd
received in her Mississippi hometown. She was eighteen when
Rosa Parks sat on that Montgomery bus, eighteen and working in
white women's houses to save money for a chance at college and
a better life. She was twenty-three when the Greensboro sit-ins
took place, pregnant with Dot, hurriedly married to a man she
scarcely knew, watching her dreams of college slip further and
further away. When thousands marched on Washington, she lay
in a hospital bed giving birth to her second baby, exhausted and
already feeling the strains of married life. I was born the year of
the Civil Rights Act, but my father refused to let her work outside
the house. A year after King was killed in Memphis she landed
in that same, sad place, escaping a husband who mistreated her,
four children in tow. In the year of *Roe v. Wade* she quit a job she
loved at the post office to stay home and save her children from
the street. The Carter years were welfare years; the Reagan years
were worse.

I did the exercise over the course of that long summer afternoon, and then I stood up and turned on the O.J. trial. I turned
on my sociological imagination. I saw the wider picture, or at least
a good-size chunk. The only thing I had to yet to figure out was

what, precisely, that picture had to do with me. That much I could not figure out.

So instead, I called my mom.

## MEMPHIS, 1969

*Memphis faced west, toward the great Mississippi and the continent* beyond. Mattie drove into town from the east, slipping through the backdoor down Interstate 40 from Nashville, down from the seaboard through cities, farms, and fields. The day was cloudy and gray and surprisingly raw, surprising because Mattie remembered the city as warm in March. She had expected warmth, but instead she got sullen clouds graying the sky. One of the girls, Lena, she thought, liked to say clouds were fluffy white butts that peed on the world, and although these clouds were neither fluffy nor white, they certainly seemed to be pissing all over them.

All morning the radio had been reporting the news: James Earl Ray, in court in Memphis, pleading guilty to the murder of Dr. King. Hard to believe it had been an entire year since that terrible day. Ray spoke only to admit his guilt, to hint at some kind of plot, the radio said. He spoke to avoid the electric chair. Mattie had seen him on television, a scrunched-up, rat-faced little man. She imagined him in the courtroom, smug and silent, this evil person, this killer of hope.

"Who are they talking about, Mommy?" asked Dot. She sat in the back, squeezed in between Grace on the right and Lena on the left, Sidney cradled in her arms. She had held him nearly all of the way from Baltimore. "Who got killed?"

"Nobody," Mattie said, clicking the radio off.

"But, Mom."

"Hush up. Look out the window."

They were coming off the highway now, still just north of the city among the farmhouses and trailer parks. She had forgotten how flat the Delta lands were, how the soybean and cotton fields could stretch for miles. They turned at an intersection and drove down a dirt road past a small, scuzzy pond. "There's the river!" cried Dot. "There's the Mississippi!"

All the way from Baltimore Mattie had been telling them about the great Mississippi, about its mighty banks and muddy rolling ways, about the paddleboats and barges as big as parking lots. She had told them every single good thing she could remember about the Mississippi and about Memphis so that they would not ask when they were going home.

Now Lena said, "That's not the river, stupid. It's not big enough."

"Watch your mouth," Mattie warned. Then, to Dot, she said, "That's not the river; its just a pond. The river is downtown, to the west of us. I'll take you to see it later today."

Five minutes later they were in the city itself, and ten minutes after that Mattie pulled off the road onto the gravel driveway of her mother's house and watched her mother come out onto the porch. Her mother's hair was freshly pressed and curled in tiny ringlets and she wore the plain, blue cotton dress with white collar that was her working uniform. Her hair looked a shade blacker—was she dying it?—and her body seemed maybe a half size chubbier than the last time Mattie had seen her, eight years before. Mattie could remember exactly, because it was the week she married Cush and left college for good. After leaving the courthouse, she'd felt such a hole in her heart she'd asked her new husband if they could drive down to Memphis for a few days to visit her family. Cush had not wanted to go—it was a long drive and he'd planned to spend his leave searching for a house for them to rent. But Mattie had insisted, saying a woman needed to see her mother on her wedding day, or, at least, her wedding week. So they'd driven down, and although Rae had not had much to say about her new son-in-law other than "Kinda dark, huh?" Mattie was still glad she'd gone. Because between Cush's refusal and the cost of travel and the children coming so quickly, she had not had the chance to get back again until now.

Other than the extra weight, though, Rae seemed largely unchanged, a woman who shone with country health no matter where she actually lived. She stood on the porch eating a peach.

"Walked out empty-handed, I see," Rae said between bites. A bit of amber juice escaped from the peach and ran down the corner of her mouth. She caught it with her tongue.

"Hello, Mama," Mattie said. She wanted to run up the steps and fall into her mother's arms, to rest there from Cush and pain and life. But instead she just leaned against the car, stretching her aching back. Sidney was nearly three months old, but still she felt her joints had not quite slipped back into place.

"I'm not empty-handed. I've got the children," Mattie said. When her mother hooted, she added, "And the car."

Her mother took one glance at the car and hooted again.

Mattie smiled and walked up the steps for a quick kiss on the cheek. It didn't matter if Rae hooted; what mattered was that she was there, waiting. Ready to help Mattie when she needed it most, for once. For the first time. Who said people did not change?

Her mother was older now, more settled. In the years Mattie was struggling with her own marriage, Rae had married and divorced one husband and buried another. She'd also produced two children along the way, which meant Mattie had a sister and brother not much older than her own children. The girl, Julie, lived with her father's mother in St. Louis, but the boy, Harry, lived with Rae there in Memphis, in the modest but sturdy brick house his father, Mr. Harold, had scraped and fought to secure before he died. The house was Rae's pride and joy, the first she had ever owned—though of course it was really owned by the bank—and Mattie thought it had changed her mother, softened her. "Come on if you have to," she'd told a tearful Mattie on the telephone. "I'll help as best I can."

Mattie had hung up the phone and started packing that very day, weathering all of Cush's curses and taunts and even threats. None of it bothered her because this time she had her mother on her side. And if you had your mother on your side, what else did you need?

*Not much, it seemed at first. Things fell into line with a swiftness* that nearly made Mattie dizzy. In May she took the postal exam and scored high enough to land a full-time job as a mail processor. In August, with the security of a good government job, and the thousand dollars she had managed secretly to save over the years with Cush, she put a modest down payment on a modest two-bedroom brick house two miles from Rae. In September she enrolled the girls in school and found a babysitter for Sidney, an older woman from her mother's church. She found a place to have the car's oil changed. She even, to her astonishment and not minimal fear, met a man. Of all these gifts, the man was the only one she had not been looking for. But there he was nevertheless.

His name was Jimmy Stillman and he was a little man, at least compared with Cush. He'd been born in Memphis, raised in Memphis, never been farther from Memphis than the dog track in West Memphis, Arkansas, except for six weeks basic training in Mississippi and two years spent dodging bullets and death with the 24th Infantry in the hills of Korea. By the end of that war, the 24th Infantry had been disbanded in shame and Jimmy Stillman was back in Memphis vowing never to leave again. It wasn't that he was incurious about the rest of the world, only that his curiosity had been well and nicely satisfied. "Some pretty places, some different-colored folks, but otherwise the same joys and same despair," he said. "Give or take a bullet or two."

He told her he had noticed her long before she noticed him— noticed her that first day she strode into the postal distribution plant, exam-score papers in hand. She was sober-faced and determined, and had eyes only for the task at hand, but he had noticed her. Noticed the creamy color of her skin, the delicate oval of her face. Noticed, too, the wedding ring she wore on her left hand and so noticed no further, until weeks later, when the postal rumor mill churned the truth of her separation his way.

Still, Jimmy, with his years of seniority, was a supervisor who worked days, and Mattie worked nights. It took months for them to meet. When they finally did, it was just before Christmas; all hands were on deck to deal with the usual rush. Jimmy came in one evening to sub for her regular supervisor, and there was a little flutter among some of the other women workers, who considered him the most eligible bachelor in the place. But Jimmy only had eyes for her.

When he kept strolling, keen-eyed and silent, past her station that evening, she feared it was because she was doing something wrong.

"Am I going too slow?" she finally asked, trying to speed her hands to match the frantic beating of her heart.

"You fine," he said.

"I'm clearing my boxes."

"You doing fine."

He strolled away then, and when the woman next to her, a sassy, overlipsticked thing with hennaed hair said, "Girl, it's not your hands that interest him," Mattie was too surprised to respond. Interested! In her? She sneaked a glance down at her body, as though she and it had made a deal to turn to stone and now, behind her back, it was turning back to flesh.

So when Jimmy Stillman showed up at the end of the shift as she was pulling on her jacket and asked if she needed a ride, she just stared at him.

"Excuse me?" she said. Wanting to be polite to a supervisor, even if he was not her usual supervisor.

"Be my pleasure to ride you on home if you need one," he said.

"Oh." She zipped up her jacket, fumbled around in her purse for her keys, tried to walk. "No. No, thank you, I mean. I have a car."

"Then I'll walk you to it."

"No, thank you," Mattie said briskly, pulling on her gloves. But he had already fallen into step beside her. She pushed through the heavy metal door and he followed. Outside in the cold December air the world was waking up. She could hear trucks rumbling by on the highway behind them.

"I'm fine, really," she said.

"Going your way anyway."

"I do not need you to walk me to my car."

"Well, then," he said. "Maybe you could walk me to mine."

She had been speeding up her pace, hoping to pull away from him, but now she stopped and looked at him. "What?"

"Maybe you could walk me to my car. Ain't safe for a man wandering around out here alone at night."

She laughed before she could stop herself and he grinned at her reaction, grinned as though he had just hit the numbers big. "Now that's what I'm talking about," he said, rocking back on his heels with satisfaction. "That smile!"

She stopped laughing then, forced a frown, turned away. But he didn't seem to notice.

"That smile," he said, "could make a man want to go out and do good in the world."

He started showing up fifteen minutes early for his daytime shift to walk her to her car. For a week she ignored him as he trailed behind her like a puppy, hands behind his back, whistling Marvin Gaye. When they reached her car he always stopped, waited for her to open the door, closed it behind her, then tipped his brown fedora with a little bow and walked away.

By the second week she caught herself searching for him among the crowds as she neared the door after her shift was done. And when she passed through the doorway and saw him waiting—hands thrust deep inside his coat pockets, the black fur collar of his camel-hair coat turned up against the damp morning cold, hat pulled down low—she just couldn't sit on her smile.

"How long do you intend to keep this up?" she asked him over her shoulder.

"Long as the good Lord gives me breath," came his reply.

By the third week she was talking to him as they walked, disrespecting postal politics, listening to his stories and his advice. By the fourth week she was telling him about the children, about how tired she was all the time, about how it felt being back in Memphis. By the fifth week they were holding hands on the long, slow walk and kissing furtively when they got there, on the lookout for gossips and spies. And Mattie had to admit to herself they had started something, though she wasn't sure what it was.

*But if there was one thing she'd already learned about life, one* thing Aunt Eba had taught her growing up, it was that what went up would surely come down again. And if you weren't careful, it would come down atop your head. That's what she thought about one late-winter Saturday morning she looked out her dining-room window and saw her mother marching up the drive. "How much do you need this time?" she asked when her mother got into the house.

"Fifty," Rae said. "Fifty would get it done."

The children were awake, of course. Getting them out of bed on Saturday was easy; it was the rest of the week that challenged Mattie's nerves. They were watching cartoons in the next room, technically the dining room but used by them as a den-bedroom-general place to eat. Lena, ten years old going on twenty-nine, was stretched out like Marlene Dietrich on the sagging, secondhand couch upon which Mattie slept most nights when she wasn't working. Dot and Grace lay curled in blankets on the bare wood floor, Dot with Sidney beside her. Getting a rug for the room was one thing Mattie hoped to do with her next paycheck if she could. Or if not the next paycheck, certainly the following one.

"Fifty dollars," Mattie repeated. As if saying the number aloud could reduce it in size.

Rae looked down, examined one coral pink fingernail. "Guess I got a little behind on the electric bill."

Mattie glanced at her mother. Rae did not normally volunteer her reasons when asking for money and Mattie never asked. Asking was disrespectful and also unnecessary: Mattie knew her mother needed money to pay some bill that had gone unpaid while she strolled the suit racks at Goldstein's department store.

Rae turned her head and picked an invisible speck from the arm of the couch. The couch, ocean blue and nubby-textured, was Mattie's pride, the nicest piece of furniture in her house, the only thing on which she had not skimped in furnishing the place from scratch. Her mother sat right on the edge; if she sat all the way back her feet would stick out like a child's.

"Friday is payday," Mattie said. "I could let you have something then."

"I got to go down to the electric company today," Rae said.

"I understand, Mama. But—"

"Them folks ain't playing. They said I need to put something on this bill or they're cutting me off."

"Did they say fifty?" Mattie asked.

"They said at least fifty."

Mattie got up and took her purse from the hook near the front door. Keeping the wallet deep inside her purse where her mother could not see, Mattie counted: two twenties, a ten and a five, all neatly smoothed and filed by denomination and facing the same way. It was Aunt Eba who had taught her never to ball her bills up in her purse or fold them messily. "Treat your money with respect," Aunt Eba said. "Treat it with respect and it'll treat you the same way." Aunt Eba held such high respect for her money she had a hard time parting with it. People back in Mississippi said she'd walk a mile to save a penny and walk all day to save a dime. She was the oldest girl of the family, Rae the baby of the bunch.

Mattie had always wondered how they could possibly share the same blood.

She counted again. Fifty-five dollars; money she had intended to last her through the week. The tank in the car was nearly empty. They needed groceries, especially milk, which Sidney, now that he was off formula, drank like it was going out of style. Plus Lena needed new shoes and Grace needed a set of crayons for school and Dot had a field trip to the zoo on Wednesday and needed spending change. Fifty-five dollars and everybody needed. Treat your money with respect.

Mattie took out a twenty. "That's the best I can do, Mama. Cush hasn't sent child support again this month. I don't know if he will or not."

From her perch on the couch her mother stared at the twenty, not lifting her hand to take it, not waving it away. Just then Grace came strolling into the living room. She was dressed in one of Lena's old T-shirts and pajama pants that had been handed down from some cousin years before. Spying Rae, she grinned. "Grandma!"

"Come give me some sugar," Rae said, sticking out her cheek.

Of all the children, Grace seemed the one who liked her grandmother best. Whenever Mattie announced a visit to Rae's house, Dot would rise dutifully from the couch and head for the door while Lena pouted and sighed and dragged her feet. Sidney, being a baby, didn't much care. But Grace, Grace always raced for the car.

"Grandma, you got any mints?" the girl asked after delivering her peck.

Rae laughed heartily. "No mints, child."

"Got any gum?"

Still chuckling, Rae dug into her lemon-yellow purse. "See? This one knows the story," she said, handing Grace a half-full pack of Juicy Fruit. "Ask and you shall receive."

"Thank you, Grandma!" Grace ran into the other room, shouting "I've got gum! I've got gum!"

Rae stood up. "Next week," she said casually, turning away and heading toward the door, "I'll be sitting in my house in the dark."

Mattie opened her purse. At the sound of the click, Rae paused. Mattie took out the other twenty and the ten.

"If you can get it back to me by the end of the month, Mama, that would be great," Mattie said.

Her mother smiled and went on out. Mattie watched her walk down the driveway and climb into her car, watched her head off down Jackson toward Lee Street. She would turn right on Lee, head down to Sturgeon and make a left, cross over the highway and head straight on downtown to the electric company. Mattie knew where her mother was headed as surely as she knew the names of all the streets in Memphis, knew because every night at the post office she sorted their mail. She knew where her mother was headed as surely as she knew she'd never see that fifty dollars again.

*"This all the food you got in the house?"* Jimmy closed the cupboard door and looked at her. "Good thing I came by."

From the table where she sat finishing up a piece of cheesecake, Mattie smiled up at him. "You certainly aren't a country boy," she said. "I've known a family of ten to survive for a month on less than that."

"Big difference between surviving and thriving," he said.

It was her evening off and Jimmy had called at the start of it, asking if he could bring Tops barbecue for her and the children. Mattie had been surprised at how quickly the children took to Jimmy. Maybe it was because they so rarely spoke with their father, and saw him even less. Mattie remembered how Cush had taunted her those first weeks and months, so certain she would give up and come crawling back to him. When she didn't, when she found a house and a job and a new life, Cush found a new woman and was about to start a new family. He was, he said, just doing what she had done; he was moving on.

Lena especially had become attached to Jimmy. She squealed when he walked in the door, and pranced and paraded before him like a pony at center ring. "Mister Jimmy," she'd coo, batting her eyes. "Can I please have a piggyback ride? Pretty please?"

"Why not?" he'd respond, swinging her up and onto his back like a sack of potatoes and galloping her all around the house.

Usually Mattie stood by and watched, though once she'd said, "She's really too big for that kind of stuff." Jimmy had just shrugged it off.

"The child's got two, maybe three more years of childhood," he said. "Let her have some fun."

Now the children were in bed and Mattie and Jimmy sat in the kitchen, finishing up a surprise he'd saved for Mattie alone: cool, creamy cheesecake with strawberry topping from the Smithfield Bakery. He had gotten up to look for coffee and found the cupboard nearly bare.

Now he sat down at the table across from her, took her hand into his. His hands were smaller than Cush's but strong and warm. "Mattie, do you need some money? Please tell me if you do."

She shook her head. It made her heart full to hear him offer, but she did not want to get into the habit of taking money from men. That led only to trouble. "I'm just low this week. Payday is tomorrow. I'll be fine."

"You having trouble meeting your obligations? Want me to take a look at your bills?"

"I'm fine. Really. This week was just tight because . . . well, it just was."

"They paying you right?" he asked. "You know to check the scale, don't ya? See how much you should be getting? Don't let them folks mess you around 'cause they will sure enough try."

"Nobody's cheating me."

"You got some repair you didn't tell me about? Them repair-men see a woman and see—"

She cut him off. "I had to lend my mother some money."

It made her feel strange to talk about her mother to Jimmy. She had told him a little about Rae, but stopped because he seemed to be getting the wrong impression. He seemed to think her mother didn't care about her.

"Just a little. She needed some help."

Jimmy rose and cleared the table. "You help your mother a lot?"

For the first time in their relationship she felt her anger flare toward him. "Do you help yours?"

Jimmy rose from the table, carried the plates to the sink. Over the roar of the water from the faucet she heard him speak softly. "My mother passed twenty years ago. I was in Korea at the time."

Her anger fizzled. "I'm sorry," she said. "Then you surely know how precious a mother is. Even if she's not perfect."

He turned toward her but she ignored his questioning look. "The Bible says 'Honor your mother and father that your days may be long upon this earth.'"

Jimmy nodded without speaking. She could tell from the way his forehead furrowed that he wanted to say something but wanted to make sure he said it as precisely as he could. "What if they don't deserve such honor?" he asked finally. "What if they don't honor you in return?"

Her heart jumped up and so did her voice. "She does!" she said. "She does!"

"Calm down, girl." He dried his hands and turned on the little white radio she kept on top of the fridge. "Let's forget it. Come on up here and dance."

He found a station playing Sarah Vaughan, then pulled her into his arms. She had kicked off her shoes beneath the table and she was glad; in stocking feet she met Jimmy eye to eye. Wasn't a man supposed to be taller than the woman? Cush had been much taller than she.

He kept smiling at her but she refused to smile in return.

"Did I ever tell you," she said as they danced, "about the dress my mother gave me when I was ten?"

"Don't believe you have."

"It was my birthday. I was living with her here in Memphis. She had sent for me, sent all the way down to Mississippi. She was working in a department store and I helped watch the little ones and went to school when I could. And about two weeks after I got here it was my birthday. And she brought me home this beautiful dress. It was my first store-bought dress, my first new dress period, and it was beautiful. Pale pink, soft and cottony, tiny red roses embroidered on a Peter Pan collar and around the hem.

"I was so excited. I got up early the next morning and heated water for a bath so I'd be clean to put it on. I was going to get to wear it to school."

"What about the babies?"

"Oh, I don't remember. Maybe our neighbor watched them that day. She did sometimes. Anyway, school was a dream. Everybody in class noticed my new dress, everyone said how pretty it was; even Verna Lee Buckner had to admit I was beautiful that day. She was always picking on me, calling me ugly."

On the radio, Sarah Vaughan went off and was replaced by Lena Horne. Jimmy pulled her closer. "What the hell does Verna Lee know?"

"That afternoon I floated home. I carried my books way out in front of me so I wouldn't wrinkle the dress."

Jimmy nuzzled her neck. "Smart girl."

"But when I got home my mother was waiting. She told me to take off the dress. She said she had to take it back to the store. Turned out the salesgirl at the store—a different store than where she worked—had not checked my mother's credit. But the manager didn't have to check; he knew how bad it was and when he found out about the sale he telephoned over to Steinman's and told my mother's boss to make her bring it back. My mother made me take off the dress and sponge out under the arms so it wouldn't smell. She said they wouldn't take it back if they knew I'd worn it. And then she would have to do something else to pay for it."

She didn't know who had stopped dancing, Jimmy or her. But suddenly a commercial was playing on the radio, something about sausages, and she was standing in the middle of the kitchen like a fool, Jimmy staring hard at her. She pulled away from him, went to the stove to take off the boiling kettle. She took down two coffee cups. She felt Jimmy watching her as she moved.

"But see, it shows how much she loved me, that she would go into a store where she knew her credit was bad and get me a dress. That she would risk such embarrassment to get me something nice"

Jimmy walked to the table and sat down in silence.

"Back then people didn't just toss money away on children the way they do now," she said. "She didn't have to do that. She didn't have to get me that dress."

Jimmy took her hand and pulled her onto his lap. He kissed her. She let herself be kissed, but her mind was still thinking back.

"And yes, sure, I was upset at the time. I didn't understand. She came home without the dress and I was crying. I was so, so sad. The idea of facing Verna without that dress. And my mother went into her closet and pulled out this piece of material she had and gave it to me to make me feel better. That's what she did."

Jimmy kissed her again and this time she kissed him back.

"You deserve the prettiest dresses in the world," he said. "All lace and finery."

"My pastor likes to say if we all got what we deserved we'd all be long gone from this place."

"And that there," Jimmy said, "the main reason I ain't set foot in a church in fifteen years."

On the radio the commercials went away, replaced again by

music. Ella this time. Jimmy let his hand slide downward to the small of her back. She felt it pressing there through the soft cotton of her blouse, insistent and warm.

"Jimmy."

"I know."

"With the girls, I can't have—"

"Hush," he said, pulling her tighter, ironing the length of his body against her own. "Just out of curiosity, though, lady, you think there's ever gonna come a day when you and me might spend a little time at my place?"

She didn't pull back from him, though her head told her to. They had known each other for nearly six months and it was the first time he had asked. She thought that was pretty good. Some men never made it past hello.

"If it doesn't happen right away . . ." She let the thought trail off a minute, then went on. "Well, is that going to be a problem?"

"Tell the truth? Normally, yes that would be a problem."

She thought she heard a child calling for her and lifted her head. But after a few seconds of listening she lowered it again.

"But with you, lady, no. With you, I'm willing to wait."

She was silent.

"'Course that don't mean it won't be damn hard to keep my thoughts straight," he said with a grin. "Pardon my French."

"Did you ever go there? France. During the war, I mean."

"Wrong war," he said gently. "I went the other way. West."

"What places did you see?"

"Hawaii. The Philippines. Tokyo. Korea."

Mattie closed her eyes and imagined trade winds, coral seas, banyan trees. "Can you tell me about them?"

"Yes," Jimmy said, holding her tight. "I can do that."


*Another thing Aunt Eba had taught Mattie growing up: The road to* hell was paved with good intentions. She remembered that the day she received a promotion from the overnight shift at the post office to the evening one. "Congratulations," said her supervisor, Betty, a broad-shouldered, silver-haired white woman who thought she was being kind. "Now at least you'll be able to sleep."

"Thank you," Mattie said, and went home to sigh.

Being kicked up to the day shift would have been one thing; working 7 A.M. to 3 P.M. would have meant she could be away when the children were in school, though even then she would still need someone to watch Sidney and to be home if one of the girls got sick. But a promotion from overnights to the 3 to 11 P.M. shift did her no favors in the child-care department. She still needed someone to watch the children.

Since moving to Memphis, she'd gone through four different babysitters, each one less responsible than the one before. Miss Jessie, the woman from her mother's church, had turned out to have a little problem with alcohol. Two college girls from LeMoyne-Owen each worked a week then never showed up again. Finally, in desperation, Mattie had brought her second cousin Doreen up from Mississippi to care for the kids. Doreen was nineteen and childless, a miraculous accomplishment where she came from, and Mattie thought the girl might have something inside that would let her see the benefits of exchanging child care and house care for a chance to see the world beyond Tupelo. For ten months everything went fine. Doreen was a hard worker, the opposite of lazy, and the children both liked and respected her. But then Mattie made the mistake of taking the girl over to Memphis State and signing her up for a literacy class so the child could learn to read. After her second class, instead of getting on the bus and coming home, the girl wandered around campus until she stumbled into a meeting of the Pan-African Students for Power to the People—and that was that. She met a boy there, stopped pressing her hair, started spouting slogans, lost her mind. When Mattie caught her encouraging Lena to skip school because what they were teaching there were just lies perpetuated by the Man to keep the people enslaved, she knew it was time to let Doreen go. Which left her in a bind.

Her sister, Josephine, pitched in a few times, but she was working, too, and had her own children to tend. Jimmy offered to come over when he could; he worked the day shift and had his evenings free. "I'm happy to do it," he said. But the idea of leaving a man, even a man she trusted as much as Jimmy, in a house alone with three growing girls did not sit comfortably with her.

She asked her mother if she could help out, but Rae was working, too, and had her own child-care issues. On the weekends she usually left Harold home alone or sent him to Mattie's or Josephine's house. But he was thirteen and quiet and a boy; his prospects for trouble were less immediate and less dire than for three girls left unguarded in the world.

Mattie knew she could more than cover what her mother was making at her second job with a day's overtime if Rae would only help with the children. But Rae said no. "I'm done with diapers," she said, meaning Sidney.

"Dot will take care of that," Mattie said. "Besides, he's almost toilet trained."

But Rae just kept shaking her head. "Why don't you ask Eba?" she suggested after a while.

So Mattie went downtown and sent a telegram saying she needed help with the children if she was going to keep her job. She also sent along forty dollars for bus fare, which was more than enough. She knew Aunt Eba still didn't have a phone but somebody down there would get a telegram to her. And sure enough, two days later a telegram came back. It read: *Be there next week.*

*Aunt Eba arrived dragging along a snotty-nosed, knock-kneed little* girl by the name of Petunia Crepe. Mattie was not surprised. Aunt Eba was forever taking in somebody's child. Mattie herself had been neither the first nor the last.

"I'm just here until you get straightened out," Aunt Eba said, climbing down from the bus. "Then I got to get on home."

"I know, Aunt Eba," Mattie said, prying the cardboard suitcase and the woven lunch basket from her aunt's viselike grip. She was secretly hoping to persuade her aunt to move to Memphis permanently. But now was not the time to say so. Instead she gestured toward the little girl.

"Who does she belong to?"

"She Delta Montgomery's daughter. You remember her."

Mattie did. Delta and her family had moved to the plantation when Mattie was eight, part of the great reshuffling of sharecroppers that took place every year. It began in the fall, when the cotton was picked and hauled to the gin for weighing. It intensified just before Christmas, when Mr. Burch summoned each head of household to his field office for the settling up of accounts. It climaxed when a man realized he was being told his entire family's whole season of backbreaking, sun-blistered work had earned him just eighty dollars, minus twenty-eight dollars for food at the plantation store and five dollars more for cottonseed in the spring and ten dollars for loan of a mule to work the fields and on and on until the balance was zero or sometimes even a debt. It ended when the man and his family slipped away in the night and wandered miles across the Delta to another plantation, ready to start the process all over again. By the time she was five Mattie knew that come January, somebody would be moving on. Nobody wanted to move before Christmas, but if you were going to crop you had sure better get there by seeding time.

In the car Mattie clicked on the radio to a song: Elvis Presley, sounding just black enough. Mattie turned up the volume to hide her voice. The girl, wide-eyed and openmouthed, bounced in the back. "Memphis! I'm in Memphis! Memphis, Tennessee!" she kept saying. "Can we go to the zoo?"

"What happened to Delta?" Mattie whispered. She hoped it wasn't something terrible. Mattie remembered Delta as a sweet, dewy-eyed baby sucking her thumb. Mattie used to watch her sometimes while Delta's mother worked the fields or did laundry in town for one of the white women.

But Aunt Eba didn't bother to lower her voice. She didn't believe in shielding children, not from life and not from truth about those who gave them life.

"That fool girl got herself messed up with Sherman." Aunt Eba sucked her teeth, as though something unpleasant had gotten stuck there.

"Sherman?" Mattie racked her brain for a boy named Sherman but could remember none. It had been so long since she'd been back in Red Hook.

"Sherman Burch," Aunt Eba said. "Rotten son of a rotten son and ain't one of them ever fallen far from the tree of the original. But what Delta didn't count on was that these young white women don't sit up in their houses and pretend not to know what's going on like the old ones did. Sherman's wife found out, drove down to Delta's house to tell her to stop messing with her man. Delta told the fool to get on back into town before she got hurt. Next thing you know they're rolling in the dirt."

They were coming to a light. Mattie slowed to a stop, turned up the radio a little more. She didn't want the child to have to hear this.

"What you trying to do, make me deaf?" Aunt Eba barked, reaching for the dial.

"Maybe we should talk about something else," Mattie said, gesturing over her shoulder. Aunt Eba snorted.

"No sense trying to hide the truth from Petunia," Aunt Eba said. "She already knows her mother's in jail. She needs to know her mother's a fool."

Mattie glanced at the child through the rearview mirror. She had been about the same age herself that morning she woke and found Rae gone. It was Aunt Eba who had been there for her. Aunt Eba had taken her by the shoulders and steered her out to the porch. "No crying in this house," she said. "You got to cry, you cry out here." Mattie had. She sat on the porch in the dust from the fields and sobbed and sobbed and sobbed. And after a while Aunt Eba came outside to toss dishwater on her sweet-potato plants. "That's enough of that," she said.

Mattie only wailed louder. Aunt Eba tossed the water into the garden, then handed Mattie the pan and told her to get fresh water from the pump. "Girl, you better toughen up," she said as Mattie struggled to stand. "Only the strong survive. The tenderhearted bleed to death. Specially with a mother like that."

"I want her," Mattie had cried. "I want my mommy!"

"Child," Aunt Eba said, "people in hell want ice water. Don't mean they gonna get it anytime soon."


*"Free at last, free at last!" said Mattie's supervisor, leaning against* the doorway to his office, grinning her way. Mattie smiled back, picked up her time card, punched it.

"Thank the Lordy all mighty you's free at last!"

"Night, Mr. Bledsoe," Mattie said.

He was a greasy old cracker and he hated having to work with black folks, so he was always cracking smart with every Negro on the shift. Some people got angry, but the supervisor just laughed when that happened. Some people complained, but the supervisor had twenty-five years under his belt and a brother-in-law further up the chain. Some people, especially the younger workers with their billowy Afros and their clenched fists, waged minor wars of protest by stealing his lunches or trashing his desk or calling the supervisor by his detested given name. *Hey, Leslie, what's up?* they sang, infuriating him. *My man, Leslie!* When Mattie suggested to them they weren't accomplishing much except making sure they got the worst shifts and the loudest machines, they called her Aunt Jemima. *This here is 1977, not back in slavery times, and this is the United States Post Office, not Mr. Charlie's farm,* they said. *We ain't got to put up with it.* But Mattie knew you had to put up with something; that was just the way life was. Things were going pretty well for her otherwise—making a decent living with the job, Aunt Eba helping with the children, Jimmy being so sweet. Not to mention being near her mother for the longest time since she was ten. Even if Rae wasn't exactly what Mattie would have hoped, that was still a great blessing. Mattie was willing to put up with some redneck mouthing off in exchange for so very much.

"See you Sunday," she said, pulling on her coat. It was an hour before midnight and she was exhausted; all she wanted was to get home and into a hot bath and then into bed. But the supervisor stopped her as she turned to leave. "Wait a second, Miss Mattie," he called. "I do believe there is a message for you."

Mattie's hand froze on her buttons. She had never received a message at work before.

The supervisor wiped his lips with the back of his hand. He had just been eating something. He was always eating something, day and night. "Yes, sir, I do believe somebody telephoned while you were out on the floor, hardly working." He grinned. "I mean, working hard."

The supervisor turned around and shuffled into his office. Mattie stood waiting, holding her breath. Her hands were suddenly freezing, and she thought of Aunt Eba's thin, scarred hands dialing the telephone. For Aunt Eba to call her at work meant something terrible had taken place. Something with one of the children. Mattie had an image of Aunt Eba running down the sidewalk, the house ablaze, the children shoved ahead of her, every child but one. Mattie closed her eyes and chanted her children's names: Dot and Lena, Sidney, Grace. Dot and Lena, Sidney, Grace.

"Here it is."

Mattie opened her eyes, watched the supervisor fish a slip of paper from his desk and shuffle back toward her. "Called about an hour ago. Somebody named Rae."

Mattie let out her breath.

"Called 'bout an hour ago. Said for you to stop by on your way home. No emergency, she said."

Mattie took the slip with a weakened smile. It was only her mother calling, her mother, who unlike Aunt Eba, wouldn't think twice about phoning somebody on the job.

"That one of your children, Mattie?" the supervisor asked. "How many you got again? Twelve? Fifteen?"

"Good night," Mattie said again. Only Rae calling. And Mattie didn't have to think twice about what her mother needed, either. It would be the same thing she always needed.

When she arrived at her mother's house she found Rae at the kitchen table drinking a cup of coffee. The rest of the house was dark, save for the glow of a night-light in the bathroom. The door to Harold's room was closed.

"Want some coffee?" her mother asked as Mattie took off her coat and laid it upon one of the kitchen chairs.

"I can't drink coffee this late." Mattie rolled her head back and forth a little on her neck. She was tired, tired of her shoes and her bra and the starchy feel of her uniform collar against her skin. She wanted to get home, get to bed. She thought about how much cash she had in her purse: twenty-two dollars and some change. Twenty-two dollars she would no longer have when she left her mother's house.

Rae chuckled. She was dressed in a beautiful quilted housecoat the color of corn silk. "Coffee don't keep nobody awake," she said. "That's just in your head."

Mattie said. "What's wrong?

Rae put down her cup. "The house," she said. "They want to take it from me."

Mattie stopped her yawn. "Who wants to take it? What do you mean?"

Rae picked up one of the stack of papers that lay before her on the gleaming table and handed it to her. Mattie scanned it: the official Shelby County seal, the terse, one-line paragraphs, the bluntest of words. *Taxes. Eviction. Sheriff.* She gazed at the blotches of black upon white, too stunned to think.

"I need a thousand dollars," Rae said, not looking at her but at her painted fingernails. "Need it by Monday or they going to take my house."

Mattie stood up, no longer transfixed. "A thousand."

"Two years taxes," Rae said. "Plus penalties."

It was midnight Friday; her mother needed a thousand dollars in two days. It might as well have been a million for all the difference it made. Mattie knew without looking exactly how much money she had in her savings account at the Union Bank in midtown: $511. Five hundred and eleven dollars to last her until the end of the month when she would be paid again. The house note had been paid, thank goodness, but not the telephone bill, the electric bill, the insurance on the car. She still needed to buy food and buy Lena a new pair of shoes and try to keep some pitiful amount in the bank for emergencies.

"How did you let this happen?"

Rae lifted her hands to the air and shrugged, as if failing to pay her taxes for two years was like forgetting to turn off the light in a room. As if it were something that could happen to anyone. "I thought they took it out the rent."

"Didn't you check? Didn't you know how much your mortgage was?" Mattie asked, her voice climbing. "Didn't you get notices?"

But she knew it was useless. The horse was long, long out of the barn.

"Mr. Abernathy used to take care of all that stuff," her mother said. "Before he died."

Mattie sighed and sat down again. "How much do you have?"

"I give my whole paycheck to the bank for the mortgage last week," Rae said. "They was pestering me, too."

"Maybe the Gershwins can lend you some money," Mattie suggested. But she could tell from the way her mother shook her head that Rae had already borrowed money from her employers, probably borrowed more than a little and as yet failed to pay it back.

"Or maybe I can go to the bank, see about a loan myself," Mattie said, thinking out loud. "I have good credit."

"Loans take time," Rae said. "I ain't got time."

"Well, maybe Josephine—"

"Josephine don't have it," Rae said. "Her car broke down last week. She let me have a hundred dollars, said it was all she could spare."

All she could spare. That sounded like Josephine, all right. Mattie envisioned her sister, arms crossed and eyes locked, telling her mother she was sorry but one hundred dollars was the most she could spare. Josephine didn't think she should hurt herself trying to help someone else, even if that someone was her mother. Josephine could do that.

"How much do you have?" her mother was asking.

All she had to do was lie. She couldn't do what Josephine did, but she could just tell her mother all she had was a hundred. A hundred wouldn't break Mattie; a hundred wouldn't destroy the tiny cushion she had managed to build. All she had to do was lie.

"Not much," she said. "A little more than . . . five."

Her mother's eyes lit up. "Five hundred?"

Mattie felt like a fool. She threw up a line, tried to save herself. "It's not enough for what you need."

But Rae was already figuring. "Well, with the one from Josephine and the one I was able to scrape together, that makes seven."

"It's still not enough."

"But maybe they'll take that, if I promise to get the rest soon," Rae said. She was up from her chair now, pacing around the kitchen as she talked. "Bet if I went down there and asked them real nice, they'd take it. White folks like nothing more than for you to beg."

Mattie felt suddenly dizzy. She bent over the table, propped her head in her hands. "That's all the money I have in the world."

"Might even be able to get a little bit from Mr. Dodd down the road," Rae said. "He's always been sweet on me."

"All the money I have," Mattie said again. She closed her eyes against the dizziness and fatigue, surprised at the pleading in her voice. As if the roles had been switched. "That five is the only money standing between my children and an emergency."

Her mother stopped walking. The room grew still. For one long moment Mattie held her breath, afraid to open her eyes. She couldn't tell if her mother had left, had turned on her heels and walked out of the room in disgust. But then she felt her mother's hand on her shoulder.

"Your head hurt?" her mother asked.

"I'm fine," Mattie mumbled.

"Let me rub your shoulders," Rae said. "I do this for Ms. Gershwin all the time. Sit up."

Mattie sat up, and her mother began to massage her shoulders and neck.

"That woman always getting tension headaches, though I couldn't tell you why. Ain't like she working too hard." Rae chuckled a little, still massaging. Her hands were warm and strong even then, years from the cotton fields.

"I know it's asking a lot, daughter," Rae said after a minute.

Did she? Did her mother really know how much it was asking? Mattie wondered. She never had before and people did not change, did they? The Bible said it was possible with God's help, and Mattie believed the Bible, of course. Still, sometimes she wondered.

"I know it is," her mother repeated. "But this the only decent house I ever had. It would break my heart to lose it."

Mattie closed her eyes and leaned into her mother's hands.

*She drove straight to Jimmy's house. She knew the location exactly,* though she had never set foot inside the place. Not that he had not invited her. Not that she had not wanted to go. What she hadn't wanted was to give him the wrong idea; or the right idea but the wrong impression at the wrong time, or something. She didn't know.

To her relief the lights were on, though it was nearly midnight. Too late she realized she should have stopped at a pay phone and telephoned first. Her thoughts were scrambled. She could barely think at all.

"Jimmy?" she called softly, knocking at the door.

When he opened the door some trick of perspective, some shifting of light from the flickering television screen and the glowing lamp, made him look taller. Made him look huge. "What's wrong?" he demanded, pulling her inside. "The children?"

"No, no." She was suddenly breathless. She had to struggle to get the words out. "Children . . . are fine. Nothing . . . like . . . that."

He led her to a couch and sat her down. "Water is what you need," he declared, and walked away. The second he left the room she came back to herself and felt ridiculous. What was wrong with her? Why was she acting so silly—trembling and gulping for breath like some catfish flopping around on the dock. Jimmy would think she'd lost her mind. She shook her head to clear it and saw Jimmy coming back across the room.

"Drink this," he said, holding out a surprisingly beautiful glass of cut crystal. She took it, sipped.

He sat next to her on the couch. "Better?"

She nodded. "Fine," she said. "Don't know why I acted that way. There's nothing wrong, nothing earth-shattering, I mean. I'm not even sure why I'm here."

Jimmy took her hand with a smile. "Well, I'm glad you are," he said. "Whatever the cause."

The couch was small, really more of a love seat, and his thigh

pressed against her own. He smelled of tobacco and soap and san-
dalwood, as though he had just washed his hands before rolling a
cigarette. Taken altogether, his physical presence was so intense
she had to look away, to lay her eyes on safer things. The house
was almost as small as Aunt Eba's shack, though much better built.
From where she sat Mattie could see straight through one doorway
into the tiny kitchen, where a miniature fridge, a miniature stove,
and a regular-size sink barely left room for two feet of counter
space. Through another doorway she glimpsed the equally minute
bedroom, dominated by a bed and its headboard of polished pine.
And everything she saw was not just clean but impeccably so. The
kitchen floor gleamed and the countertops glistened, and the bed
was made so neatly Cush would have been pleased.

She told him everything, not sure herself what she expected
him to say or do. When she finished Jimmy stood up and walked
slowly around the room for a few minutes, his hands in pockets,
his eyes low.

Then he sat next to her and took her hand again. "You can't
give her the money."

"What?"

"Just last week you were complaining about her always asking
for money."

Mattie pulled back her hand. "I wasn't complaining," she said,
though in fact she had been. "And this is different. She's not asking so she can go out and buy a new hat. This time she could lose
her house."

"That's not your fault," Jimmy said.

"I know it's not my fault, but—"

"And it's not your responsibility," he added, cutting her off.
He was using his firm, patient supervisor's voice, the one he used
at the post office when people came to him crying, whining, bickering. "Plus, you need that money yourself. Your children need it.
Your first obligation is to them."

She stood up so fast she missed her footing and came down hard on his toes. Jimmy winced but did not cry out. *Good!* she thought, stepping away from the couch. She hoped it hurt, hoped it hurt a lot. She was suddenly, wildly furious. Who the hell did he think he was, telling her what to do? The last thing she needed was to be lectured on obligation by a forty-year-old man who had never been responsible for anything but himself. She knew her obligation to her children, knew better than anyone would ever know. But the phone company could wait a month on their payment—she had never been late before. And Lena could get perfectly good new shoes at the Salvation Army store for fifty cents. And wasn't it for her children, too, that she had moved back to Memphis in the first place? So they could know their grandmother and their cousins, so they could grow up around family? So they could have someone in this world besides themselves?

"Mattie," Jimmy said, still using his patient supervisor voice even as he rubbed his toe. "Sometimes when you can't find a thing where it's supposed to be, you need to give up and look someplace else."

But Mattie was shaking her head. She didn't want to hear any more of his nonsense. She began looking around for her purse.

"Mattie? Did you hear me?"

"She's my mother!" she said, still seeking her purse.

"She has other children."

"But I'm the one she asked," Mattie said. "I'm the one."

The next thing she knew she was crying and Jimmy was next to her, taking her into his arms. "Baby!" he whispered. "Baby girl, Mattie Mae. Don't cry. Please don't cry."

"I'm tired," she said, because she was. She was tired of her shoes and her bra and the starchy feel of her uniform collar against her skin. She was suddenly so exhausted she could barely stand and she let him kiss her, let his hands feel their way down to the small of her back, let them press her body against his own.

"Call home," he said, kissing her face. "Stay here with me."

Yes, she would stay, she decided. She would stay there with

Jimmy for a while and let the world run on its own. And later she could get up and go home and take a bath. And tomorrow morning bright and early she would get up and go on down to the bank and empty out her account. And what happened after that, the good Lord only knew.

*Two hours later, when she was certain he was asleep, she rose and* washed and left the house.

The next morning she was at her own kitchen table when he showed up bringing ice cream for the kids. She had been there since dawn, going over the checkbook, adding and re-adding the numbers, hoping they would somehow change.

"Is it safe to come in?" he asked when she opened the kitchen door to his knock.

Mattie nodded. She knew he was referring to Aunt Eba, who had made her disapproval of "mens in the house" abundantly clear. It wasn't that Aunt Eba didn't like Jimmy in particular; she had simply seen one too many teenage girls led down into the cotton fields, one too many men move into a house with a woman and her daughters and try to bed them both. "I don't trust most mens as far as I can spit," she liked to say. Mattie understood that; she wasn't exactly wide-eyed herself. But Jimmy was different; she'd made certain before he stepped one foot inside her house, one foot near her kids. She had asked around, she had watched him around other women, had watched his eyes and his body when some young girl came swinging toward them down the street. And even then, even after she was certain, she never left him alone with the children; why give opportunity a helping hand? But that was just her cautious nature at work. In the end she trusted Jimmy. He had touched her in a way Cush never even bothered to try. Such a thing would not have been possible, wasn't possible, in a man with a dirty heart.

"You're safe," she said, ushering him inside. It was cold out, the sky gray and threatening. She hoped it wouldn't rain before the children got back. "Aunt Eba went down to the bus station to put Petunia on the bus. Her mother is back in Mississippi, looking for her."

Jimmy stepped inside. "Where the kids? Bought them some ice cream."

"I sent them down to the library. They'll be back soon enough."

Jimmy opened the freezer door to store the ice cream, then stepped over to her, rubbing his hands. "Well, well, well. Looks like I timed my visit perfectly."

He pulled her into a kiss. "You left too early, woman. I wanted to wake up beside your beautiful face."

She tried to smile but she must have seemed distracted, because after a moment he pulled away. He looked at her, then reached into his pocket and pulled out a brown paper bag, wrapped tightly around some rectangular shape. He tossed it on the table in front of her.

Her heart leaped. "What's that?" she asked.

"Six hundred and fifty dollars," Jimmy said. "Cash."

She was so stunned she dropped her pen. "Six hundred and . . ." she stammered. "Where did you get it?"

"Keep it around for emergencies," he said. "I don't much trust banks, not completely. They got a lot of my money, but I never give them all." He moved toward the stove, and she couldn't help but notice his strut. "Mind if I make myself a cup of coffee?"

"Let me." Mattie leaped up from her chair but Jimmy put his hand on her shoulder and pushed her gently back into her seat.

"I can do it," he said, smiling. "Been cooking for myself for thirty years. You ain't got to do everything, Mattie."

She sat and looked at the package, stared hard at it as if she were Superman and could see straight through that brown paper wrapping. All those bills, all that money. All that release. She should have taken it; her hand itched to reach out and wrap around that paper bag. But it was too much, too weighty, especially after what she had done the night before. It implied certain things.

Taking a deep breath, she said, "I can't take it, Jimmy. I do thank you for the offer, though. I really do."

He looked at her hard. "Why not, Mattie?"

"She's my mother. I have to be the one to help."

"Even if it breaks you?" he asked.

"It won't break me," she said. "I'll . . . I'll find a way."

"Oh, sure," he said, and she could tell by the edge in his voice that his pride had taken a slap. "After all, you got so much money to burn."

He paused, seemed to be waiting for her to say something. When she didn't, he went on, his voice growing steadily angrier.

"Seems like from what you're saying, the money you give her won't even be enough to save the house. Is that right?"

"They might take it," Mattie said. "They might give her a second chance."

Jimmy made a skeptical noise. "When have you ever known white folks to give a poor black woman a second chance?"

The kettle began to sing. Jimmy turned off the fire, spooned instant coffee into two cups, and poured the boiling water on top. "And what are you going to do without that money? What if something happens next week or the week after and you need it?"

"She's my mother," Mattie said again.

But Jimmy seemed to be really working himself up now, as if it were his money they were talking about. He set her cup on the table before her and crossed his arms. "Hell, you need it now," he said. "I was looking at the roof coming in here. There's a spot that looks like trouble."

Ignoring the coffee, she stood up, wanting suddenly to be tall. "Don't you worry about the roof."

"I'll fix it, that's not a problem," Jimmy said. "I'm trying to make a point."

"Don't you worry about the roof," she said again. "It's my damn roof."

"Now, Mattie Mae," he said, using his pet name. He came to her, tried to take her hand into his own strong one. "Don't get mad at me. I'm just trying to help you see something here."

She could hear the children outside, playing in the yard. They would notice his car in a minute, come tearing into the house to see what he had brought them. "She's my mother," she said. Trying one more time.

"You keep saying that."

"Your mother is gone, you don't understand," she said. "I have to help if I can."

"Even if it means taking bread from your children's mouths?"

He said this so softly, so gently, that it took her a second to hear what he'd said. When the words sank in a fury rose up inside her heart. She snatched her hand from his. "To hell with you!"

"Mattie—"

"Everything I do is for my children," she said. "Everything!"

This time Jimmy didn't pull back as she expected. He got right up on her, got into her face, and looked into her eyes. "Then do this for them, Mattie," he said, his breath so warm across her cheeks. "Give up on trying to make your mama love you."

Mattie caught her breath. For a moment she was back at the club with Cush, watching him sneer into her face. *She didn't love you, so why should she love your nappy-headed kids?* Mattie backed up, staring at Jimmy in astonishment. How could she have been so fooled by him? How could she have thought he was such a good man?

"Mattie," he began, but was cut off by Sidney's voice through the window. "Hey, look! It's Mister Jimmy's car!"

How had she been so wrong? And if she had been so wrong about that, then what else about him might she have missed?

"This ain't about saving her house," Jimmy was saying. "That house is gone. That house was gone the minute her last man died."

"Get out," she said.

"You think if you give your mother this money she's going to change."

"Get out."

"You think she's gonna suddenly become the mama you never had, treat you the way she should have done years ago," he said. "But she won't. You got to realize, Mattie. Your mother is a selfish woman. I'm sorry to say it, but she don't give a damn about anyone but herself!"

She wanted to slap him. Her hand burned to do it, her fingertips flamed. She was raising her hand when the children burst through the door, screaming his name. "Mister Jimmy's here! Mister Jimmy's here!"

She let her hand drop. She turned away toward the stove. Jimmy had left his coffee sitting there and she picked up the cup, pretended to be busy cooling the liquid with her breath, though when brought it to her lips it was stone-cold.

"Hello, Mister Jimmy," Dot said, demure as could be.

"I checked out five books!" said Grace. "Did you ever read *Charlotte's Web*?"

"What did you bring us?" cried Sidney. "Did you bring ice cream?"

"Don't tell me you knuckleheads been to the library," she heard Jimmy say. "What'd you do—learn something?"

Mattie turned around. Jimmy was hugging her children, hugging them all one by one by one. They hugged him back, their faces all shiny and excited and glowing from the cold outside. A man in their life. Mens in the house.

The last to step up was Lena. The girl slunk over and grabbed him around the neck like she was swinging on a rope swing. "When you going to get a decent ride, Mister Jimmy?" she asked.

"When you get a job and pay for it," he joked.

Mattie watched him holding her daughter, still seething inside. She was sure his hand lingered on the girl's waist just a little too long.

*It was raining when Mattie took Grace and Sidney along with her to* the bank first thing that morning and then to her mother's house. But by the time she staggered out half an hour later, the rain had stopped and the sky cleared to a miraculous blue. As if all the world were just fine.

And by the next morning, by the time the sheriff arrived at her mother's house, the temperature had climbed back to its usual spot in the nineties, wrapping the city in a humid daze. The sheriff had small rings of sweat around his armpits as he strode to the porch, hat on head and gun on hip, banana pudding speckling his many chins. He gave her an hour to pack up, but apparently Rae was two steps ahead of him. She had already loaded the car twice and driven to Josephine's house. By the time the sheriff arrived she was almost ready to go.

"Go?" Mattie asked her sister. She thought maybe she had misheard. She was working a double shift at the post office and it was noisy in the break room. "Go where?"

"She said she always wanted to see Chicago."

High above Mattie's head a casement window revealed a sky the color of joy. "What happened to the rest of her things?" Mattie managed to say. "Her furniture, her clothes. She couldn't take all that in the car."

"It all happened so fast, Mattie," said Josephine. "She got her jewelry and her clothes and Harry's things and I got some other stuff. The rest the sheriff seized."

A man Mattie knew by sight but not by name walked up and got on the phone next to her. He gave her a wink before turning his back.

"The good news is, most of the stuff he took belongs to the store anyway." Josephine's laugh was forlorn.

"Did she . . . did she leave me anything?" Mattie asked.

"No, girl."

"She took the money?"

"What money?" Josephine asked.

"The money I gave her," Mattie said. "To save the house? She took all of it?"

There was a pause during which Mattie heard the guy next to her cursing into his telephone. "Mattie," Josephine said finally. "Mattie. Don't you remember Mama saying a leopard doesn't change its spots?"

For a minute, bright red spots clouded her vision. When they cleared, she said, "What?"

"Don't you remember Mama saying that?"

But, no, she couldn't say she did. In truth, Mattie didn't remember her mother ever teaching her much of anything at all.

# Chapter Fourteen

In the days after the funeral Eddie and I floated around each other, pushed this way and that by the unspoken currents of what I'd done and what it meant and what he wanted and what I did not want, did not want at all. We gave wide berth to each other in the kitchen, maneuvered in the living room, slid past each other in the hall. I folded laundry and watched television until late at night, then went to bed when I was certain he was well asleep. He got up early, made his coffee, kissed the children, and tiptoed from the house. We went along until one evening, climbing the stairs for bed, I smacked into him as he made his way to the bathroom for a drink of water. He'd been in bed for more than an hour, but I could tell, from his darting eyes and uncreased face, that he had yet to fall asleep. I took a breath, made myself speak.

"I guess we need to talk."

"Not now," he said.

"Okay. When?"

"Later," he said, pushing past me back into the bedroom. He closed the door.

Which, really, was fine with me. I had other things to do, such as: (1) do something about the violent teenager lurking around my mother, and (2) find my grandmother. I took the second project on first. It occurred to me, after Eddie left for work the following morning, to telephone my sister Dot. Of all of us children she was the closest to my mother, the one most likely to know and tolerate family secrets, the one to stay involved, the one who had never tried like hell to tear herself away only to come slinging back. It was possible, just possible, she knew something about my grandmother's whereabouts that I did not. But when I got her on the phone she scoffed at me.

"Why would I know where she is, Grace?" she asked. "Mom doesn't even speak to her anymore."

"So?" I tried to sound reasonable. "Does that mean we can't? Does that mean we have to hate her, too?"

"What's wrong with you?" Dot asked.

I was sitting on the top step of the basement, with the door—unlocked and double-checked—pulled closed so Paula would not hear me as she dabbled in the kitchen with her finger paints. "Nothing," I said, but in the close and darkened space I could hear the faint undercurrent of strain in my voice. "I just . . . have been thinking it would be nice to connect with her. While there's still a chance. She is our grandmother."

"She abandoned Mom," Dot said. "More than once."

I flinched at the word *abandoned*. "Maybe," I began, "maybe she didn't think of it like that. Maybe she thought of it as saving herself."

Dot hooted. "I'm sure she did! I'm sure she thought of it as choosing herself over her daughter, exactly. And that was her choice."

"Maybe she didn't have a choice."

"We always have a choice," Dot said. "She made her bed."

"So you won't help me? Even if you did know where she was, you wouldn't tell me?"

My sister did not answer this, which was an answer in its own right. "Fine," I said. "Fine."

Dot let a second pass, then asked, "Have you actually talked to your mother lately?"

So now we were on to the good-daughter contest. Dot, who talked to my mother at least once a day, would win that one hands down. "Just recently enough for her to tell me that little sociopath she has living in her house now got kicked out of school for carrying a weapon. I'm sure she mentioned that to you, too."

"I don't like it either, Grace," my sister said. "But that's her job. It's what she does."

"Well, maybe it shouldn't be anymore," I said, without knowing I was going to say it. The words came out of my mouth without me knowing what they meant, but as soon as they touched air, I knew.

Dot sighed, sounding so much like my mother I wanted to reach through the phone and pinch her. "I tried talking to her about it. But you know how she is: she won't give it up."

"But she can be made to," I said, very coldly. "In her own interest."

Suspicion colored my sister's voice. "What do you mean?"

"I was just thinking if someone told the DFS about some of the, you know, strange stuff she used to do, they might decide to take away her license."

Silence. I heard Paula singing to herself, a song about a baby whale.

"It would be for her own good," I told my sister. "She's too old for this; those children are getting far too dangerous."

"You're joking, right?" Dot said. "That would be the worst kind of betrayal, Grace."

I stood up, as if Dot were in the room and I needed to get height over her. "It would be for her own good," I insisted again, stubbornly. "It would save her health."

"It would kill her," Dot said.

"Oh, come on—"

"It would be killing her!" Dot's voice had climbed several notches. "Taking her children away would be the end of her. Don't you understand that, Grace?"

I opened the basement door and looked at Paula, who had smeared bright yellow paint across her forehead and into her hair and onto the cabinets.

"I thought you of all of us would get that, Grace," Dot was saying into my ear. "Don't you know anything about motherhood?"

I said, "Apparently not."

*I do not mean to leave the impression my grandmother disappeared* completely from our lives. We received telephone calls and Christmas cards after she settled in Chicago, and a few postcards years later, when she decamped from there to Detroit. I think my aunt Josephine went to visit her once or twice when she lived in Detroit; or maybe it was Las Vegas or St. Louis or Cleveland. I don't remember; my grandmother covered a lot of ground. What I do remember is sitting in the room I shared with Lena and Dot and hearing Dot whisper as she filled us in on the family news. "Apparently she's doing all right for herself," Dot said. "Married, quote unquote, to some guy who owns a funeral home. She was working there as something or other—heaven only knows what—and that's how they met."

"Uh-huh." I was stretched out on the bed, staring up at my *Starsky and Hutch* poster, lost in a fantasy about Paul Michael Glaser squealing up in his hot red car to sweep me away.

"Nice enough guy, apparently," Dot said. "Too nice for her, probably. Older, Aunt Josephine said. With grown children who don't think much of Grandmother."

"Really."

"Josephine told Mom she ought to go see her." She said this as if it was the most ridiculous idea in the world, but I didn't catch the undertone.

"Well, uh, maybe she should."

Dot laughed. "Are you kidding? Mom said Detroit was cold and dirty and crawling with drug addicts. She said there was nothing there she wanted to see."

"Not even her own mother?" I asked. Dot just rolled her eyes and left the room.

I think my grandmother even made it back to Memphis once for a visit; the grand return of the queen. I was away at college at the time and intensely self-focused, as young people are. It wasn't high on my list of important events, and, at any rate, my mother was pretty stiff-lipped about the whole thing. "Dot said Grandmother came home," I remember saying during a telephone call home.

My mother laughed. "*Home* is a funny word," she said. Then she went on to something else, and I remembered the last time I had seen my grandmother. That last day in Memphis. The day before my grandmother left.


## MEMPHIS, 1972

*That day I held Sidney's hand as we went up the steps and through* the front door into my grandmother's immaculate living room. She was there, polishing the coffee table with an old rag, but she stopped when we came in. "You get it?" she asked my mother. I knew she had. Sidney and I had gone with our mother to the bank, had stood in the long line and watched her carefully count and recount the stack of twenties before stuffing them inside her sock. My mother always carried large amounts of money in her shoes or socks. If some stupid purse snatcher came after her the only thing he'd get for his trouble was a coin purse and a handkerchief. But instead of pulling out the money from her sock, my mother sat down on the couch and folded her hands. Sidney and I just stood there. We were not allowed to sit in Grandmother's living room, but we weren't sure if we could go play in the kitchen or outside.

"Mama," Mattie began.

Grandmother tossed back her head and cried "Sugar!" to the skies. It was the strongest swearword she ever used and it meant she was well and truly pissed. "You didn't get it, did you?"

"No, I—"

"What happened? The bank give you some trouble? It's your money, right?"

"I have it, Mama," my mother said. "I got it. It's just . . . well, I had another thought."

Grandmother stood still a moment, coming back to herself. Then she folded the rag into quarters and slipped it into the pocket of the housedress she was wearing. I could tell from the outfit, and from the bandanna tied around her head, that she had been cleaning all day. The only time my grandmother was not dressed to the nines was when she was cleaning her house.

"Thoughts ain't going to help me now," she said. "Only cash."

"But maybe not even that," my mother said. "What if they won't take this? Where are you going to get the rest? And even if you do find it, what happens next month? And the one after that? Mama, I know you love this house. I wish I could help you keep it. But without help it's probably just too much for you."

I was still holding Sidney's hand but we were both growing restless. I didn't want to be there, didn't want to listen to this. It was embarrassing, the messiness of grown-up business. It was something I did not want to see.

"Mom, can we go outside?" I asked. But my mother did not seem to hear me. She was focused on her own mother's face.

"I think the best solution," my mother said firmly, "at least for a while, is for you to come live with me."

Grandmother said nothing. Sidney tugged on my hand.

"Not forever, maybe a year or two," my mother said. "You can help with the children—Aunt Eba's been itching to go home anyway. But if you're in the house I can work as much overtime as I can and save up some money. And then, in a while, we'll see about getting you another house."

Grandmother untied the bandanna from her hair, then put it in the other pocket of her dress. She smoothed her flat curls with her hand. She said, "I don't think so. No."

My mother came back quick, as if this was just the response she had expected. "And why not, Mama? Give me one good reason you shouldn't do the most sensible thing in the situation?"

"Because I don't want to, Mattie," Grandmother said. "That's the long and short of it right there."

Sidney giggled; probably hearing words he spoke ten times a day himself out of his grandmother's mouth seemed funny to him. But nobody else in the room laughed.

"People can't just go around doing what they want," my mother said, her voice rising.

"I done plenty I didn't want to do, Mattie," Grandmother said. "At this stage in my life I want to enjoy myself."

"Enjoy yourself?" My mother laughed. "What else have you ever done but enjoy yourself! Life isn't just about having fun, Mama! It's about hard work and responsibility. It's about sacrifice."

My grandmother threw up her hands. "Who taught you that? Who in the world taught you to be so pitiful, to be always laying down in the mud for folks to walk over? Was it Eba; did she do that to you, child? I know it wasn't me."

My mother said, "No. It wouldn't have been you. Would it, Mama?"

"Are you going to give me the money, Mattie? Yes or no?"

Next to me Sidney was holding his breath. He was four years old, but he was, as Lena said, a "baby four." He acted so much younger than his age, so we all took care of him, or maybe it was the other way around. I tried to back us out of the room, to pull him backward with me, but he seemed frozen to his spot, his mouth open in astonishment. All of a sudden my grandmother called our names.

"Grace," she said, sitting down in a wing chair by the window. "Sidney. Come on over here and give your grandmother some sugar."

Both Sidney and I were too surprised to move. But she urged us along. "Come on. Come on over here!"

My mother said, "Do what your grandmother says," in a deflated little voice. So we did as we were told, moving across the room to kiss our grandmother's smooth cheek. I thought it was a precursor to finally releasing us, to sending us into the kitchen or outside to play—away from grown folks' talk. But my grandmother surprised me again by not releasing me from the hug.

"How old are you now, Grace?"

"Nine." I shifted my feet, trying to rock away without seeming to move.

"What grade you at in school?"

"Third." I waited. Whenever grown-ups asked these questions it was usually followed by some expression of amazement that I should have reached such an age, as if doing so required great effort and accomplishment.

My grandmother asked, "They teaching you about slavery in that school?"

I was so surprised I forgot my manners. "What?" I caught my mother's glare and corrected myself. "I mean, yes, ma'am."

Every year my class took a field trip to Shiloh, Tennessee, home of some Civil War battle. For a week before the trip my teacher would talk about the war and all the brave soldiers who died—on both sides but mainly the Confederates—and how some people got confused and thought the war was about slavery but really it was about states' rights. All the black kids in the class slumped in our seats and stared out the window when we got to the page in the textbook that showed slaves. They always had their hair sticking up straight in plaits or wrapped in some bandanna, and were dressed in rags, and had bad teeth, and stood barefoot in some cotton field, staring at the camera like it was the bogeyman.

"Good," my grandmother said. "You need to know this stuff." Then: "Your mama ever tell you my great-grandmother was born a slave?"

I must have looked startled because my grandmother laughed. "No, I didn't think so. Slaves in the family is not something folks like to talk about."

Well, that much was true. Saying my mother—saying black folks in general—didn't like to talk about slavery was like saying she didn't like to talk about her period. Slavery was just that common, that omnipresent, and that hidden away. I could count on one hand the number of times I'd heard the issue discussed with anything more than a passing remark. In church it came down to singing about Moses going down to Egypt. In school it came down to "Lincoln freed the slaves." Having a slave in the family was like having a daily bowel movement—everybody had them, but they were nasty and shameful and why in the world would you want to have it discussed?

My grandmother ran her hand across my hair, trying to smooth it down. "Slavery was something my grandmother talked about all the time. She had been born a slave and she was mad because she didn't have to be."

"What do you mean, she didn't have to be?"

"My great-grandmother was a free colored woman," my grandmother said. "Not all coloreds were slaves, you know."

This was astonishing news. There were no free colored people in my schoolbooks. There wasn't a single nonslave black person in *Gone with the Wind*. "How did she get free? Did she run away?"

"Her master freed her when he died," my grandmother said. "He was a small tobacco farmer in South Carolina, a religious man, except he managed to turn the Bible to his own use most of his life. But when he got old and sick and stuck in bed, he had a vision: an angel, her feet in chains, her sword pointing down to hell as if his place had already been assigned. It nearly scared the life out of him. The next day he freed his slaves, all eight of them.

Some stayed at the farm anyway, but my great-grandmother and her man and a few others started hightailing it north. They got as far as Philadelphia and thought they were safe."

She paused to chuckle. "The City of Brotherly Love."

"What happened there?" I asked.

"They were fine for a few years, long enough for my great grandmother to marry her man and have a son. And then one day slave catchers grabbed that husband and that son as they were walking home from working in a white farmer's field and dragged them away and sold them down south."

I tried to imagine myself riding my bike back from the store and some white man coming out of nowhere on his horse to drag me off. The idea terrified me. "Why didn't they call somebody?" I asked, agitated. "Why didn't they call the police."

My grandmother rasied her eyebrow at me. "No police back then. Not for colored folks anyway."

"Mama," my mother said. I could tell she wanted my grandmother to stop.

"What did she do?"

"Tried to get them back, of course. Begged white friends to help her—"

"She had white friends?"

"So to speak. One of them even wrote a few letters around, but it didn't help. Finally word came her husband had been killed trying to escape and her son was about to be sold further down south."

"No!"

"So you know what my great-grandmother did? You'll never guess in a million years."

I was afraid to ask. I knew it would be something terrible and I didn't want to know. But Sidney did.

"What? What'd she do?"

"She followed that slave catcher. Followed him all the way down to North Carolina and to the plantation where her son got sold. Her husband died along the way, fighting, trying to get free. But she found out where her son was and she went to that white man and volunteered to be his slave if he promised never to separate her and her son. She was pregnant at the time."

"With your grandmother."

"Yes," my grandmother said. "My grandmother Hyacinth. She was fifteen when the Yankees came marching through and told them all we were free. By then she was pregnant, carrying her master's son."

My mother was up out of her chair. "Why do you have to make it sound like she was stupid for doing what she did!"

"She was a fool," my grandmother said calmly.

"She saved her child."

My grandmother laughed. "Saved him? Tell me how she saved him when he was still a slave?"

"At least they were together."

My grandmother pushed me away and stood up. "Don't you know if you're trying to save some fool from drowning in the river and he gets his arm around your neck and starts pulling you down, you're supposed to cut him loose? Save yourself first."

I turned around to look for Sidney. My grandmother had released him during her story, had grabbed my hands and held me there as if the story was meant for me. I saw Sidney over near the front door, his back to us and his face pressed up against the glass, as if he wasn't listening, was no longer a part of the scene. My mother, too, was backing toward the door, her face all twisted.

"That's good advice, Mama," she said. I could tell she was struggling not to cry. "I wish I could take it."

She bent over and pulled the roll of money from her sock, then tossed it onto the coffee table, the one my grandmother had just polished to a gleam. "Let's go," my mother choked. Then she turned and left the house, pulling Sidney along with her.

I tried to follow them but my grandmother held my arm.

"Grace," she said. "Remember: I never held myself up as some big example on how to live."

She was staring hard at me and I could tell she wanted something from me, something important. But I had no idea what it was. "I have to go," I said.

"I'm just living, that's all."

"I have to go, Grandma."

She released my arm. As I was leaving I saw her walk to the coffee table and pick up the money.

My mother had the engine running, the car in gear. I climbed into the backseat and she took off. I glanced at Sidney, who was sucking on the collar of his shirt, looking frightened. I took his hand.

After a second of what sounded like gulping my mother asked, "What did she say to you?"

What's strange is how easily came the lie. I hardly had to think. "She said she loved you."

I don't know what reaction I expected, curses maybe, though my mother was not one to use foul language. Or maybe tears. But what we got, my brother and I, in the backseat of that car in the Memphis midmorning, was a scream. My mother screamed, full-throated, flat out, and piercing, so hard Sidney began to wail and I began to pray. And somehow my mother managed not to lose control of the car, just screamed with her eyes wide open, and then she stopped and kept driving all the while. "Be quiet, Sidney," she said finally. I wrapped my arms around my brother and shushed him, told him everything would be fine.

"I waited my whole life to hear those words," my mother said. "And she says them to you."

Instead of going home, my mother got on the highway. I didn't know where we were going and did not dare ask. She drove north for twenty minutes without speaking, then veered into a rest area and put her head on the steering wheel. I thought she might still be crying but I couldn't be sure; the only noise was the ticking of the engine, the distant whir of the cars racing past. After a long, long time she said, so softly I could barely hear, "I wish . . . I wish to God . . ."

I looked out the window at the truck on my side and said nothing at all.

She sat up, wiping her face, and opened the door. "Going to the bathroom," she said over her shoulder. "Stay here and lock the door."

Watching my mother walk away into the darkness, I marveled at my own numbness. I felt nothing, or at least nothing I could detect—not sadness for my mother, not sympathy or fear. I glanced into the backseat at Sidney, who had curled up into a ball and gone to sleep. I was glad he'd hunkered himself down into slumber; had he been awake he might have been scared. He might have thought our mother wasn't coming back, that she planned to just keep walking and leave us there. But one thing I knew about my mother: if any one of us was drowning she'd jump feetfirst into the river and not hesitate. Another thing I knew was this: my mother couldn't swim.

# Chapter Fifteen

After an early lunch I settled Paula down for a nap. By then it was nearly one—just over an hour left before it was time to pick up Harriet. I sat down and turned on the computer, determined to do work of some kind, to revisit one of the projects I had set aside. Instead, I spent ten minutes weeding through the junk in my e-mail account, and another ten staring out the kitchen window at a cardinal dancing in the snow, and another fifteen halfheartedly searching an Internet phone directory for Royal Rose Van Buren in Chicago, Detroit, and Washington, D.C. By then it was one-thirty and time was ticking by. With a sigh I gave up and rechecked my e-mail, then trolled the Internet. I clicked to the *New York Times* site and read through the headlines, then did the same at the *Washington Post* and the *Wall Street Journal* and the *Boston Globe*. I went to the *Chronicle of Higher Education* and read an article on the blossoming sociology department at UNC. Then I went to Google and, for no particular reason, typed in the words *best age to abandon your child*. There were no documents to match.

I typed in *maternal abandonment*. There were 312 results, several of them about some insipid horror flick I'd never heard of, many more about Bill Clinton and the psychic wound that drove him past Hillary and the Secret Service into Monica's eager arms. A few about Toni Morrison's great book *Beloved*. Assorted others I did not read. For contrast I typed in the words *paternal abandonment*. Results: 11,600.

I got up and went into the bathroom to check for my period, fruitlessly as it turned out. Amazing how much time women spent anticipating or dreading the coming of the blood. Amazing and fascinating, if you weren't involved. I had nearly written my graduate thesis on the sociology of menstruation and puberty, specifically as it related to African-American girls. I had noticed, that summer at the clinic, how many of the girls coming through the door seemed—from the way they paraded their chests and ran their mouths and swung their hips—like teenagers when in fact they were eleven or ten or even nine years old. Babies still, except they were not. A little research turned up some frightening statistics: by the age of eight, nearly half of all black girls will have begun developing breasts or pubic hair. By the age of ten, fifty percent of black girls will have gotten their periods. Not fourteen or fifteen but ten. Ten. The sociological implications were staggering. Imagine the effect of such precocious puberty on early sexual behavior, on teen pregnancy, on the transmission of AIDS and other sexually transmitted diseases. On high-school dropout rates and welfare dependency. On society's hypersexualization of black women. On how all those ripening, bewildered, hormone-maddened children thought and felt about themselves. It was as if they'd been handed the keys to Porsches and let loose on the Autobahn when they could barely see over the dash. But in the end my adviser steered me away from the politics of menstruation. "You will never be taken seriously as a scholar," he warned. And of course I wanted to be taken seriously. I wanted to be a scholar, I wanted to contribute to the life of the mind.

The doorbell rang as I was washing my hands. By the time it rang a second time I was halfway down the stairs to the first floor and racing for the front door. Paula still had twenty minutes in her nap; if she woke early she'd be a bear for the rest of the afternoon. Lord knew I did not need the grief.

"Please stop!" I cried, flinging open the door. I expected to find, waiting on my step, the mailman, or maybe some earnest college kid collecting for PIRG. What I did not expect was to see my sister Lena standing there, exquisite little suitcase in hand.

"Hey, girl," my sister said, grinning as if she had arrived on my doorstep from around the corner or up the street. Her hair was longer than when I'd last seen her, suspiciously so. She wore it relaxed and sprouting out from the top of her head and falling down her back in feathery waves. She was dressed in high heels and a smart gray, wraparound cloth coat that probably sufficed in Texas but was laughable against the New England winter wind. She was shivering. I had to fight for breath against my fear.

"What's wrong?" I demanded. "Why are you here?"

"Calm down," she said. "Everything's fine. I didn't mean to scare you."

"Is it Mom? Did something happen to Mom?"

She reached out and placed her hand on my shoulder to stop me from panicking. "Mom is fine," she said steadily, meeting my eyes. "Everyone is fine."

"Then why are you here like this? Where's Gil? Did he leave you?" Funny how my first thought went to that, to abandonment. My mother's daughter after all.

"Calm down, Grace," my sister said. "I just have a little . . . trouble is all."

"Trouble?" I looked behind her into the street, as though trouble were a dog that had followed her home. "What kind of trouble."

Lena smiled, a you-won't-believe-this smile. "Gil's in jail," she said. "And they're after me, too."

# Chapter Sixteen

When I was fourteen the city of Memphis held an essay contest for junior-high-school students, under the theme "New South Rising." The winning essay would be published in the local newspaper and the writer and her family would get an all-expense-paid trip to Washington, D.C.

I was in the eighth grade, awkward, unattractive, and certain of very few things in life except my ability to do well in school. My English teacher that year was a Mr. LeCarre. We called him, not too originally, "the Car" or sometimes "the Dump Truck" because his sole joy in life seemed to be dumping huge tons of crap all over us. He was forty-five or fifty, thin-haired and watery-eyed, an Anglophile from Blackwater, Mississippi, who dressed like a dandy, spoke with an affected British accent, and frequently sighed aloud in class about the tragic unfairness of being forced to waste his life on the likes of us.

Mr. LeCarre announced the contest in class by saying, with

his usual sneer, "I don't suppose any among you would be even vaguely interested in this. It is my duty to inform you nonetheless." By the time he finished yawning out the rules, I had my theme: *What Memphis and the New South Have to Teach the World.* I had no idea what, if anything, Memphis had to teach anyone, but I knew I could come up with something, and I sensed the idea was precisely the kind of thing the leaders of Memphis wanted to believe about themselves.

For two weeks I worked hard on the paper, but without much success. I did research at the library every afternoon and wrote drafts late into the night, but everything I wrote sounded encyclopedia-like and dull even to my juvenile ears. Then one day I heard a white librarian who had just returned from a trip to Boston talking with a white customer.

"They had some nice restaurants," she said. "But you know, I wouldn't live there for nothing in the world. Too crowded and dirty and cold. And you know, they like to pretend they don't have any"— she lowered her voice—"Negro problems, but really they feel the same way as us. My cousin told me the whole town nearly burned when they starting busing Negro children into white schools a few years back. I tell you, it was ugly! Now he and everybody he knows just send their kids to Catholic school."

Now this was interesting. It was 1978 in the heart of the South—the mid-South, as Memphis liked to call itself, but the South nonetheless—and I'd attended school with white children since kindergarten and never given it a second thought. Yet up there in the North, a place we'd been taught to loathe and distrust and secretly consider superior in all matters racial, they were throwing bricks and hurling stones.

I had to go to the big library downtown to find archived issues of the Memphis *Commercial Appeal,* but when I did I learned that school desegregation (if not integration) in Memphis had been accomplished with almost no violence. By the time I entered kindergarten in 1969, desegregation of the schools was pretty much a fait accompli. I wrote a long essay about busing and desegregation and Crump Junior High, where the photos of Best Dressed, the Most Popular, the Most Likely to Succeed students in the yearbook all looked like some teach-the-world-to-sing Coke commercial, with black and white holding hands and smiling into the camera. This was what Memphis had to teach the nation, I wrote: how to let go of the past and embrace the future, how to realize we were all in the same boat, pulling together toward the shore. I included quotes by everybody I could think of: Martin Luther King, Abraham Lincoln, and, for good measure, General Robert E. Lee.

Monday morning I turned in my essay, confident I'd done well, if not won. Monday afternoon I was called to the principal's office and accused by Mr. LeCarre of plagiarism. He said I could not possibly have written something so good. I left the office running and on the way out I passed the school secretary. She was leaning on the high counter, sipping at a frosty bottle of Coke. She smiled at me.

After school I ran home and told my mother what had taken place. She sat the kitchen table clipping coupons for her weekly trip to the grocery store. When I had finished she kept cutting for a few minutes. Then she put the scissors down and closed her eyes. "Folks don't want you to succeed, Grace. Might as well get used to that."

I stared at her through my tears, horrified. Wasn't she going to do something? Wasn't she going to raise a fuss, to march up to the school and shake Mr. LeCarre by his webby white neck until he cried? But, no, instead she told me it was a waste of time and energy, that you couldn't go over white folks, had to go around them. She said I needed to keep studying hard and not antagonize Mr. LeCarre because I still had to get out of his class with a decent grade.

"But it's not fair!" I cried.

My mother made a noise in her throat. "Who taught you life was fair? I know it wasn't me."

At the time all I saw was a system rigged against me and a mother who would not fight. I learned a lesson from the incident, though not the one either my mother or Mr. LeCarre would have wanted me to learn. I learned that nobody—not your teachers, not your sisters not even your mother—could really be counted upon to go down swinging for you. In the end, all you really had was yourself.

It never occurred to me that my mother acted the way she did because she felt the exact same way herself.

## MEMPHIS, 1972

*She had done the right thing. At least she knew that much.*

Mattie had honored her mother; she had not been selfish, had not put her needs above the needs of someone else. She had suffered for another person, had made the sacrifice. Why then was God so unpleased?

That He was not pleased seemed obvious to Mattie, because after her mother left town nothing seemed to go right. Section by section, bit by bit, her life seemed to tumble apart.

Her bank account was empty. She was late on her bills. Jimmy was gone, though of course she had been the one to do that.

Then there was the house, the place she had once thought of as a sanctuary, as a shelter from the storm. Turned out it was just another petulant child, demanding always the impossible. First the bathroom faucet began to drip. She managed, with much scraping and banging of her knuckles, to change the washer herself, but it did no good: the drip went on. Later that same night a fuse blew in the fuse box. She went down into the basement and changed it, but an hour later it blew again and then again. Finally she yelled at the children not to plug in more than one appliance at a time in the front of the house. Since the television was usually on, that meant no ironing in the front bedroom.

Then, when the snow began to melt it revealed a hole in the roof and a leak right over the living-room couch. Jimmy had been right. For a moment she considered telephoning him, asking if he might stop by and take a look, not to fix it but at least to help her deal with the roofing man. But, no, no, she couldn't do that. She had done the right thing, breaking up with him. Not, as he claimed, because of what he'd said about her mother but because in the end Aunt Eba had been right: a woman couldn't drag mens into the house when she had young daughters around. Especially daughters like Lena.

The girl, more willful by the day, acted out almost constantly. She hiked her skirts and took in the seams of her jeans until they were tight across her butt. She stayed on the telephone all evening and in the streets all afternoon. No amount of yelling or screaming or threatening could get her to act right. She seemed intent on throwing her life away. Her teachers said if she spent as much time paying attention in class as she did whispering to her friends, she would receive straight A's. Aunt Eba said if the girl spent as much time reading the Bible as she did running up and down the street after school, she'd be a saint.

All this Mattie viewed through the scrim of unending work. She had to make up the money her mother had taken, so she signed up for as much overtime as possible. Some days she went in at seven in the morning and did not return home until time for the eleven o'clock news. She would sit in her car in the darkness, too exhausted to walk inside. Her back ached, her feet throbbed, and her fingertips sizzled from a hundred paper cuts.

Then, one night, the supervisor came to her station holding a slip of paper in his pudgy hand. "Miss Mattie." He sneered. "You get more telephone calls than the president."

This time the caller was Aunt Eba and the message, though not an emergency, was urgent enough. Mattie waited for her break fifteen minutes later then ran to the pay phone.

"Your hussy of a daughter jumped on me!" Aunt Eba's voice quavered but not with fear, with indignation. She was furious.

"What? She did what?"

"Jumped on me," Aunt Eba repeated. "Knocked me right to the ground."

Mattie leaned her forehead against the cool metal plate of the pay phone and prayed. "Are you hurt?"

"Bumped my hip against the floor, but I'm still standing."

"What happened?"

Aunt Eba made a retching noise, a kind of sharp clearing of the throat. It was the noise she made when she was disgusted with something, with laziness or good food gone to waste, with pig shit tracked into the house. "Caught her trying to sneak out the house. Crawling out the window like a common thief. Said a friend of hers was in trouble and needed help. I told her there was no help in the world a child could provide another child at ten o'clock at night that wouldn't land them both in jail or the unwed mothers' home. Told her she better get her butt in bed. But when I went to shut the window she said she was going out and there was nothing I could do to stop her. Next thing I know I'm on the floor and she's running out the door."

Mattie groaned. "Where is she now?"

"Lord only knows," Aunt Eba said. "Laid up with some trifling, no-account Negro no doubt."

A woman Mattie did not know came into the break room and got on the phone next to her. Mattie tried to stand up straight, to make it look as though she weren't suffering a family crisis right there in the Memphis distribution center. It was all she could do to raise her head. "Aunt Eba. I'm so, so sorry."

"Not as sorry as you're going to be," her aunt said.

Mattie knew Aunt Eba did not mean the words as a threat, more as commiseration. Still, she heard it like a sentence that would hang over her head the rest of her life. *Not as sorry as you're going to be.*

"Not with a daughter like that," Aunt Eba said. "I'm done, Mattie. Packing my bags tonight and heading home on the first bus."

In the year since Aunt Eba had come to live with them, always saying it was temporary, Mattie had tried now and then to find someone else to watch the kids. Mostly for show, it was true, mostly to show Aunt Eba she had not given up. But even a halfhearted attempt was enough to let her know she would never find anyone to do it, nobody who was trustworthy and decent and whom she could afford. Nobody who wouldn't end up causing more problems than they solved.

No, if Aunt Eba left, Mattie would have to quit her job and stay home to watch the children. Not even so much Sidney, the baby, the youngest, but the girls. Mattie had once thought things would get easier as her children aged, that they would need less watching, but just the opposite was true. Dot was okay, of course. Dot would be fine regardless. But Lena was barely fourteen and already running wild. And she had great influence over Grace, who might get dragged right along with her. Somebody had to be home to keep that from happening. The warden had to be on-site to keep the prisoners from running amok.

"If I wanted to be jumped on and beat up in my own home, I'd have found me a man long time ago," Aunt Eba said. Then, she added, "Warned you, didn't I, about dragging mens into this house. Monkey see, monkey do."

Her supervisor didn't want to hear about family issues. "You still got three hours of your shift," he said. "Unless somebody's in the hospital you got to stay."

"My aunt is elderly and there's been . . . an accident."

"Call an ambulance."

"I need to be there," she said. "My children are frightened."

Her supervisor leaned back in his chair and put his hands behind his head. He stared at Mattie, letting his eyes roam across her breasts. She tried not to flinch.

"I knew a colored lady once. Bred like a rabbit. Had twelve or thirteen kids."

"I'll make up the time," she said.

For a minute he said nothing. Then he brought his feet to the floor with a disgusted slam. "Get," he said. "Make sure you clock out before you leave."

"Yes, sir." She began backing from the room.

"No wages for time not worked," he called after her. "The United States Postal Service is not a welfare agency."

She couldn't seem to get away from the building. She kept rushing to the door only to remember something—the ID she'd left in her locker, the "Addressee Unknown" stamp she'd mistakenly shoved into her uniform pocket—and having to turn around. Once outside, she forgot where her car was parked and had to wander up and down aisles and all around the asphalt maze for nearly ten minutes before finding it. Then she got in and turned on the engine and saw the gas gauge sink farther down to *E*. Somehow the tank was empty, though she tried never to let it get that way. A full tank was important. A full tank said something about how things were in your life. She would have to stop at a gas station on the way home, if she could find one open so late. She looked in her purse and found a dollar and two quarters. She would have to ask the man at the pump for one dollar's worth of gas.

She drove out of the lot, turned the corner, and drove back past the front of the building, past its grand public face. Just as it was supposed to, it reminded her of that building in Greece, the famous one with the big columns marching all around. She had learned about it in college, remembered looking through her history book at photographs. She remembered how tall it stood on that rocky hillside, crumbling but still majestic, the sky behind it a brilliant, framing blue. She remembered thinking how one day she would climb over those rocks and walk up those stairs and look out upon the world from such a magnificent place, a place her mother could never have dreamed of. But now she couldn't even remember the building's name.

# Chapter Seventeen

I stood in the kitchen making coffee. One room away my mysterious fugitive sister was making conversation with one of her only two nieces in the world. "Hello, Paula. How are you today?" Lena asked. She might have been addressing a client, one she could already tell was more interested in looking than in buying.

"I'm making a castle," Paula answered. She had woken up crankily from her nap at the sound of the doorbell, but seemed to be shaking it off.

"That's nice," Lena said.

"I'm a princess."

"Yes," Lena answered. "Aren't we all?"

Talking to children in a way that is neither patronizing to them as kids nor degrading to oneself as an adult is a gift, or, at very least, a skill—one few people possess. I certainly did not possess said skill at all before having children myself, and only marginally afterward. But Lena did. I had seen her engage sullen teenagers, soothe cranky babies, and once charm the training pants right off the tantruming toddler of a wealthy client and his bored and blondly disaffected wife. But the thing with Lena was, she only talked to children if there was some reason to do so, some goal to obtain. Otherwise, she politely but firmly acted as though they did not exist. Some people found such behavior offensive, but I, for one, considered my sister nearly brave. It took bravery to decline to coo and gush over a slobbering baby or nose-picking preschooler being presented before you by his parents as if he were the main course. Usually I gave in and cooed, or at least smiled, just to get it over with. But not Lena. Which is why I was not surprised to hear companionable silence between Paula and her. The only sound from the living room was the crack and clack of plastic as Paula snapped her LEGO bricks together one by one.

When I carried the tray of coffee and juice and crackers into the family room, Lena sat organizing the contents of her purse. Paula lay sprawled across the carpet, intently constructing the LEGO castle of her dreams.

I set Paula up at the coffee table with her grapes, graham crackers, and juice, then handed Lena her coffee. Settling myself into a chair opposite my sister, I said, "So."

"Sew, sew, your drawers to'e," she said with a smile. It was something we used to say as kids, a comeback, devastatingly witty, we thought.

"You going to tell me what's going on?" I asked.

Lena poured cream into her coffee and dipped up two teaspoons of sugar. After a moment she said, "Gil's been arrested for real-estate fraud. They want me to testify against him. If I don't, they're threatening to charge me, too."

I was stunned, too stunned, for a moment, to think. When she'd said Gil was in trouble my mind had immediately leaped to the petty or the sordid: seducing some fifteen-year-old child, perhaps, or running numbers. Which showed, I supposed, what I thought of my brother-in-law.

"What happened?" I said when I could think again. "What is this about?"

Lena looked at me over the top of her coffee cup. "You ever heard of flipping?" she asked.

"As in burgers?"

"As in buying a property then flipping it the next day for a profit," she said. "Pretend you're a speculator. First you find a house in some slumping, run-down neighborhood and you snap it up. It's falling apart: the roof is in shambles and there are drug dealers on the corner, so nobody with any choice wants to live there. You pick it up for five, maybe the one next door to it, too. Then you turn around and sell them, a week later, for a hundred grand. You walk away with ninety-five thousand profit each."

"Sounds like the American way."

"Oh, it is," Lena said. "Nothing illegal about selling something for more than you paid for it. If you can find someone willing to give you a million dollars for your dirty socks, you have every right to do so. The problem is, no one in his or her right mind is going to pay a hundred thousand dollars for a shell in South Dallas."

"Which is where the trouble begins."

Lena nodded and sipped her coffee. "Since you can't find a legitimate buyer for the house, you have to . . . manufacture one. Someone willing to lend you his name, basically. A friend, a distant cousin. Some guy you knew from school who could use an extra five thousand. You set him up as the buyer and arrange a mortgage."

Lena paused to add another teaspoon of sugar to her coffee cup. She was as cool as iceberg lettuce, my big sister. I wanted to tell her if she had to talk to the cops she should not be nearly this cool. It would be difficult for anyone to believe Gil could conceive and arrange such a scam on his own. He was a good-looking man, Gil, in an oil-slicked, Southern kind of way; he could work a certain kind of charm, but bright-burning he was not. It had been Lena who'd introduced him to real estate, Lena who'd coached him through his repeated attempts to pass the real-estate exam. They had only been married two years, but from what I saw it was also Lena who kept them afloat financially.

"Mommy, can you help?" Paula asked.

"In a minute. I'm talking to Aunt Lena now." I turned back to my sister. "How does this speculator convince the bank to make a hundred-thousand-dollar mortgage on a five-thousand-dollar house?"

Lena smiled. "You have to find an appraiser. One who's willing to . . . bend the truth. He appraises the house at a hundred and five. You do some fancy footwork with the buyer's papers, touching up his credit report, creating a few pay stubs from a nonexistent job. Probably even hand him the down payment. And most importantly you hook him up as a first-time homeowner so his loan can be backed by HUD. That makes the bank happy, because if the buyer defaults on his loan—"

"Which he will," I said.

"—the bank can hit the federal government up for their cash."

"Mommy, can you help?"

"You're doing fine, honey," I said, not looking at Paula. If the federal government was involved, then Gil was really in trouble. And Lena, too. "So the bank is happy but HUD is left holding the bag. Which means it's the federal government who's pissed. Oh, Lena. What were—" I had been about to ask what she was thinking but stopped myself. I didn't want to get any closer to a confession than we already had. But Lena misinterpreted my fear as disapproval. Her voice got warm.

"Listen, you try getting a non-HUD-backed loan for one of us from a bank in Texas," she said.

"Mommy?"

"Just a minute, Paula."

"You see how easy it is," Lena said. "You think they want to help us? You think they want to believe we can afford a nice house right next to them? I had this couple, both doctors, both degrees from Duke, and still this fat, white pig of a loan officer put them through every hoop imaginable."

"I'm sorry," I said. "I wasn't . . . I was just surprised that the feds are involved. I'm worried for you."

Lena looked out the window. The sky was low and heavily gray, threatening snow. It was not a sky you would ever see in Texas. "You know how they say, 'They come at dawn'? Well, they do. I was in the shower when I heard the knock. Scared the life from me. By the time I got my robe on and downstairs, they had Gil in handcuffs."

"Mom-my!"

"I said just a minute, Paula." Then, to Lena: "Was it the FBI?"

Lena nodded. "They plan to make an example of him. You know, this uppity nigger. Who in the hell did he think he was pulling one on them?"

It was strange, the note of pride in her voice, of admiration. Not the way she usually spoke of Gil. Maybe he really had pulled the scam by himself. Maybe he'd done it to show her, to finally win her respect.

"You hired an attorney?"

"Yes."

"What does he say?"

Before Lena could answer there was a scream. Paula, pressing too hard on a LEGO, had broken her castle. It fell to the floor in chunks. "Stupid castle!" She picked up a section and flung it across the room, where it struck a framed picture of Eddie and me, standing in a garden on our wedding day. She stood there and watched the piece sail through the air, her little fists clenched together, her face furrowed and scrunched. I responded the way I would have if no one else had been around. I snapped at her.

"What is wrong with you? Are you trying to break something?"

Paula ignored my tone, the way both my children so often did.

I wondered if I shouldn't have spanked them more, the way my aunt Josephine had recommended. "You got to whip them," she always said, "to make them mind."

Paula picked up another chunk of LEGOs and hurled it against the couch, not far from where Lena sat.

"Stupid castle!" she screamed.

"Stop that!" I yelled at her. As if outyelling a child ever did any good.

"I hate Aunt Lena!" Paula cried, then burst into tears.

"Don't say that," I said, but by now I'd regained myself, at least partially. I slid to the floor and pulled my daughter into my lap, holding her.

"It broke! It broke! It broke!"

"Paula. It's just a castle. And we can fix it, see?" I picked up a few LEGOs and snapped them back onto the base. "Why are you so upset?"

Lena watched us, her expression unreadable. My sister had told us all long ago she would never have children. I often wondered if that was one of the reasons she had waited so long to get married, until she was almost forty; to lessen the chance the man would try to push her into motherhood. At first my mother said she'd change her mind about not having babies. Then she said she'd come to regret it. I never asked Lena whether she did in fact regret her choice; it was not a question to ask easily, not if you yourself had children. There was no way not to make it sound like a crow.

"She's tired. Probably woke too soon from her nap," I said to Lena. Half apologizing, half justifying my child's behavior, the way mothers did.

"She's mad," Lena said casually. "At you. For ignoring her and talking to me."

I looked back down at Paula, quieting now. Of course, Lena was right. Of course, of course. That she could know this about my daughter when I had not seen it suddenly filled me with despair. What was I doing, in a role I stank at? In a life I did not want?

Lena was looking dreamily away now, toward the window. My moment of crisis undetected. She asked, "Do you ever blame Mom?"

"For what?" I asked.

"Oh, you know," Lena said. "The way your life turned out."

"My life is just fine," I said, but even I could hear the defensiveness in my voice. So I lightened it, then raised my hand and swept the air, the way Eddie had that night in the bathroom. "I mean, who wouldn't want all this, right?"

I laughed, a little. But Lena just looked at me, and then at Paula, falling asleep in my lap. I followed my sister's eyes to my daughter's face, and for some reason I remembered an incident that had taken place the week before Valerie died. I'd been downstairs trying to tackle the mountain of laundry that seemed to be my life. I heard a bump and a pause and then a wail from upstairs. Harriet. "Mommy!" she screamed. "Mommy!" And instead of terror or fear or even concern, what came to me first, what climbed up my back and seized my throat, was black-eyed fury, an irrational rage at never getting a second to myself. *What now,* I thought, stomping up the stairs. *Why can't these people leave me the hell alone?* And when I got upstairs and found Harriet with a swelling lip from having bounced against a wall, I felt terrible. And I knew it would happen again.

Lena said, "You know Gil's favorite question to me? 'Why you so hard, woman?' Of course a marshmallow is hard compared to Gil," Lena went on. "But he's not the first man to point out a certain stoniness around my heart. And, yes, for that I blame Mom a little bit," Lena said. "More than a little bit."

"Oh, come on." I was in no mood for a blame-the-mother talk. "Aren't we past all that?"

Lena sat up, slammed her cup down hard upon its little saucer. I flinched. "Do you remember that summer I was seventeen and I left home?" Lena asked. "I went to Texas to stay with Uncle King and his wife?"

"Of course. But what—"

"I had an abortion that summer." Lena looked at me sharply, as if trying to catch my reaction before it disappeared. "I was pregnant and I went there and got rid of it."

My eyes went to Paula; I had the urge to place my hands over her ears but she was curled in my lap, sucking her thumb and drifting off to sleep. "I know, Lena," I said in a voice just above a whisper. "Mom told me a long time ago."

Lena threw up her hands. "Oh! Oh, of course she did! What was I thinking—that something like that could remain a secret in this family? Well, did she also tell you the things she said to me, the names she called me?"

Paula stirred in my lap. "Lower your voice," I ordered, but Lena was gone, falling fast and deep into in the past.

"I thought I was doing a hard but necessary thing, that I was saving myself from the one terrible outcome she had always warned against," she cried. "God knows I didn't expect her to dance a jig when she found out, but I thought she would at least see how necessary it was, how brave I had been to do it alone. Instead she called me a murderer and said I was going to hell!"

"Lena!" I hissed, and she seemed to come back to herself. She looked at me and then at Paula, and fell back against the couch, her hands to her face.

"Lena," I said quietly, stroking my daughter's hair so she would not stir. "That was twenty years ago. She was upset. You can't still be hanging on to that. You can't still be taking it so . . . personally."

"Why not? I learned from the best."

In that I knew she was right. My mother had a bag full of hurts in her bedroom, and every morning she opened the bag and sorted through to keep things fresh. Some were big, like my father, and some were small, like Dot's man friend who declined to eat at our house. Was that what happened when your mother abandoned you—was every slight, every rejection after that, personal? How did people live through so much pain? How did they even breathe?

Suddenly I felt as if I could not breathe myself. I staggered upward, found my feet, then hefted a still-sleeping Paula onto my shoulder. "I have to go pick up Harriet. Now. It's time."

Lena caught my gaze and held it. "What's wrong?"

"Nothing."

Lena watched me a minute longer, then dropped her gaze. I knew she thought I was angry about what she'd said about our mother, but that wasn't it. Not completely or even mostly. But I was afraid to try to explain it.

"Okay," she said finally. "You go on. I'll be here. Unless the feds come for me."

She smiled to show me she was joking. Except I wasn't sure if she really was. "Are they looking for you, Lena?"

She shrugged, feigning casualness. "I talked to them before I left Texas. With my attorney. They think I'm going to cooperate. That's why they let me go, to 'get my affairs in order.' That's what the man said, but what he meant was to get ready to go to jail."

"So you just ran away?"

"Hopped a plane to Chicago. I have a friend there and I spent the night with her. Then I took the train here."

"If anybody's looking for you they can track you through Amtrak's reservation system," I said.

"I paid cash. Used my friend's driver's license. She was going to report her wallet stolen today or tomorrow."

I looked at my sister. "Quite the criminal mastermind, aren't you?"

Lena stood, too, and stretched. "I watch *Law & Order*," she said. "Look, I don't even know if they are looking for me. They got Gil; they might be satisfied with only destroying one of us. But it doesn't hurt to be careful."

"So I guess what you're saying is you're a fugitive from justice," I said. "And you're not going back."

Lena tossed back her hair. "I'm following the drinking gourd."

_____

*Paula dozed in the minivan on the way to Harriet's preschool, but I* felt more awake than I had in ages. The thermometer had inched its way up to forty-nine, and the mild air washed over my face as I drove with the window cracked. Out on the sidewalks, wet with melting snow, people lingered, taking in what they could of the weak winter sun. It was still only January; no one was so stupid as to believe winter was over. But every now and then you caught a break.

I thought about what Lena had said about blaming our mother for what had become of her life. It had made me angry, but I couldn't judge her for it; that's what people did. I'd done it, too. Maybe there were five stages of daughterhood, just as there were five stages of grief. Adoration, aggravation, separation, normalization, and always, always, blame. Lena blamed my mother for being too something; my mother blamed my grandmother for being not enough. The pendulum swung back and forth. So what difference did it make in the end?

Lena was planning to run away, to slip into Canada. She thought she could just cross the border as a tourist and not look back. The American border guards were more concerned about who was sneaking in than who was sneaking out, and the Canadians would not know and would not care about some black chick not even formally accused of real-estate fraud in Texas, a state they disliked anyway.

Lena was going to Canada. She needed money; the feds had frozen her bank accounts. She needed a plane ticket to Toronto or a car she could drive up to Montreal. She needed my help to become a fugitive from justice and I would help her, of course— she was my sister and duty counts. I would give her money and maybe the car or a ride to the train station. I would point her in the right direction, start her on her way to a reimagined life. And maybe I would go along.

For the first time I let myself really taste the idea, rolled it around in my mouth, and waited to be struck blind or dumb. It occurred to me again that there was something wrong with me, something diseased. I had always been suspicious of other parents of my acquaintance; I'd always thought they were exaggerating their parental devotion, pulling on the mask of fulfilling motherhood. But maybe I was wrong. Maybe no one else felt the way I did. Maybe all those forty-year-old women making goo-goo faces at their toddlers in the park were truly giddy with joy, were having the time of their lives. Maybe some women really lived for clutching fingers and endless readings of *Goodnight Moon* and noodle Mother's Day cards. Maybe they really never looked at their children with hatred. Not even briefly. Not even once. Maybe I really was the monster. And maybe my children would be better off without me.

I guess I was looking for a sign. I didn't have to look very far. As I pulled up at the school, I felt a first, faint trickle between my thighs. Reaching down, I touched the blood.

Free at last.

# Chapter Eighteen

I called Eddie's mother from the car, asking whether she had any time free that afternoon.

"Of course, dear," said Louise. "Is there a problem?"

"Oh no," I said. "It's just that I have a doctor's appointment and the babysitter canceled." Amazing how smoothly the lie rolled from my lips, how smoothly and easily. Not to mention the unplanned cunning of the lie; Louise would wonder hopefully if the doctor in question was, in fact, my ob-gyn. Nearly as much as her precious son, Louise wanted a boy child born to carry on the family name.

"You know I always love to see my granddaughters," Louise purred into the phone. "I'm free all morning and all afternoon. You bring them right over this second."

The girls cheered when I told them they were going to see Grandmother. "I'll bet she makes cocoa," Harriet said.

"With marshmallows!" squealed Paula.

Harriet lowered her voice to a stage whisper. "*She* always gives us as many as we want!"

At my mother-in-law's house I squatted down to hug them both together, sucking in the sweaty, vanilla smell of them. My stomach hurt, and I had to fight the fluttering of my voice. "I love you guys," I said. The girls squirmed and squiggled against my grip, eager to break free. I let them go. "Bye, Mommy," they called, racing toward their grandmother's kitchen with hardly a backward glance. I wanted to be boosted by that; I tried to tell myself, *See? See? They'll be just fine.* But I knew it was a lie. Somebody always has to be sacrificed. And I was choosing them.

It took me a minute to stand, so wobbly were my knees.

"Are you all right, dear?" Louise asked, clearly fighting down her delight. "You look a little peaked."

"Fine," I said. "Just fighting a cold." Hand on the wall, I pushed myself up and left.

Once outside, I went straight to the car and then straight to the bank and then straight home, the window open, the radio tuned to a classic rock station, the volume cranked as high as it would go. It was painful, music at that volume. My head throbbed from the noise, which was what I wanted, what I needed to have. By the time I got home my eyes were tearing from the pain.

"You got a curling iron?" Lena asked, yawning. Instead of a nap she had taken a shower and washed and dried her hair and now stood in the bathroom, rooting around in the cabinet beneath the sink. "I don't want to dig mine out of my suitcase."

"It's in there," I said. "Somewhere."

With a grunting noise, Lena bent lower and stuck her hand far into the cabinet. "Got it," she said, straightening up. "Where are the kids?"

I said, "Took them to Eddie's mother's place." There must have been something funny in my voice, because Lena stopped fiddling with the curling iron and looked at me.

"You did."

I nodded.

"Okay," she said.

I glanced behind her; on the floor of the bathroom, in a basket, lay a jumble of Paula and Harriet's bath-time toys: windup frogs that swam, a boat that scooted, a waterlogged doll or two, assorted measuring cups in plastic green and blue. For the longest time I'd been meaning to get the bleach up from the laundry room and scrub them all clean. What kind of mother let her children play with mildewy toys?

I looked straight at my sister. "I want to come," I said. "I want to come with you."

Then I spread my feet and waited for the reaction, whatever it was. I think I expected shock, perhaps horror or outrage or disgust or all of the above. I think I expected—and maybe I wanted—Lena to pick up the whip of society and flail me for the great sin I had decided to commit.

But Lena said nothing. For one long minute she looked at me, her face expressionless. Then she turned and plugged in her curling iron, pushing the dial to maximum. "Give me thirty minutes," she said.

*While Lena curled I packed. I raced down into the basement for my duffel bag.* It was huge and blue and nylon, purchased years before for a grad-school graduation trip to Cancún. Eddie had wanted to come but I said no; it had seemed important for me to take some solo time then, to fly to a beach and sit alone and face the future undistracted. I bought a duffel bag instead of a traditional suitcase because no matter how full you packed it and no matter how heavy it was, if you were strong, and I was strong, you could always just hoist it up over your shoulder and go.

I rushed around the house trying to decide what to take. What did I need, what I did need for—what did I need for now? My sweaters and jeans and dresses and boots and underwear, of course. My first-edition W.E.B. DuBois, my journals, the diaries of my teenage years. I packed the thin gold cross Dot had given me for Christmas one year and the small ruby earrings Eddie gave me for our fifth anniversary, but I left his grandmother's engagement ring. I backed up every file on my computer onto a flash drive the size of a lipstick tube and slipped it into my purse. I packed my toothbrush and facial lotion. I packed, without looking at it and trying not to think, the framed photo of Harriet and Paula on the beach at Kitty Hawk, digging their toes into the sand.

I left: blender and microwave, towels and sheets, duvet covers and crystal candlesticks. I left the silver tea set from Eddie's grandmother. I left the keys to the Subaru; I didn't want Eddie driving the children around in the rusting piece of junk he drove. I took no snacks.

It would be nice to say how pained I was, how weighed down with guilt and remorse. But really what I felt was a kind of wild exhilaration. A great wind of purpose had risen and I didn't think about its source or direction; I just blew along.

"Are we taking your van?" Lena asked.

"Excuse me?"

"Are we taking your van? Are we keeping it?"

"No," I said, then stopped in my tracks, surprised at the strength of my reaction. I guessed I'd been thinking we would get a rental car or take the train. Or rather, I had not thought that far ahead. But somehow the idea of taking the van from the children seemed selfish, downright nonmaternal. Ludicrous, of course, given the nature of what I was about to do; the human brain is a terrifying piece of machinery. *Run away, abandon your children, but for goodness' sake leave the minivan! It has antilock brakes!* I laughed out loud at the insanity of it. Lena gave me a sharp look.

"We'll drive to the airport and rent something," I said, lifting my bags. "We can leave the car in long-term parking for Eddie to pick up."

"What about a note?" Lena asked.

"What?" I was scanning the living room, trying to see if there was anything else I needed to take.

"A note?" Lena drawled, with exaggerated Southern deliberateness. "You know? Some words on a piece of paper explaining the situation to those left behind?"

She seemed to be trying to slow me down, but I did not want to be slowed. I wanted movement, action. My feet itched inside my boots, my knees twanged and throbbed. I felt electrified. "I'll leave a note about the children."

Lena studied me. "Okay."

I raced upstairs to the computer, grabbed a piece of paper from the printer, and ran back down again. *Eddie,* I wrote, not daring the *Dear.* How could I. *The children are at your mother's and safe. I took the emergency fund from the kitchen and some money—$2,000— from the savings account, the least I will need. Forge my name on anything you want, that's fine with me, and don't forget the savings bonds in the bottom drawer upstairs.* I did not even bother reading it over, knowing how ridiculous and inadequate it would sound. At the bottom of the page I scrawled *I'm sorry.* Below that I signed *Grace.*

I propped the note on the dining room table between the salt and pepper shakers, our usual place. Eddie would pull into the driveway, see the darkened house. He would wonder but not worry, my man of probabilities. He'd open the door, flip on the light. He'd see the note and pick it up and start to read.

"Let's go," I said to Lena. "Let's go, let's go right now."


*Lena had taken her bag out to the car but she'd returned and was walking toward the kitchen.* "I'm ready," she said. "Just want to grab something to eat. Did I see some turkey in the fridge?"

"Let's go." I pushed open the screen door, stepped onto the porch. "We'll eat on the road."

"We need to watch our money," Lena said, still moving. "We have to be practical."

She was right; with just twenty-five hundred dollars in my pocket and who knew how little in Lena's purse, we had nothing to squander, not even the cost of a Happy Meal. But I didn't care. The air in the house was suddenly cyanide; even the porch wasn't far enough away. "Now, Lena!" I screamed. "I want to go now!"

Lena turned around and I saw the look I had expected earlier. I had no right to feel hurt, but when has that ever stopped anyone?

"It's funny," she said, walking slowly toward me. "Earlier, when I was curling my hair in the bathroom, just before you came in, I was thinking of Grandmother."

This startled me, that Lena should be thinking of the woman I had been chasing the past few weeks. But I didn't have time to focus on it; I wanted to move. "Let's go," I said.

But Lena was in a suddenly pensive mood. She stalled in the hallway, staring into space and fluffing her fresh curls with one hand. "Weird, isn't it? I don't really know why I was thinking of her, but I was thinking maybe I should try to get in touch. I was thinking she and I might hit it off now that I'm grown. We might have a connection, be more alike than me and Mom. Mom and I never really got along, not even when I was little. Not like her and Dot. Or even her and you."

Lena stopped to lift her purse from the hook at the side of the door. I remembered hanging that hook our second day in the house so I would always have a place for my keys.

"I was thinking that if Grandmother had stuck around, she might have liked me better. I might have finally been somebody's favorite." Lena laughed. "But then again, maybe not."

Lena stood next to me on the porch now, the late-afternoon air cooling as it blew across our faces. "Then again, maybe you would have claimed that spot, Grace," Lena said. "Seeing you today, I think Grandmother would say you're doing her proud."

*Lena offered to drive but she was dangerously unfamiliar with Boston and its crazy tangle of streets.* "Just until we get out of town," she suggested, holding out her hand for the keys. From the way she studied my face I could tell I looked as wobbly as I felt. I took a breath, struggled to rally.

"I'm fine," I said.

"Just until we're on our way."

"If I'm going to do this, I need to do it," I told her.

Lena raised an eyebrow at me. "If?"

I said nothing, just opened my door and climbed inside.

It was late afternoon by then, the day defeated, the sun already slinking away. Snow that had melted with the day was beginning to glaze. We made our way from the exile of my suburban town into Boston proper, inching along behind school buses and cabdrivers and frantic minivans. Teenagers set free from school clustered on the steps of corner bodegas, the girls hatless and shivering in their tight jeans and tiny jackets, the boys hulking and warm in their puffed-up coats and pointy sweatshirt hoods. At a stoplight I eased down the brakes and wondered if those boys knew what they mimicked with those hoods, what racial nightmare they recalled. Probably not. They thought their enemies were one another. They thought the fight was about props and respect and territory that no one really owned. Was that why Eddie wanted a son, to counter the damaged versions of himself he saw every day on the train? He had been a Big Brother since I'd known him and planned to connect to the organization in Boston once we settled in. Only he wouldn't have time now. Not while raising two girls on his own.

An angry horn blew behind us. I looked up; the light was green.

"You okay?" Lena asked as I stepped on the gas.

"Fine," I said. But I realized I'd been thinking of Harriet and Paula as children, as kids, as daughters, but not as girls who would someday grow into young women like those standing on the corner, underdressed and shivering because it was more important to be seen, to be visible, than it was to be warm. But no, not exactly like those girls. They would have advantages: nice house, nice schools, lessons of every kind and stripe. The absence of physical and economic violence in their faces, the luxury of walking home without having to watch their backs. Most important, a father who loved them and who remained. Unlike their mother. Would that be enough?

I turned a corner and took the on-ramp to the highway. On the other side of the median, traffic crawled along, commuters fleeing the urban core. But on our side traffic flowed easily. It was too late in the day and too early in the week for a mass exodus inward. I thought about how little I had liked Boston: the hard winters, the hard accents, the steely segregation still. Boston remained foreign to me, even after months of residency, in a way other cities had not. Strange to think my children would grow up in such a place, loving it probably. Cheering the Red Sox and walking the Common. Calling it their hometown.

"Maybe you could drive a little slower," Lena said.

I looked down at the speedometer; I was doing forty in a fifty-five zone. From the corner of my eye I saw a blue sports car pull out from behind and speed past, the driver shaking his fist.

"Just because everybody else in Boston drives like a lunatic doesn't mean I have to," I said. But I sped up anyway.

We made the airport in record time. I missed the sign to long-term parking and had to circle the perimeter twice. Finally, though, we found it, a vast wasteland of abandoned automobiles. We drove up and down six rows before finding a space. I eased the van into position and turned the key. The engine sighed off.

Lena unbuckled her seat belt and turned to face me. "So?"

"Sew, sew, your drawers to'e," I said.

"Come on, Grace."

"Come on what?"

One corner of Lena's lip twisted up. "Listen, sister dear. One thing I don't need is to be dragging you and your regrets around for the rest of my life. You need to make up your mind and do it now. Before we go any further."

I said, "I'm here, aren't I."

"Are you?"

"Yes."

Lena scoffed. "I don't know why you're doing what you're doing and I don't need to know," she said. "But you sure as hell do."

I opened my mouth to talk, then closed it, at a loss as to how to explain it. What, really, could I say? That I felt as though I were suffocating? Because that lovely life of mine had wrapped itself around my neck and was choking me to death? As soon as I put the reasons into words they began to fall apart.

So instead I feinted. "Goethe said, 'Never by reflection but only by doing is self-knowledge possible.' "

Lena looked at me. "I guess I'm supposed to know who that is, right? Or feel bad for not knowing?"

I sighed. That's what happened when you tried ducking away from something; you got clumsy and ended up stepping on somebody's foot. "I didn't mean it that way."

But Lena was ruffled and not about to be soothed. "You know what your problem is, Grace?"

"I have several ideas. But go ahead with your version."

"You're greedy," she said, pulling her coat tighter. With the engine off, the car was beginning to cool. "Greedy, greedy, greedy. You want to have your cake and eat it, too."

Okay. So here it was at last, the attack I'd expected since I told her I wanted to leave. Lord knew I deserved it. But since when has that ever meant anything? "I beg your pardon. I didn't know it was against the law to be conflicted about leaving your family."

"What's against the law," Lena said, "is abandoning your kids."

"Screw you!"

Lena brushed a stray hair from her eyes, as casual as a runway model. She had stabbed me good and she knew it. She could afford to be cool.

I twisted in my seat, put my back against the door. "It must be nice," I said, facing her straight on, "to cut and run without a second thought. It must be nice to not care who you've left behind, swinging from a tree."

Lena pushed a lock of hair behind her ear but said nothing.

"Why did you even marry Gil?" I asked.

Lena smiled. "Do you remember the Oklahoma City bombing? It's gotten pushed aside now, after the World Trade Center, but in Texas it's still fresh. I was in my office the day it happened, alone, everybody else gone out of town on some conference. I turned on the television and there was all this smoke and fire and people stumbling around bleeding and it was terrible. So many people, dead. And I sat there watching and, for some reason, all I could think was, what about the single people in that building? The husbands and wives and children, of course, would be missed and mourned, but what about the single people? What about the secretary on the second floor who lived with her cat? Who would look for her? Who would even know she had gone?"

Stunned, I turned away and looked out the window. Sleet was coming; the first icy drops pelted the windshield and splintered in the harsh blue-white light of the streetlamp. I turned on the ignition. Just to warm the air.

"I'm sorry," I told my sister.

"I'm not," she said. "People make choices, at least the brave ones do. I'm willing to live with mine. The question of the hour is whether you are."

It was the question of the hour all right. I knew the price of love, at least for me: some extinction of myself. Which was the better choice? Or maybe that wasn't the question at all. Maybe the only real question was about the children. Maybe the question was whether I was going to keep this pendulum of pain that I'd inherited swinging through my family or not.

Right then my cell phone began to ring. It was stuck down in the bottom of my purse, but it cut through the car's atmosphere like a gun retort.

"Crap," Lena said, "It's Eddie."

But it was too soon for Eddie to have gotten home, and very few other people had the number to my cell phone. I rarely gave it out because I hated the damn thing; I had only gotten one in the first place because of the kids.

"Oh God." I began digging frantically through my purse.

"What's wrong?"

I was convinced it was Louise. Something had happened, something was wrong. In a flash I saw my mother-in-law standing in some hospital corridor, gray-faced and crying, cell phone to her ear. By her hand she held one of my daughters, but not the other one. This was my punishment. Not from God; I didn't believe in a God who acted that way, who visited the sins of the mother upon the daughters, who punished the innocent along with the damned. I didn't believe in a God who did such things, but I did believe in Life. Life was a bitch.

"Where's the damn phone?"

"Calm down," Lena said.

"What if it's the children? What if something happened to the children?" My hand slipped onto something cool and metallic. By the light of the streetlamp I looked at the faceplate. It wasn't Louise, after all. It was my mother.

"Hello?"

"Grace?"

"Mom? What's wrong?" I asked.

In the background one of my mother's children made her strange, animal sound. "I just got a call," my mother said. "From some woman in Omaha. A nurse at a nursing home."

"What?" I couldn't make sense of what she was saying. I couldn't make sense of anything anymore—who I was or what I wanted or what I was doing there in the airport parking lot with my fugitive sister by my side. Was this a leap toward freedom or a moment of insanity? Surely it was a personal trouble, but was it only that?

I couldn't seem to figure it out, I had no framework upon which to hang the tsunami of the last few weeks, all the frustration and fear and desperation and grief. That's what academics did, hang things on frameworks. But my framework had collapsed. My imagination, sociological or otherwise, had failed. I couldn't seem to think my way out.

"She said Mama's there, at the nursing home," my mother said. "She said Mama is about to die."

"Grandmother? Grandmother's in some nursing home in Omaha?"

"I have to go there," my mother said. "I want you to come with me."

"What?"

"I want you to come along," my mother said.

"What?" I shook my head, trying to grasp what she was saying. "You want me to come to Omaha?"

"Yes, Grace," my mother said. "Dot's in London at some kind of conference. She said she would come, but . . . I don't know. It would take her forever, wouldn't it? And I don't know where in the world Lena is. She seems to have fallen off the face of the earth!"

I looked across the car at my sister, who was staring at me with concern. "I talked to Lena yesterday," I said. "She's fine."

"Fine? Where is she? Why hasn't she called."

"She's, uh, she's . . . on vacation with Gil. Somewhere in Mexico. A second honeymoon. You know . . . trying to patch things up."

My mother made a dismissive sound, but across from me Lena nodded with appreciation and applauded silently. "What about Sidney?" I asked, to steer the conversation onto safer ground. But I knew better than that. Sidney was the boy, after all. She would never bother him unless she really, really needed to.

"This new woman of his has got him wrapped around her finger," my mother said. "I don't want to get in the middle of that. No, I need you to come, Grace. I need you."

"But—" I started to say that I couldn't go to Omaha, that I

was busy, that it was impossible. But I stopped myself. What was I going to say—that I couldn't go to Omaha because I was running away to Canada?

Closing my eyes, I said, "Mom, just let me think a second."

Over on her side of the car Lena made a noise. "Ah," she said. "Saved by the bell."

*I offered to put Lena on a flight to Montreal, but she insisted I drive* her to South Station instead and get her a one-way ticket on the train. "Even if they are looking for me, they won't think to look on the train," Lena said. "People in Texas don't even know how to spell Amtrak, let alone figure out its schedule."

We stood together in the middle of the station, next to a large, circular coffee bar. All around us people swarmed and swirled and jostled for space in the coffee line. Because oil interests were running the nation and because Amtrak was slowly sinking beneath the weight of governmental indifference and bureaucratic ineptitude, Lena would have to take a complicated route down through New Haven and then back up through Vermont to reach Montreal, but the good news was that the train was leaving in twenty minutes. The big board flashed the train's imminent arrival outside on track number nine.

Still, I wasn't ready to give in. My guilt about abandoning my sister at the last minute was pressing me to press her to take the plane. "It'll take all night," I said. "The flight would have you there in an hour. This is more dangerous."

Lena patted my arm. "I'll be fine," she insisted. "I can pretend to be a glamorous movie star having an adventure. On the run from my landlord, like that movie we used to watch. You know the one I mean—the one with the sisters? And Bing Crosby?"

I knew instantly. *White Christmas.*

Lena snapped her fingers. "Right! Bing and somebody else, somebody funny . . ."

"Danny Kaye."

"And Rosemary Clooney," Lena added, "before she got old and fat. And that scary skinny white chick who danced with Danny Kaye. You know Rosemary must have hated to see her skinny butt swish on the set."

"Yeah," I said. "But Rosemary got the last laugh. I have no idea who that skinny white chick was."

Lena made a little twirling motion with her hand, as if she were waving a fan, and said a fragment from one of the movie's many songs. "Lord, help the mister . . ."

". . . who comes between me and my sister," I said, finishing the phrase. A memory flooded back to me, one in which Lena and Dot and I flounced around the living room singing that song and waving sheets in substitution for the giant feathers Rosemary and the skinny chick had used in the film. We always made Sidney be our audience. He would sit on the couch and clap enthusiastically as we sang full tilt and completely off-key. Funny that four poor little black kids growing up in Memphis should love so deeply the starlight story of two white women and two white men dancing and singing their way through life.

Lena smiled and shifted her overnight bag from one shoulder to the other. "Sure you don't want to come along? Last chance for escape."

"Not sure at all," I said truthfully. "But it seems that God has taken a hand."

"He usually does," Lena said. "One way or the other."

"Mom needs me," I said. "I have to go help her through this thing."

Lena raised one of her perfectly manicured eyebrows. "This is about Mom, then?" she asked.

The skepticism in her voice was so arch it could have propped up the thirty-foot ceiling in the station where we stood. I laughed. "Oh, I don't know. Isn't everything? Isn't everything everybody ever does about their mother in some way?"

"You tell me," Lena said. "You're the sociologist."

"But not a shrink."

"Close enough," my sister said.

There was a hiss and a loud gurgle of sound, and the public-address system buzzed to life. *Now boarding, on track number nine* . . . A woman in a dark blue uniform threw open a set of doors leading to the tracks and a crowd of people began moving outside. We followed them.

"Well, I guess that's the reason to have children, huh?" Lena said, wrapping her arms around herself as we hit the frigid air. "Somebody to help you in your old age. Your hour of need."

The word *children* caught me like a sharp poke in the ribs and I flinched, thinking of Harriet and Paula. Nobody would expect them to show up forty years in the future in my hour of need, not if I did what I was planning to do. And what were they doing at that moment, as I stood shivering on the platform with Lena by my side? Were they sad? Were they missing me? Or did Louise have them well in hand.

"I guess it is," I said. "One of the reasons, anyway."

"Which leaves me where?" she asked lightly. I put my hand on top of hers.

"With siblings," I said. "That leaves you with Dot and Sidney and me. Especially me."

Lena smiled but said nothing. She opened her mouth and breathed, watched her breath condense in the cold, damp air. She shook her head, as if such a thing were too ridiculous to be believed. "I don't know how you live up here," she said. "I guess Montreal will be worse."

"But not Omaha," I said. "Come with me. Mom would love to see you; it would mean so much to her to have us both there while she's going through this thing."

"It'll mean a lot to her to have you there," Lena said.

"You're her daughter, too," I said. "She loves you."

Lena said nothing for a moment. Then: "Well, at least one of those sentences is true." Before I could respond the conductor stepped onto the platform and called, "All aboard!" Lena picked up her bag and stepped forward, but I grabbed my sister and pulled her into a hug.

"Be careful," I said. "Call my cell phone as soon as you get wherever you're going."

I felt her head nodding against my shoulder. "Tell Mom I'm sorry," she whispered.

"I will."

"About her mother, I mean," Lena said. "Tell her I know how much that is going to hurt."

*There was a little Internet café across the street from the station,* so I went over there and logged on to a travel Web site, searching for a flight to Omaha. There were none for that evening, as it turned out. There was, though, a late, last flight to Chicago, through which I would have to pass to reach the Cornhusker State. I considered taking the Chicago flight, then spending the night in an airport hotel and heading on to Omaha. Or I could simply stay in Boston one more night and fly straight to Omaha the following day, a plan that, objectively speaking, made much more sense. In fact, now that my heart had slowed a little and my thinking cleared, it seemed just a bit melodramatic even to think of flying off to Chicago just to get out of town. As if I were the one running from the law. As if I were running for my life, hotfooting it across the river, hounds on my heels.

The whole time I was making deliberations I kept expecting my cell phone to ring—Louise tracking me down or Eddie wondering. It was nearly 7 P.M. by the time I put Lena on the train. Eddie would have arrived home by then, walked up the driveway to the darkened house with a sliver of ice forming in his gut. He would have turned on the light, found the note, sat on the stairs in the hallway to read it again and again and again. He would have run upstairs to check my closets, the bureau drawers. He would have telephoned his mother and told her he was on his way.

And the children. Louise would have fed them dinner by now. Louise believed in dinner on the table at six sharp, and no chalky mac and cheese from a box and soggy hot dogs lying limply beside. No, Louise would have magically fried up a chicken, whipped up some mashed potatoes, and baked some fresh, hot popovers. And, even more magically, my kids would have eaten every bite, without complaint. They always ate so adventurously at Louise's house, so that Louise thought my complaints about their finicky habits exaggerated and ridiculous. Which probably they were.

There was a Marriott just off the highway, a little south of downtown; I'd seen the sign on my many lost wanderings up and down the hell of Interstate 93. It was a squat and boxy little building, one step up from a motel, really, one story stacked atop another and stretching straight back from the street like a giant toothpaste box. But the lobby was brightly lit and manned twenty-four hours and the room doors opened inside to a hallway instead of out onto a balcony, and the exit doors locked from the inside. All important safety considerations for a woman traveling alone.

Once in the room I pulled my cell phone from my purse and, without letting myself pause to think about it, dialed home. Eddie answered on the second ring. His voice had that clipped, I-am-not-pissed tone he used with wunderkind white boys and secretaries who thought he was the deliveryman.

"It's me," I said.

In the pause that followed I heard an ambulance race past on the street outside, its siren wailing into the night.

"Is this a joke, Grace? Because it's not very funny," he said finally.

"How are the children?" I asked, but Eddie didn't hear me. His voice was rising into the phone.

"Or is this about the . . . baby? Is that it—you're pissed off at my reaction to what you did? So you're acting out, running away? Where are you—in some hotel sipping white wine?"

"Eddie," I said, in fact eyeing the minibar with faint desperation. "How are the kids? Are they still at your mother's or did you bring them home?"

It was an astonishingly arrogant question to ask, given the circumstances; still, I could not help myself. Eddie let out a harsh laugh.

"You have a hell of a lot of nerve, you know that?" he said, but his voice was calm again. Eddie was not the type to yell or curse me out or smash his fist against the wall. All of that was way too ghetto for him. "They're sleeping at my mother's house. I had to work late and she had already bathed them and put them to bed when I got there. Because of course you were nowhere to be found."

I fell backward onto the bed, closed my eyes. "I'm sorry. I am."

Eddie said, "You know, I always knew you didn't need me. I knew that, I did. Grace the Strong, Grace the Independent Woman, doing things her own way."

He said "independent" with a sneer, but I didn't jump on it, not even in my head. I knew that it wasn't strictly true that Eddie could be happy only if I was weak, but that the truth was far more complicated. He had always told me how much he appreciated my strength, and I'd believed it, and so had he. And the fact that he was never happier than when I was pregnant with Harriet, and so sick I could hardly move from the couch, or when I was down with the flu, or when I broke my ankle slipping on the ice—these circumstances I'd written off. And the few times he'd used my so-called strength against me I tried to attribute to something else. His mother, his stress. Like the time we went hiking in the mountains of North Carolina, and I'd just won an invitation to a fellowship that would take me away for a month, and he'd been a little upset, and had started hiking ahead of me on the trail, a little at first, then a little more, until suddenly he rounded a boulder and was gone. And when I finally caught up to him nearly forty minutes later and asked why he'd left me behind, he'd seemed genuinely surprised. "I thought you'd be fine," he said. "I thought you were self-sufficient." What could I say? Because, of course, I had been fine. I'd stayed on the trail, rationed my water, hiked within myself. No problem at all.

"I always knew you didn't need me," Eddie said again. "But I guess I thought you needed the children. I guess I thought you were a real woman in that way, at least."

"My grandmother is dying," I said. "She's in Omaha. My mother called me today to fly out there and be with her."

"What?" Eddie was startled now.

"I'm going there, to be with her while her mother dies," I told him. "After that, I don't know."

"Grace—"

"Don't forget to give Harriet her echinacea," I said. "I'm turning the cell phone off. But I'll check it every hour. If there's an emergency, leave me a message and I'll call back."

"Grace, this is ridiculous," Eddie yelled. "What do you want? What's it going to take to make you stop this craziness?"

My scientist husband, who believed all of life could be reduced to a formula. Sex plus sacrifice equaled motherhood. Regret plus selfishness equaled life.

I hung up the phone.

# Chapter Nineteen

An airport is an airport is an airport; still, you can tell something about the city in which it exists by the way people move through such an edifice. From its size and structure and brightness, from the kinds of shops lining the concourse, from the level of controlled hostility or cold indifference affected by the service personnel. In the Omaha airport I watched two gate attendants, one black and female, the other white and male and clearly gay, joking around as they tapped their keyboards. I bought a bottle of water from a frosted blonde at a kiosk who smiled and offered that the bus was the cheapest way into town.

My mother, when she finally appeared, was the last one through the security gate, lumbering past the guard long after everyone else had rushed through.

Before the children came along I'd made it a priority to visit my mother three or four times a year. But after Harriet and Paula were born, flying to Memphis became more expensive and more difficult and my visits dwindled to one or two. And so it had been more than eight months since I'd last seen my mother. In the middle of life, in our twenties and thirties and forties, eight months seems but the blink of an eye. But one thing parenthood taught you was how long eight months could be, how many worlds and lifetimes it could encompass. How many selves. In eight months Harriet had grown nearly an inch, gained a shoe size, memorized her address and telephone number, learned to write her name. She had left toddlerhood behind and entered what anthropologists call "middle childhood," and suddenly her brain, responding to some preset biological command, could do things it could not before. In eight months Paula had crossed the magic threshold of her third year, had not only acquired language but learned that it holds *meaning,* that language could evoke emotion, could heal or destroy relationships, could alter her very reality. If I told Paula now that I loved her and would bring her a present when I got home, my words were not just sound but salve and blanky and warmed milk in her favorite Pooh-bear cup. Eight months for all that.

And maybe, too, in the waning of life, for in eight months my mother had aged exponentially. Her hair was grayer than I remembered, her eyes more yellowish; the dry, brown hands clutching her person more wrinkled and gnarled. She seemed to have lost weight since I had last seen her. Not much, maybe a few pounds. Still, a lessening.

"Hey, Mom." I put my arms around her. We weren't big or frequent huggers, my family, but I bent the rules and pulled her close. She returned my squeeze but then flinched, and when I pulled back to search her face I saw it grimaced in pain. My thoughts flew immediately to Tamieka—that crazy little sociopath lurking around my mother's house.

"What happened?" I asked. "What's wrong? Who hurt you?"

"It's nothing." She placed her hands on the small of her back and rubbed. "Just my back. It hurts a little."

"Come over here and sit." I took the overnight bag she carried and tried to steer her toward a bank of chairs, but she shook her head.

"I need to walk," she said. "It was all that sitting on the plane that made it worse."

She began shuffling down the crowded concourse, moving with such stiff deliberation it hurt to watch. Walking close beside her, seeing the effort on her face, I had to fight the urge to stretch out my hand and hold it behind her back in case she fell, the way you did with children, the way I'd done when Harriet took her first, terrifying steps. It was just after ten in the morning Nebraska time, not quite lunchtime, but in the airless, timeless, notional world of the airport, people crowded around the standing tables and unnaturally darkened bars and shoved overpriced plastic sandwiches into their mouths. Back in Boston it was lunchtime. Where were the children? I wondered. At home with Eddie, eating peanut-butter-and-jelly sandwiches while he tried to grin through his fury and pain? Or at his mother's house, enjoying a three-course gourmet meal?

"The sitting made what worse?" I asked my mother. "What did you do to yourself? Or should I ask what Tamieka did to you?"

We were passing a water fountain and she stopped before it, dug a bottle of small white pills from her purse. The sight of the brown prescription bottle sent my heart skipping across my chest. My mother hated doctors; I doubted if she had seen one more than five times in all the decades since her last child was born. If the pain had driven her to seek medical attention, it must have been severe. Trembling now, I put my hand on my mother's shoulders and leaned into her face.

"Did she hit you?"

"Who?"

"Did she attack you? I knew this would happen!"

"Grace, calm down." My mother took my hands from her shoulders, placed them firmly at my side. "Nobody hit me."

But I wasn't buying it. I had a sudden, frightening vision of my mother lying senseless on the floor, Tamieka rifling her pockets. "Did you call her social worker? Did you call the police?"

"I told you nobody hit me," my mother said.

"When will you stop—"

She cut me off. "I pulled a muscle in my back when I was trying to put up some new shelves in the garage."

Looking at her face, I knew she was telling the truth. My mother might evade or leave out, but she would never lie. All the air went out of me with a pop. "Oh," I said.

My mother looked closely at me. " What's wrong with you? Did something happen?"

It took every ounce of will not to burst into tears and throw myself into my mother's arms. "I'm just tired," I said. "And worried about you. Just because that girl hasn't hurt you yet doesn't mean she's not capable of it."

"We're all capable."

"She needs to go," I insisted.

"The child has to live someplace," my mother said. "The girl has got to have a home."

"But does it have to be yours?" My voice was rising again. "It's not your problem, Mom. You don't have to save the world. You've done your share."

My mother started walking again. Over her shoulder she said, "Only God can say that."

I followed her, remembering all of a sudden a Thanksgiving long past. My mother had a really difficult child at the time, a whippet-thin, wide-eyed, furious five-year-old named Renni, who sometimes ran howling through the house. The social workers said she was traumatized from a life among drunken Beale Street prostitutes, including her mother. My mother said the girl was spoiled rotten and needed to be brought into line. I thought my mother was both crazy and cruel.

The afternoon before Thanksgiving, while Dot and I were busy making pies, Renni sat on the living-room floor and defecated in her pants. My mother cleaned her up, and that evening as we sat down to dinner Renni did it again.

This was before I had children of my own and I was thus still fairly finicky; I could barely stand the smell of a public bathroom, and even a baby's diaper made me wrinkle my nose. I got up and went for a walk. When I came back Dot was in the kitchen washing dishes, my mother in the bathroom running water and muttering, and Renni was at the table, clean and wet-haired and keening like the wind.

I joined Dot in the kitchen. "What did Mom do to her?"

"Took away her Ding Dong," Dot said, rinsing a plate.

"Her what?"

"Ding Dong. You know, those chocolate-cream things? It's her favorite thing in the world. She gets one every night after dinner, she lives for those things. But Mom took the last two and flushed them down the toilet. Told her if the poop didn't go in the toilet from now on, the Ding Dongs would."

Over at the table, the keening rose to a wail.

"But she didn't mess herself on purpose," I protested.

"Mom says she did."

"But not consciously," I said. "It's a cry for help."

Dot looked at me. "Mom is helping her."

The wailing became a howl. From the bathroom my mother barked, "Cut out that noise before I come out there and give you something to howl about!"

How many times had I heard those very words during my own childhood? Okay, fair enough with four children to raise alone and in poverty, but this was different. This child was damaged, incapable of doing better. To deprive her of her one pleasure in life seemed concrete proof of my mother's insanity.

"She's crazy," I whispered to Dot. She washed a pie plate.

"No, I mean she has really lost it now!"

Dot shrugged and rinsed a bowl. And the next day, Thanksgiving Day, Renni made it twelve straight hours without howling or biting anyone or shitting in her pants and after dinner sat at the table with her Ding Dong in one hand and a grin as wide as Texas upon her face. And the next day my mother gave her two Ding Dongs and braided the girl's hair, Renni humming happily as she sat on the floor between my mother's knees. But still somehow I didn't see it. Caught up in the drama of my own unfolding life, I didn't see what I saw now, that it wasn't the money. It wasn't the money at all. With these children—unwanted and tossed aside—our mother had replaced us. She had created for herself an eternal family, one composed of children forever dependent, children who would never, in a sense, grow up. Sure, the individuals themselves would come and go, but the family, the need, would remain forever. There would always be another one toddling up the front steps.

My mother and I reached the escalator and stepped on, gliding our way down toward baggage claim. My mother turned to me, patted my hand. "Just help me get through this, okay?"

I tried to give her a smile. *Only God can say that,* my mother had said, meaning only God could say she'd done her share, she'd sacrificed sufficiently, it was enough. But I wondered if she would stop even if God sent her a telegram, because her refusing to let those children go had as much to do with what she needed as what they did. A powerful force, human need, not to be underestimated. I thought of Abraham Maslow's famous triangle, the hierarchy of human need. First, spreading out across the base, the need for food and water and protection from the elements. Atop that the need for safety, then for belonging and love, then for self-esteem, and finally, if all those are fulfilled, the need to self-actualize. But human beings are nothing if not variable; not every triangle looks the same. Some people need love more than air, and some people, their daughters, found love so frightening all they could do was run.


*We were headed to an address in north Omaha. From the bright,* forced way the rental car clerk said the neighborhood's name, I knew north Omaha must be the black part of town. Strange how often black folks ended up on the northern sides of cities: north Philadelphia, north Memphis, Harlem, north Omaha. The sociological explanation, I knew, flexed on race and segregation and fear, but in my turbulence I wondered about some parallel explanation: Was the south side of anything a place we did not wish to linger, or were we forever prepping ourselves to flee? Maybe it was just that we were a southern-hemisphere people moving ever northward, forever struggling to right ourselves.

Snow blanketed the ground as we exited the highway; more threatened from the clouds. We ended up on Dodge Street, the main thoroughfare separating north Omaha from south, and, following the rental clerk's directions, twisted our way through the neighborhood. Despite the fact I'd never set foot in Omaha before, the place felt sadly familiar: the squat wooden homes still strung with Christmas lights, the storefront churches with their burned-bulb marquees, the littered commercial strip full of check-cashing joints and liquor stores and beauty outlets and junk-filled dollar stores. Back in my little suburban Massachusetts town the local history guardians were up in arms against a planned invasion by The Gap, but The Gap wasn't coming within ten miles of this desperate commercial strip. Not The Gap, not Starbucks or Trader Joe's or anybody else.

We drove along, paralleling the river; every time we crossed an intersection I could see its iron-gray face. I had to fight the urge to turn toward it, to find a bridge and cross. Then I thought about my daughters, and how they loved to ride the Red Line subway train across the river Charles.

Shaking my head to clear the thought, I said, "Look—the Missouri. Reminds me of the Mississippi a little bit."

When my mother did not answer I went on. "I wonder if that's what Grandmother thought. I wonder if that was part of what attracted her here—the river. How long has she been here?"

"I have no idea," my mother said.

Which is what I'd thought, but with my mother, one never

knew. She held so many secrets so close to heart. I kept driving, searching the city for signs of where to go. My mother looked out her window for a moment, then back into the car.

"She was the worst mother in the world," she said after a while.

"Maybe," I said, "maybe she did her best."

My mother hooted, but I ignored her, kept talking. "No," I said. "You think of her as this monster, but maybe she gave what she could. Maybe any more would have killed her."

My voice slipped a little on the last sentence, and I feared I had exposed myself. But all my mother said was, "Then she should have died."

I gripped the steering wheel, tried to keep my eyes locked on the road. I did not want to cry.

"You don't understand," my mother said. "You and your sisters and your brother can never understand because I was there for you."

"Yes, you were. But—"

"I gave y'all everything I had," my mother said, cutting me off. "I gave up everything. Everything!"

The traffic light in front of me turned yellow and then red, and with gratitude I eased the car to a stop. "Mom," I said, turning in my seat. "Mom, calm down. Just—"

"I gave up my job!" My mother sat pitched forward in her own seat now, the seat belt straining against her chest. "I liked that job, I did. And I was good at it! I could throw mail faster than anybody down there but I gave it up for y'all!"

"Mom—"

"I gave up my privacy, my hopes!" she cried, putting her hands to her face. "I even gave up Jimmy."

Slowly, feeling as though I were pushing my way through water, I turned my head away. My eyes fell across the rearview mirror and I saw that in the car behind me a red-faced white man of about fifty wearing a fur-collared coat and a baseball cap was gesturing angrily and smashing his hand against his steering wheel. What was wrong with *him*? I wondered. Was he hurt? Disappointed, dismayed? Was every person in the world walking around filled to bursting with such despair that every now and then they had to pry open their hearts and slosh some across the world just to keep from choking to death? Then the sound of his furious, blaring horn came through the muffler of my shock and I looked up to see the green light in front of me leaping to yellow, and I put my foot on the gas and moved.

When I was sure I could speak I said, "Mister Jimmy? I thought . . ."

But in fact I didn't know what I had thought had happened to Mister Jimmy. One day he'd been there in our lives, bringing us ice cream and peppermint sticks, and the next day he was gone, and my mother never said a word about it. I remembered Lena crying and stamping her foot, but my mother had smacked her on the behind and said grown folks didn't have to explain themselves to children. And since she had never explained the comings and goings of other people in our lives—our father, our grandmother—I figured that was true.

"But . . . we didn't ask you to," I mumbled after a few moments.

My mother sat back in her seat and turned her head away. "Never mind," she said.

When you are a parent, one of the platitudes people love most to spout your way is that children grow up so fast. *In the blink of an eye,* they say. *Pay attention,* they warn, *they'll be gone before you know it; before you know it, those little birds will spread their wings and fly the nest.* And, sure enough, Dot and Lena and Sidney and I had all grown up, had left the nest. We'd soared away, leaving our mother behind to watch us gain the horizon, her own wings atrophied. Unable to renew.

Ten minutes later we turned a corner and there it was: a large, brown-brick building, six stories high, sitting atop a hill. On one side someone had begun and abandoned a mural, getting only as far as the blue sky, and two misshapen butterflies and the words *Love is ageless.*

I turned off the engine and said, for lack of anything better to say, "It's big."

I had envisioned something smaller, quaint and antiseptically white, something more appropriate for housing the wizened bodies of the old. My mother just rolled down her window and leaned out. Looking up at the butterflies, she said, "I hope she's on the top floor. All she ever wanted was to come up in the world."

All hospitals have a smell, but that smell is nothing, that smell is roses and lavender compared with the odor of a place where old people go to die. Which is what the place was—not a retirement community, not a rehabilitation center, not a senior-citizen anything, but a holding pen with a smell like urine and disinfectant and boiling beans and hopelessness, a way station with one long, dim corridor after the next and at the end a cheerless room with hard-backed chairs and checkers and a piano and tables and walkers scattered everywhere and the television bolted to the ceiling forlornly blasting out *The Price Is Right.* One perfect part of a social system erected to institutionalize death, to hide the dying from those of us who would greatly prefer not to see them.

The front desk, when we entered, was unstaffed. We wandered the halls, seeking a clerk or a nurse, passing wandering old women and hobbled old men: citizens of no world but the past. One woman, splinter-thin and grimy, bibbed and diapered and barefoot, sat parked in a wheelchair near the emergency fire door, her chin smeared with the chocolate pudding she'd had for lunch or perhaps dinner the night before. But her hair was long and clean and braided down her back. She raised a withered hand as we passed and called out in a little-girl voice, "Mama, that you?" I stalled before her, too stunned to speak. My mother patted the woman's hand, then pushed me on.

Circling the front desk the second time, we passed a room

and spotted a nurse, a scrawny white woman in dull, green scrubs helping an old black man back into a bed she had obviously just changed, except not very well. The top sheet was untucked and the thin, white blanket lay at a slant. "Understaffed today," she said, casually, her gum smacking inside her mouth. "Six people called in sick. Must have been some party last night."

She led us back down the hallway to the front desk, where she flipped through some papers on a clipboard and said, "Royal Rose Polk Knight, room 315. Top floor." She pointed toward the elevator. Once on the floor, we found the room right away. The door was closed. My mother grabbed the handle but did not turn it.

"Mom?"

Silence.

"Are you okay?" I asked, as gently as I could. When I was a child my mother used to tell us to be careful what we wished for. Because it just might come true.

"Maybe I should go in first," I said, touching her shoulder lightly. One of us was trembling.

But my mother answered, "I have come a thousand miles for this," and pushed the door.

It was a standard hospital room: twin beds separated by a curtain, now pulled back, a television bolted to the ceiling, a window in the far wall overlooking the street below. Instead of white, however, the walls had been painted a hideous shade of yellowish orange. Probably whoever did the painting had been striving for cheer, but what they arrived at was a kind of Halloweeny garishness, a headache-inducing evocation of the very holiday of death. Two cheap-looking framed prints hung on the walls: one of kittens playing in a basket, one of two blond children running hand in hand through a sun-dappled field. The television was on and blinking, some kind of game show perhaps, the volume turned down low.

Both beds were empty, but on one of them the covers were disheveled, tossed as though someone had just crawled out and would soon be crawling back in. Across the room, in a wheelchair by the window, sat a woman, thin and shriveled but unmistakably her. She craned her head around and saw us and looked startled, but only for a moment. Then she took a slow, rattling breath and said, "Well."

I waited for my mother to speak. After a second, she said, "Hello, Mama."

My grandmother coughed, a wet and hacking sound.

"Hi, Grandmother," I said. "How are you?"

She smiled, as if hearing a joke she'd heard a hundred times before. "Seen better days," she said. "Seen worse ones, too."

My mother had stopped just inside the door as if frozen, but now she tipped forward into the room, pulling me along by the hand. Behind us, the door swung shut. No one spoke; the only sound was someone singing in the hallway, a woman's high, thin, querulous voice scratching out Sarah Vaughan. "Love for Sale."

My grandmother was coughing again, so I said, as much to break the silence as to help, "Can I get you anything? Some water?"

"Pitcher's there," she said, trying to clear her throat. She raised a papery hand. "On the table."

The pitcher was small, aluminum, its outside sweaty with condensation from the ice. "Here you go." I walked across the room and handed her the glass. She smiled at me, as toothless as a newborn.

"Thanks, baby." She took a long draw, then held the glass back out to me. "You see my teeth around here? Nurse took them, said she was getting some stuff to clean them."

"I'll call and find out."

My grandmother shrugged. "Don't worry about it," she said. "Food they give me, better not to chew." Then: "Turn my chair around a little so I can look y'all in the face."

Up close, my grandmother looked even thinner than she had from across the room. What I had taken for bulk was really layers of dress: a faded blue cotton nightgown, a thin pullover sweater of some acrylic material, and a button-down one of wool, a terrycloth robe. And still she shivered.

I repositioned her chair. "Are you cold? Should I turn up the heat?"

"I'm fine, baby," she said, smiling at me. "Won't warm me none no matter how high you turn it up."

The way she said "baby" made something prickle behind my eyes, though I knew she was probably calling me that because she couldn't tell which one of my mother's daughter's I was. I returned her smile but did it quickly, aware of my mother's eyes. My mother was staring at me, and I realized I was standing too close to my grandmother, that this was a betrayal of some kind. "Well, I'm a little warm," I said, though I wasn't. "Early menopause, I guess." Nobody laughed. I took off my coat. There was a closet door on the near side of the room near my mother, but I walked to the dresser beneath the television and laid my coat there. Neutral ground.

My mother, who had moved far enough into the room only to allow the door to close behind her, now reached down into the shopping bag she carried and pulled out a piece of folded cloth.

"Brought you something," she said. She shook the cloth from its folds, walked to the near, unruffled bed, snapped it like a sheet. It was a large, silky piece of material, cornflower blue. For a moment it billowed over the bed like a parachute, then drifted gently down. At first I did not recognize it; then I remembered I had seen it once, many years before. I was nine or ten and digging around in the back of my mother's closet looking for something to wear for Halloween when I stumbled upon it, wrapped carefully and sealed in a box. When I asked my mother if I could have it for a princess cape, she said no, and took it from my shoulders. She said it was the only thing her mother ever gave her that she never took back. Then she spread the cloth on the floor and began folding it, but instead of square over square she made a long, thin strip, then bent the top diagonally, forming a triangle. The way the military folded a flag when a soldier died.

"Come on over here and see what it is," my mother said. "You always liked new things."

The room seemed colder now, as though someone somewhere had propped open a door.

"Can't," my grandmother said.

"Can't what?"

"Can't come over there."

I realized she could not turn the chair around, let alone wheel it back across the room. Someone else must have pushed her to where she sat.

"If you want me to look, you got to help," she said.

My mother snapped up the cloth, took two steps, and threw it into my grandmother's lap. "How's that?"

My grandmother laid her shaking hand atop the material and rubbed. "It's nice," she said.

"You don't remember it, do you?"

From my spot in the room I tried to will her to remember. But she only coughed and did not speak.

"You gave it to me," my mother said. She had backed away again, all the way to the door, and was leaning against it for support. If someone came swinging in they'd strike her. They'd knock her out.

My grandmother examined the cloth closely now, her eyes squinted half closed. "I gave you this?"

"When I was four," my mother said. "Before you left me. The first time."

"Ah." My grandmother let the material fall back into her lap. "And you done kept it all these years?"

"Yes."

"And brought it here for what—to be my winding sheet?"

I winced. My mother, though, was unflinching. "To show you I kept it," she said. "To show you that some people keep important things."

For a moment no one spoke. Above us, on the television, a commercial tripped on, a catchy, happy song, vaguely familiar, somebody singing about the joys of cargo pants. Then the door opened and a nurse bustled in, pushing a cart before her. "Oh, hello," she said, sounding surprised to see us. She took a needle from the cart, tapped it in the light, and pushed it into the IV. "Visitors for Royal Rose!"

"What was that?" my mother asked, gesturing toward the needle.

"Atropine," said the nurse. "It'll dry up that cough. Been asking that idiot doctor to prescribe it for two days and he finally did." She put the needle down and picked up a second one, but then she hesitated. "This is Dilaudid. For the pain, but it'll knock her out. Y'all want me to hold off a bit?"

She was looking at my mother and me, asking us as if my grandmother was no longer present, had ceased to exist. "Are you in pain, Grandmother?" I asked. "Do you want the shot?"

She looked from the nurse to my mother's face. "Hold off awhile," she said.

The nurse nodded and laid the needle back across the tray. She began bustling around the bed, plumping pillows, straightening sheets. "Y'all from out of town?"

I nodded. "California and Boston."

The nurse placed a fresh pitcher of water on the nightstand. "Just fly in today?"

My mother said, "I'm her daughter, Mattie. Her firstborn."

"That's nice."

"She probably never mentioned to you that she had children, I suppose."

My mother's voice caught on the bitterness, but the nurse just smiled. Maybe she did not hear it. Or maybe, like blood and death, she saw so much of it every day it was hardly worth noticing anymore. "Nice you could come," she said on her way out, pushing the cart before her. "You hungry, cafeteria's in the basement. Soda machine on the second floor. I'll come back with the Dilaudid the end of rounds."

When she was gone we remained as we were for a long moment, listening to her scuffling passage down the hall. Then my grandmother coughed again, lightly this time, and covered her mouth with a lace handkerchief she plucked from the pocket of her robe. "Mattie," she said when the coughing subsided. "What you doing here? I didn't send for you."

I looked at my mother; she stood pinned against the door like some magician's assistant tied to a tree, and the knives were flying and the knives were real. Somebody was going to get hurt. Was I supposed to stop it? Wasn't that what daughters did? Wasn't that what mothers did, kept people from hurting one another or themselves?

My mother found her breath. "The Bible says honor thy father and thy mother."

"That your days will be long upon the earth." My grandmother finished the verse with a weak smile. "Doing your duty, Mattie? Doing what's right, the way you always have."

My mother went livid. "You ought to be glad I am! Look around, Mama—where are the rest of your children? Where are the rest of your children while you lie here and die?"

"Living they own lives," my grandmother said. Her voice was toneless.

"Without you!" my mother yelled. "They're living their lives without you, because you never gave a damn about anybody but yourself! Do you even know where your children are? Do you even know your grandchildren?"

My mother turned and stalked toward me, grabbing my arm. Her fingers dug into my flesh, but I did not pull away. "Who is this child, Mama?" my mother yelled. "Do you even know? Do you even know which of your granddaughters this is?"

I caught my breath as my grandmother let her eyes rest on my face. For a split second something rose in those eyes, something unfamiliar, maybe even regret. But she shut it down. My heart fell through the floor for all of us.

"I'm Grace," I said.

"Grace," she said. Then: "Did I ever tell you about my great-grandmother, Grace?"

My mother made a strangled noise. "You told her!" she said, spitting out the words.

But I stepped forward anyway. Because, suddenly, more than anything else, I wanted to hear that story again. Maybe I had missed something the first time, maybe I had gotten the whole thing wrong. I'd been nine at the time, a child, and when I was a child I thought like a child and spake like a child and understood like a child. But I was grown now, a woman who needed to see the bigger picture. Who desperately needed her imagination to make sense of her world.

"Tell me," I said.

Grandmother nodded. "My grandmother was born a slave," she began. "But she didn't have to be."

"She was a saint," my mother said.

"She was a fool," my grandmother said. "Listen, Grace."

I listened as my grandmother, thin and coughing, spoke the story of her own grandmother's life. A woman who was born a slave and achieved freedom and tasted it for a while, and it must have been sweet, and then her world was ripped apart and she decided to hand that freedom back. A fool or a saint, or a woman caught at a blind and vicious bend in history. Her private trouble. A public issue and a nation's disgrace.

My grandmother finished with a cough and my mother said, "I don't know why you keep telling that story. I don't know what you think it has to do with what *you* did."

My grandmother just closed her eyes and shook her head. Maybe she didn't know. Or maybe she knew but could not articulate it; maybe that job was left to me. To see that because such a thing could happen to a woman a long, long time ago—because her family could be legally and even righteously shredded before her eyes, could be torn asunder with societal sanction and no more thought than it took to divide a set of flowering bulbs—because that could happen, the woman's great-granddaughter could shush her own child with a piece of cloth one summer night in Mississippi and walk away.

"You lived your life, Mattie," my grandmother said.

For my grandmother, to be a mother was to also be a slave, and a slave she refused to be. So she walked away; the pendulum swung to its apex. Then my mother had children of her own and, in her woundedness, ended up walking away from herself. The pendulum swung again. We were a rootless people, reaping the whirlwind still; my mistake had been to believe that because I was blessed and beyond, the beneficiary of so much sacrifice and so much pain, I was also somehow exempt. That I wasn't still living at the intersection of history and biography. That I could stop that swinging pendulum dead in its tracks. The past had meaning in the present, my old mentor Dr. Madison had told me a long, long time ago. The past had meaning in the present, whether the present wanted to acknowledge it or not.

Grandmother was speaking to my mother. "Whatever I did, it didn't kill you," my grandmother said. "You lived your life!"

My mother asked, her voice breaking, "How do you know?"

In the silence that followed my mother began to weep. I went to her and stroked her back, dug a tissue from my pocket and stuffed it into her hand. "Hush," I said. "I'm here."

My grandmother turned toward the window, stretching her neck. Outside, the heavy snowflakes thudded dully against the window and slushed away. For a long time none of us said anything, the only sound in the room my mother's diminishing sobs. From the hallway I heard the sound of two women passing: striding fast, laughing voices, boot heels clicking along the linoleum. Nurses getting off duty, perhaps. Or visitors like us fleeing the scene.

After a long while my grandmother opened her mouth to speak. "Y'all go on," she said. "I'm better alone." Then a coughing fit struck her and she hacked and trembled and shook like a paper doll. "Go . . . on!"

My mother wiped her face and blew her nose. Then, with a deep breath, she stood and tossed the tissue into the wastebasket. "Let's get her into bed."

She fought us. We went to lift her from her chair, and even though it sounded as though her lungs might be ripped from her chest, she rallied enough to struggle, twisting her frail body and slapping at us with her open palms. Her strikes were like snowflakes landing. "Go on," she wheezed.

My mother spoke to her with gentle firmness, the same tone she used with her kids. "Now stop that. Cut that nonsense out so we can get you into bed."

"Go on."

My mother said, "You need to rest."

Grandmother coughed again and a little blood came up, dribbled bright red down her chin. My mother sent me into the bathroom for a washcloth, then wiped it away. "Help her sit up," she ordered me. I put my arms beneath my grandmother's shoulders and straightened her in the bed. She seemed to weigh no more than a child, no more than Harriet on certain nights, when she leaped into my arms and demanded a twirly twirl-around before bed. That weight, the weight of a child, was elastic; it rose and fell with the child's energy. But my grandmother's weight was brittle and dry and evaporating fast.

I settled her against her pillows, then cranked her bed. The nurse came bustling in again, carrying a tray. "Y'all have a nice visit? Time for Royal Rose to get some sleep." She plunged the needle into the IV, then checked the line and left the room. We stood over the bed, watching my grandmother. After a few minutes, her breathing eased. My mother leaned in, searching her face.

After a long moment my grandmother stirred and mumbled something; it took me a second to make out what it was.

"Cold. Cold."

My mother dropped my hands. She got a white blanket from the closet and spread it over my grandmother. "How's that, Mama? Better?" she asked, pressing the blanket close.

"So cold," my grandmother said.

"Shush, Mama. It's okay."

"Cold."

It must have been seventy-five degrees in the room already; still, I jumped toward the thermostat and cranked it up. "It'll take a minute to come on again," I told my mother.

But she was not listening. She was leaning low over my grandmother, whispering something into her ear. Something between the two of them, something not for me. I turned away, to go out into the hallway for a drink of water, maybe outside for some air. But just as I moved my grandmother spoke again.

"I'm so cold," she murmured. "Build the fire up."

Feeling helpless, I peeked at my mother, worried for her. How would she bear this final parting, this last, great, unavoidable abandonment. But my mother looked more calm and, in a strange way, more content than I'd ever seen. She stood up straight and began adjusting her clothing, pulling the tail of her blouse from her pants and lifting it against her ribs. "It's okay, Mama," she said. She raised my grandmother's hands, laid them against the warmth of her own skin. "It's okay," she murmured over and over. "Mattie's here."

# Chapter Twenty

She died as she had lived: solitary, defiant, nobody holding her hand. I had stepped out of the room for a cup of coffee; my mother had risen from her chair and gone again to the thermostat to check the heat. It took less than a minute, she told me, but it was time enough. When she returned to my grandmother's bedside the passing was over. It was the last time Rae left her daughter without saying good-bye.

My mother wanted to stay awhile and so we did. We prayed, then sat vigil until the doctor wandered in, wiping pizza sauce from his mouth with the back of his hand. "Time of death, eight thirty-two," he said, signing the paperwork a nurse held out to him. "My condolences on your loss."

After he left, the nurse handed my mother a clipboard full of other papers to sign. My mother, without a word, handed it to me. I scanned the papers and signed them, then took the list of funeral homes from the nurse and went out to the nurses' station and started dialing. Some of the funeral directors didn't want to quote prices over the phone until I pointed out they were legally required to do so. Others ignored my request for specifics and riffed instead on the importance of grandmothers, those mighty women not always honored in life but deserving in death. I hung up on those people. On the seventh call I got a man with the rich, cultured voice of Roscoe Lee Browne who answered my questions directly, sang no false praises to grandmothers, and waited in silence whenever I stopped to think. I gave him the information about my grandmother and the name of the hotel where we were staying.

When I got back to the room my mother was standing by the bed, putting lipstick on my grandmother. She had already washed my grandmother's face and brushed her hair, and when she leaned back to examine her work I thought how young my mother looked.

"Let's go to the hotel and get some rest," I said gently.

My mother capped the lipstick and laid it on the table beside the bed. "Yes," she said. "It's time to go."

At the hotel I made my mother a cup of chamomile tea and gave her a valerian pill I'd brought along, though she hardly needed it. Ten minutes after we checked in she was asleep atop the quilted bedspread of the queen-size bed nearest the door. I got her up and into her nightgown, but when the sandwiches from room service arrived and I shook her shoulder gently, she pushed my hand away.

"Okay," I said. "I'll save yours for later."

Eyes closed, she nodded heavily and sank deeper into the bed. But when I turned away to examine my own dinner—turkey like plasterboard, bacon like sawdust, limp fries, a salad of unrecognizable greens—I heard her mumble.

"What?" I asked, turning back to my mother. Dragging her head up from her pillow, she asked, "Is there something going on with you? Is there something wrong?"

"Everything's fine," I said.

"You sure? The children? You're not thinking . . . of doing something terrible, are you, Grace? You would never do something terrible like that, would you?"

I leaned over my mother and kissed her forehead. We are not big kissers in my family, but I did it anyway. And maybe the rules say you should never lie to your parents, but I did that, too.

"I never would, Mom. Go on to sleep."

She sighed a sigh of release, then fell back against her pillow and closed her eyes.

I dug my cell phone from my coat pocket and checked the messages. Only one: Lena calling from her friend's house in Montreal. "It's pretty nice here, except for all the snow," she said. "Melissa's house is tiny; in Texas we would use it to store our linens, but here its considered luxurious. Funny world. Anyway, I'm fine. Call me at this number if you, you know, change your mind."

After listening to Lena's message, I hung up and dialed the number in Boston, not knowing what I would say when Eddie answered, not knowing still what I was going to do. But it was Harriet who picked up the telephone. She squealed upon hearing my voice and it took my breath away.

"Mommy!" she cried. "Where are you? I miss you!"

"I miss you, too, honey," I said. "What are you doing up? It's past your bedtime."

"Daddy's letting us stay up late. We watched a movie and had ice cream. He said tonight was a special night."

"Where is Daddy now, peanut," I asked. "Is he there?"

"He's upstairs giving Paula a bath," she said. "Want me to get him?"

"No, honey. Tell Daddy I'll call him tomorrow morning," I said. "I love you, Harriet."

"I love you more than ice cream," Harriet said. It was a game we sometimes played.

"I love you more than all the ice cream in the world," I said. "And all the chocolate sauce."

"And all the cherries!"

"And all the whipped cream and all the sprinkles and all the Reese's Pieces and peanut M&M's." I made a kissing sound. "Go to bed."

Harriet asked, "Mommy? When are you coming home?"

I stood there in the hotel room waiting for some revelation to occur, some definitive feeling to manifest, some great wave of emotion to rise up and either rock me forward once and for all or shove me back. Nothing came. All I had were two broken women and a stream of frantic images: myself in the basement, my mother crying in the car. My great-great-grandmother knocking on the big house door. My grandmother walking down some dusty Mississippi road. Lena at the airport rental counter, waving me good-bye. Eddie in the living room of the house he loved so much, bewildered and wondering. My daughters in the hallway, peeking through the mail slot . Me in the basement. My hand on the door.

"Go to bed, honey. Good night."

"But, Mommy, when are you coming home?"

My hand on the door. Me turning around. "When I can," I told my daughter. "As soon as I can."

# Acknowledgments

The author would like to thank Donald Massey and Nancy Denton, authors of the absorbing *American Apartheid: Segregation and the Making of the Underclass,* which I read while struggling to give depth to this work of fiction. The author would also like to thank David S. Adams for his article "Writing with Sociological Imagination: A Time-Line Assignment for Introductory Sociology," from which came the idea for the time-line assignment for Grace's students. The author would also like to thank Judith Shapiro for the wonderful and important concept of sociological illiteracy.

The author is grateful to her agent, Kim Witherspoon, and her editor, Claire Wachtel, for sticking with her during this long and often perilous journey. She is also grateful to, and thankful for, her children, her family, Emerson College, Union United Methodist Church, and especially the members of her writing group—Beth, Chi, and Simone. Writing is sore and lonely work, but a community of writers—a sisterhood—is like balm to the wound.